Praise ...
Jory Strong an...

"If other erotic romances are just de..., then this book is a seven-course meal—plus dessert! . . . Beautifully written."
—*Just Erotic Romance Reviews*

"Never a dull moment within this blazing read . . . Be prepared to be in a constant state of arousal."
—*Fallen Angel Reviews*

"A beautiful, passionate story . . . Tender, loving, erotic, and consuming."
—*Joyfully Reviewed*

"The passion is going to blow your darn mind . . . This is truly an excellent out of this world tale that drew me in and kept me enthralled from beginning to end."
—*Dark Angel Reviews*

"A phenomenal and spellbinding read. Jory Strong has once again created a story you will be unable to put down . . . from an author whose imagination seemingly knows no bounds."
—*The Romance Studio*

SPIDER-TOUCHED

Jory Strong

B

BERKLEY SENSATION, NEW YORK

THE BERKLEY PUBLISHING GROUP
Published by the Penguin Group
Penguin Group (USA) Inc.
375 Hudson Street, New York, New York 10014, USA
Penguin Group (Canada), 90 Eglinton Avenue East, Suite 700, Toronto, Ontario M4P 2Y3, Canada
(a division of Pearson Penguin Canada Inc.)
Penguin Books Ltd., 80 Strand, London WC2R 0RL, England
Penguin Group Ireland, 25 St. Stephen's Green, Dublin 2, Ireland (a division of Penguin Books Ltd.)
Penguin Group (Australia), 250 Camberwell Road, Camberwell, Victoria 3124, Australia
(a division of Pearson Australia Group Pty. Ltd.)
Penguin Books India Pvt. Ltd., 11 Community Centre, Panchsheel Park, New Delhi—110 017, India
Penguin Group (NZ), 67 Apollo Drive, Rosedale, North Shore 0632, New Zealand
(a division of Pearson New Zealand Ltd.)
Penguin Books (South Africa) (Pty.) Ltd., 24 Sturdee Avenue, Rosebank, Johannesburg 2196,
South Africa

Penguin Books Ltd., Registered Offices: 80 Strand, London WC2R 0RL, England

This book is an original publication of The Berkley Publishing Group.

PRINTING HISTORY
Berkley Sensation trade paperback edition / August 2009

Library of Congress Cataloging-in-Publication Data

Strong, Jory.
Spider-touched / Jory Strong.—Berkley Sensation trade paperback ed.
  p. cm.
ISBN 978-0-425-22793-0
I. Title.

PS3619.T777S65 2009
813'.6—dc22

                                    2009001832

PRINTED IN THE UNITED STATES OF AMERICA

10 9 8 7 6 5 4 3 2 1

For my aunt Hazel,
who got me hooked on romance stories

SPIDER-TOUCHED

One

THE city was straight out of Araña's nightmare. A reclaimed port rising from the devastation wrought by The Last War and the anarchy that followed when the supernaturals emerged from hiding.

Pain lanced through her chest in a spasm at the sight of it. An echoed emotion, the blending of reality and the demon vision she'd walked in ten years earlier, on the day she'd climbed onto Erik and Matthew's boat to avoid the mob hunting her.

Oakland. She'd had no name for the city then, but its image had haunted her for years. Now, as she knocked aside the moisture gathering at the corners of her eyes, she wanted to claim it was the cold ocean breeze causing the tearing, but she knew otherwise.

A gruff male voice cut across her thoughts. "Stop daydreaming, girl," Matthew said. "Free the jib and ready about."

Araña did as ordered, freeing the line from its cleat as Erik took up the slack and the *Constellation* turned away from Oakland, a short reprieve even as the wind drew them deeper into the bay.

Emotion closed her throat as her eyes traveled over Erik, taking in the gaunt appearance of his features, the excess of clothing he required to keep warm. There'd be no cure in this city. No healer who could change the course of the wasting disease and restore him to health.

She wished she could turn aside the future she knew was waiting, the death to come, but her gift was useless except to bring pain and suffering.

Their eyes met, warm brown irises to the solid black of hers, and she saw only what she always saw—confidence, intelligence . . . love.

"That's San Francisco," Matthew said, drawing her attention away from Erik by pointing out the city across the bay from Oakland. "Vampires rule there, and only a fool deals with them directly."

Erik's laugh was soft, weak, but heartfelt all the same. "And the desperate. There was a time when we were forced to deal with them, until we worked our way into Thierry's good graces and he mediated."

Matthew grunted but didn't reply. Araña smiled, remembering the old bookseller who'd visited them shortly after they'd taken her in.

The sails fluttered as the wind shifted. "Ready about," Matthew said, and she automatically reached for the jib line, pulling it in when Erik loosened his.

They swung around, once again facing Oakland, steadily working their way deeper into the bay and then into the channel. They were operating under sail rather than using the *Constellation*'s motor because its heavy throb would draw attention to them and reveal the speed the engine was capable of when needed.

Guardsmen in camouflage-patterned uniforms patrolled the docks along with the heavily armed private security forces stationed on container ships. The sight of them tightened Araña's stomach to the point of pain.

There was safety in the waters she called home, in the boat towns formed when crafts of all shapes and descriptions were tethered together on a calm sea.

There was safety in the small armed settlements held in land surrounded by packs of werewolves. But here . . .

Matthew and Erik were wanted men, though their days of piracy had ended shortly after she arrived in their lives. Not that they'd given up thievery.

She'd learned from the best and felt no guilt over the jobs she'd accompanied them on. Why would she?

It was hard to find evil in the deed when they earned their money helping one rich man steal from another while the vast majority struggled to survive in a land forever changed by war and plague and the emergence of the supernaturals.

In the books that were Erik's passion, there were stories of a United States where civil rights prevailed, opportunity abounded, and humans lived in ignorance of the unseen. There were pictures bearing little resemblance to the places that now existed. Towering, gleaming cities turned to burned-out rubble and hollowed-out sanctuaries for the lawless as well as the desperate, most of it slowly being reclaimed by the forests.

Where human civilization made a stand, its nature was determined by those in power, all of them wealthy, all of them beyond the daily struggle for food and shelter. But whether those places were controlled by the religious—as the settlement where she'd spent the first twelve years of her life had been—or by politicians backed by guardsmen and police, they held only the daylight hours. The night belonged to the predators—natural and supernatural alike.

Araña's eyes settled on Erik again. Only pride and the stimulants coursing through his system gave him the strength to help with the jib. He was in no condition to walk long distances.

"What part of the city is the healer in?" she asked as they neared the dock, her throat tightening on the words as the emotion of her long-ago vision surged from the past, washing over her in an agonizing wave to remind her that only death waited in this city called Oakland.

"The Church has influence here," Matthew said. "There's a

section set aside for humans born with *controversial abilities*. The healer will live there. Best go ahead and put your glove on."

Araña reached for the fingerless glove she was never without and slipped it over her left hand, hiding the brand burned into her flesh by a now dead clergyman. Her gaze flicked to Matthew. The hard set of his features hid his worry, but she knew it was there, just as she knew something inside him would die with Erik.

They turned into the wind. "Drop the jib," he said.

Araña lowered the triangular staysail then went to the front of the boat to gather and stow it in a waterproof bag. The mainsail followed and she secured it to the boom, their momentum carrying them close enough to throw a line to a thick-necked man who pulled them into an unoccupied slip.

"Pay at the end of the dock," he said when the boat was secure. "If you bring trouble here, the boat gets impounded along with everything on board."

He left without waiting for acknowledgment. Araña climbed from the boat and turned to offer her hand to Erik as Matthew waited, allowing Erik his pride but there to aid him onto the finger pier all the same.

"Where's the spider?" Erik asked, taking her hand before she could answer him and continuing to hold it longer than necessary after he'd stepped onto the dock, the gesture telling her some part of him was already braced for his own death.

"On my shoulder," she said, knowing without conscious thought where the demon mark rested, four of its legs streaking downward to touch her collarbone, its body so much a part of hers there was no change in the smooth texture of her skin—brown yielding to the solid black of the spider shape then becoming brown again.

She never felt the demon mark move, could only guess at the reasons it positioned itself where it did. But it was always present, as deadly to others as her flame-trapped visions were.

Matthew followed them onto the wooden dock. Araña resisted the urge to ask how far they had to go before they reached the healer.

Their destination mattered only in that it offered them a place of safety and rest.

The pier was crowded with fishing boats and a few houseboats. She used the silence as they traveled its length to study her surroundings, to notice those who took an interest in them.

When they neared the small concrete building at the dock's end, Erik murmured, "Camera. On the lamppost."

She glanced surreptitiously at it, keeping her head ducked.

"You two keep walking while I pay for the slip," Matthew said. "By the time they identify any of us—if it's even possible—we'll be long gone from Oakland."

"Let me pay the fee," Araña said, misgiving filling her, the framed "Wanted" pictures on the wall of Erik and Matthew's bedroom crowding her mind, tightening the knots in her stomach.

Matthew shook his head. "If the camera is there for any reason other than scaring people into good behavior, then there will be others. For all we know the dock attendant wore one and took our pictures when he pulled us in. The technology existed well before The Last War. We're safe enough. It's been a long time since Erik and I were here."

Araña had no choice but to follow Matthew's dictates. No reason to dispute his logic. She and Erik kept going as he detoured to pay for the slip. They stopped only when they were beyond the lamppost and the camera.

She longed to take Erik's hand in hers—the contact too brief when she helped him from the boat. She ached to turn into him, to wrap her arms around him and let the hot wash of tears escape to wet his neck as she told him how much he meant to her, how much she loved him. How he was father and older brother, best friend and confidant, irreplaceable and unequal in her life—even though she loved Matthew, too.

But she didn't dare press her skin to his. The demon mark had killed for the first time when she was five and a stranger had grabbed her. It had killed again when she was sixteen and thought she was in love. She wouldn't risk losing Erik that way, even though she ached to be held close and feel the brush of his lips and the soothing stroke of his hand, the rub of his cheek against hers in comfort offered and received.

Be strong, she told herself. Here in this city, that's what Erik and Matthew needed from her.

As they left the dock area, Araña's hands settled near the hilts of the knives she wore in inconspicuous sheaths sewn into the dark fabric of her pants. A gun would have made her feel safer, but they'd left them locked on the boat with the longer knives.

Along the coast and canals, in the settlements without enough wealth to pay for more than a few policemen, an open display of weapons was viewed as a wise precaution for avoiding trouble. The larger cities were different.

There they were viewed as a threat to society. People remembered that after the plague ran its course and the supernaturals revealed their presence, anarchy reigned for long years and the streets filled with violence and fear.

Eventually the armed services and guardsmen brought order and harsher gun laws. There was no way to ban them, not when any abandoned and unclaimed building was fair game for salvage. But obtaining ammunition was difficult and expensive, and the penalty for using a gun without just cause was death.

Araña's hands curled around the hilts of her knives in an unconscious search for security as Erik's breath grew labored with each step, until finally he said, "We can separate. It's still early enough for the buses to run. I can take one and wait for the two of you just inside the area set aside for the gifted."

"No," Matthew said. "You and I stay together. Araña can—"

"No." Her stomach clenched on the thought of not being with them. "I don't want to be separated from you and Erik."

"Then we stay together," Matthew said, one hand leaving its position near his knife to curl around Erik's arm in unprotested assistance. "We'll turn up ahead."

Erik whispered, his breathing already strained from the sprint to shelter. He shifted his knives into one hand and dug out his wallet, then slid it into the pocket of Araña's shirt. "Don't go back to the boat. It's not safe and by tomorrow she'll be confiscated. Hide among the gifted."

Icy fear squeezed her heart. A terror born in her childhood and fed with ranted sermons about Hell and damnation, beatings that came with being judged as demon-tainted.

"I won't leave you," she whispered, refusing to let the thought of what waited in the afterlife make her abandon the men who'd saved her life and made her a part of their family.

When she would have given the wallet back to Erik, Matthew stopped her. "Keep it for now. Only two of the guardsmen have rifles. The rest have handguns. Eliminate any one of them and get his weapon and the odds start to change in our favor. We'll hide and wait for them to come to us. We won't outrun them."

Araña nodded, hearing in Matthew's words his own declaration. He wouldn't leave Erik regardless of what happened.

Matthew moved around the corner to hunt the hunters. She found a place among a curtain of vines, one that allowed her to see the building where Erik melted into the gloom of a room that had collapsed except for a small area.

There was no sound save for the thunderous beat of her heart. It felt as if the world around them held its breath, silencing birdsong and insect noise alike, stilling the wind so there was no rustle of leaves or whisper of grass.

A guardsman appeared, the pale redhead with his own plans for her. He walked quietly, his arm outstretched and gripping a gun. His movements held a bold confidence, as if he were stalking prey and his possession of the weapon protected him from attack.

The thin leather of her belt could serve as a garrote, a way to kill without risk of a shouted warning. But it took strength and time, and with the others patrolling, she couldn't take the chance of using it.

Her breath caught when he glanced briefly at the building housing Erik, and released it when the guardsman shunned it in favor of aiming toward the open doorway near where she hid.

In her mind she prepared to attack. Saw herself striking without hesitation as Matthew had taught her to do.

She let the raw need for survival turn fear into strength, conscience into primal instinct as adrenaline surged, honing her focus so all reality faded save for the need to kill her enemy.

He neared, his eyes flicking over her hiding place, dismissing it. The scent of sweat and cologne trailed him as he stepped past her.

She struck. Driving and twisting with the knife in her left hand.

The gun fired as his grip tightened on it reflexively. A cry escaped before the knife in her right hand found its mark, slashing across his throat and making arterial blood spray onto the vine and concrete.

Araña pushed him away and crouched, picking up the gun. Out of the corner of her eye she saw Erik emerge from his hiding place and grab the arm of a guardsman summoned by the noise.

They struggled. Erik's back was to her, preventing her from using the dead man's gun.

She rushed forward. A shot fired. And then Erik crumpled to the ground.

Animal sounds of rage ripped from Araña's throat. She leveled the gun and pulled the trigger without thought, didn't stop moving forward as the bullet slammed into the guardsman's forehead, the force of it taking most of his skull and driving him backward into rubble.

And then Matthew was there, a rifle in one hand, his knife in the other. He knelt by Erik, the weapons dropping to the ground as he lifted Erik off the cracked, broken cement and cradled him in his arms.

Araña crouched next to them, agony swelling in her chest, incapacitating her, the present and past colliding in an overwhelming instant of anguish.

It was the scene from her vision. The death she'd known waited with the first glimpse of Oakland.

Matthew's face was a mask of unbearable grief as he put Erik down and snatched up both the rifle and the pistol she didn't remember dropping. "Don't follow me, Araña. Run. Hide. Live for all of us."

He disappeared around the corner before she could say anything. There was the sound of a gun firing, then another.

Araña cast a quick glance at the guardsman who'd killed Erik, but she didn't see where his weapon had landed. She grabbed Matthew's discarded knife as well as her own dropped one. A sob escaped as she turned her back on Erik and did as Matthew ordered. She ran, dodging rubble and blackened cars in an effort to escape the guardsmen.

Behind her she heard a shout go up, followed by the crack of a shot being fired from a rifle. A bullet grazed her side, the shock of it distracting her for a precious second from the hazard-laden ruin of what had once been a street crowded with houses. Her foot snagged on something hidden in the weeds, pitching her forward.

There was blinding pain as her head struck a rock. Terror made her fight through it and scramble to her knees to look for her knives.

The men were on her just as she staggered to her feet. The hard smash of a rifle butt to her chest sent her tumbling backward and struggling for breath.

A heavy boot landed a blow to the middle of her stomach, making her roll to her side and vomit what little she had in her stomach.

The dark-haired man delivering the blow drew back his leg, and she braced herself for a second kick even as she tried to gather the strength to surge upward, to at least kill one of her attackers with the knife she'd managed to recover.

The man with the rifle stopped his companion from delivering the blow by saying, "Enough already. I don't want to fuck a corpse, Nelson."

There was a raunchy laugh from the third man. "It wouldn't be the first time."

"Shut the fuck up, Cabot. My cock was out of that girl before she died."

The rifle barrel dropped to point at Araña's hand. "Let go of the knife or I'll fire. Putting a bullet into you won't ruin our fun. You won't bleed out before we're finished."

The demon mark was no longer on her shoulder. It was on her bare mound like an exotic tattoo, ready to kill the first man who touched his flesh to hers in an attempt to rape her.

Its presence gave her courage. Matthew's last words gave her strength. She opened her fingers and let the knife fall away.

The blond guardsman named Cabot immediately holstered his gun and unzipped his pants. "I go first," he said, pulling his cock out and fondling its hardened length.

The man holding the rifle kicked Araña's knife out of reach before pressing the barrel of the gun to her forehead. "Push your pants down."

Her heart pounded violently inside her chest, a seething mass of fear and grief and hate. Bile rose in her throat at the thought of revealing herself to these men.

She wanted to kill them. To see them writhing in agony. But only their faces and hands were exposed and the spider needed bare skin.

The waistband of her pants was wet with blood. Touching her fingers to it broke the barrier of numbness her mind had erected.

Araña fought against crying out as pain rippled through her, originating where the bullet had grazed her side. Her jaw clenched as she refused to show them anything more than their deaths.

She undid the buttons at the front of her pants. Her fingers trembled slightly despite her efforts to keep them steady and focus her mind on what she needed to do in order to survive. In the coming confusion she'd grab the dying man's gun and—

He grew impatient and bent down, took a fistful of material and jerked, wrenching her pants and underwear to her knees. The sight of the spider sent him stumbling backward, his penis shriveling.

His two companions laughed. The one not holding the rifle unzipped his pants. "I'll take your turn. Looks like we've got ourselves a lawbreaker. A tattoo like hers is illegal. I'm betting she likes it rough and bloody."

"Give me your gun, Nelson," the man with the rifle said, holding out his hand.

"I'm not going to fuck her with it. Not till after you have a turn with her."

"Gun."

A petulant expression came and went on the dark-haired guardsman's face. He unholstered the weapon and slapped it onto his companion's outstretched hand. "I want it back. I want to finish her with it."

A shudder went through Araña. She found it easy to imagine any one of these men brutalizing her with a gun and then firing it inside her as his companions looked on.

Erik and Matthew had always ensured her safety, but life among fugitives and societal outcasts had stripped her of what was left of her innocence when it came to the atrocities men were capable of. The settlements and floating boat cities were full of women left disfigured by the violence done to them.

"Hurry up," the man holding the rifle barrel to her forehead said. "We've still got to haul the bodies to the truck then find out if Sarge was shitting us about there being bounties on the two men."

Araña closed her eyes against the wave of pain that crashed through her heart with his words. A tidal wave of grief threatened to drown her.

She wanted to scream out her rage and anguish. Instead she fought her way through it, for Matthew and Erik, as well as herself.

Her eyes opened when her assailant climbed on top of her with a grunt. She was barely aware of the feel of his hand and cock brushing against her skin as he tried to find her opening. And then he was rolling away, screaming and shrieking, his penis and hand swelling as black streaks of poison spread.

She grabbed the rifle barrel, deflecting it. A bullet slammed into the screaming man, putting him out of his misery and sparing him long moments of torment.

Araña hung on to the rifle, fighting to wrest it free at the same time she tried to use her grip on it to pull herself up, in the hopes the spider would be able to find skin and kill again.

The tangle of her clothes around her knees interfered. A kick to the chest sent her backward.

There was the sound of a bullet being chambered, and the end of the rifle was once again placed against her forehead. But death didn't come, though the blond guardsman whose penis had shrunk at the sight of the spider said, "Kill her so we can get out of here."

"I've got something better in mind. We'll take her to Anton and Farold. They'll pay good money for her, no questions asked. Then we turn around and double it by going to a betting club and watching while she runs the maze."

"She's a witch," the blond said, aiming his pistol at Araña, his voice shrill. "Look at what she did to Nelson. Look at the glove on her hand! Look at it! I bet she's been branded by the Church."

"Don't turn into a chickenshit just because your dick shrunk. Good thing it did or you'd be dead. If she could have killed us with a spell, she'd have done it. I'm betting we're safe as long as we don't touch her."

"I don't care! Out of seven of us, look how many of us are left. You and me, Jurgen. You and me. Everyone else is dead."

Anger tightened the rifleman's face. "Use your brains before you piss me off, Cabot. Think about the edge knowing what we know would give us at the club. Tonight they're running convicts in the maze. They'll let them loose to have some fun with her before setting the hunters free. We'll make a killing betting on her."

The guardsman pulled the barrel back from Araña's forehead,

trusting that she'd prefer to remain alive, to take her chances else-where rather than die where she lay. "Take off the glove."

She pulled it off, revealing the brand burned into her flesh when she was twelve, when an exorcism failed to rid her of the demon mark.

"We'll get more for her once Anton or Farold sees it," the one called Jurgen said. "Maybe Anton will even let the demon out in the maze tonight."

His blond companion backed away, but he nodded. "Okay, but I'll shoot her if she tries to touch me."

She was ordered to her feet and allowed to restore her clothing so she could walk. At their command, she emptied her pockets. They took her keys to the boat, but not Erik's wallet. Somewhere between the first dead guardsman and the one the spider killed, it had fallen out of her pocket.

"Move," Jurgen said, indicating the direction with the rifle barrel.

Fresh blood poured from the wound in her side. Pain stabbed through her, but it was nothing compared to the searing agony as Araña passed Erik's body and then Matthew's.

The need for revenge burned at her core, intensified when the blond, Cabot, said, "What about collecting the bounty? What are we going to say about Sarge and the others being dead?"

"We'll radio it in to headquarters and say we were ambushed while trying to bring three people in for questioning. We'll tell them we're still chasing the third one. Let them send another unit to collect the bodies. Even if it turns out Sarge is wrong about there being bounties, after what happened here, nobody is going to care."

Two

HE hated humans now as fiercely as he'd hated them for centuries. If not more so.

They were dust, the walking dead. Frail and unworthy.

They were *less* than the most simple of beasts.

It was their cunning, their intellect that allowed them to rule. And yet their base nature always reasserted itself. Time and time again they raised civilization to unimaginable heights only to plunge it into a dark abyss of decadence and decay.

He'd witnessed it for more years than he could count, seen the cycles of humankind repeat themselves over and over again. Blissfully he could no longer remember all of the details.

He was old. Hundreds of years old. That much he knew from what memories he still held.

Perhaps his age could be measured in thousands. The heavy weight of his soul whispered it might be so, though why he should be so convinced he had a soul was beyond him.

His form was human, but it wasn't his true form. He was positive in that regard. Just as he was equally sure the name resonating through him was his own. Tir. Though he hadn't heard it spoken in centuries and would never willingly share it with any of his captors.

Was he the last of a supernatural race no longer walking the earth? Tir didn't know the answer. He had never met another of his kind.

Great stretches of his remembered life had been spent in darkness, in damp underground catacombs, his ankles and wrists manacled. In the early days the priests and their acolytes cut out his tongue periodically so he couldn't speak. Then, later, as science gave them other tools, they sewed his lips together and fed him through a needle in the arm.

He could no longer remember why his human captors feared what he might say. Apparently neither could they—though they still feared what he might do.

They were right to.

One day he would be free of the sigil-inscribed collar around his neck. When that day came and his memories poured into him along with the power he sensed at his core, he would wreak vengeance not only on the human race but on whatever beings had first enslaved him.

He would have his revenge. The promise of it had kept him sane over the centuries, given him the strength to endure torture and dismemberment, depravation, and degradation.

In the cage next to Tir the human finally succumbed to his injuries. His rattling breath was a death knell making the hyenas laugh and the lion charge.

The wereman, his body caught in a grotesque blending of cougar and human, paused in his savage assault on the bars of his cage, his lips pulling back to reveal broken teeth and a bloody mouth.

At the far end the lethal dragon lizards turned their heads, flicked their tongues out to capture the scent and taste of death. Their huge size and venomous bite, their aggressiveness, made them terrifying creatures, illegal to house or transport, though Tir had seen little evidence that humans obeyed the laws they were so fond of creating.

The sound of footsteps drew Tir's attention away from the companions he was caged alongside. He shifted his weight, and the chains tethering his shackled wrists and ankles to a metal belt around his waist rattled.

There was enough play in them to allow for a shuffling walk, to allow him to scoop food into his hand and bend his torso to eat, but not enough to allow him to kill—though given the opportunity, he wouldn't hesitate to attempt it.

His hands curled around the bars of his cell. The door at the far end opened, allowing pure sunlight into the building. His eyes stung, but he didn't close them. He let the light burn itself into his soul, let it strengthen him and feed his resolve for freedom and vengeance.

A slight figure stood in the doorway, her fear palpable. Familiar. Tir's lips curled in disgust when the woman finally stepped into the building, driven not by courage but by a terror of disobeying her husband.

She scuttled crablike past the wereman, who pleaded for help in a voice that sounded strangely human despite the distortion and indecipherable words caused by the cat's muzzle. She moved past the dead man's corpse and Tir, her face averted, shoulders hunching in defense, like a turtle trying to pull its head and neck into a shell.

If Tir had once been capable of feeling pity for humans, it had long ago been extinguished. Disgust burned in his belly with his rage. Those who stood by and did nothing deserved to have their fate tied to that of the guilty.

The woman stopped at a crank mounted on the wall. She grasped it with both hands, strained to turn it.

Her arms shook with the effort of trying to manipulate something set for a man's height. Whimpers and panted sobs blended with the groan of metal against metal, the slow unfolding of a heavy tarp rolled against the ceiling.

Tir watched without compassion. He wondered idly when the trapper would come in and berate her for her inadequacy, equate her value to the dead man whose carcass already buzzed with flies.

Her plight interested Tir only in that it served to break up the monotony of his captivity. He would have been the answer to her prayers had she been willing to free him. But his promise to kill the human known as Hyde and leave her alive had fallen on deaf ears. His words had been wasted on a spineless creature who allowed herself to be terrorized by the man she'd accepted for a husband.

Tir could not remember a time when he was free, but not all his jailers had treated him poorly. Some, especially the acolytes, had shared with him the changes taking place in the world outside the catacomb prison. Others had left books in his cell, hoping to gain his favor, or perhaps reduce their own complicity should he gain his freedom in their lifetime.

He might have spared them. It was a moot point.

The acolytes matured into priests. Into deacons and bishops, and popes, grand rulers and god kings, chancellors—depending on who held the key to his cell. They aged and died, and in the end, many of them were laid to rest in the same catacombs holding his prison, their bodies becoming food for worms, then dust and brittle bones.

Tir's attention shifted away from the woman and her pathetic struggles. It returned to the open doorway.

Through it he could catch a glimpse of blue sky and white clouds. The sublime promise of freedom.

His latest captor appeared, a brutal, unkempt man with bearish features. Hyde.

Oh yes, Tir thought, *I would enjoy killing this human.*

A look of distaste crossed the man's features when he noted the tarp curtain extended only a few feet from the ceiling. "Worthless cunt," he directed at his wife. "What's taking you so long? You think they'll stop to ask who owns the lizards? They'll shoot us on the spot if they see them, and walk out of here without paying for what they came for."

Hyde's gaze shifted to the cell containing the corpse. He half turned in the doorway. "Raoul, get in here. Help this worthless bitch get the tarp down. Then haul Rudy's body out of here. Put it someplace where the dogs won't get it. We'll deal with it later. After you've done that, stay out of sight until the buyers are gone."

A toddler son followed the trapper into the building, then Raoul. Hyde's hand settled on the knife he wore strapped to his thigh as his gaze followed the teen.

Raoul moved with the grace of a shapeshifter and had the edgy energy of one, though Tir had never seen him in any form but human. The teen's attention went to the woman and then to the corpse. Covetous desire followed by satisfaction flared in his eyes before it was masked, making Tir stir with the anticipation of freedom.

There was buried hatred in the boy, fear. But there was also an animal urge to oust the alpha and claim his mate.

"Hurry up," the trapper said, jerking a chain attached to his belt and pulling a collection of keys from his pocket.

He unlocked the dead man's cell, remaining aware of what Raoul was doing.

Raoul finished lowering the tarp curtain and moved on to the task of hauling the corpse from the building.

Tir smiled slightly. Hyde didn't trust the boy. He never left Raoul unsupervised in the building for more than a few minutes. Perhaps with good cause.

There was just enough of a similarity in the eyes to make Tir think Raoul might be his captor's son, gotten on some other woman. The toddler's mother was too close in age to Raoul's, though given what Tir had seen of humans, she could just as easily be a half sister.

Tir's attention flicked to the wereman trapped between shapes. He wondered if Raoul saw the same fate waiting for him when his usefulness was extinguished.

The woman tentatively approached, beckoning the toddler to her arms. Her voice was little more than a whisper when she said, "I'll take Eston to the house."

"No. The two of you stay with me."

Hyde selected a key from the cluster in his hand and Tir tensed. Rage built when his captor opened a locked cabinet and lifted a taser gun from the shelf.

Despite his will to show no reaction, Tir's fingers tightened on the bars of his cell. No matter what his tormentors did to him, he didn't remain dead. The damage done would heal and his organs re-form. He was physically stronger than any human, but he wasn't immune to pain or the effects of their weapons.

Hyde turned. He met Tir's eyes and sneered. "Looks like I've already got a buyer for you."

He walked toward the cell. "Get in the chair."

Tir fought to keep his lips from curling back in a savage snarl. He refused to grant his captor a victory, already knowing the trapper enjoyed inflicting pain in any form.

With a casualness he didn't feel, Tir moved to a chair stained with a hundred years' worth of his blood. He sat, centuries of existence allowing him to win the struggle and keep his face expressionless. But hate slid through him like a cold glacier. There would be retribution, revenge for all he'd suffered.

The trapper unlocked the cage door. "Put Eston down and get in there," he ordered his wife.

"Please, Hyde, don't make—"

Fist and taser connected to the woman's cheek in a casual blow. "I'm not going to tell you again. Get him tethered to the chair. They'll be here in a few minutes."

The woman trembled as she set her son down and entered the cage. The stink of her fear swamped Tir. And if he hadn't long ago erected a barrier against human emotions, he would have felt it as well.

She scurried to the chair and hastily secured his already shackled wrists and ankles to it before darting out. He closed his eyes and leaned his head back, escaping the horror of his situation by letting his awareness drift through the open door to blend with the sound of birds and the rustle of leaves, the smell of the forest and wildflowers beyond the trapper's compound.

Freedom. Despite the immobility imposed on him by the chair, Tir felt closer to it than he had ever felt.

He'd changed hands many times in the last century. And each time, more of his history was lost to the humans.

Hundreds of years had passed since the last acolyte meticulously restored the tattoos covering Tir's arms—trying as he worked to get Tir to translate the unfamiliar images and symbols into sounds and words he could understand so they could be added to the parchment scrolls holding their meaning in long-dead languages.

Tir wouldn't have done it, couldn't have even if he'd wanted to. If he had once known their meaning—which perhaps he had, given those years when his tongue was removed and, later, his lips sewn shut—he no longer did. But he was sure of one thing: the tattoos held the key to opening the sigil-inscribed collar around his neck and breaking the spell keeping him locked in human form, his memories and his power denied him.

Fear—the only emotion he was capable of feeling—rose up and threatened to engulf him. Even if he gained his physical freedom, the possibility of enslavement would exist as long as he wore the collar.

It had been decades since he'd seen the rolled parchment pages containing the history of the translations that used to accompany him each time he changed hands. Given the nature of mankind, he didn't doubt the information had been stolen and copied into occult texts, but with the destruction and the devastation wrought by what the humans called The Last War, the knowledge enabling him to recover the meanings to the tattoos might well have been lost.

Tir blocked the fear as he had learned to block the pain and con-stant assault of human emotion. Outside, the rumbling of a heavy truck grew near, its brakes squealing as it stopped at the gateway to the trapper's compound.

Without opening his eyes, Tir followed Hyde's footsteps. He heard the gate open and men alight from the truck.

"You didn't tell me you were bringing—"

"I'm here as a favor to an important man," a smooth voice inter-rupted the trapper. "He wants my opinion before he pays your ask-ing price. Shall we go inside?"

"Only the three of you. The rest stay here."

The trapper sounded belligerent, though Tir could hear traces of suspicion and uneasiness.

"Unless we decide on the lion," the smooth voice said. "I'm sure you'd prefer we transport him and save you the trouble."

"Maybe."

The compound gate closed. Its lock clicked into place.

Tir's captor retraced his steps, his guests behind him. Before they came into view, the smooth voice murmured, "Is he blindfolded?"

"What for? He's in chains and shackled to a chair."

"Blindfold him. Or put a hood over his head." There was power in the voice now, a hint that the man it belonged to was used to being obeyed without question.

The trapper stomped into the building and found a burlap sack. This time he didn't bother to order his wife into the cell. He strode in, anger hiding his increasing nervousness, taking it out on Tir by roughly pulling the sack down over Tir's face.

"He's covered," Hyde said.

Tir heard the soft slide of the knife from the sheath strapped to the trapper's thigh and braced himself. He knew only too well the feel of that particular blade.

The wereman went silent as the strangers entered the building, his fear scent growing more pungent as Tir sensed him moving to the back of his cage and cowering there.

The lion and hyenas grew agitated. A voice Tir recognized from days past said, "The lion is almost as large as Zenzo. He'll make a nice addition to the collection, don't you think, Papa?"

"Only if the price is right, Tomás," the third stranger said, and then to Hyde: "How did he come into your possession?"

"Trapped him up north."

"And the prisoner?"

"Stumbled across him in a settlement while I was hunting in the Sierras. He was locked in a cell in the basement of a church. As far as I could tell, he was the only survivor. Everyone else was massacred. Werewolves maybe, or something else. There wasn't enough left of anyone to tell what got to them first."

"And you didn't think to turn him over to the Church or the authorities?" the stranger whose smooth, powerful voice had insisted on Tir's not seeing them asked.

"I've got expenses, and a man's entitled to profit from his labors. Either can have him if they'll meet my price."

"I've yet to see a demonstration that his blood is truly capable of doing what Tomás believes he witnessed when he was here last."

"I need to cut one of you. Which one will it be?" There was relish in the trapper's voice, not only at the possibility of inflicting pain but at the prospect of making money.

"I'll do it," Tomás volunteered.

"No," the smooth-voiced one said. "I don't recognize any of the tattoos on his arms as those of a lawbreaker, which leads me to believe they might well be marks to hold a demon here. I'll need to study them further before there can be any contemplation of presenting him to your great-grandfather. Until we know what we're dealing with here, it would be unwise for you to mingle his blood with yours. Our host can provide a demonstration to satisfy us or we can turn our attention to the lion and start our trip back to Oakland. I want to be home before the sun sets."

"Get in here, bitch," Hyde said, greed winning out over the pleasure of tormenting his visitors.

Tir heard her low whimpers as she shuffled in to join the group. Her cry merged into sobbing as it had on other occasions, the child in her arms adding his sounds of distress to hers.

In that moment, Tir was glad for the burlap sack that would hide his agony from the humans. He braced himself, not for the pain that came when the blade of the knife slashed across his arm and cut to the bone, but for the noise assaulting his mind as her wound was pressed to his.

A thousand discordant notes thrust together in a stabbing cacophony, almost making him wish for a death more permanent than any he had known. It lasted only until her skin was made smooth, her veins healed to prevent her life from bleeding out—but it seemed like an eternity.

"Impressive," the powerful-voiced one said, directing his comment at his companions. "Worth an investment, though again, it's important we take precautions at this stage and not proceed until we know more about the prisoner. Have him delivered to the house in the red zone we spoke about on our way here. It wouldn't do for too many people to know about him. And with the guard involved in a power struggle, it'd be unwise for us to transport anything besides the lion."

"I'll give you twenty-five percent of your asking price," the stranger Tomás called Papa said. "The balance when you make delivery in Oakland."

"If I make a special trip just for him, I'll have to go by boat," Hyde countered. "There are cameras now, and extra patrols. I'll be stopped as soon as I set foot in the city."

"Take him by truck," the one who seemed in control said. "We're well aware of your dealings with the maze owner and Farold. Do you think we can't guess where the hyenas and the abomination are heading?"

There was the jingle of coin, the sound of it being counted out. Tomás's father said, "I am willing to offer a bonus to cover the cost of delivery, if he's in Oakland by tomorrow at sunset."

"Where do you want him taken?"

"Tomás will remain here. When you get to the red zone, he'll guide you to the house. Do we have a deal?"

"And if we get caught?"

"I would suggest you don't," came the smooth voice. "The politics in Oakland are unsettled at the moment."

"I'll be there by tomorrow night," the trapper said, the words resonating in Tir strangely, as if this moment was preordained, the strands of destiny woven together by an unseen hand.

"Good." There was the sound of money changing hands, followed by footsteps and then the slide of metal against metal, the banging of cage bars as the lion was driven outside and the partition lowered again, trapping him there.

Tir waited, half-expecting to be left in the chair. But as soon as the three strangers left the building, the woman was ordered back into his cell and told to free him.

She did as she was told, scuttling in and undoing the bindings holding him in the prison of the chair, rushing away, gone from the cell before he bent over and pulled the burlap sack from his head.

Peace, of a sort, descended with the closing of the building door and the diversion of the trapper's attention to supervising the loading of the lion into the truck that would take it to Oakland.

Oakland, Tir mused, settling on a bed of straw and raking through his memories as he idly studied the intricate spiderweb in the upper corner of his cell. He found nothing to distinguish this city from all the others he'd heard about. Nothing to explain the sense of anticipation, exhilaration—hope—that filled him, leaving him unconcerned, uncaring he'd been sold like an animal.

The rumble of an engine nudged his thoughts to the three visitors. Outside, the truck was allowed into the compound and brought alongside the building. There were shouts and the sound of metal striking metal as the lion was driven from one enclosure to another.

Tir visualized Tomás from his previous visit. The boy—though the humans would consider him a man—was only a few years older than Raoul. But there any similarity ended.

Even dressed in traveling clothes it had been easy to see Tomás came from a background of wealth. Perhaps he'd be softer as a result, more careless. His companions wouldn't leave him unarmed. Not in this place. Not with a man like Hyde.

All it would take was an error in judgment, a moment of inattention . . .

Tir closed his eyes and savored dreams of freedom and vengeance, until hours later the sound of footsteps signaled someone's approach.

The hyenas moved to the front of their cage as if scenting death and the possibility of a meal, while the wereman's distorted limbs and half-furred body remained curled into a ball.

Raoul entered the building, the corpse of the man who'd been called Rudy slung over his shoulder. He stopped in front of the cages containing the dragon lizards, and with a shrug, the body dropped to the floor.

He kicked an arm aside then moved to the wall crank and began to raise the heavy canvas curtain hiding the dragon lizards. By the time it was halfway to the ceiling, the trapper returned, his wife behind him, arms crossed in front of her body as if to hold in what courage she possessed.

The dragon lizards stood in anticipation of a feast; the yellow-eyed female lashed her tail as the orange-eyed male moved to the front of the cage and flicked his black tongue out to touch the dead man's face. They were huge, deadly, the male easily weighing three hundred pounds, the female two hundred.

Tir didn't know the truth of their origins. He'd heard it claimed their existence was proof of evolution reversing itself after the near destruction of the planet. But he thought it just as likely they were the result of man's biological weapons, either created accidentally, or a calculated adaptation of the Komodo dragons.

They possessed a chameleon's ability to blend and could survive a wide range of temperatures. During the years of war and plague, they'd thrived on humans, feasting on corpses as well as live prey, until now the fear of them seemed genetically encoded in mankind.

Eventually order grew out of chaos and the creatures were systematically slaughtered. But it was too late by then to completely eradicate them.

Once the heavy tarp was rolled into place against the ceiling, Raoul slung the corpse over his shoulder. He climbed the metal ladder welded to the front of the cage, its rungs far enough away for him to avoid being bitten.

The dragon lizards grew more animated, their tails thrashing as they backed up, their eyes never leaving Raoul. They were capable of climbing trees, though the heavier they grew, the less they chose to do it. They were also capable of bursts of speed. But their true deadliness came from the venom and bacteria in their mouth. A single bite killed a man of the same weight within twenty-four hours. And if their prey escaped, their keen sense of smell allowed them to follow until they found the dying or dead.

At the top of the cage Raoul opened a hatch. He shrugged, and for a second time sent Rudy's corpse to the floor. The dragon lizards were on it as soon as it struck the concrete, savage jaws ripping flesh and clothing, crunching bone.

The trapper grunted and turned his attention to Tir, though Tir could see the man watched Raoul out of the corner of his eyes. "I've got a little evening entertainment planned for you," Hyde said.

Tir offered no response, verbal or physical. He remained on the straw bed and waited for events to unfold.

After centuries of being at the mercy of humans, he no longer had the capacity for curiosity when it came to what his captors planned for him. He endured. He survived. He dreamed of freedom and vengeance.

Raoul dropped from the ladder, his gaze going to the woman

and growing heated, hungry, then flaring with anger when Hyde said, "Open the cage, bitch, and get in there with him."

Disgust came to Tir with understanding. Over the centuries hundreds of women had been put in his cage for him to breed. Many had been killed in front of him the next morning when his jailers arrived to find them untouched.

"No, Hyde—"

A slap silenced her.

"Get in there and service him. I'm not likely to get my hands on something like him again."

"No—"

This time she was interrupted by Raoul's lunge.

A long, agonized scream followed as the trapper shot a taser round into the Were.

The scream gave way to whimpering and thrashing as electricity continued to surge into the boy's body.

Urine wet the front of his pants in a growing stain. Material shredded as Raoul convulsed, skin and bone contorting as black hair covered flesh until a wolf lay panting, insensate on the floor.

"Get the silver wire the witch in Sacramento warded," Hyde said, jerking the keys from his pocket and handing them to his wife before sliding the gun from its holster and leveling it on her.

She obeyed, remaining cowed even in proximity to the weapons stored in the cabinet. He holstered the gun when she returned with a spool. The charmed silver was spun like thread and mixed with another metal to give it physical strength.

Hyde took the offered wire and removed a tool from his belt. He knelt beside the wolf and sent a jolt of electricity into it to ensure the unconsciousness wasn't a ploy.

The body twitched and jumped, but Raoul's eyes remained closed while his breathing grew more erratic. It was enough confirmation for the trapper to set the taser down and wrap a thin band of silver thread tightly around Raoul's neck, trapping him in the wolf form.

Until now, Tir's time around shapeshifters had been limited to hearing their screams echoing through pitch-black catacombs in centuries past, as torturers tried to extract the names of others like them before war and plague brought the existence of supernaturals out into the open.

Given the band around his own neck, he was surprised at how little it apparently took to keep a Were confined to the furred form. Whatever the sigil-inscribed collar was that stole his history and his power, it was like no metal he'd ever encountered, nor was it the work of a human, of that he was certain.

Across from him the wereman was trembling, his misshapen body pressed tightly into a corner, his face hidden as Hyde dragged Raoul into the cell next to Tir's and left him there, lying in the stink of the dead human's body fluids.

The trapper retreated to the doorway then gave a savage jerk to free the taser barb before closing the cell and locking it. A few steps and he was once again in front of Tir's cage. It took only a glance at his wife for her to shuffle forward.

"The next time I see you, you better look good and fucked, bitch," Hyde said, unlocking the cage then slamming the door after she entered.

The hyenas cackled as if they approved. The wolf convulsed as if consciousness struggled to return.

Hyde put the taser and the spool of silver in the cabinet then left the building, locking and barring the door behind him. The woman remained cowered against the front of Tir's cage, her image overlaid onto hundreds of others in his memory.

For the most part they'd all been terrified. Afraid of eternal damnation if they lay with him. Equally frightened of the death waiting for them at the hands of his captors if they didn't. But some of them had been willing, and paid well, to seduce him.

None had succeeded. None stirred either desire or pity enough for him to take them.

Even when he'd been bound so he couldn't prevent them from putting their hands and mouths on him, from rubbing their slits against him in an attempt to entice him, he'd easily maintained control over his body so his cock didn't harden.

He would never mate with a mortal.

Three

ARAÑA sat with her back to the wall, her knees up to provide a pillow for her head. Her hair, freed from its braid at gunpoint, was a welcome curtain against the eyes of the men watching her.

Some sat on the concrete floor of the cage holding them. Others paced along the bars separating them from her.

They all wore the tattoos of lawbreakers. The majority were there because they'd been found guilty of rape or murder. A few of them were thieves caught for a third time, and from their conversation Araña knew they'd been given a choice between running the maze or being put to death under a three strikes law.

If the history books spoke truly, once there'd been an uncountable number of prisons and jails in the United States. Places that filled up as fast as they could be built, providing jobs and financial security for those who worked on and in them.

Now prisons existed only for the wealthy and powerful, those who could afford the cost of keeping a loved one incarcerated in order to avoid the death sentence or a criminal's tattoo. In most places small crimes were punishable by restitution and community service, more serious ones by hard labor and a tattoo—or death.

The framed "Wanted" pictures of Erik and Matthew rose in her mind. They'd been convicted in absentia on charges of piracy and murder. The first would have gained them a tattoo, but they'd been sentenced to die for killing the son of a councilman when they boarded his boat and discovered he was a child molester.

Araña's arms tightened around her legs as she fought against the wave of agony thinking about Erik and Matthew brought with it. A shuddering breath was her only concession, but it was noted by the men watching her.

Catcalls came, lewd offers of comfort if she'd push her pants down and bend over to press her buttocks against the bars of the cage separating her from them. She ignored the men, ignored even the sudden silence that came with the opening of a door.

She followed the visitors' footsteps as they walked down the aisle and stopped in front of the cell she was in. A melodic, unfamiliar voice said, "She'll make a nice addition to the entertainment to-night."

Farold, the man who'd paid the guardsmen a handful of bills when they'd presented her at the maze, said, "I thought you'd ap-prove, Anton. The betting audience has grown tired of seeing noth-ing but hunting. It's been a while since a woman ran. I thought you'd want to put her in the maze with only the convicts at first . . . Per-haps they'll even kill each other for a chance at one last f—"

"Language, Farold. There's no need for us to descend to their crudeness."

"I apologize. You're correct. There's no excuse for it. The in-come from the wagering proceeds will increase if we give the clubs a chance to offer odds as to what the men will do if given a chance at a woman. I took the liberty of sending her photograph along with the pictures and profiles of the men. She's really quite beautiful, which is an added appeal. Plus she bears a brand, one of the Church's, I think. But I didn't recognize its meaning."

"You did well, Farold. What was her crime?"

"Jurgen and Cabot brought her in. They warned me against touching her, quite vehemently. In fact, they were disappointed you weren't on hand to deal with the transaction personally. Both of them claim she's a witch and one of their companions died as soon as he touched her."

"Some of those who practice black magic are capable of setting such a spell in place. Jurgen and Cabot certainly displayed a great deal of restraint in not killing her outright. Cabot in particular. He's the youngest son in a family where the oldest inherits everything. If I remember correctly from my days with the Church and serving as his mother's confessor, he was terrified of anything that even hinted of witchcraft."

"You're correct. I got the impression Jurgen was responsible for keeping her alive and bringing her to us. Have you decided which of the hunters will work the maze tonight?"

"No. I'd hoped Hyde would be here by now with a new delivery. On his last visit he said he'd spotted several dragon lizards. He hoped to trap at least one of them."

There was a sharp inhalation. Araña almost glanced up at the mention of the lizards.

"Do you think that's wise with the turmoil going on in the guard? Carlos Iberá's influence is growing. If he succeeds in having his grandson named commander of the guard, his push to have the red zone done away with will grow even stronger. Hyde getting caught bringing dragon lizards here . . ."

"He won't get caught. And in the event he does, then I know nothing about his intentions, nor did I commission him to capture the creatures for the maze. Once he crosses the red zone boundary, and as long as we ensure they don't escape, there won't be a problem. On the contrary, I imagine they'll attract a larger crowd to the gaming clubs, especially on the evenings I set them against some of the hunters who have lost their drawing power."

"The werelion among them?"

"Yes. I'm afraid club patrons have become jaded in their tastes. Running the dregs of society against animals or Weres no longer draws the crowd it once did. But dragon lizards . . . I hope Hyde is able to deliver, and if I were a betting man, I'd bet on him. He's been an excellent supplier over the last couple of years."

"What you say is true."

"I'm curious about the brand and the claim the woman is a witch," the man with the melodic voice—Anton—said. And though Araña didn't lift her head, she could feel his attention focus more firmly on her, could hear power in his voice when he directed her to stand.

With a thought she knew the demon mark rode her shoulder again. She hoped it would move to her palm if either of the men dared to enter her cell.

Farold said, "I can get the taser. She'll stand quickly enough then and comply with your request."

"No need. I have a better idea. Perhaps I should let the demon amuse himself in the maze tonight. What do you think?"

"He's always a crowd-pleaser, especially when he's put in with humans."

"Announce it to the clubs then, so they can calculate the spreads and let their members know Abijah will be part of the entertainment." There was a brief pause, then Anton began speaking in an ancient language.

Words ran together, vowels and consonants blending so closely and in such odd combination Araña couldn't differentiate one from another. But the cadence and sound of them stirred something inside her, sent fear whipping through her, deeper even than that caused by the mention of the demon.

A breathless, nameless dread built in intensity as Anton's incantation did. Crashed over her in icy shock when it ended abruptly with a summoning name. Abijah en Rumjal.

She felt a wrenching, inexplicable sense of déjà vu at hearing it.

A primitive instinctual memory like the ones she sometimes experienced when she was trapped in a spider's vision and forced by her unwanted gift to destroy lives.

Araña lifted her head, unable to resist looking at the demon. Just as she couldn't fight when the fire called her to look into its black heart.

Terror left her breathless as Abijah shimmered into existence. He was a dark-skinned thing of nightmare and punishment—a harbinger of the Hell and damnation she'd been told since birth awaited her unless her soul could be cleansed of the evil taint the spider mark meant she carried.

The demon's eyes flared from gleaming yellow to bright red. His fingers ended in curling, wicked claws. Leathery black wings emerged from his back, like those of a bat, while a snake-like tail coiled around his thigh as though it were a living thing.

A forked tongue flicked out to taste her fear. A smile curled on his lips when he found it. And as if wanting to add to her terror, he reached up and caressed the mark on his chest with a deadly talon, drawing her attention to the golden scorpion there.

At the sight of it, the primitive instinctual memory and the wrenching, inexplicable sense of déjà vu slid through Araña once again. Her heart pounded against her chest as though it would beat its way through ribs and muscle and flesh in order to escape his proximity. The spidery shape of her own mark rested at the base of her spine as if cowering in the presence of a greater demon.

Abijah was naked. She noted it and pressed harder against the back of the cage when his penis stirred to life.

"She interests you," Anton said to the demon. "That rarely happens. Perhaps you'll give the gamblers a show they've yet to witness."

The demon made no reply, but apparently one wasn't expected. Anton said, "Bring her to the front of the cage, Abijah."

The maze owner's eyes narrowed when the demon made no move toward compliance. The fast race of Araña's heart slowed with sudden understanding. Abijah wasn't a willing participant in the evil of the maze. He was bound somehow, forced to serve a master not of his choosing.

"Bring her to the front of the cage, Abijah," Anton repeated, his tone holding a threat. And this time when the demon didn't immediately obey, the command was followed by a flurry of sentences spoken in the same unfamiliar tongue that had summoned him.

Abijah disappeared. Or seemed to. Until she saw the scorpion step through the opening between the cage bars, the deadly stinger at the end of its tail curled over its back.

Without conscious thought, Araña rose to her feet. Scorpion morphed to yellow-eyed demon.

The spider hid on the sole of her foot, as far away from the flicker of the forked tongue as it could get. The golden scorpion now marked Abijah's cheek rather than his chest, and what small hope Erik and Matthew had been able to foster in Araña, about her own mark, was extinguished. It was demon in nature.

There was no way to avoid Abijah's touch. No point in resisting it.

Taloned fingers curled around Araña's upper arm. His skin was hot, but she'd expected as much, knew from the spider birth dream that demons were born in a place of fire and molten lava.

Abijah pulled her from the wall of the cell and forced her to the front of the cage as he'd been ordered to do. Anton smiled and turned slightly toward his human companion. "You're right, Farold. She's quite stunning. Quite exotic, actually."

"It almost seems a shame to run her with the criminals."

"I know what you mean. We'll allow her two knives in the maze and give Abijah permission to play with her all night if the convicts don't kill her first." Anton took a step closer. "There's something about her . . . Is she a shapeshifter, Abijah?"

"No."

"One of the human gifted?"

Abijah's hand slid down Araña's arm in a frightening caress. It stopped at her wrist, and the shiny tip of a curved nail scraped over her veins before digging in deeply enough to draw blood.

He leaned down. The forked tongue darted out to lap at her blood before he released her. "She is mortal, but not one of the human gifted."

"Interesting. Her use of witchcraft must be learned instead of inherited. Too bad, but it might not matter. Given your physical reaction to her, are you capable of breeding offspring on her, Abijah?"

The demon refused to answer, forcing Anton to ask the question a second time, and then a third before an answer was unwillingly torn from him. "Yes."

Araña couldn't suppress a shiver of terror. She'd longed to know the feel of skin against skin, to have a lover. But not this one. Not a demon that sent the spider-shaped mark to cower on the sole of her foot.

Farold said, "Why not add a caveat that Abijah can't intentionally kill her unless she's escaping the maze? If she survives his attention, that'll make her next run a profitable one."

"You prove yourself a worthy assistant yet again."

Anton spoke in the flowing, frightening language, and at the end of it, the demon disappeared. "Done. Abijah has his instructions."

"I'll send the information along to the oddsmakers so they can factor it into their calculations."

"Do that. It should make for an interesting night." Anton focused on Araña's hand. "Let me see the brand."

She complied.

"Do you recognize it?" Farold asked.

"Yes. It's one the fundamentalists favor. It's not used much here, but in the San Joaquin, especially in some of the more isolated communities near Stockton, there are several groups who routinely use it to mark individuals they view as tainted by evil. The brand literally means *touched by Satan*, or alternatively, *one of Satan's own*. A witch practicing the black arts necessary to kill by touch alone would certainly fall into that category."

"I'm surprised they didn't burn her at the stake."

"I imagine her looks saved her from that fate, and perhaps the fact she's learned rather than gifted. More than one pious man has been led astray by a beautiful face and form, and thought they'd be able to redeem and reclaim the soul inside it."

Farold's eyebrows drew together. "But once she's branded? How would it be possible?"

"Where there's a will, there's a way. Once she'd been judged redeemed, a second brand would be laid over the first, attesting to the restored purity of her soul." Anton chuckled. "Very primitive views considering the revelations that have come since The Last War."

"True."

"I believe I've seen enough here, Farold."

Murmurs rose in the cage next to Araña's as soon as the two men left the room. Only now they were the sounds of men speaking in frightened turns about the demon, negotiating to work together in an attempt to survive and escape the maze.

Araña sank to the ground where she was. Fear and adrenaline washed away to leave a deep numbness.

Once again she pulled her knees to her chest to serve as a pillow. She wrapped her arms around them and let the curtain of hair hide her face.

Blood from her wrist soaked into her pants. Her side throbbed with pain, as did the places she'd been kicked and hit.

Thoughts of all she might be forced to endure in the maze overlaid the images of Matthew and Erik lying dead. The combination threatened to paralyze her, to provide an opening for despondency to envelope her in an icy haze.

It pulled at her, nearly succeeded in sucking her under and holding her there. But pride wouldn't let her remain in the deadly embrace.

Matthew's last words shamed her for allowing even a hint of

hopelessness to invade her. *Live for all of us*, he'd said. And she would.

She would live for them. And she would avenge their deaths by killing the two guardsmen who'd brought her to the maze.

Slowly she became aware of her surroundings again. The words one of the prisoners was speaking sank in, and Araña turned her head slightly, just enough to peek through the black of her hair and read the tattoos on the man's face.

Wife abuser. But he'd frequented one of the gambling clubs where his money was welcome despite the violence he'd been found guilty of. He'd watched men and beasts run through the maze, and though he'd never seen anyone escape it, he still had answers when the other convicts asked him questions about pitfalls and design, dead ends and traps.

Those answers chased the last of Araña's emotional paralysis away. Hope blossomed and surged through her veins.

There were places like the maze in other cities. She'd heard them talked about in boat towns and outlaw settlements, wherever men and women gathered to brag and swap stories over beer and moonshine and homemade wine.

The names of the cities were often volunteered, but when a man ran a maze and survived it, he didn't usually speak of its location or of the offenses leading to his imprisonment—and no one asked. That was unspoken custom among them because desperation could turn a former drinking buddy into a bounty hunter.

How many times had she heard the tale of Gallo's escape from a maze? How many times had he bought her meals and filled Erik's and Matthew's cups with beer while she captured his stories on paper with her pens and pencils?

She'd run Gallo's maze a hundred times in her imagination as she'd turned those oral stories into pictures. He'd never revealed the city, but as she listened to what the wife abuser said, familiar landmarks rose from her memory with perfect clarity.

She saw Gallo's run through the maze. Saw the statues he'd

passed, the walls streaked with blood where desperate men tried to claw their way up concrete surfaces studded with shards of glass. She saw the traps he'd discovered, the doorway to freedom he'd found, and she knew she had a chance of escaping death. This maze was the one Gallo had survived.

MOISTURE dampened Rebekka's palms as she reached the edge of the red zone. In front of her was the section of town set aside for gifted humans, though in this part most of it was weed-filled open space or row after row of destroyed houses covered with clinging vines.

There was no wall. No rigid boundary. But sigils marked it and wards were set in place to repel the predators that thrived in the red zone during the night.

She paused and turned to her companion. "You don't have to cross with me. The occult shop is only a short distance away. I'll be okay."

Levi shook his head, causing the sunlight to reflect off the thick mane of his hair. He lifted his lip in a silent snarl. Tawny eyes flashed, revealing the lion trapped in a human body. "I can handle it."

She nodded, knowing he wouldn't be deterred and feeling guilty for wanting his protection despite how uncomfortable it would be for him to cross the wards and remain in the territory of the gifted.

In a rational world, gifted humans and shapeshifters would view each other as allies, but the world wasn't any more rational now than it had been before The Last War. There was too much history between the gifted and the Were. Too much bloodshed. Too much suspicion and distrust, especially when it came to witches.

Rebekka stepped past the boundary and continued walking, keeping her back toward Levi. She imagined he'd almost rather die than get caught flinching as he crossed the wards.

She'd homesteaded a house in this section. But she rarely left the red zone and the brothels.

Her fingers curled around the token in her pocket. It had been delivered hours earlier to the brothel where her room was by a young boy, one of hundreds who roamed the streets in the main part of the city looking for work, willing to do almost anything for enough money to buy food—even carry a message from a witch into the red zone.

The token was a pentacle. Carved into its center was the Wainwright sigil, and at its outer edges, elaborate glyphs. With it came a summons only a fool would refuse to answer.

Rebekka shivered, not just from thoughts of the Wainwrights, but at the sight of the occult shop as it came into view. All along there'd been rumors about its owner, Javier. He'd been a frequent visitor to the brothels, though, thankfully, at those she worked in he'd come only to slake his need, leaving the women he visited no worse for encountering him. But at others he'd bought out the contracts of some of the prostitutes and they had never been seen again.

There'd been rumors of black masses and sacrificial offerings. But in the red zone there was no law, no police or guardsmen to investigate. It was only when Javier's body was discovered that the rumors were proven to hold truth—he was a dark magic practitioner who used human sacrifices in order to summon demons.

She shuddered. The tales might have been embellished, but she didn't doubt for a moment the existence of demons. More than one of the men who visited the brothels had spoken of the demon who sometimes hunted in the maze.

Rebekka cast a quick glance at Levi as they neared the occult shop. He rarely spoke of his time in captivity—what had been done to him by Gulzar to force his body into a horrifying blend of lion and man, or those he'd killed in the maze when he hunted there. But she knew not a day passed when Levi didn't think about it, didn't curse himself for escaping and leaving his brother behind to die or to become an insane monster—to hunt for the pleasure of humans who sat safe in their clubs and bet on the outcome.

She stopped at the edge of an inscribed circle painted in red on the sidewalk surrounding the shop. This time she didn't say anything. She let Levi reach his own conclusion and voice it.

"I'll wait for you here," he said and Rebekka gave a slight nod before stepping over the line.

There was a mild touch of magic, one that had probably served to warn Javier of a visitor's presence. She wondered if whoever now claimed Javier's shop and house benefited from the magic Javier had laid down.

Her heart rate accelerated as she drew closer to the shop. Weres were leery of magic, and perhaps because she spent so much time around Were outcasts, she'd absorbed some of their beliefs and uneasiness, despite having gifts of her own.

Her nervousness increased as she reached the shop door and entered. The air was heavy with the scent of incense, cloying, enveloping—tempting and yet repugnant at the same time.

A man glanced up from something he was working on behind the counter. A clerk, she thought, though she didn't discount him.

Pentagram jewelry, fetishes and candles, herbs, wands, cauldrons and athames—all were available and with plenty to choose from. But it was the books on magic and witchcraft that both awed and frightened her each time necessity brought her to the shop.

She moved deeper into the store, toward the place where the Wainwright witch would be. An entire wall contained a library of handwritten spell journals, individual shadow books no living witch would have willingly parted with. They were all that remained of entire families lost to plague and war, people who'd died long ago, so quickly they hadn't been able to burn the books in order to keep them out of the hands of strangers.

Rebekka stopped next to a woman dressed in black. Not the Wainwright matriarch. Even with the streak of gray in her hair, this woman wasn't old enough. But she was still powerful. Standing in the witch's proximity made Rebekka feel as though magic crawled over her skin like a hundred tiny spiders.

She pulled her hand from her pocket and offered the pentacle. The woman gave a small shake of her head. "Keep it. You might need it to summon help. I'm Annalise. But it's on behalf of the matriarch that I'm here. Tonight they run in the maze."

Only the instinct for self-preservation finely honed from being around Weres kept Rebekka from stiffening with the mention of the maze. If Anton Barlowe or Farold had any idea she and Levi were doing what they could to interrupt the supply of captured hunters, planning for the day when they could somehow find a way inside and free those held . . .

Rebekka suppressed a shiver—but only barely. "They're running convicts tonight," she said, somehow managing to keep her words neutral, as befitted someone who called the red zone and the brothels home.

Annalise pulled a book from the shelf. It parted on a page showing a werelion in a partial form, the head and arms those of a beast while the body remained human.

"A woman will run tonight as well," Annalise said. "It is beyond our control as to whether she will escape. But should she survive, she will be as important to you and the . . . man . . . who waits outside for you, as she is to us."

Rebekka didn't ask how the Wainwrights knew about the woman or Levi. It was possible they had spies who passed on information in the same way she gained it when the men and women who frequented the gaming clubs came to the brothel. But it was equally likely they'd gained the knowledge by other means, with a toss of bones or a reading of fire. There were whispers about the Wainwrights and their ancestors, tying them to black magic as well as white.

A tremor passed through Rebekka before she could stop it. The token she still held in her hand grew heavier. She understood the significance, understood if she acted on the witch's information, obligations would arise between them because of it.

Her gaze flicked to the picture of the werelion. Sometimes it was hard to maintain hope that Levi's brother could be freed or his sanity salvaged.

The destruction of the maze itself and the release of the animals and Weres held captive there seemed like an impossible dream. And yet it was one of hers. If the witches wanted the same thing, or might be persuaded to involve themselves . . .

Rebekka closed her hand around the pentacle and put it back in her pocket. Annalise returned the book to its place on the shelf and picked out another, opening it to a page with a handwritten spell and a picture of a pentacle similar to the one in Rebekka's possession.

"Can you read this?" Annalise asked.

It was a short spell, requiring candle, blood, and token, easy to memorize because it served only to trigger a larger one already set in place. "Yes."

"Should you need to use it in order to summon help, change the last word to *aziel*," Annalise said, placing the book on the shelf and leaving without another word.

Four

ARAÑA guessed it was nearing sunset when footsteps approached beyond the door.

The men grew quiet.

She rose to her feet as Farold entered with a satchel under his arm. He stopped in front of her cage, far enough back that she couldn't touch him, and emptied the contents of the bag onto the floor.

Two dozen knives poured out of it, many of them with dried blood on their blades. Araña's throat tightened when she recognized one of Matthew's, then saw Erik's as well as her own.

Farold glanced up at the camera mounted above the door he'd just come through. "You've got five minutes before the others are freed," he said, speaking to someone else as well as her. "Anton is allowing you the choice of two knives."

Behind her she heard the slide of metal, the solid steel that had served as a wall opening to become a doorway. A breeze swirled in, bringing with it the smell of evening air.

The choice of knives was easy. Araña indicated one of Matthew's and one of Erik's.

As they slid across the concrete toward her, she allowed herself the brief fantasy of using them on the guardsmen who'd brought her to the maze. But when they reached her, her thoughts turned only to survival.

She grabbed them and fled, emerging from the cell into a chute formed of outdoor cages. Wild animals lunged as she ran past them. They hurled themselves against the bars, excited by the prospect of a hunt.

A pack of feral dogs frenzied, spinning and salivating and finally turning to savage the weakest member. A bear rose on its back legs. A cheetah crouched in the cage next to it while hyenas laughed.

Adrenaline surged through Araña, but its source wasn't solely fear. This gauntlet meant to induce terror fed her hope. It was exactly as Gallo had described it.

Beyond the caged animals she paused only long enough to determine which direction the heart of the city lay in. Then she ran away from it, toward the forest.

Her lips pulled back in a fierce smile when she reached the next choice of turns. It was marked by pornographic statues, a beast raping a woman to the right, another doing the same to a man on the left.

She took the left without slowing, just as Gallo had once done, and ran past walls covered in vines, ignoring glimpses of light hinting at shortcuts, and deep shadows suggesting hiding places.

Cameras perched boldly on top of poles and concrete. Araña imagined just as many of them remained unseen, all of them turning violence and carnage into entertainment for anyone with the money to pay for it.

There were other statues along the way, most of them sexual in nature. She used them as others would use a street sign, hoped as she was doing it that they hadn't been repositioned since Gallo ran this maze.

Behind her a bell sounded. The feral dogs began barking, warning her the convicts had been freed.

Araña pushed herself to run harder, unsure how long it would be before the demon was released into the maze. Blood ran down her side from where the bullet had grazed her. She ignored it and kept going, her breathing becoming labored.

The maze encompassed miles, and one wrong turn would mean rape, possibly death. Her lungs burned along with her thighs, making her fight for each running step.

Relief fed her strength as she turned a corner and faced a bridge she'd hoped to find there. In the evening air a trace of steam rose from a channel too wide to jump.

The water disappeared through a bricked archway offering a tantalizing glimpse of freedom. She knew it was an illusion. Just as she knew the bridge was a trap.

Anyone rushing across it would drop into the water. And though its surface was calm and unbroken, beneath it waited schools of piranhas kept hungry for human flesh. The night Gallo ran, he'd seen the man in front of him fall into the water and be eaten alive.

Araña sheathed the knives. She wiped sweat and blood from her hands before grasping the metal railing and moving forward, keeping to the very edge of the bridge.

Gallo hadn't known where the trigger was, but there was one. And once it was tripped, a section of wood would swing downward.

At mid-span a scream tore through the maze, followed by another, and then another, telling her the demon now hunted. An involuntary shiver wracked her body as she pictured Abijah. She flinched when a different voice gave an agonizing cry of torment—the sound of it wavering, hovering in the air and turning her skin icy cold as it went on and on and on.

Footsteps drew close, more than one pair of them, pounding hard and fast. Making Araña hurry along the bridge. She nearly screamed herself as it fell away beneath her feet.

Only her hold on the railing saved her from plunging into the piranha-infested water. The upper body strength she'd gained from a lifetime of hard physical work served her well as she climbed hand over hand to reach solid footing.

Out of the corner of her eye she saw two convicts round a corner. She recognized them. One was the wife beater, the other a rapist.

Araña started running again as soon as her feet touched dirt. Seeing the trap of the bridge, the men would know the danger the water posed and cross it quicker than she had.

She followed their progress with her ears. They were catching up to her. But with freedom so close, she didn't think they'd linger to make sport of her—*if* the opening Gallo had escaped from was still there.

Araña turned the corner and saw it. Only instead of a doorway leading to sky and forest—and a nightmare trap in the copse of trees beyond it—a silvery web spread across the space.

Clinging to a corner was a spider half the size of a man. She started forward anyway, heart thundering in her ears but willing to take a chance it wouldn't attack. She'd never suffered a spider's bite, even when her hand had been forcibly thrust into a nest of them as a test of her soul's purity.

The leathery sound of wings made her glance upward. A whimper of fear escaped when she saw the demon.

Abijah landed in front of her, blocking her chance at freedom. His skin gleamed with blood. The metallic scent of it reached her on a breeze caused by his descent.

Just as it had done earlier, his tongue flicked out to taste her fear. His cock hardened to resemble those on the statues she'd run past.

The demon's smile held wicked menace. "I have something special in store for you," he said, taking a step forward.

She pulled the knives from their sheaths and braced herself for his attack. He leapt, but instead of attacking her, the batlike wings carried him past her and to the first of the convicts to round the corner after her.

Araña darted forward as the screaming started. With a glance up at the spider and an instinctual thought of apology, she sliced the web and pushed through it to where a path cutting through the forest beckoned and a trap waited.

Gallo had elected to clamber over rock and debris along the wall of the maze after his companion chose the path and entered the copse of trees, only to discover how deadly a choice it was. Araña pressed on, running along the bone-cluttered trail as the agonizing cries of the dying followed her into freedom.

REBEKKA shivered as the air cooled and full night drew closer. Despite Levi's presence next to her and her own gifts, she wasn't foolhardy when it came to roaming the darkness. If the woman didn't escape the maze soon . . .

Levi tensed. "Someone's coming," he whispered, lifting the gun he held and pointing it toward the trail.

She strained to hear something beyond the croak of frogs and the song of insects, but her ears were no match to those of a shapeshifter, even one who no longer had an animal form.

Rebekka worried her bottom lip as her thoughts strayed to the Wainwright witches. She wondered if there was a subtle message in the picture Annalise had chosen to show her in the occult shop.

Had the witch meant to imply more than the possibility of Levi's brother being freed? Was she hinting there was a way Levi could regain his ability to shift into a lion?

Icy fingers slid down Rebekka's spine as she touched the pentacle in her pocket. What price would the Wainwrights ask for such knowledge?

Levi nudged her, bringing her attention back to the trail. Their choice of hiding place had more to do with practicality than anything else. If the woman escaped at all, the forest was the only place they could intercept her and guide her to safety without revealing themselves. And the spot where they waited was the only one where several paths joined. Still the odds didn't favor either escape or—

A woman moved into view soundlessly, with determination, as if she had a destination in mind. Uneasiness assaulted Rebekka, the worry this was a trap. But logic and the token in her pocket said otherwise.

She stood, drawing attention to herself. Somehow she managed not to recoil when she saw the brand on the woman's hand, the Church's usual way of marking someone who practiced black magic.

Rebekka shoved her fear deep inside and said, "If you want a safe place for the night, we offer one."

Levi stood, and the woman's gaze shifted to the gun in his hand. It stayed there until he lowered it in a demonstration that they didn't intend to force her to go with them.

"Who are you?" the woman asked.

"No names," Levi said. "Not here."

In case I'm recaptured, Araña thought, nodding, the answer reassuring. They couldn't know she'd already seen them clearly enough to draw a picture that could be used to identify them.

She glanced past them. The tree Gallo had taken shelter in the night he escaped the maze wasn't far, but then what?

Home was a long way away, nearly impossible to get to without a boat. And she didn't doubt the *Constellation* had already been confiscated.

She intended to get the boat back. Just as she intended to stay in Oakland until justice was served on the two guardsmen. But she had no money unless she stole it, or returned to the place she'd been captured and found the wallet she'd lost after Matthew ordered her to run.

Beyond that, she was injured, her clothes bloody enough to attract predators of all kinds. She was in a strange place without allies . . . except for these strangers.

They would want something from her. It was the way of things.

But Araña found herself nodding slightly and slipping the knives into blood-crusted sheaths.

Tension left the woman's body. She bent down and retrieved a cloak before closing the distance between them.

The man came with her, his body language alert, protective. The woman thrust the bundle into Araña's hands. "When we're near the edge of the red zone, you can put this on so no one from the gaming clubs will recognize you. We need to hurry. At nightfall the were-wolves and feral dogs prowl in packs."

Araña nodded and followed the strangers. They stopped once, where forest merged into vine-covered ruins. She put the cloak on and they continued.

Rubble gave way to lit streets in an extravagant use of power. But it didn't surprise her, not given the old Victorian houses and the elegant people seen through bay windows.

Bouncers blocked club entrances, neckless men with thick arms and dead eyes. They began disappearing into the clubs as light faded quickly.

Behind her Araña heard the sound of locks clicking into place one by one, a domino effect spreading along the streets as humans gave over the night to the predators.

Her companions picked up the pace, and she could feel their tension mounting, the need to hurry measured against the desire not to draw attention. They ducked into a darkening alleyway, then another and another, until emerging on a street that made Araña halt in her tracks.

Brothels lined it, some connected by walkways, others standing alone. The woman glanced over her shoulder but didn't stop. "You won't make it to safety if you change your mind now. I've got a room here. You won't be bothered."

With a thought, Araña found the demon mark on her shoulder and drew comfort from it. She caught up with her unnamed companions and followed them into one last alley.

They stopped in front of an unobtrusive door. The man punched in a series of numbers to open it and Araña hid her smile. If they thought to betray her and lock her in, they wouldn't keep her using a system like this.

As soon as they stepped inside, her companions sagged with relief and identified themselves as Levi and Rebekka before indicating they were going upward. Araña told them her name as they began climbing a narrow set of stairs.

Levi left them at the first landing. On the third, Rebekka pushed through a doorway leading to a dimly lit hall. "Clients aren't allowed up here," she said, producing a key and letting them into a bedroom.

An open doorway revealed a small bathroom. Rebekka lit an oil lamp to take the edge off the darkness of the room. "I can't stay to tend to your wounds. But there are salves and bandages in the bathroom. Use what you need."

"Why are you helping me?"

"We'll talk about it tomorrow."

Rebekka opened a drawer and pulled out clothing. As she had with the cloak, she shoved it into Araña's hands. "We're close to the same size. These should fit you. I need to get downstairs. I'm the healer here. I won't be back until morning. You can take my bed."

She left and Araña showered, washing her clothing at the same time. Watching as clear water turned bloodred before disappearing down the drain.

When she was finished, she bound the wound on her side then freed the clothesline coiled on one shower wall and attached it to a ring on the other so she could leave her clothes to dry.

Exhaustion hit like a sledgehammer as she emerged from the bathroom. It made her movements slow and laborious as she pulled on a long shirt and slid under the blankets on the bed. But when she closed her eyes, sleep wouldn't come.

In the room beneath her the rhythmic creaking of bedsprings began. The thump of wood against wood intermingled with grunts.

Pain lanced through her heart, harsher than what spasmed

through her body. Memories washed over her, of lying in her own bed and hearing soft laughter coming from the bedroom next to hers as Erik said something to Matthew at day's end. Of their love-making, muted by the heavy, exotic tapestries they'd hung on their wall when she'd entered their lives.

Tears slid across Araña's cheeks. This time she didn't knock them away as she'd done on the boat. She let them flow freely to wet the pillow beneath her, and tried only to stifle the sobs that threatened to wrack her body.

Her chest ached with the effort. Her fingers curled into fists.

The feel of the skin stretching and pulling against the scarred tissue on her left hand made her aware of the demon mark. The spider rested on top of the brand.

Guilt rose sharp and fierce with the worry that she had caused Erik and Matthew's deaths. It lashed at her as mercilessly as the rod she'd once felt across her back each time her father claimed even the smallest wrongdoing was a result of the evil taint she carried in her soul.

She'd gone by another name then. One she'd shed ten years earlier, on the night she killed her parents and the clergyman who'd pressed the hot brand to her skin. The night she'd climbed aboard the *Constellation* and taken the name of the demon mark as her own.

Spider. Araña.

She dug her nails into her palms, unable to prevent the memory of that first night on the boat from assaulting her. In it she lay huddled in a blanket, too overwhelmed by all that had happened to protest when Erik dabbed salve onto her newly burned flesh with a cloth.

When it was done, he'd extinguished the lantern and gone on deck. She'd been only vaguely aware of Matthew untethering the boat and silently pushing it away from the dock and into the deeper part of the canal with a pole.

She understood now that together Matthew and Erik had used oars to maneuver the boat into the black shelter of night on the water. They'd rowed as she ebbed in and out of consciousness, hadn't stopped until finally the wind stirred to life and was caught by the sails.

Araña steeled herself. She tried to stop the memory from continuing to play out, but it was impossible. In it Matthew remained on deck while Erik entered the cabin. A match flared, its flame put to the wick of a lantern and trapping Araña in her demon gift.

She trembled as the reality of the day's events merged with the long-ago vision of Oakland and death. Felt her heart swell in agony as once again Matthew was cradling Erik in his arms. Only now she knew there would be no going home with Matthew—to grieve and try to pick up the pieces of their lives without Erik.

Araña rolled over in an effort to escape the pain, the question of guilt. But there was no escape, just as there'd been no escape from the demon gift that night.

The yellow-orange flame in the oil lamp Rebekka had lit trapped Araña so she couldn't look away. Her heart raced in her chest, as if its thundering beat could hold her soul against the essence of fire, the birthplace of demons—but it had no power against the gift that was a curse.

Yellow-orange gave way to red the color of newly spilled blood. Bright red darkened, became a black void as the last thumps of her heart faded along with her awareness of it, leaving her in utter silence.

The only sense of herself she had was spiderlike, as though she had become the darkness stretching across time and encompassing endless possibility. There was a peace to it, a unity with the mark she didn't have anywhere else. But there was also a price to pay for it—a terrible price despite the nearly overwhelming beauty that came in an explosion of color.

Silence yielded to sibilant whispers. Thousands of voices blending together like a rushing stream.

Black nothingness gave way to strand after strand of color. Thousands of threads given substance, each strand representing a soul, a life. And the urge to grasp them, weave them together into patterns of her own choosing was a tempting, haunting call that had grown stronger as she got older.

Araña fought against it as she always did, though she knew in the end she would lose. There was no leaving this spider's place of vision until she yielded.

And she would yield—sooner rather than later. Before the pain of *not* choosing grew so intense she would grab wildly, grasping two threads without caring about the result, what the intersection of two paths would mean or how their coming together rippled into the future and changed the design of it.

Phantom pain slashed through a heart she could no longer hear or feel as she remembered that long-ago night when Erik lit the lantern and the flame caught her, bringing her to this place. She didn't remember taking up the thread belonging to the witch, but she must have.

The view of Oakland from the water belonged to the old witch at the bus stop. Even now, it was a clear snapshot in Araña's mind, an image followed by the memory of pain and nothingness as she'd fought against touching another soul to the witch's.

But in the end, she'd lost. She'd chosen a second strand, a deep, rich earth brown, not knowing until she touched it that it belonged to Matthew—the stranger whose boat was carrying her away from the mob hunting her. And in that instant when she touched the thread of Matthew's life, she'd seen Erik's death without understanding the full truth of it or what crossing the witch's path would mean.

The first shimmer of pain pulled Araña from her memories. A nameless urgency made her push formlessly through twisting, multicolored strands—forward into some future moment—until a blue-black thread caught her attention and drew her to it.

She couldn't tell from looking at it what made this soul and life different from all the others, but she knew it was, knew the being it represented was like nothing she'd ever encountered before.

The pain intensified, isolating her until the only choice was to reach out and grasp the thread in a spidery demon touch.

There was a wrenching disorientation as darkness and nothingness gave way to midday sun and the Oakland skyline. She saw it through tattered canvas, the ripped side of a rapidly moving transport truck.

They were several miles away from the red zone. She recognized the tallest building and knew it was near the maze. Beyond it was one of the buildings she'd seen when they sailed toward the docks.

The truck was in an old graveyard. She noticed tombstones fallen among the weeds, a destroyed mausoleum with the words "Our Lady of Peace" above a doorway framing sky and forest.

Movement to the right turned her attention to what was inside the truck, and even without a physical presence, the sight of the dragon lizards with their tails swinging back and forth in agitation sent terror whipping through her. They were contained, as were the hyenas trapped in a small cage above them.

Next to the hyenas a wolf had bloodied its mouth gnawing frantically at the bars of its cage. The warded silver around its neck made her think it was a Were. Her suspicion deepened when she turned farther and saw the werecougar trapped between forms, his body vibrating with despair.

The sense of the future, *tomorrow*, reverberated through her. Given the proximity to Oakland and the presence of the dragon lizards, she knew she must be in the truck belonging to the trapper the maze owner had spoken of.

There was one last occupant in the truck, the one whose life she'd followed to this place and moment in time. But when she would have turned farther to look, searing agony prevented it, ripping her backward to the present.

She expected an explosion of color, a thousand threads to choose from. Instead there was only the single, blue-black strand in an infinity of darkness.

The pain stopped. Completely. In a way it had never done before while she was still held in the spider vision.

Pure blackness gave way to night. A man lay on a bed of straw, bathed in moonlight.

His wrists and ankles were shackled to a band of metal around his waist. An eerie sigil-inscribed collar encircled his neck, glowing icy blue.

There was no sound in her vision walk save for the sibilant whispers, now joined by discordant notes of music, a fractured rhapsody she instinctively knew belonged to him.

He had a face like the angels she'd seen in Erik's art history books, too beautiful to look at and yet so enthralling she couldn't look away. Black hair as long as her own rippled over his chest and back in erotic waves, making her want to reach out and tangle her fingers in it, making her crave what she'd never known and couldn't have—the touch of a lover.

Despite the length of his hair and the shackles imprisoning him, he was masculine perfection, the epitome of unfathomable power. And though Araña had no true awareness of her body, she had a phantom sensation of her breath catching and her cunt weeping with a need that would never be safely satisfied with anything but her own touch.

The man's eyes opened, his gaze meeting hers deep in the vision, trapping her in dark pools of blue. And in that instant she felt the shimmering touch of soul against soul and she understood even as the lantern flame released her to tumble into exhausted sleep, this time it was her life that was to become part of the weave.

Five

THERE was nothing for Tir to do other than wait—and endure—as the truck rumbled deeper into the day and closer to its destination. But unlike the centuries he'd spent doing the same, escaping the monotony of captivity by dreaming of freedom and vengeance, this time his thoughts were consumed by the woman.

Not the pathetic creature who had spent the night huddled near the door of his cage, knees pressed to her chest, arms wrapped around her legs, weary terror filling her eyes as she waited for her husband to enter the building at dawn. No, not that woman, but the one who'd invaded his dreams like a vision and filled his body with heat, doing what no woman had done in all the centuries he held in his memory—hardening his cock and filling his testicles with seed, leaving him with the burning need to find her and lie with her.

Tir's arm muscles bunched, straining against the tethers holding him to the chair as he remembered his actions the previous night. His lips pulled back in savage fury thinking about how he'd turned his back on the trapper's cowering wife as lust unlike anything he'd ever known burned through his veins.

Never in all his remembered existence had the need for release driven him to take himself in hand as it had after the dream, forcing him to seek relief as he fantasized about a female whose eyes were as black as night and whose imagined touch was a fire strong enough to melt his icy control.

His body hardened with the mere thought of her and stayed that way despite the jolts traveling up his spine with each pothole and bump the truck hit. Lava-hot lust poured into his bloodstream, making him close his eyes and begin fighting against the effect the fantasy woman had on him.

Thinking about the trapper helped. It banked the flames and filled him with cold hatred.

In his mind's eye he replayed the scene before daybreak—the trapper arriving and entering the cell, sneering with coarse satisfaction and greed when he noticed the erection pressing against the front of Tir's pants and caught the whiff of semen on the straw bedding.

"Hope you enjoyed her enough to leave a little something behind. It's about time I had another cash cow here," Hyde said before ordering Tir to pick up the heavy chair, the shackles on his wrists and ankles making the task difficult.

At taser point he carried the chair outside, then up the truck ramp and into a cage just barely big enough to stand in. Tir seethed when he was bound to the chair, and the cage door closed afterward, immobilizing and securing him for the duration of the agonizing trip.

The animals, including the wereman and Raoul, were loaded next. The dragon lizards were driven into cages at the rear of the truck last and the tarp flaps pulled closed and tied down, trapping them all in the cool predawn darkness.

Hours and miles had passed since then, each one of them adding to Tir's discomfort. The air was heavy, heated, filled with the dry, scaly scent of lizard. His skin was covered in a light sheen of sweat. Around him in the dim interior, the furred creatures panted, their body heat adding to what the close confines and sun-beaten tarp created.

The visitor left behind, Tomás, had barely spoken as they traveled, while the toddler, Eston—brought to ensure his mother would remain in the compound—fretted occasionally, but was already afraid enough in his father's company not to give in to tears.

The heavy rumble of the truck's engine drowned out the sounds of insects and birds. Tir closed his eyes, willing himself to ignore the torture of his confinement. He strained to hear something of nature, to escape the tether of his body and lose himself in the sweet hope of escape. Instead he heard the distant thump of rotors, the sound of a helicopter flying low and rapidly approaching from the direction they were heading.

Moments later Tomás uttered a single panic-laden word: "Guardsmen." And the truck accelerated savagely then lurched violently as it took a turn.

Machine gun fire erupted behind them. The toddler began screaming, terror of his father giving way to an instinctive fear of death as the truck careened forward, plowing through anything blocking its path.

Jolt after jolt of pain shot up Tir's spine as the truck bounced along, jerking and swaying dangerously each time it turned. Tree branches clawed and grabbed, stabbed and shredded the canvas, revealing the thick, dark forest hiding them from view.

Eventually the sound of the helicopter faded and the truck slowed. In the truck's cab Eston's screams of terror ended abruptly with the sound of a slap and Hyde's growled "Shut up."

"What now?" Tomás said, fear leaking through in his voice. "There'll be ground patrols looking for the truck."

The trapper's only response was to brake at a turn, then accelerate.

ARAÑA moved through the woods as quietly as her companions. The last time they'd reached a spot affording a view of the bay and the Oakland skyline, she'd compared it to the one she'd seen in her vision. They were nearing their destination, the abandoned cemetery with the destroyed mausoleum.

Her eyes went to the gun Levi wore holstered at his hip and the crossbow slung across his back. She hadn't known he was Were the night before, though it wouldn't have made a difference to her. A Were among humans was almost always an outcast.

She'd tumbled out of deep sleep and into an urgent sense of wakefulness as soon as Rebekka and Levi stepped into the bedroom at sunrise. The first words out of her mouth were a request for paper and a pencil so she could capture the vision scene. And as she'd drawn, she'd answered their questions about what she'd seen and heard while waiting to run the maze—and quickly learned of their interest in the werelion Anton intended to pit against the dragon lizards.

Uneasiness slid through Araña. It seemed too much of a coincidence, like an elaborate pattern created by an unseen hand—Rebekka and Levi waiting beyond the maze, the vision and the blue-black thread, the nightmare glimpse of Oakland on the night she climbed into Erik and Matthew's boat.

Her throat threatened to close thinking about them. She touched the sheaths that now held their blades, seeking comfort even as she steeled herself against the pain of their loss.

Her fingers curled around the knife hilts, and she tightened her grip until her knuckles paled and the fist squeezing her heart loosened. *Live for all of us.*

Matthew's voice whispered through her consciousness, reminding and reinforcing what she knew to be the truth. They'd always lived in the here and now, cared only about the present.

It was enough she'd loved them while they were alive. They wouldn't want her to grieve for them.

Araña took a deep breath and forced her fingers to loosen. The back of her hand brushed against the borrowed wrist-brace slingshot dangling from her belt. It wasn't a weapon she favored, but she was proficient with it, Matthew had seen to that.

Shadow gave way to sunlight around her, forming a wall to block the sadness and press her toward anticipation as the cemetery came into view, a small patch of forgotten civilization not yet reclaimed by forest or covered in vine.

A narrow road ran through it, faded gray cobblestones no longer holding against the weeds. She read the sign even as Levi said, "Nothing's passed through here recently."

He didn't ask if they were in the right place. Neither did Rebekka. From the road they had only to turn and look toward Oakland to see the picture she'd drawn at sunrise.

Rebekka knelt near the road and slid the knapsack off her back. She opened it and dumped its contents on the grass. Narrow strips of rubber, pierced with sharp metal and nails, lay in coils.

"If the truck has good tires on it, these might not be enough to flatten them," she said.

Araña nodded. Most of the outlaw settlements had spike strips in place to prevent guardsmen from driving in at will in a hunt to collect bounties. Those strips were more substantial than the ones Levi had fashioned, but they couldn't take the chance of arriving and relying only on their weapons to stop the trapper.

"I'll look for something else," Araña said, leaving Rebekka and Levi to position the spike strips and secure them so they'd remain in place when the truck drove over them.

She found a section of wrought iron fencing near a grave site, the ends jagged and sharp from whatever long-ago force had sheered it away from the base still buried in concrete. She liberated it and dragged it to the road.

Rebekka and Levi joined her in positioning the section of fence at an angle and fixing it there so the ground became its new base and the power of the truck would force metal through rubber.

Levi cocked his head. "Just in time," he said, freeing the cross-bow.

For a moment Araña heard only the sound of birdsong and whispering grass, but then the breeze shifted to bring the distant rumble of a truck. Her fingers brushed over the knife hilts again, but she didn't draw the blades from their sheaths. She unclipped the slingshot and placed it on her wrist before pulling metal bearings from her pocket.

They split up, Rebekka going to a place of safety while Levi sought a perch where the crossbow could be used effectively. None of them knew what they'd be facing, whether there would only be a driver, or whether the truck would have a mounted machine gun and guards.

Araña slid into the forest and waited, one of the metal balls tucked into the slingshot's leather pocket. She felt the vibration of the truck through her feet long moments before it roared into sight and accelerated when it hit the clearing, as if the driver was afraid of being caught out in the open.

The windows were tinted, hiding the cab's occupants, but the lack of a mounted machine gun made Araña smile in anticipated victory. She heard the truck drive over the spike strips and saw the tires gape when it struck the wrought iron fence, the impact making the vehicle sway dangerously.

The driver kept going, his speed increasing, spinning the rubber off the rims even before he reached the end of the clearing and was swallowed by forest. Caution held Araña in place long enough for the shadow of a helicopter to sweep across the clearing, the sound of its blades no longer masked by the truck.

It made another pass, the nose dipping, pointing at the bent weeds marking the truck's path, before lifting and spinning away. She moved then.

A sense of urgency gripped her. Where there was a helicopter, there would soon be guardsmen in trucks.

She didn't see Levi and could only guess he was on the opposite side of the road, moving forward, as she was. A child's screams poured ice into her veins, making her steps quicken though her training held, keeping her in shadow.

A hyena streaked by, followed by three others. Fear tightened her grip on the slingshot. Her thoughts flashed to the dragon lizards. If the hyenas were free . . .

Gunshots sounded, cutting across the engine noise like a sharp knife. A spray of automatic fire that didn't match Levi's weapon.

Araña pushed forward, the slingshot leading. The rear of the truck came into view, a twisted mess next to a tree broken and held upright by branches entwined with those belonging to its neighbors.

In a glance she took in the empty cages that had contained the dragon lizards and hyenas when she'd seen them in her vision. The werewolf desperately flung himself against the bars of his.

A bearish, rough-looking man crept around the side of the truck, a gun in his hand. Blood poured over his face from a gash in his forehead.

Hyde, she thought, remembering the name Anton had spoken, as she inched forward, looking for a clear shot.

"End of the road for you," the trapper said, wiping blood off his face with his arm, then taking aim at the werewolf. "You'd be useful but I can't trust you. It was the same way with your mother. When I was done with the bitch, I took care of her just like this."

The werewolf growled savagely in response, hurled itself more ferociously against the front of the cage. Araña moved again, found the shot she was looking for, and released the slingshot's leather pocket even as the man fired.

The bullet struck metal and ricocheted. The bearing projectile didn't. It plowed through eye and brain and bone, dropping the trapper instantly.

Levi emerged from the woods with Rebekka behind him. "There was someone else in the truck besides the trapper," he said, explaining his delay. "A man. He got away but I don't think he intends to double back."

Araña nodded as she left her position, securing the slingshot to her belt as she walked. It would have been foolish to ignore a potential sniper.

Levi and Rebekka reached the truck first. Rebekka leaned into the cab and turned the engine off. The child's crying stopped, and in the abrupt silence, they all heard the unwelcome sound of the helicopter above the canvas of the trees and the distant rumble marking the approach of guardsmen in jeeps.

"Leave the child where he is until we're finished in back," Levi told Rebekka.

"The dragon lizards are loose," Araña said as she knelt next to the dead trapper and rifled through his pants until she found the keys she'd guessed would be there.

Levi picked up the gun and checked it for ammunition before tossing it aside as worthless. "Only one of the lizards is free," he said. "The trapper used all but his last bullet on it."

Araña shivered and wondered if the freed dragon would put distance between it and the truck, or if the death of its companion and the smell of the trapper's blood would keep it close.

She stood and climbed into the truck, pushing her way through torn canvas. Levi did the same.

Part of her noticed the crumpled form of the werecougar, but it was the man at the far end who held all her attention, trapping her in dark pools of blue and making her heart race as he'd done in her vision. She moved toward him without being aware of doing it. Felt again the shimmering touch of soul against soul and saw recognition in his face where there shouldn't have been any.

Questions pressed in on her, but there was no time to ask them. She selected a key from the ring and fit it to the lock of the cage.

"Wait," Levi said, lifting his hand to stop her but halting as the spider appeared near her wrist in the place his fingers would settle. "He's not Were. He smells completely human. Look at his arms. They're covered in tattoos. Look how afraid those of your kind are of him. He's a prisoner being shipped to the maze to run. We don't know what his crimes are or whether we can trust him. Leave him for last. We'll free him from the cage and the chair then give him the keys so he can remove the shackles and go his own way."

Ice slid through Araña as the man's gaze flicked to Levi and she read the promise of death there. She tried a second key, then a third before the lock to his cage clicked and she opened the door.

"Give me the keys," Levi said. "I can free the wolf and the were-cougar while you release him from the chair."

Araña hesitated, not sure she could trust Levi. She glanced at the keys and tried to identify the one that would open the shackles.

"It's not there," the imprisoned man said, his voice rough, as though he rarely used it. "It was never in the trapper's possession."

Araña turned the keys over to Levi without looking at him and bent to the task of dealing with the restraints holding the prisoner to the chair. Her fingers brushed against his bare skin as she fought against cruelly tight bindings. Each touch made her breath catch and her eyes flash to the spidery demon mark, but it remained where it was on her wrist, a deadly bracelet with an agenda of its own.

Rebekka climbed into the truck and gasped at the sight of the prisoner before turning and murmuring in a soothing voice to the wolf. Levi opened the werecougar's cage and found a pulse in the human throat. "He's alive but unconscious. I'll have to carry him."

He stepped to the werewolf's cage and pulled his gun from its holster. Aimed it at the wolf who was already rolling on its back, exposing its belly and throat in a submissive gesture.

Rebekka moved to the side, out of danger as Levi unlocked the cage. The wolf continued to lie still when the door swung open.

Levi pressed the barrel of the gun against the Were's skull. "Don't repay us by making us kill you," he said as Rebekka stepped forward and removed the band of warded silver from around the animal's neck. It turned its head slowly and lapped at Rebekka's hand with a pink tongue.

The last restraint fell away and the tattooed stranger stood, his chains rattling as he took the first shuffling step. Even shackled like the worst of criminals, power radiated from him, stirring a deep instinctual recognition in Araña. Fear matched by and juxtaposed against desire, as if he could be either deadly enemy or eternal lover.

She shook off the strange musings as the werewolf jumped from its cage above the one that had housed the dragons. It closed its eyes, whined as if it was trying to shift into a human form but couldn't.

Levi hefted the Were trapped in a grotesque blend of cougar and man over his shoulders. "Let's get out of here."

Araña left first and felt a fresh rush of adrenaline. The jeeps carrying guardsmen were closer, but it was the sound of the helicopter that made her hands go automatically to the knife hilts.

The wolf jumped from the truck and went straight to the trapper's body. He issued a low growl before sinking his teeth into the dead man's throat and ripping it out.

Rebekka climbed through the torn canvas side of the truck, then Levi, with the werecougar slung over his shoulder. He glanced in the direction of the clearing and voiced Araña's fear. "We don't have much time. The pilot is trying to set down in the cemetery. Even if he doesn't, with the jeeps close by, he might lower guardsmen on a cable."

Levi set his burden on the ground. Despite his early argument to leave the tattooed stranger behind, he helped the man from the truck and tossed Araña the ring of keys before pulling his gun. "I'll stand guard."

Araña could hear the tension in Levi's voice. She knew without being told that if the stranger couldn't be freed, he would be left behind, his shackles giving him no chance of escaping the guardsmen.

There should have been cutters or a saw in the truck, but there weren't any. Araña salvaged a collection of stiff wire as she searched, claimed a short machete in a sheath as well as a knapsack packed with food, camping blanket, and matches kept safe in plastic.

Rebekka retrieved the child.

From the direction of the clearing, the helicopter rose above the trees, circled, and dropped again, the rotors thumping the air, a mechanical heartbeat sending terror out before it. Araña finished rifling through the locked tool trunk welded onto the truck body, the last of the places where anything useful might be stored, and found nothing.

She returned to the shackled stranger, who waited stoically, his gaze rarely leaving her. "We've got to leave now," Levi said.

"Go. I'll catch up later." The words held a confidence Araña refused to waver from, though her nerves were strung tight and her heart raced. She knelt and tried to steady her hand for the work of picking locks. She wasn't adept at it, not like Matthew and Erik, but given enough time—

Levi hesitated a second, then stepped to the trapper's body. He removed the knife and sheath strapped to the dead man's thigh and dropped them on the ground next to the claimed knapsack.

"You know where to find us," he said, hefting the still unconscious werecougar over his shoulders and leaving with Rebekka and the toddler.

The werewolf looked back before following the others into the forest. Araña's gaze flicked upward to meet the prisoner's and then she went to work on the locks.

In a thousand dreams of freedom, Tir had never imagined a human would risk her life for him, and yet there was no mistaking that the woman kneeling at his feet was mortal, despite the mark that had appeared at her wrist when she stood in front of his cage and refused to yield the keys.

His hands clenched and unclenched as he fought not only to remain still but to resist the urge to spear his fingers through her hair.

He'd convinced himself she was a sliver of recovered memory—a woman he'd lain with when he knew who and what he was; or a fantasy conjured up to accompany the dream of freedom, but neither had done her beauty justice.

She was exquisite, her skin the dusky brown of earth, her hair and eyes the color of night sky. "I am Tir," he said, giving her the name he hadn't heard spoken in centuries and had never willingly shared with any of his captors.

"I'm Araña."

Araña, the Spanish word for spider. He glanced at the mark on her wrist again and wondered if she had a witch's training, or carried a witch's spell.

There was the barest trembling of her hands as she tried to coax the lock open. He could sense her fear. It washed over him in waves despite her outward calm.

The tiny click of the lock yielding to her coaxing sent emotion surging through him, a fevered song pouring hope and anticipation into his blood as the first shackle fell away. The second followed quickly, and then she rose to her knees, her fingers going to the band at one wrist, the heat of her and the proximity of her mouth to his cock searing him, burning a fantasy into his mind even as the wrist restraints fell away and she turned her attention to the steel belt with its dangling chains.

When the last of the restraints put on him by humans dropped to the ground, Tir reached for her as she stood. She stumbled backward, evading him, her fear spiking. "Don't. It's not safe to touch me."

A small sound of anxiety followed as the tone of the chopper blades changed, indicating the pilot's success in landing it a short distance away. She pointed to the sheathed weapons and knapsack on the ground and said, "You can have them," before whirling away, heading in a different direction than the one taken by her companions.

Tir grabbed the items up and followed her, his muscles rejoicing in the movement. He didn't fear recapture, not in that moment.

There was no room for it in the heady reality of freedom—the sweet scent of forest and the play of sunlight in shadow, the smooth rhythm of movement denied him for centuries.

He wanted to laugh. To sing. To raise his arms toward the heavens in embrace.

Behind them he could hear shouts as the dead dragon lizard and the trapper's corpse were discovered. A machine gun rattled, a nervous burst slicing through leaves and silenced by a shout from a superior officer.

He smiled, a savage baring of teeth. Let them come after him. Let them try to take him. They'd be the first to feel his vengeance.

From time to time he caught a glimpse of the city. They were moving away from it and he wondered if Araña had a destination in mind.

He didn't ask. He didn't care. If he'd ever walked freely among men, it was locked away, the memory of it blocked by the collar.

Eventually he would go to Oakland and begin his search for the texts that would help him translate the tattoos on his arms. But for the moment he savored the freedom.

He easily paced Araña, found his attention returning to her repeatedly, caressing her lines, appreciating the sleek feminine form, the confidence in her stride.

His eyebrows drew together as the scent of blood reached him. His gaze was drawn to the black material of her shirt and the darkening spot on her side.

She was injured. The knowledge of it sent emotion roaring through him—not unfamiliar in the violent resolve it contained, but unfamiliar in its cause. The thought of someone touching her, hurting her . . .

Tir's fingers curled into fists, tightening on the sheathed knife and machete. He told himself the savage anger rose from the debt he felt toward her for freeing him, from the belief she would be of further use to him in navigating a human world he had no experience with.

He told himself the fierce possessiveness came from the lust she generated in him, a heat unlike any he could remember. Thoughts and images from the previous night flitted through his mind.

Suspicion flared as he remembered his revulsion when the trapper's wife was ordered into his cage to breed with him, her face overlaid onto a hundred other faces—women who'd failed to tempt him into breaking his vow never to lie with a mortal. And now, when he should care about nothing but savoring the freedom he'd gained, he burned for a human whose life was nothing against the span of his.

He didn't think he would be able to stop himself from taking her. He wanted to cover her body with his and know the sweet heaven of finding her opening and thrusting into her slick, heated core.

He wanted her kneeling in front of him, as she'd done when she removed the last of the shackles, and taking his cock into her mouth. The fantasy was so visceral it sent a jolt of icy-hot pain through his shaft.

Tir slowed, allowing her to pull ahead of him and move out of sight. His lips pulled back in a silent rage. Was she a witch? Was that how she'd shown herself in his dreams and sent lava-hot lust boiling through his veins?

Was this the work of some dark deity? Or some elaborate human ploy, his freedom an illusion to trick him into surrendering what he'd never surrendered before, his seed? Already he'd given her his name.

Tir slowed further, stopping at the edge of a clearing. There were no sounds of pursuit, and with the fading of Araña's footsteps, he was left surrounded by the rustle of leaves and grass, the scolding of a jay and the chirp of a squirrel.

He became aware of the knapsack he carried and the weight of the weapons in his hands. He didn't need them to survive, but they gave him an unanticipated advantage as he prepared to enter a world that was unfamiliar to him in so many ways.

Without meaning to, his gaze traveled to where Araña had disappeared. Instinct told him to follow her. His cock urged it.

The sheer force of his desire to go after her served as a warning of how dangerous she was to him. It made him turn away and take another path. But each step grew harder than the last the farther he got from her.

A tightness gathered in his chest, silken strands of unnatural worry weaving, encasing his heart until finally he stopped and turned back—unsure he could find her given the time that had passed.

Six

EXHAUSTION had finally pulled the child into the deep oblivion of heavy sleep. His face was pressed to Rebekka's neck, but she didn't stop stroking the small back, the gesture as soothing to her as it was to him. It had taken a while to gain his trust, then longer to understand his baby talk and to learn his name. Eston.

Where is his mother? she wondered, though she held no illusions when it came to men—or women. It was possible the toddler's mother was as evil as the trapper had been.

There were plenty of humans who wouldn't protest capturing and selling Weres to run in the maze. An uncomfortable number of them would applaud it.

Weres had rights—but only when they were in their human form. And even then, who would enforce them? Not the police or guardsmen. Not in Oakland anyway.

Was it any wonder the Weres, whose ability to shift form gave them an advantage when it came to survival, chose to live away from places where humans ruled? She didn't blame them, though it meant the Weres who lived in the human world were the outcasts who'd fled to escape punishment or chosen to leave because staying meant death.

Eston whimpered in his sleep, his arms tightening around Rebekka's neck and sending a twinge of longing through her heart. She wanted a child of her own, but she also wanted a husband, and she saw little chance of gaining one.

What few men she encountered regularly were those who visited the brothels. She'd never accept one of them. And the Weres, like Levi . . .

Marrying one of them was to be forever trapped between worlds, just as they were. It meant hardship, not just for her as a human, but for any children who might come.

That left only the gifted as potential mates and she knew so few of them. Beyond that, her talent wasn't one to help overcome the stigma of being the daughter of a prostitute and growing up in a brothel, even if she'd never lain with a man for money.

Rebekka sighed, a soft sound of sad acceptance as her fingers combed through Eston's silky locks of hair.

Next to her Levi asked, "What are you going to do with him?"

His voice was carefully neutral, as if he could guess the nature of her thoughts and didn't want to tread on the land mine her heart had become or be the one to point out the harsh reality of the world they lived in. There was only one choice. He knew it as well as she did.

"I'll take him to the Mission tomorrow," she said, arms tightening at the idea of leaving the child at the orphanage. But she couldn't keep him in the brothel and she didn't have the resources to try to reunite him with his mother—nor did she want to call attention to herself by attempting it.

Both the police and the guardsmen turned humans over to run in the maze. If word got to Anton Barlowe or Farold that she had the trapper's son, it could lead to questions, to retribution for the loss of the dragon lizards and the others being transported to the red zone.

Rebekka shivered. She glanced at the werewolf padding along next to her now that the trail had widened, then at the werecougar, still slung over Levi's shoulders and just beginning to stir and fight his way back to consciousness.

"If either of them is able to take a human form, maybe they can tell us where the trapper lives," she said. "Davida cares for the children left with her. She has the support of the Church and the government, as well as some of the wealthy. They have the resources to get Eston back to his mother if they know where to look."

"I'm not convinced they'd incur the expense, but if we learn where Eston is from and take him to the Mission, at least a story claiming he was handed off to a prostitute in the red zone will be believable. We know a man was traveling with the trapper."

The wereman jerked into sharper wakefulness. Levi quickly lowered his burden to the ground, pinning the shapeshifter on his stomach with his hands behind his back while animal instinct prevailed and made the werecougar dangerous to all of them.

Rebekka knelt where he could see her, the child snuggling closer, seeking safety in his sleep. "It's okay," she murmured softly, both to the toddler and to the struggling Were.

She pitched her voice to soothe them, touched the werecougar's emotions and calmed him through the use of her gift. He stopped fighting, though he continued to shake with fear.

Rebekka's heart went out him. She wondered how he'd come to be trapped between forms. A pure Were mother would kill an infant at birth if it didn't quickly settle into one shape or another. A mixed child born to a human mother wouldn't fare any better.

"We don't mean you any harm," Rebekka said, willing the wereman to meet her eyes, but he was too timid, or too traumatized by all that had happened, to look anywhere other than the ground.

"Levi is going to let you go in a moment," she continued. "Before he does, I want you to understand you have a choice."

Her throat tightened for an instant, her thoughts straying to

Levi, to the memory of offering him this same terrible choice, the loss of one part of himself in order to avoid a lifetime of being trapped between forms.

"I'm a healer. I can push the parts of you that are human back or I can push the animal away, so you're one or the other. Or I can do nothing and leave you as you are. Whatever you choose, you're free to go your own way. But if I change you, there's no going back. You will remain animal or man. Do you understand?"

The Were spoke, an unintelligible word forced through a mis-shapen cat's mouth. She assumed it was yes and met Levi's gaze, gave a small nod. He eased his grip on the werecougar, slowly releasing him, though Rebekka knew Levi would act quickly and lethally if there was the slightest hint of aggression.

For a long moment the Were remained still as he gathered his courage. Finally he tilted his head enough to look at Rebekka. He spoke again, a sound that might have been *help* or *cat* or something else entirely.

"Do you want me to help you?" Rebekka asked, feeling pity where others would feel revulsion at the sight of pelt and skin, human features as well as animal on the same body, as if a madman had hacked apart two separate beings then cobbled pieces of them into one.

This time the wereman nodded instead of trying to speak, accompanying the gesture by cautiously raking his claws in the dirt.

"You want the cougar's form?" Rebekka asked, wanting to be sure.

Another nod.

She didn't remind him there was no going back. She understood his choice and guessed he knew he would continue to be a victim if he elected to look human.

There was no advantage to it. In his animal form he might be accepted into a Were community, perhaps even allowed to breed. In Oakland he would have to hide his nature outside of the red zone because there were plenty of humans who feared and loathed Weres—in any form.

It might be different in other places, though she'd never heard of any. Only the vampires lived openly among humans. But in the cities where they did, like San Francisco, they ruled with an iron fist, ensuring safety to the humans who worked for them but guaranteeing death to any who defied or challenged them.

Rebekka passed off the sleeping child to Levi. Eston's face scrunched up, but he didn't wake.

"I'll need to touch you," she told the werecougar. "It won't hurt. But it'll feel strange, like you're a piece of clay in the hands of a sculptor. The calmer you are, the faster it will go."

She waited for him to make eye contact and consciously relax his taut muscles before she slowly leaned over and placed her fingers against the bare human skin. At first there was only a tingle, as if the magic of her gift was gathering information about the nature of her patient. The sensation passed and then she applied her will and her fingertips became like blunt knives sliding into soft clay, only more so.

It was a melding that took her completely, sucked her in and blocked everything else out. She saw the human parts that needed to be pushed back from the surface. She tugged at the fabric of the cougar, expanding it, pulling it forward to conceal anything not matching it.

When she came back to herself, a mountain lion was rising to its feet where the wereman had lain. It shook itself off, gold-colored eyes meeting hers briefly before its attention centered on the wolf.

The cougar went into a crouch, revealing yellowed, deadly fangs as it gave a feral snarl and prepared to leap. Levi's gun was out before Rebekka could move.

"Leave or die," he said, and even in a human form, Levi was alpha, the gun replacing the teeth and claws of his lion form.

The cougar slunk away, waiting until he'd gained the sanctuary of the forest before he screamed in protest at being denied the opportunity to attack the werewolf. The werewolf whined and groveled, crawled over to lick Rebekka's foot before slipping into the woods where all signs of obsequiousness disappeared.

ARAÑA stopped when she reached the stream. She knelt and splashed cold water on her face before drinking, her eyes searching for and finding the markers Levi had described during the hike to the cemetery.

There was safety upstream, a small concealed lair he'd built with his brother before they were captured and sold to the maze owner. To get there she'd travel in the creek, a risk because water drew prey and predators alike, but an advantage because water also would make it more difficult to track her.

It had been an unconscious decision to head there rather than back to Oakland. Some instinct guiding her, or perhaps it was training—splitting up lessened the odds of being caught.

Separating herself from Levi and Rebekka had also allowed her a chance to think, to make her own plans. After today's events, she considered her debt to them paid.

Her side throbbed painfully. Of greater concern was the blood soaking her shirt, a scent guaranteed to attract predators. She listened for the sound of Tir and heard only insects and birds.

It was for the best, she told herself. She'd known the moment his footsteps slowed, but she'd kept going despite the cry in her heart.

For a moment she allowed herself to remember his beauty, the heat she'd seen in his eyes when she'd knelt in front of him, and afterward when he'd reached for her. It was better this way, she repeated, turning it into a mantra. Whatever had caused her to touch her life to his in the vision place, it didn't change the truth of what the demon mark meant.

Staying with him and being unable to touch him or be touched in return would be torture. Coming to care for him would only lead to horror and pain.

Her throat closed up as memories rose, stark and brutal. Once she'd foolishly thought love could make a difference. She'd thought the convictions of her heart and the driving need to act on them would make a difference. She'd believed in whispered words and sweet promises, in a confident tone and a knowing masculine smile.

Araña opened her eyes and found the spider still on her hand. She shivered as she remembered the man she'd thought she was in love with when she was sixteen, how he'd coaxed her into sneaking away to his boat even after Erik and Matthew had warned her against it until they could learn more about him.

As with the guardsman who'd tried to rape her, the demon mark didn't hesitate to kill. Only unlike that death, she still carried the guilt of the other one with her.

She would never have what other women had. She'd never know what it was like to be held and caressed, to give her body over to a man, to claim and be claimed physically.

Araña forced her thoughts to the present. She stood, her hands settling on the knife hilts. The need for revenge burned like a hot ember in her belly, as did finding a way to reclaim the boat. Without *Constellation* there was little chance of getting home.

A stab of pain sliced through her with the word. Home was more than a place. Home had always meant Matthew and Erik. She stiffened her spine and found her earlier resolve not to allow grief to swallow her.

The sudden silence of the forest cut through her thoughts and sent her heart racing. She turned, expecting to see guardsmen, or Tir.

Instead there was a flash of gray as a dragon lizard erupted from the growth. It was on her in a burst of speed.

If her hands hadn't been resting on the hilts of her knives, there would have been no time to draw a weapon. She pulled the blades, and slashed at the deadly reptile even as it knocked her to the ground.

Her forearm against its neck was the only thing keeping it from biting her. Its tail and head thrashed violently as she sliced its underbelly, adrenaline giving her strength though its weight hampered her movements.

Fetid breath struck her face. Claws raked against her chest and sides.

Pain spurred her on and terror turned her into a creature of pure instinct.

Fluids gushed from the lizard's body and into her wounds. Burning. Stinging. Increasing her fear and making her more savage.

She dragged the knife upward and felt slick entrails emerge from the opening. The dragon lizard rolled away, trailing viscera.

Araña tried to get to her feet but slipped on blood and gore in a wave of nausea. She hit the ground and the lizard's head snapped around. It lunged, the orange irises marking it as male.

Her blades were there to meet the attack, this time going into the neck, driven deep by the lizard's momentum. Its blood sprayed across her face, into her eyes, blinding her so she didn't see the moment the reptile died, though she felt the severing of its spine as one of the knives slid through it.

Araña's arms trembled as she held the lizard's upper body away from her and wiped her face against the sleeve of her torn shirt. When she could see, she pushed the reptile to the side but remained crouched rather than trying to get to her feet.

This time the dragon lizard didn't move. Its orange eyes dulled as she watched.

She stood slowly then. Became aware of the sound of panting intermingled with whimpers and realized it was coming from her.

Her heart thundered, beating so hard that pain reverberated through her, drawing her attention down to her shredded shirt and flesh, to the blood trailing in bright red rivulets to soak into her pants.

The demon mark was on the back of her hand. She didn't know

whether it had sent its poison into the lizard or not. She guessed it had for the fight to end so quickly and without her feeling the lizard's teeth sink into her skin.

The venom and bacteria from the reptile's mouth would have turned her into walking death, a corpse waiting only for organs to fail and a final breath.

Adrenaline washed out of her, leaving her trembling, vomiting for long moments. She got into the creek and lay down, letting the cold water wash away the stink of lizard and the fluids coating her clothing and skin.

Her teeth were chattering by the time she rose to her feet. Dizziness made her stagger.

Araña fought it. She forced it away and started up the creek toward the lair and sanctuary.

The chills continued unabated despite the distance she put between her and the dead dragon lizard. Her clothing dried and then became soaked with sweat, each step becoming harder to take. Twice she stopped and bent over with dry heaves.

Her heart fluttered erratically in her chest, her mind attributing it to loss of blood, to shock, refusing to consider anything else, shying away from thoughts of the lizard's body fluids pouring over her open wounds, from contemplating the possibility that more than its bite was deadly.

The mound of rocks and downed trees hiding Levi's lair came into view. She climbed out of the streambed, relief making her sink to her knees in a pool of sunlight, the heat of the sun a hand pushing her forward to lie against warm soil.

Something was wrong. It was a fleeting thought lost in darkness as consciousness slid away.

TIR ran. Harder and faster than he had before. The nameless urgency he'd experienced as he turned away from Oakland and toward Araña had only intensified when he discovered the dead dragon lizard.

How she'd survived the attack at all was beyond imagining. But she had.

She still lived. He refused to believe it was too late. He *wanted* to believe she hadn't been bitten at all.

The evidence suggested otherwise.

His fists tightened around the knives. Her knives. He'd found them near the dragon lizard's corpse, as if she'd forgotten she was holding them. She would never have left them behind if she was well.

He owed her for his freedom. That's what drove him forward, he told himself. But he had no explanation for the bolt of agony spearing through his chest when he rounded the corner and saw her lying on the ground only a few steps from the water.

She whimpered when he pressed his fingers to her throat, a faint sound that could have been protest or a longing for the comfort of touch. Her pulse was weak, her breathing thready, and her skin fevered though she trembled as if freezing.

Tir rolled her to her back. Bile rose in his throat as the smell of infection and death reached him. It radiated from the scratches on her chest and sides, oozed from her flesh.

In all his memory he'd never willingly tended to another. But his hands worked without his conscious decision, stripped her of clothing so he wouldn't miss any of her wounds. And then he slashed her knife across his palms.

Never in all the times his blood had been used to heal had he endured the agony of it without promising himself one day vengeance would be his. But this time, as he pressed his hands to her fevered flesh, he willed his blood to make her whole, to restore her to health.

The agony of it was excruciating, worse than it had ever been, perhaps because on other occasions the healing had been involuntary. Pain sliced through his skull and the muscles of his arms and neck stood out in violent relief. His breath came in tortured pants. His jaw clenched against the need to scream as he battled to heal rather than kill.

Time slowed. Every minute contained an eternity of suffering as, wound by wound, he kept his palms pressed to her flesh, only leaving one spot for another when her skin was unblemished, unmarred. Perfect.

As abruptly as the torment started, it was gone, leaving him disoriented, his eyes unfocused for long moments, until the smooth texture of her skin and her nakedness burned away the haze left by the painful echoes of his sacrifice.

She was beautiful. Beyond what he'd imagined the night before when her appearance in his dreams had made him wake and take his cock in hand.

He caressed every inch of her with his eyes. The earth-rich color of her skin stirred primitive emotions, a fierce possessiveness twined with the searing flames of lust.

They were the same feelings that had made him turn away from her earlier and take a different path. But looking at her, he knew he wouldn't be able to leave her again without taking her first.

His attention lingered on dusky breasts tipped with dark areolas, then moved to her smooth, bare mound. Carnal hunger clawed through his belly, ravenous and dark.

It was a bestial urge to dominate. To mate. To cover Araña as she offered herself to him on hands and knees, her thighs parted and her folds slick and open.

The strength and suddenness of the erotic fantasy, the power she had over his body—even when she was unconscious and helpless—brought the return of uneasiness.

It damped down the lust, cooled it, until his gaze went to the place between her thighs, drawn there again against his will.

A moan escaped as he fought the need to tumble forward, to prostrate himself like a supplicant and press his mouth to her tempting flesh.

Seconds earlier the lust pulsing through him had been primitive in nature. Now he wanted to worship her with heated kisses and an adoring tongue. He wanted to inhale her scent, taste the honey of her arousal, and hear her whimper as he pleasured her.

Once again the force and suddenness of the desire, the intensity of the fantasy, shook him. Only this time his uneasiness was met with a wall of lust, a lava-hot need that had built up over centuries and wouldn't be denied.

Tir couldn't stop himself from rising to his feet and shedding his clothes before lifting her into his arms. He stepped back into the creek, going to a sun-warmed pool his subconscious had noted.

As he sat, cradling her on his lap, his hands smoothing away all evidence of her near death, he told himself he meant only to clean her of blood. It was a lie, one he admitted as soon as her eyelids fluttered open and she tried to escape.

Tir's arms tightened automatically, ruthlessly, as if some part of him feared he'd lose her if he freed her. "I won't hurt you," he managed, her struggles inflaming him, the rub of slick flesh against slick flesh making his buttocks clench and his cock throb.

"Stop," he said, holding her against his chest, nearly moaning at the feel of her breasts with their dark, dark nipples brushing his skin, sending icy hot streaks of sensation down his spine and through his penis. "I don't intend to hurt you."

The words barely penetrated Araña's consciousness. Panic. Fear. Confusion. The emotions held her in their grip as she tried to make sense of where she was and what had happened.

It came to her in hazy, fever-shrouded glimpses. The fight with the dragon lizard. The trip up the creek. Collapsing on the bank. Tir.

Clarity brought shock. She was alive when she should have been dead.

Araña stopped fighting. With a thought she found the demon mark above one nipple, trapped against Tir's bare chest.

A more familiar fear made her heart trip into a frantic beat.

Panic from a different source gathered and she started to struggle again as she said, "Let me go. It's not safe to touch me. The mark—"

Tir's arms tightened, preventing the words from escaping. His laugh was a heated stroke along her spine, a hot cupping of her breasts and mound.

"You can't kill me," he said, burning away her fear and panic with the absolute certainty in his voice.

Araña stilled, for the first time becoming aware of the smoothness of her flesh now, where earlier it had been ragged and bleeding, torn in the fight with the dragon lizard and the encounter with the guardsman. Becoming aware, too, of the heat of his skin, the hot throb of his cock trapped between them.

She felt bombarded by sensation, by something she'd only imagined. Heat pooled in her labia, her breasts. Her breath came faster, taking in his scent, imprinting it on her consciousness along with the feel of his body against hers.

She wanted to turn in his arms, to wrap her legs around him and press more tightly to him. To guide him into her and touch her lips to his as her fingers explored him. She wanted to capture this moment of physical contact and turn it into a memory she could cherish and savor for a lifetime.

Araña closed her eyes and did nothing but feel. His heart beat steadily against her breast, sending subtle vibrations through her nipple and straight to her cunt. The taut muscles in his arms as he restrained her made her feel safe rather than confined.

Warm water lapped against her, caressing her folds as sunlight slid over her back and shoulders. His heat seeped into her.

Birds sang and leaves rustled. The stream rippled over rocks. All of it the music of the living.

A shiver of need went through her. A primal craving that came with surviving, that fed on Tir's touch and the hardened length of his cock trapped between them.

Carnal hunger knotted in her belly, urging her to press her lips to his neck and leave a trail of kisses on her way to his mouth. To coax him into opening for her, to twining his tongue to hers in wet heat and shared lust.

He'd healed her. She tried to remember something of it, but couldn't. Perhaps that was why the spider allowed his touch. But it didn't guarantee the spider would allow more—or ever allow it again once the contact was broken.

His arms loosened enough for her to ease away from him. The instant her gaze met his, spider vision and reality melded in the deep water blue of his eyes, submerging her in the memory of the soul thread unlike any she'd seen before, the sigil-inscribed collar glowing icy blue when she followed the strand to him.

Levi had said Tir smelled completely human, but held in Tir's arms, Araña thought the Were was wrong. Fear and worry, hardlearned habit, made her try again to warn Tir. "The spider—"

Tir stopped her with another laugh, with fingers tracing her collarbone—the feel of it something out of fantasy, so exquisite she never wanted it to end.

She'd hungered for touch all her life.

A moan escaped. It was followed by a gasp when his palm covered the demon mark.

"If it was possible for me to die at the hands of a human, it would already be done," he said, the words nearly lost when his palm glided downward over her hardened nipple.

Araña shuddered. She fought to think, to question, to choose— though deep inside she knew she wouldn't turn away from the lust she read in his eyes, from the needs of her own body to know a man, to have, for a little while, what others could have for a lifetime—a lover.

He wasn't human. His words confirmed her suspicions.

He wasn't Were. That much Levi had right.

She didn't think he was vampire.

"What are you?" Araña asked, her voice barely audible.

His eyes became instantly hooded. "Does it matter?"

He shifted their positions abruptly, rolling so she lay underneath him, caged in the shallow pool, her upper body held out of the water by her elbows.

"Does it matter?" he asked again, his cock rubbing against her swollen folds and stiffened clit, making her tremble with need and the desire to cant her hips and have him pierce her.

Did it matter?

A small voice said yes. She might hunger for touch, but her soul longed for true intimacy—the joining of spirit and flesh as Matthew and Erik had.

A more insistent voice said no. Tir could touch her where others couldn't. And at least for a little while, she wanted to lose herself in passion, to forget what she'd lost.

"It doesn't matter," she whispered, putting more weight on one elbow in order to free an arm. She mimicked his earlier touch, tracing his collarbone, though her touch was more tentative than his had been. "I was dying and you healed me."

He brought his face closer to hers, the movement causing the long, silky strands of his hair to become a curtain enclosing them in a private world. "It was a fair trade. You freed me."

Araña gave a small nod of acknowledgment, reading in to his words that they were even now—a debt had been incurred and paid. There was no longer any obligation between them.

She ducked her head, feeling suddenly shy with the stranger who lay so intimately on top of her. She wanted this. She wanted him. But her normal confidence seemed to have deserted her.

Another shiver of need went through her, accompanied by a small sound of longing. Her fingers tangled in the black silk of Tir's hair as her hips lifted, pressing the unprotected head of her clit against the hot steel of his erection.

"Please," she whispered, a small word holding so many different meanings for her.

Raw need twisted in Tir's gut, urging him to possess her even as it was tempered by an unfamiliar, inexplicable desire to protect her.

She was beguiling him, drawing him into a web with her at its center.

He didn't understand her, couldn't guess at what motivated her. Her emotions were quicksilver he couldn't grasp, her thoughts hidden in dark eyes.

Only her body was easy for him to read. And it sang to his, a siren's song of temptation he had no will to resist.

"You're beautiful," Tir said, brushing his lips against her cheek, the touch gentle despite the savage ache in his cock as she ground her bare mound and clit against it.

Her soft laugh made him smile. "You're the beautiful one," she said, and he caught the words with the press of his mouth to hers.

Deep inside him, in the hidden recesses of lost memory, a warning sounded against sharing breath with her—but it came too late. He moaned against the satin of her lips, the sweet yielding of feminine to masculine as she opened for him, welcomed his tongue with hers in a slow, sensual slide.

He was sorry now he'd brought her to the water. The first taste made him hungry for more.

Later, he promised himself. Later he would kiss down her body and press his mouth to her swollen cunt lips. He'd lap the honeyed arousal he found there.

He shouldn't care that no other man had ever touched her this way. But a savage, primal satisfaction surged through him at the thought of having her as only he could.

Liquid hunger poured into his bloodstream as one kiss melded into another, then another. He settled more heavily on her, changed their position, his arms sliding underneath her shoulders and his hands cupping the back of her head, his elbows supporting them both in the shallow pool.

His strength made it easy. His reward was the feel of her arms wrapped around him, her fingers tangling in his hair, holding him to her as if she were afraid he'd leave.

Soft, desperate sounds spilled from her mouth to his, enflaming him further. The head of his cock found her opening, sending a jolt of unparalleled ecstasy through him.

He rubbed back and forth, tormenting them both, swallowing her gasps and soft cries. She retaliated by lightly raking her fingernails down his back, by grabbing his hips and trying to hold him steady so she could impale herself on him.

Tir resisted with a husky laugh, with the rub of his chest over the tight points of her nipples. Fiery need arrowed straight to his cock each time his nipples struck hers.

He wanted to lift up, to press his nipple to her mouth and feel the lash of her tongue, the grasp of teeth and pull of lips as she laved and bit and sucked. He wanted to kiss downward to her breasts and do the same to her.

Later, he promised himself. Later he would explore more of her, conquer every inch of her.

A shock of pleasure made him gasp. Lost in his fantasies, he'd forgotten about resisting, about drawing out the moment when his length would be held deep in her body.

She'd captured his cock head in the hungry mouth of her opening. And it wept, cried in ecstasy, his arousal joining hers in a heated wash as she clenched him.

Twin urges assailed him. The desire to swallow her virgin cries warred with the desire to watch her face as he forged inside her for the first time.

The latter won, though his lips clung to hers and his tongue was loath to leave the wet heaven of her mouth. When he was finally able to draw away, her sound of protest added to his pleasure.

The sight of her midnight eyes clouded with desire filled him with a satisfaction he wouldn't have believed himself capable of, not when it came to a human. But she wasn't just any human. She was the one who'd freed him.

She cried out when he pressed deeper. She was so tight, so hot he nearly came from the exquisite pleasure of having the muscles of her sheath tighten and spasm on him.

"Araña," he whispered, the name torment and benediction.

It strained his control to keep from thrusting all the way in a single stroke, to keep from giving in to the mindless, clawing hunger she created in him—a hunger magnified by centuries upon centuries of abstinence.

Alpha and omega. The first and the last.

He couldn't remember anything as pleasurable, didn't know if he'd ever lain with a woman before.

He'd never imagined how close ecstasy and torment could be.

With excruciating slowness he worked his way in. He couldn't resist the urge to cover her mouth with his, to feel her open for him, letting his tongue slide past her lips as his cock had done through the slick, swollen folds of her labia.

He shivered when he was fully seated. Stilled.

It was beyond imagining.

Tight vaginal muscles rippled and clenched, welcomed and resisted.

Heat surrounded him, bathed him, made him want to cry out.

Araña.

Her name echoed through him. In warning? In recognition?

He didn't know. He knew only that nothing had ever felt as good as this, as having her beneath him, her body open and his penis held deep and fast inside her.

Araña's arms tightened around Tir's neck. The thick length of his cock was a throbbing presence in her channel, an echoed heartbeat filling her, stretching her in a seamless blending of pain and pleasure.

His lips left hers and she cried out at the loss. When their eyes met, the intimacy was nearly too much for her. She felt exposed, stripped bare, the shields necessary to survive no longer hiding her vulnerability, her need for love and touch.

Araña lifted her head and pressed her mouth to his, wanting to hide, willing to give her body but not her soul, not to a stranger who would soon be gone from her life.

His kiss didn't allow the escape. His tongue plundered, commanded, insisted she cling to him, surrender a part of herself she knew she would never recover.

It didn't matter, she told herself, knowing it was a lie and forcing everything from her mind but the moment, the reality of having Tir inside her.

She felt him fighting to give her time to adjust to his size even as need pulsed between them in a fierce, rapid beat that made it impossible to remain still.

Her sheath tightened on him. Feminine pride surged through her with the catch of his breath, the sharp thrust of his hips.

"Please, Tir," she said against his mouth, and it was as if some barrier inside him broke.

His tongue fucked against hers as the hard length of him surged in and out of her.

She clung to him, moved with him.

Ecstasy. There was no other word for it.

She understood then why fortunes and lives and honor itself were sacrificed for the promise of passion.

Hot flesh and masculine desire turned her into a primal woman, a creature caught in the endless spirals of fierce joy.

She struggled for breath.

To get closer.

To reach the pinnacle that expressed itself in a sharp cry and brought exultation when her orgasm triggered his, leaving her swamped in feelings she never thought she'd experience.

For long moments afterward he continued to lie on top of her, nuzzling, kissing, his cock still inside her, as if he were in no hurry to part from her.

He was everything she'd dreamed a lover would be.

It was foolish, she knew it was, but she closed her eyes and allowed herself to pretend she'd always have this. Tir's touch. His body covering hers. The pleasure he'd shown her was possible between a man and a woman.

When he finally rolled away to sit in the shallow pool, she wanted to follow him, to climb onto his lap and cling to him. Instead she sat, bathing herself in the sun-warmed water, struggling in the aftermath of sex to find words, chiding herself for the fierce longing to be held, for craving true intimacy as well as touch.

Her eyes teared with memories of Matthew and Erik together. Their shared glances and casual caresses, the way it was impossible to think about one of them without thinking about the other. Her throat tightened and she forced the pain back to the place in her heart that would always contain it. She couldn't afford the weakness.

Live in the moment, in the here and now. That's what life had taught her.

Make the most of every opportunity. That was the lesson favored by Erik and Matthew.

Tir watched the play of Araña's thoughts across her face. Her emotions buffeted him, sliding through mental barriers erected over centuries.

What was it about this human that affected him so strongly? Stripped away his control as though it were nonexistent?

She rose from the shallow pool, black hair and water trailing down her back, tanned skin covering sleek muscle and a beautiful feminine form. She was like the Eve of the religious—unbearable temptation capable of leading any man to his destruction.

Tir caressed her with his eyes, hunger flaming to life, filling his cock so it rose along his abdomen, filling his testicles so they hung heavy with seed. There was a fleeting thought to ask her about the scars crisscrossing her back, the brand on her hand, but when she stepped onto the mossy bank and turned toward him, dark eyes sultry, holding a knowledge he'd given her, only carnal desire remained.

"I want you again," she whispered, meeting his gaze boldly before lowering her eyelashes, shy temptress and brazen seductress rolled into one.

Seven

TIR surged out of the water to go to her, the gentle first lover he had been giving way to something darker, more primitive, as the promises he'd made to himself roared to life with the sight of her bare mound.

"Lie down," he ordered.

Color bloomed in her cheeks. But her nipples beaded, making him hunger for a taste of them.

She sat, drawing her knees to her chest, her movements graceful. The erotic fear he read in her and her subtle disobedience heightened his desire.

Tir crouched in front of her, a male in his prime, his thighs splayed, affording her a view of his thick erection and heavy testicles.

If he hadn't been sure of his own ability to discern the nature of others, he'd have thought she had to be a gifted witch to affect him so profoundly, to do what no human female had ever done before, harden his cock and take away his will to resist.

He tangled his fingers in her hair, tightened them until she tilted her head backward, exposing her neck in an unconscious show of submission.

The scent of her arousal swamped him, told him she would accept a dominant lover. And his lips pulled back in silent anger at the thought of any other male having her.

He pressed his lips to her throat, feeling the wildness of her heartbeat there—a primal fear mixed with the desire to mate, both of them knowing he could easily kill her. Both of them knowing he wouldn't.

Because of her, he wore no shackles. Because of her, sunlight danced on his skin, flirting with shadows as a breeze dried him, reminding him he was physically free for the first time in memory.

He wouldn't let the desire he felt for her enslave him, he told himself, kissing upward until he covered her mouth with his, swallowing her cry before he took her breath and gave her his. He'd been at the mercy of humans for centuries. Now he had one of them completely helpless, subject to his will.

His tongue dominated hers. His fingers slid through raven-black hair, tugging, pulling her backward until she lay sprawled on lush green moss. It took more effort than it should have to keep from following her all the way down, from covering her body with his and thrusting inside her again.

Her hands found his chest, delicate fingers going unerringly to his nipples and sending an icy-hot spike of need straight to his cock. His hips bucked and his buttocks clenched, echoing the throbbing desire of his penis to impale and thrust.

"No," he said, freeing her hair to take her wrists in his hands and pin them to the ground at her sides.

She was a warrior in her own right. He'd seen the evidence of it—in the corpse of the dragon lizard she'd fought and killed as well as in the courage she'd demonstrated in remaining to unlock his shackles while the guardsmen drew closer. Yet she was fragile compared to him, so very mortal. He could easily crush the fine bones of her wrists. But he knew that even in the throes of passion, he wouldn't.

She was safe from him unless she proved to be his enemy. And even then, he'd take no pleasure in exacting vengeance.

With a moan he left the sweet temptation of her lips. Her breathy protest and the needy sound of his name as she whispered "Please, Tir" were a song that made him want nothing more than to please her.

He kissed downward, to a dusky breast capped with a dark, puckered nipple. Her back arched when he laved it with his tongue then took it between his lips and began suckling.

The scent of her arousal deepened, the desire she felt sliding past mental barriers and hitting him in waves, melding with his own. He was torn between freeing one of her wrists so he could take the nipple's twin between his fingers, or continuing to restrain her, keeping her at his mercy.

He delayed the decision, kissed across her chest to capture the other nipple. She shivered underneath him, her hips lifting, angling so her wet cunt lips brushed against his thighs where he knelt between hers.

The feel of her hot, smooth mound eradicated every thought but the one that had his lips leaving her breast and trailing downward toward the feminine folds waiting for him. At her abdomen Tir forced his mouth away from her. He lifted his head, testing his control by doing nothing more than looking.

She was intoxicating. Exquisite.

He wanted to memorize the sight of her bare cunt, its secrets unfolding for his pleasure, its lips glistening, hungry for his kiss and the feel of his tongue slipping between them to thrust into her heated core.

It was torment to remain motionless, especially when her hips rose in carnal offering, bringing the scent and heat of her so close he had only to flick his tongue out to taste her.

Tir shuddered, resisted giving in to her. He wanted to pin her thighs to the ground, to see his hands holding them open. But he knew he'd be lost if he freed her wrists.

He knew he couldn't trust her not to touch him, to tangle her fingers in his hair and force him to her mound. And unlike the unwanted women who had tried to entice him by rubbing themselves against his face while he was held motionless by chains, with Araña he'd be a willing prisoner.

On a groan Tir closed the distance, pressed his face to her cunt. He inhaled her. Savored her. Lost himself in the ecstasy of hot flesh and slick arousal.

His head spun with the scent of her. His cock head grew wet and his heart raced.

She rocked against him, tormented him even as he tormented her. Begged with words and movement for him to suck her hardened clit, to pierce her with his tongue.

Fire scorched through his penis in warning, and he fought to keep his hips from jerking, refused to hump the air like the small dog a long-ago captor had been overly fond of. He ran his tongue up her center, felt the clenching of her channel as she tried to capture him and pull him in.

Silky, slick folds deepened in color with his touch. The tiny hood of her clit pulled back, drawing his mouth to it. She cried out with his possession and yet fought to get away from the pull of his lips with the same desperation as she fucked the tiny organ through them.

Tears streamed from the corners of Araña's eyes. Desire ruled her.

She'd never imagined such pleasure was possible. Each lash of Tir's tongue, each suck sent need spiking through her, sharp as a razor-thin blade and just as dangerous. Time and time again he held her on the edge of desperate climax, in a place of exquisite agony and unbearable pleasure, only to deny her its release.

He became all that mattered in her world. And when he allowed her to come, she only barely remained conscious as wave after wave of unparalleled ecstasy washed over her.

It left her boneless, weak, her helplessness stirring instincts of self-preservation. She shivered when he pressed a kiss to the spidery mark that now lay demon-inked on her mound.

The act reminded her he wasn't human. It sent her emotions into turmoil as her mind raced to build walls around her heart and soul.

He lifted his mouth from her cunt. Dark blue eyes glittered in a face of otherworldly beauty. She couldn't look away as he crawled up her body and took her again, sharing the taste of sex and submission with her as he did it.

Afterward he rolled to his side, taking her with him so they lay together in lazy contentment. Her fingers traced a line of symbols on his arm, strange glyphs and sigils, none of them recognizable.

They weren't the punishment tattoos given to a lawbreaker. She'd lived among the outcast and criminal for ten years; she knew what those marks looked like.

"What do they mean?" she asked when her fingers reached his shoulder.

His eyes became hooded, just as they'd done when she asked him what he was. He answered with a question of his own. "How is it I saw you in a dream, and then you were waiting to free me?"

Her hand fell away from his shoulder, but he caught her wrist, his fingers a shackle. The suddenly hard lines of his face did nothing to detract from his beauty. If anything, they compelled her to answer.

"The demon mark causes me to have visions," she said, giving him a small part of the truth.

His gaze moved to the spider now resting in the curve of her neck. He studied it, eyebrows drawing together in a concentrated frown as he freed her wrist in favor of brushing his fingertips over the mark.

"I once knew what this meant," he murmured. "How did you come by it?"

"I was born with it." The truth and yet not the truth, but Erik was the only one she'd ever revealed the spider birth dream to.

"You were branded because of it?" Tir said, reclaiming her hand and taking it to his mouth, pressing a kiss to the scarred flesh.

The gesture was so tender and unexpected she ducked her head to hide its impact on her. "Yes."

"And the scars on your back? They are also because of the mark?"

"To beat the evil out of me."

He carried her hand to his chest and left it there, then cupped her chin in his palm, forcing her to look up and meet his eyes. "When I'm free of the collar my enemies have enslaved me with, I will hunt down the ones who hurt you and kill them."

"They're already dead."

"You're sure?"

"I saw them burn," she said, shivering, remembering.

She was twelve again, seeing the righteous fervor in the eyes of her parents and the clergyman as they prayed over her while she sat tethered in a chair much like the one Tir had been in.

The room sweltered from the fire in the fireplace. The brand glowed red as it was lifted from the flames and brought toward her.

She cringed at the remembered sound of her cries and pleas, her recitations of scripture denouncing evil as she begged them not to press it to her skin. But they did it anyway.

The brand seared her flesh, leaving only pain and rage, a desire to stop the torment at any cost. Caution and fears for her soul were lost to agony. In that moment she'd been beyond caring about consequences. She'd wanted the pain to stop and the restraints burned away so she could escape the chair, the house, the settlement.

She'd used the gift she'd never dared reveal for fear it would be more proof she was destined for the fires of Hell. She'd called the flames and they came in an explosive gust. And because her parents and the clergyman were between her and the fireplace, the

fire consumed them, filling the air with their screams just as they'd
filled it with hers.

Tir wondered where her memories took her. Her emotions were
a roiling mix, horror and fear, hatred and guilt, hurt and loneliness
and confusion.

The intensity of his need to comfort her nearly made him resist
the urge to lean forward, but it was only a fleeting thought, lost as
soon as his mouth was on Araña's.

Her sweet moan was enough to make him crowd closer, until she
was on her back and he was on top of her, his tongue rubbing and
twining with hers.

It was pointless to deny his physical desire for her. Lust burned
away any possibility of being with her and not touching her.

He wanted to keep her with him. Told himself it was only to sate
his carnal hunger and help him navigate a world he'd never moved
about freely in. But part of him remembered his attempt to leave her
earlier, how a tightness had gathered in his chest, silken strands of
unnatural worry weaving, encasing his heart until he finally stopped
and turned back toward the path she'd taken. And that part both
feared she was part of a trap and considered the possibility that her
presence wasn't an accident, that she'd been sent by some unremem-
bered ally to help him.

Tir lifted his mouth from Araña's. He stroked the smooth skin
of her cheek, brushing his knuckles over the spider now resting
there, so thoroughly a part of her he couldn't feel where it began
and ended.

Imprisoned as he'd been in the back of the trapper's truck, he
had only been able to follow the events leading to his physical freedom based on what he heard. It was clear Araña and the others were
waiting in ambush. "Who are the others to you? The Were and the
gifted human?"

"They're strangers who offered me shelter last evening when
I escaped the maze."

Shock reverberated through Tir. It wasn't the answer he'd expected. "You didn't know them before?"

"Until yesterday I'd never been to Oakland."

Her grief slid over him, a deep swell of anguish that rose from the black depths of her eyes and then receded as she got control over it. "The dragon lizards were meant to be used against Weres in the maze, including Levi's brother. Rebekka's gift is to heal both Weres and animals. That's why they ambushed the trapper's truck."

He rubbed his thumb over the spider, making the connection from an earlier answer. "You saw it in a vision?"

"I saw the graveyard the truck would pass through. I knew what it held and thought it would pass through today."

"Where's your home?"

She blinked rapidly and looked away from him, locked down her emotions so tightly all he felt was the strength of her will. "It's days away," she said after a long pause. "I've got business in Oakland to attend to, and before I can leave, I need to reclaim the *Constellation*."

"Your boat?"

She swallowed. Nodded, then said, "It will have been confiscated by now. I need to get her back before I can go . . . home."

"From the guardsmen?"

She gave a slight shrug. "Or the pier owner. We had to take a public berth in the port. The dockhand warned us if there was any trouble the boat would be impounded along with everything on board her."

"We?"

"My family." The grief broke through her mental barriers, revealing its source.

"I will help you avenge them," he said, knowing they were dead. "And I will help you recover your boat."

Araña didn't say anything as the wild ride of her emotions and the events of the day caught up to her, leaving her feeling unsteady

and unsure. She was intensely aware of Tir's weight and the feel of
his skin against hers, how much she already craved his touch, how
easy it would be to not think, not feel anything but the physical pleasure he could give her—to forget he was a supernatural being whose
life span was probably measured in centuries, if not longer.

"Why?" she asked, looking at his face again.

He didn't pretend not to know what she was asking. "I need your
help as well. This is your world more than mine. Avenging your dead
and recovering your boat is a small price to pay if because of you I'm
able to translate the tattoos on my arms. They hold the answer to
getting the collar off my neck."

She thought of his hooded eyes when she'd asked about them.
"You don't know what they mean?"

"If I once did, I no longer do. This land was a vast wilderness yet
to be discovered by Europeans when the last acolyte sat next to me
restoring the faded writing."

Her heart gave a hard beat then slowed to a painful throb. She
glanced away, telling herself not to be foolish and weak. She'd known
there was no future with Tir when she lay with him. She'd taken his
cock inside her with no expectation that he would remain with her
even through the night. And now he was offering . . .

Her cunt clenched, giving its answer. Her mind hesitated. She
knew only too well how few important books had survived in the aftermath of The Last War.

Hadn't she and Matthew and Erik lived well by selling their services as thieves to rich men who loved to play the game of stealing
one another's treasures, including books? "What if the information
is lost?"

Tir nuzzled her cheek, and with a thought she found the spider
beneath his lips. "I believe I'll find what I seek in Oakland. Otherwise I don't think you would have found your way into my dreams."

Araña had only to remember the moment his eyes opened, his
gaze meeting hers deep in the vision, followed by the shimmering
touch of soul against soul, to believe he was right. "I'll help you,"

she said, agreeing, shivering with renewed ecstasy as he rewarded her answer by joining his body to hers—and doing it over and over again after darkness drove them into the shelter of the lair.

IT was well after midnight when the werewolf crept closer to the wrecked remains of the truck. He remained cautious, alert for scents that might hint at booby traps.

The stink of guardsmen was everywhere. They'd fanned out, split into groups.

Some of them followed the path he'd taken in order to stay close to the werecougar and healer. Others had gone in the same direction as the once-chained man and the woman who'd managed to free him. None of the guardsmen had gone far.

Cowards. From the safety of their trucks and helicopters they reigned with their guns. But they didn't have the courage to take their fights into the forest, where the question of who was the most efficient predator would be settled with their deaths.

They'd left Hyde's body to rot, and the scavengers had already made a meal of it. Little remained. Still, the werewolf paused when he reached it. He lifted his leg and urinated on the bloody, shredded shirt and gleaming rib bones.

He stopped midstream, wanting to finish the task in human form, and once again attempting the change. He whined as, this time, muscle and bone reshaped themselves.

The change was excruciatingly slow and painful, feeding the terror he'd been carrying with him, that the witch-cursed silver wire he'd worn around his neck for almost a day would result in his becoming caught between two forms when he tried to regain his human one.

He fell onto his side, writhed in dirt and leaves and torn bits of Hyde's flesh until finally it was done. And then Raoul looked down the line of his body and laughed. He was whole, his limbs ending in fingers and toes, his skin free of fur.

His hand went to his cock. He stroked himself, savoring the scent of the trapper's death—his father's death—though he hadn't been sure of it until Hyde stood in front of the cage, gun lifted, taunting him, intending to kill him.

Raoul turned his head. Eyes more wolf than human contemplated the bloody strips of torn clothing, the bones not yet carried away by scavengers.

He fantasized about his return to the compound. Imagined mounting his father's wife, claiming her just as he would everything else belonging to his sire.

A snarl escaped thinking about the way she'd been forced to remain overnight in the prisoner's cage. He'd caught the scent of semen when he finally returned to consciousness as a wolf. If her womb thickened with child, he'd rid her of it, just as he would have rid her of Eston if he'd been freed during the wreck as the hyenas and dragon lizards had been.

Better that he hadn't. Part of Raoul recognized that. He'd seen the way Hyde used the toddler to tether the mother.

He could decide later what to do about his half-brother, whether it would be smarter to return to the compound with him and receive a hero's welcome, or leave him at the place where the healer intended to take him in the morning.

Raoul's thoughts lingered for a moment on the healer and the Were. They were going to be his best chance at recapturing the being their companion had freed. He hoped he'd be able to track them to the place they called home—after they got rid of Eston. He'd left them when he realized Eston would recognize his human form and show no fear, making them suspicious of him and eradicating any advantage he might have if he needed to use them.

Raoul stood, cock still in hand. He widened his stance and let loose another stream of urine, pissing on what little remained of his father, shaking the last drops from his penis when his bladder was empty.

He stepped over the shackles that had once held the prisoner, the being he'd thought of as a human-demon from the moment they'd found him alive in the foothill settlement, imprisoned in a church basement, his clothes bloodied and torn as if he'd been massacred along with the rest of the people there but had come back to life. He'd smelled human then, too. But no ordinary man would have survived whatever happened to the settlers.

The presence of the priest at the compound the day before, arriving with the men who'd taken the lion when they left, was enough to confirm Raoul's belief that the tattooed man was a demon kept trapped in a human body by the sigil-inscribed collar.

Finding the dead dragon lizard next to the creek was added proof. The woman couldn't have killed it; no human armed only with knives could have.

Raoul was glad the guardsmen hadn't recaptured the human-demon. If they had, there would be no chance of getting him back, no point in lingering in Oakland. They'd be the ones to make a profit.

He'd only risked returning to the ambush site in order to scavenge clothing and the cash Hyde thought was so cleverly hidden. Now the sight of the truck stripped of its useful parts, blackened by fire, enraged him.

The human-demon was all that remained of the valuable cargo, and if he didn't hurry, he'd lose his chance to collect what was rightfully his. The man left behind to travel with them to Oakland had probably already reported to the priest what had happened.

It would be easy enough for the priest to learn from the guardsmen that the prisoner had escaped. By daybreak tomorrow, those in his pay would be hunting the human-demon.

Raoul gnashed his teeth in frustration. Working for the Church was out of the question. They'd use him and then call him an abomination before making sure he met his death.

He had no way of gauging the human-demon's strength, but the chains and restraint chair along with the dead dragon lizard were warning enough. From the tracks he'd followed, it seemed that the prisoner had split away from the woman who'd remained behind to unlock his shackles. He'd gone a couple of miles before turning around and backtracking, then following the female and rejoining her.

It didn't surprise Raoul. In the wolf's form he'd smelled the desire between the two of them when they first saw each other.

It was probably the woman's blood that had drawn the dragon lizard. Drops of it lay along the trail leading away from the truck, and he'd caught the scent of it when she first appeared after the ambush.

As with Hyde's corpse, the scavengers had already gotten to the dragon lizard's carcass. It was hard to tell exactly how it had been killed.

There were slashes. Raoul had seen that much. He thought the demon might be powerful enough even in a human form to possess talons when the need arose. It would explain why his wrists had been shackled on short chains to his waist.

Regardless, the demon-possessed human lusted enough for the woman to follow her. Knowing it gave Raoul an advantage.

He could use her in setting a trap. He could use the healer and the Were as well. But he still needed more help if he was going to recapture the prisoner and deliver him to a buyer.

The most logical place to go was to the maze. Who else besides the Church would be interested in acquiring a demon-possessed human?

Once he'd gone with Hyde to one of the gaming clubs that didn't screen for nonhumans during the daytime. They'd watched on a big-screen television as Anton's demon hunted the maze.

Anton and his assistant Farold wouldn't question his story about surviving an ambush. They'd seen him with Hyde before and thought he was human—or if not, they didn't care.

Telling them about the loss of the dragon lizards would add credibility, as would the Church's interest in the prisoner. Involving them would mean the loss of at least half of his profit, if not more.

He hated the thought of it, but he didn't see any other way. If the priest's men located the human-demon first, he'd get nothing.

Raoul finished searching through the items thrown from the truck by guardsmen as they tore it apart looking for things of value. He rolled the salvaged shirt, pants, and shoes into a bundle then changed back into the wolf's form so he could travel through the night. His father's things weren't the right size, but they'd allow him to slip into the red zone at dawn and go to the maze.

Eight

ARAÑA woke alone and knew an instant of panic—not from the close confines of the space she was in, but from Tir's absence and the loss of his skin against hers. She sat up, aware of the meshed ceiling only inches above her head, high enough to allow a lion to walk easily and a human to sit, wide enough for a couple of Weres, in either of their forms, to lounge comfortably. Levi's lair was just that, a hollowed out place fortified by wire and steel scavenged from the human world and hidden beneath the rock and wood of the natural one.

Air and light and sound filtered in, enough of it so she knew it was morning and Tir was close by, cooking something. Her stomach rumbled at the smell of roasting meat.

She glanced around the lair and found her clothes missing, guessed he'd taken them outside and placed them near the fire to dry. In the hopes of being less noticeable when they got to the city, she'd washed the blood out of them before they'd taken shelter for the night.

A blush rose to her cheeks at the thought of emerging from the lair naked. It was foolish to feel shy after all she and Tir had done together. She knew it, but flaunting herself didn't come naturally to her.

For the first twelve years of her life she'd been trained to modesty—even her nightgowns had been flannel and cotton versions of the long dresses that covered her from neck to wrists to ankles. It had been easy to shed the restrictive clothing for shorts and tank tops, but she'd never lost her reticence even though she often saw men and women swimming naked when boats joined together to form impromptu floating cities.

She wasn't ashamed of her body or embarrassed by the sight of others naked, but she'd never slipped into the water during those times. At first it was because she feared someone would brush against the spider and die as a result. Then later, as she matured, she didn't join them because her bare mound set her apart from the other women. She'd worried . . .

Never again.

A shiver went through her as she remembered the heat in Tir's eyes when he'd lifted his face from between her thighs. Arousal slid from her opening at the memory of what he'd done with his tongue and mouth.

She wanted him to touch her that way again. She wanted to give him the same pleasure.

Her hand slid over the smooth flesh of her cunt, fingers seeking and finding the wet evidence of desire. She stroked and probed, gathered the silky moisture on her fingertips, and caressed her stiffened clit.

A moan escaped, loud in the confines of the lair, and her face heated as she imagined Tir hearing it and knowing she was touching herself as she thought about him. Her nipples hardened, ached for his touch. Spikes of need shot up her spine with each pass over the tiny, naked head of her clit.

Araña closed her eyes and tilted her head back, imagining Tir hovering over her, watching, commanding that she give him her release.

Heat suffused her body. Orgasm shimmered through her, a pale imitation of what she'd experienced with him.

Worry rose in its wake, about the pain sure to come later when he was gone, leaving her bereft of touch and heartbroken. She didn't think she could keep the needs of the body and the needs of the soul separate.

The demon mark lay on her hand. She touched it, wishing she could draw answers from it.

She was meant to find and free Tir. That much she believed beyond any doubt. The vision leading her to him was too different from the ones she'd had before for it to be otherwise.

But she was mortal, a human damned to Hell by the mark, and he was something else, something so much more. He was hundreds of years old, perhaps thousands, perhaps truly immortal.

Araña hugged herself, suddenly afraid of how much she already craved his touch, how much more she'd come to need it the longer she experienced it. Part of her recognized it was already too late to free herself from the web of destiny. It had been too late the moment she touched the thread of Tir's soul.

Taking one of the blankets with her, she crawled to the lair entrance, wanting to escape thoughts of the future. Life had taught her such thoughts did little good. In the end, as long as she wore the demon mark, it defined her future—a fiery hell and a demon master.

The metal hatch hiding the entrance to the lair was heavy, but she managed to open it and escape into morning light. She detoured at nature's call, then wrapped the blanket around her like a sarong before joining Tir by a fire pit far enough from the lair not to draw attention to it.

He was naked, crouched near the fire, black hair fanning over his shoulders and cascading in waves to his hips. His skin was marbled perfection, bone and muscle sculpted into a form that would inspire poetry and song and magnificent paintings.

Once again she was reminded of the angels in Erik's art history books, divine beings captured in oil by masters dead centuries upon centuries before The Last War. She didn't believe in angels, at least not on earth. None had been sighted since the early days, when some of the texts making up the Bible had been written. And if there once was a God—the creator of mankind—then she thought he'd long since lost interest in this world. Otherwise, why would angels not have made themselves known along with all of the other supernaturals?

It was a blasphemous thought, one that would have earned her a beating had she ever expressed it in the settlement where she'd spent the first twelve years of her life.

Araña turned her attention to the food. Her stomach growled and her mouth watered.

"Quail?" she asked, looking at the spitted birds, their roasted bodies cooling to the side of the fire.

"Yes."

When she would have reached for one of them, Tir's fingers shackled her wrist. Her eyes went to his and her breath caught at what she read in his expression.

"Mine," Tir said, not knowing where the word or the impulse had come from, but denying neither. He dropped her wrist and snagged his fingers in the blanket stretched across her breasts. A sharp tug, accompanied by Araña's small cry of surprised protest, and the material no longer hid her from him.

The sight of her flushed cunt lips was nearly his undoing. Only a grumbled reminder from her stomach kept him from pushing her onto her back and feasting on her.

Tir picked up one of the first roasting spits he'd set aside. A quick check told him the meat was hot, but not too hot. He tore a piece from it with his fingers and carried it to Araña's lips in silent offering.

Mine, he thought again, the word rippling through him, bringing uneasiness with it, but not enough to make him stop feeding her by his own hand.

Pitch black eyes widened and the scent of her arousal intensified, as if their bodies communicated on some primitive level. As if some animal instinct had taken over in the aftermath of their spending the night in the Were's lair. Whatever the reason, he found a savage satisfaction in tearing pieces of meat from the bird he'd hunted and prepared for them.

His cock throbbed each time her lips touched his skin when she took what he offered. His breathing became more labored as she grew bolder, capturing his fingers and sucking them into her mouth, licking away the juices with her tongue.

Heat leapt from her to him, a liquid fire starting where they touched and burning through his veins, eradicating all thought of eating. Primitive emotions held him in their grip, uncaring of any rational arguments he might offer to explain the raw possessiveness and molten need Araña stirred to life inside him.

He was free and with a woman for the first time in memory. For the moment it was reason enough to take what he wanted.

Araña's eyelids lowered, hiding her expression beneath heavy black lashes as her belly filled and she became sated. But she couldn't hide the rise of a different hunger.

Her lust beat against him like the wings of an exotic captive. Her scent intoxicated him.

A fantasy raged through him, of lying sprawled on cushions as she fed him by hand—a submissive seeing to the needs of her master. Vague images shimmered to life in his darkened memory, of men and women prostrate before him. But he could spare only a thought to the unanswered question of his true nature, could give only fleeting consideration to the possibility his race had once walked the earth as gods.

Araña's hands settled on his chest, her palms against his nipples, sending hot sensation to his cock. She closed the distance between them, shy innocent and sultry seductress, a primitive female intent on having her needs met.

Tir let her push him backward onto his elbows. She straddled him and a groan escaped as her smooth, hot cunt rubbed against his penis, leaving it wet with her desire.

Need raged through Araña, making her shiver. The only thing that mattered was joining with Tir.

Blue eyes glittered, adding to the savageness of his features and stirring a primitive fear inside her. He wasn't human. He wasn't safe, even for his lover.

It didn't matter. She couldn't stop herself from reaching down and taking his cock in her hand, from guiding it to her entrance.

"Tir," she whispered, impaling herself on him, nearly sobbing with the pleasure of having him inside her.

He didn't help her, didn't rise onto his knees and use his strength to lift her up and down on his shaft. He watched as she fucked herself on him.

It made her feel powerful at first. But then the emotional distance became unbearable.

It wasn't only the feel of skin against skin she craved. It was the sharing of breath and body heat, the feeling of being truly intimate with another hum—

But he wasn't. And she knew their being together was temporary.

I don't care, she told herself. In all likelihood she would die in Oakland as Erik and Matthew had, or die trying to get back home.

She thought the demon mark would kill the next man who tried to touch her. This time spent with Tir felt like stolen moments. But then she was a thief and had been for the last ten years.

She leaned forward, rubbing her palms against his tiny hardened nipples, the change in angle sending sharp spikes of pleasure through her each time her clit struck his abdomen. Her lips covered his and she closed her eyes.

He swallowed the cries she couldn't contain, the gasps. And finally gave her what she wanted.

Effortlessly he held himself up on one elbow as his fingers tangled in her hair, his arm across her back making her a prisoner as he took charge despite her being on top of him. His tongue thrust aggressively against hers, the force of it controlling the rhythm of her fingers on his nipples, the squeeze and release of pain that blended to pleasure for him.

His cock throbbed inside her, a second heartbeat held motionless in her channel until she whispered a nearly silent *please* against his mouth when they parted for breath.

He relented, the arm trapping her upper body sliding downward, the hand going to the small of her back, remaining there as his hips thrust upward, in counterpoint to hers, driving his cock into her channel hard and deep.

Araña tangled her fingers in his hair. Her own fell curtainlike on either side of their faces, spider black strands twining with his on their way to the ground.

She took the sounds of his pleasure along with his breath, their lips never far apart, their tongues rubbing, stroking, their bodies writhing in a wild joining, fighting for and finding that place of perfect union.

Araña nuzzled Tir afterward, loving the feel of his arms around her, his solid strength beneath her as she lay sprawled on top of him like a human blanket. They needed to leave. It would take them half a day to get to Oakland and they didn't know what waited for them there.

Her stomach knotted—worry about the *Constellation*, about Rebekka and Levi, chasing her contentment away. She turned her head, thinking only to delay when she'd have to leave Tir's warmth in order to wash and dress, but the instant she faced the dying fire, her soul tumbled into the flame, defenseless against its summoning.

No, she screamed silently, her voice unheard in the surreal whispers held deep in the fire. The pain arriving without pause, insistent, sharp, excruciating, as if this time she *wouldn't* be allowed to linger or fight against choosing one of the soul threads.

Araña tried anyway, out of habit and fear. But the battle was over almost as soon as it began. There was no conscious decision, there was only a forced yielding, a reaching blindly, convulsively, for a twisted strand with various shades of brown and a swirl of gray.

The pain dulled, enough so she slid from the spider's domain to the waking vision of someone's life. Oakland again, but she wasn't surprised. She wondered if she'd ever truly escape it now that she was caught in its web.

The city crept past her in slow, familiar jolts, the glass she was looking through smudged and cracked. There was no true sensation other than what she held in her memory, but she could smell the interior of the bus, could feel the rumble of its engine vibrating through metal and torn vinyl seats.

They were heading toward the heart of the city, backward along a route similar to the one she'd taken with Erik and Matthew. And though she had no corporeal presence, she felt the phantom close of her throat, the swell of grief she'd managed only to give a shallow burial.

Real pain spiked through her in a sharp reminder that the past was done with, its strands already woven into place. And in pain's wake came knowledge. She walked in the immediate future now. Minutes away. No more than an hour.

If she'd had a physical form, she would have frowned even as her heart raced with foreboding at what lay ahead. Until Oakland, until the vision of Tir, the only hint she'd ever had of present and future was what she could glean from her surroundings. Until Oakland, she might go months without being trapped by flame. But here, in two days she'd been drawn into the fire as many times.

Trepidation filled her as she forced her attention away from the window. It escalated into horror when she saw the trapper's child, positioned on the lap of the soul she was ghosting, Rebekka's slender arm around his waist.

Denial screamed through Araña. But there was no undoing the choice, no releasing the strand she'd taken.

Nothing good would come of this. Nothing ever had. Her demonborn gift brought only death and pain and suffering.

Araña became aware of a presence next to Rebekka. Her dread
deepened when she saw Levi.

The pain returned, an excruciating flash of agony forcing her
back into the black heart of the demon flame. There was no respite
from it as a kaleidoscope of colors swirled around her, accompanied
by the streaming whisper of voices.

In desperation Araña fought her way forward, remembering
the blue-black of Tir's soul thread, looking for it but not seeing it.
She endured the searing punishment of delaying until the instinct
for survival forced a choice.

The thread was gold with flecks of scarlet. Araña had the fleeting impression of wealth and unrealized power, of old bloodlines and
unacknowledged gifts, before she was in a building, ghost-walking
down a long corridor with framed photographs of men in guardsmen uniforms.

Horror filled her. She fought to escape, but she was trapped, the
pain blackening the edges of phantom sight but not spreading so she
passed out.

Glass doors came into view. She caught the image of the man
whose life she ghosted before he exited the building.

Oakland again. Downtown, where the guardsmen and police
would have their headquarters. There was the bustle of people. Food-
stand vendors called out their menus, and the man who'd been in the
guard headquarters bought a pastry from one of them before moving
to stand next to a black sedan to eat it.

The bus would appear in a few minutes. Araña knew it with
grim certainty.

Visceral waves of fear and guilt and mingled rage made her fight
more desperately to escape back into the heart of the flame. The pain
was excruciating, deadly—her struggles pointless.

What she expected came to pass—a bus rounded a corner.

It stopped, disgorging passengers and taking on new ones—
none of them Rebekka or Levi.

Disbelief settled for the span of a phantom heartbeat, hope flared into existence—she'd been wrong.

But she hadn't.

The bus began moving again, closing the distance until it came alongside the black sedan. And there was Rebekka in the window, gazing outward.

Araña knew the moment when the two threads she'd chosen intersected, changing the weave of the future. She felt it rippling forward as she slipped from the hold of the flame to find herself in Tir's arms.

"You're bleeding," he said, making her aware of the blood stream-ing from her nose, the price for her continued struggles against the demon gift.

"I'm okay," she said, attempting to pull away though she craved the comfort he offered.

Tir's arms tightened, as if he'd force her to remain with him. But then he let her go abruptly, as if on some level he knew she was dangerous to him, understood the same gift that had led to his free-dom might one day cause his enslavement.

Araña rose to her feet and went to the stream to wash. She felt raw, haunted, besieged by guilt. When they got to Oakland, they would learn of Rebekka's fate—perhaps—if Levi survived to tell of it.

Her throat tightened, remembering the night she'd run from the settlement and been taken in by Erik and Matthew, remembering her run in the maze, her escape to find Rebekka waiting, a stranger offering shelter.

Those who helped her or knew her weren't any safer from her demon gift than the multitude of strangers whose lives she touched when the flame took her. If she were braver, perhaps she'd go will-ingly into the embrace of death, and face the demon that had left its mark on her, rather than continue to do the demon's work on earth.

But the prospect of what awaited her in the afterlife was more horrifying than what she wrought with her gift. And it wouldn't honor Matthew and Erik if she surrendered, if she failed to *live* as they'd wanted her to, as they'd taught her to do by example and the strength of their love.

Tir followed Araña to the stream though he didn't join her in it. Concern for her gnawed at him as she washed the blood away, but it was mixed with tendrils of suspicion. There was more to her visions than she'd told him previously.

His eyes flicked to the spider mark now riding her shoulder. Buried memories fought to surface, but they were kept suppressed by the band around his neck.

She was human, her gifted nature not obvious to him in the way he'd known Rebekka possessed talents most humans didn't. He trailed a finger along the hated collar of his enslavement. When he was free of it . . .

"Tell me about the vision," he said, his misgiving deepening when Araña hunched in on herself.

A slight tremble of her body and he went to her without it being a conscious decision. The delicate line of her spine drew his attention, making him fight against pressing kisses along its length.

"Tell me," he coaxed, his lips brushing over the spider on her shoulder as his hand wedged itself between her thighs to curl possessively around her mound.

"Something's going to happen to Rebekka."

"What?"

Araña gave a small shrug. "I don't know."

Tir heard the truth in her words, but her emotions confused him. Guilt bombarded him, thick and heavy in comparison to the fear he sensed in her.

His hand left her cunt to go to her chin. Gripping it, he turned her face so it was no longer hidden by the silky black curtain of her hair. Haunted midnight eyes met his, their depths hinting at secrets but also flashing with a resolve not to share them.

They stared at each other for long moments. "What do you see when the flame takes you?" he asked.

She stiffened instantly and would have pulled away if his hands hadn't prevented it. Silence was the only answer she gave him, and he discovered he didn't like it—not because he feared her visions but because she stirred intensely primitive feelings in him, making him want to possess not just her body but her very soul.

He released her abruptly, rebelling against feeling those things about a mortal female—even one who had freed him. "Keep your secrets as long as they don't involve me. But remember this, if I find they make you my enemy, not even the sweet temptation of your body will save you from death."

Nine

REBEKKA lifted Eston into her arms. Her heart ached over what she was about to do, but there was no choice. "This is for the best," she said, managing the lie though Levi would smell it on her.

"I'm going with you to the Mission."

"I'll be fine. I can do this by myself." Her already tense stomach grew more so at the thought of Levi leaving the red zone.

According to law he had the same rights as anyone else when he was in human form, but Oakland was a city controlled by *pure* humans, many of whom only barely tolerated the gifted, and it wasn't uncommon for guardsmen and police to carry amulets that changed color in the presence of Weres.

The red zone was the safest place for shapeshifters who didn't live among their own kind. In the red zone Weres could defend themselves without fear of trumped-up charges or indiscriminate slaughter by the authorities.

Rebekka imagined it was because the red zone was much like the towns of the Wild West she'd read about in a history book once. A certain amount of lawlessness existed and violence was common. Only instead of a sheriff keeping some semblance of order, it was fear of the vice lords that kept those who lived in and frequented the red zone in line.

"I should leave now," she said, already fighting tears as she imagined surrendering the child she'd cared for less than a day.

"I'm going with you," Levi repeated, his tone telling her it was pointless to argue.

Rebekka nodded, accepting the inevitable, and the gesture caused her cheek to brush against the soft texture of the toddler's hair.

A fist tightened around her heart. *It's the only way*, she thought, steeling herself for what she was about to do—but also promising herself she wouldn't forget Eston.

His father deserved death. Rebekka felt no remorse in playing a part in ambushing the trapper and freeing those meant for the maze. But in doing it, they'd made an orphan of Eston unless he was reunited with his mother. And that *did* weigh on her conscience.

Prostitutes rarely carried their children to term. And those who did—

Rebekka knew she'd been lucky in so many ways. To be born at all had been the first stroke of it. And it had been followed by so many more, including being gifted.

Her mother hadn't abandoned her on the street or in the forest, leaving it up to fate whether she survived or not. She hadn't ended up in the Mission or been sold.

Even in the red zone, those who trafficked in children didn't operate openly. But it was common knowledge, especially in the brothels, that unwanted pregnancies could be turned into profit in any number of ways.

There were men whose sexual fetishes involved pregnant women. And after the baby was born, there were brokers whose clients ranged from humans with sexual perversions and dark mages looking for sacrificial victims, to supernatural beings with an appetite for human children.

Rebekka's arms tightened involuntarily on Eston. He'd be safe at the Mission.

Davida was one of the Church's faithful. She didn't like the gifted or the supernatural, but she treated the children in her care well.

They left Levi's safe place in the red zone, staying well away from where most of the activity was centered and crossing the border where forest crowded a section being reclaimed by the non-gifted. The bus stop was blocks farther, and clustered with waiting people.

When the bus arrived, Rebekka paid her fare and Levi's before claiming a window seat. He sat next to her, tense at being trapped in a confined space, though only she could tell it.

Levi tilted his head forward and feigned sleep, as if he were an ordinary human bracing for a long, tedious ride filled with a seemingly endless number of stops until he reached his destination. Rebekka looked out the window, trusting Levi's sense of smell and his instincts to warn of danger.

The bus grew more and more crowded as they made their way toward the heart of Oakland. Eston trembled and clutched at her arms, making her wonder if this was his first trip to a city. She murmured soothingly and wished his vocabulary and ability to speak were more advanced; then maybe she could understand more of what he said than just his first name and his cries for his mother.

Rebekka told herself she should take advantage of the long bus trip by taking a nap, but her mind was too busy and her heart too heavy. She leaned her head against the glass and watched the scenery change.

The bus route skirted the area where the wealthy and powerful lived. She wondered what it would be like to live among those who didn't worry about food or shelter or even the law.

She envied their freedom and security despite the damage she'd seen them do when they played in the red zone. Downtown came into view a little while later and, with it, an increase in the number of guardsmen and policemen patrolling the area.

Rebekka tensed out of habit but didn't turn away from the window. Where there were citizen witnesses, it was always safer, and she often visited the library, though the building next to it housed the headquarters for both police and guardsmen.

As they approached the library, a flag fluttering on the antenna of a sleek black sedan with darkly tinted windows caught her attention. The flag had a gold background with a red lion rampant in its center as part of an elaborate shield design—a heraldic crest. All of the founding families of Oakland had them, and many of the wealthy had followed suit by claiming ancestral emblems or designing new ones for themselves.

A man leaned casually against the car, eating a pastry, his pose all she needed in order to identify him as one of the entitled and not the sedan's chauffeur. Eston's face joined hers at the window and he made a chortling, happy sound.

She smiled. His interest in his surroundings gladdened her heart even as it added to the heavy burden of guilt and worry she felt about abandoning him at the Mission.

They drew abreast of the sleek sedan. The man looked up, and for an instant Rebekka could have sworn she saw surprised recognition on his face. But when their eyes met and held, no memory stirred, and then he looked away, his attention shifting to something else.

The bus lumbered on, almost empty of riders now. It skirted more areas claimed by the wealthy before those gave way to increasing poverty as they drew closer to the Barrens.

Houses huddled together in clusters like tiny outposts of reclaimed civilization. These places belonged to whoever was willing not only to restore them, but to defend them against bands of outlaws and the twisted dregs of society who called the Barrens home.

"Let's get out here," Levi said, breaking his trip-long silence as he reached up and pulled the cord that signaled the bus driver to stop.

Rebekka didn't protest the added walking distance. The bus would turn around at the next stop anyway, before reaching the Mission.

A moment later she stood and followed Levi off the bus. There were no children playing outside under the watchful eyes of women working in gardens or hanging laundry on lines. The yards surrounding the houses they passed were empty, though she could feel people watching from behind barred and cloaked windows.

Levi headed toward the waterfront, where they'd be less noticeable from the street. There they found suspicious-eyed men fishing from rocky banks and half-starved mongrels scuttling around, hoping to snag an unguarded catch.

Rebekka's arms were weary from bearing Eston's weight, but she didn't want to ask Levi to carry the child. If there was trouble, he'd need his hands free to protect them.

That was the curse of her gift. It made her helpless. For a healer to injure another, to kill another . . .

She shuddered. Even to save her own life she wasn't sure she could do it, for fear of destroying her ability to heal, tainting it so it became something dark and evil.

They were halfway to the final stop on the bus route when she heard the rumble of its engine. "Wait," Levi said, lightly touching her arm before they broke away from the cover provided by what remained of an old gas station.

The bus came into sight, empty save for the driver. A heartbeat later, a camouflage-painted jeep with a single guardsman slid into view, trailing behind the bus, its uniformed driver scanning the area on either side of the street.

Rebekka's mouth went dry. It had to be coincidence, she told herself, the presence of the guardsman unnerving her.

"Did you recognize him?" Levi asked, quickening her pulse with the question.

"No. What about you?"

He answered with a slight shake of his head then stepped out from behind the shelter of the collapsed building. They moved quickly, minimizing their exposure from the street.

Rebekka felt hyperaware of her surroundings, on edge. She attributed it to Levi, told herself she was picking up on Were edginess.

There was no reason for them to be the focus of a hunt—not by guardsmen anyway.

Unless the guardsmen also served Anton Barlowe.

Rebekka's stomach knotted as the last stop on the bus route came into view and she saw the guardsman waiting there. He was on foot, a rifle held casually at his side as he talked into a handheld radio.

This one she recognized. Jurgen. He was a frequent and brutal visitor to the brothel, a man who left those he visited in need of a healer.

Movement drew her attention to a cluster of houses beyond the bus stop. Another guardsman emerged, his pistol drawn. She recognized him as well. Cabot.

"This is no coincidence," Levi murmured as a silver car slid into view from a side street leading to the waterfront.

The sight of it chilled Rebekka to the core. She'd seen it often enough in the red zone, with Farold or Gulzar driving it.

Levi tensed when Gulzar became visible behind the steering wheel. Rebekka didn't need to use her gift to feel Levi's rage and hatred and desire to kill the man who'd tortured him into something neither lion nor man.

"How could they know we were coming here?" Rebekka asked, guessing at the answer even as the words left her mouth.

"The man who escaped the ambush must have hidden and overheard us talking," Levi said, making the same guess.

Rebekka's heart thumped violently in her chest. Gulzar or the guardsmen would have already talked to the bus driver and learned a man, woman, and toddler had gotten off at the previous stop.

"Where do we go?" The prospect of entering the Barrens without guns and overnight supplies terrified her.

Levi turned to her. "We split up and head toward one of the other bus routes, or get downtown and catch the bus there. If we'd been recognized they would have gone to the brothel looking for us and we'd have heard about it. Give me the child."

Rebekka's arms tightened around Eston at the steel in Levi's tone. Eyes that usually reminded her of molten gold were ice cold, frozen in ruthlessness.

She didn't need to ask what he intended. She knew.

Survival came at a cost. Always. And Levi wouldn't risk theirs for the sake of a human child.

He wouldn't hurt Eston, not physically, but he intended to leave the toddler somewhere and trust to fate that someone would find him and take him the remaining distance to the Mission.

"No," Rebekka whispered. "I'll take him ahead."

"And walk right into a trap?"

"I'll find someone I can trust when I get closer. I—"

"No. You're too valuable," Levi said, his fingers curling around Eston's sides, forming a wedge between the child's body and hers.

She pulled back automatically, and Eston began crying, frightened by the argument and Levi's attempt to wrest him away from Rebekka.

Rebekka stifled the noise quickly by pressing the toddler's face to her neck, and he quieted as though recognizing and responding to the threat of danger. But it was too late. The sound of his cries had already carried, alerting the guardsmen to their presence.

"Go!" she told Levi, turning her back so he couldn't make another attempt to take Eston from her.

She heard the soft slide of a blade leaving its sheath. Terror for Levi coiled and knotted in her stomach; fear that he'd go after Gulzar melded to what she held for herself. If she was taken and questioned—

Rebekka blocked it from her mind and began running. Levi was smart. The desire for revenge wouldn't overcome his survival instinct. He would kill the guardsmen and Gulzar if he had a chance, but primarily he would try to lead them away from the route she would take.

A shout went up behind her. A gun fired.

It was followed by more shots and the squeal of tires. But rather than coming toward her, the silver car headed in the direction of the Mission and the Barrens.

Rebekka's breath labored and her chest burned from running even a short distance with Eston. Some of the fishermen looked up as she hurried past them, their eyes and postures telling her to keep going, they would offer no aid.

She stumbled and nearly fell, the jerky movements making Eston cry again. Her heart skipped a beat when she saw the jeep that had been trailing the bus. "Hush, please hush," she pleaded, crouching in the nearest shadow, rocking, trying to muffle his sobs.

The jeep sped by, its engine noise masking the sound of Eston crying. For a split second Rebekka thought all of the men had gone after Levi. But then a bullet ricocheted off the ground near her and a male voice shouted, "Stay where you are."

Jurgen.

Rebekka froze—but only for an instant. Being taken alive was worse than dying.

She scrambled toward the corner of a burned-out building.

Brick chipped as a bullet struck. Fragments hit her face, making it sting and bleed. She bolted, desperately looking for someplace to hide with each step. The prospect of being flushed out into the open like game and easily picked off with a rifle made her bite her tongue to keep from whimpering.

The rubble and debris along the waterfront became too difficult to maneuver around with Eston in her arms. She turned, and within a block the street loomed ahead, an asphalt-coated killing ground.

A sob caught in her throat at the thought of crossing it. But the thought of being raped by the guardsmen or sold to be raped by criminals running the maze kept her moving.

She should have let Levi take Eston. Abandoning him near the Mission was no crueler fate than what might happen to him with her.

Rebekka paused next to the burned husk of a military tank that had been used hundreds of years before her birth to reclaim the city from anarchy. She strained to hear something beyond Eston's whimpers and the sounds of her own harsh breathing, something that would tell her it was safe to emerge from hiding. She found no reassurance.

Every second she delayed added to her peril. And yet she had to steel herself to edge forward and peek around the black and rusted metal of the tank.

Hope rose in her when she saw no guardsmen. Up ahead there was a curve in the road. In her mind's eye she pictured what lay beyond it, the true beginnings of Oakland. There were shops there, places it wouldn't be easy for a guardsman to take a woman and child away without witnesses.

She doubted the guardsmen hunting with Gulzar wanted what they were doing known. Not all those in authority were corrupt— Rebekka knew that, though only dire circumstances like the one she was in would make her risk her life on it.

"Just a little bit farther," she whispered, more for her benefit than Eston's.

She rubbed her cheek against the soft down of his hair as she gathered her courage to leave the shelter of the tank. Another peek and she ran, angling for the corner and the promise of safety it represented.

She'd almost reached it when the jeep came into view, racing from the direction she'd come from and carrying two guardsmen, Jurgen and the one she didn't know.

Jurgen stood, taking aim with his rifle, and she pushed herself harder, drawing on the last of her strength to get around the corner. Her terror spiked when she saw a car approaching.

Before she could reach an opening between houses and dart through it, the black sedan cut her off. The man she'd noticed as the bus passed the library emerged and opened the back door, forcing her into the car. He followed her, slamming the door shut behind him.

It happened so quickly she had no chance to offer any resistance. And then he was urging her to stay quiet, and the instinct for self-preservation made Rebekka comply as the jeep carrying the guardsmen stopped next to the sedan.

A partition shielded the backseat from the front but didn't filter out sound. Boots crunched as one of the guardsmen got out and approached. An electric window in front slid down. The man driving, a chauffeur or bodyguard maybe, said, "Are you chasing a woman carrying a child?"

Rebekka closed her eyes, willing Eston to remain silent. She fought to slow her breathing and could barely hear over the thundering race of her heart.

"You saw them?" Jurgen asked, wariness in his voice, or suspicion.

"Nearly hit them," the driver said. "If I'd been going any faster I wouldn't have been able to swerve out of the way in time."

Jurgen didn't say anything immediately. Rebekka could almost sense him struggling for a legitimate reason to search the car. Finally he said, "Which way did she go?"

"I don't know. By the time I looked again, she was gone. What'd she do? From what I saw, I wouldn't have thought she was someone the guard would be interested in."

"She's wanted for questioning. Her companion just killed a guardsman without any provocation."

Fear for Levi flashed through Rebekka, overwhelming the fury she felt at Jurgen's claim the attack hadn't been provoked. She silently urged the driver to ask if the killer was alive and in custody.

But Jurgen stepped away from the sedan, and the sound of his heavy footsteps marked his return to the jeep.

The window in the front seat hummed as it closed, the sedan already in motion. It wheeled around to head in the direction of the city, and the pressure in Rebekka's chest eased though the worry for Levi remained.

She turned toward the man who'd probably saved her life. But before she could speak, Eston chortled and opened his arms, leaning away from her in order to go to the stranger.

"Mas," he said. "Mas."

Rebekka reacted without thinking. Her hand snaked over to the door handle but just as quickly the stranger grabbed her arm. "You'll hurt yourself," he said, ordering the driver to secure the car.

Locks snicked into place. The man released her and Rebekka pulled away, pressing her back to the door. "What do you want?"

"The prisoner you and your friend freed when you ambushed the trapper's truck."

A small shock of amazement went through Rebekka, that Araña had managed what seemed impossible. But on its heels came fear as Eston wriggled and struggled to get to the man who was no stranger to him—the man who must have escaped into the woods before Levi could stop him.

"I don't know where the prisoner is," Rebekka said, reluctantly giving up her hold on the toddler rather than continuing to restrain him. "Who are you?"

Her rescuer grunted as Eston clambered onto him, but his hands were gentle as he repositioned the child.

"Who are you?" she repeated.

Indecision played over his face. It lasted only a split second before he shook it off. "Tomás Iberá."

Her heart stuttered, the blood it pumped turning to ice. *Iberá*. She recognized the name.

His family was old, one of those who'd "founded" Oakland—reclaiming it from the chaos of lawlessness after The Last War and the subsequent emergence of the supernaturals. Enzo Iberá was a general in the guard and said to be one of those in contention for taking it over after its last leader was killed by werewolves and feral dogs in the red zone.

Tomás tapped on the partition separating front seat from backseat. "Home," he said to the driver.

Rebekka forced thoughts through a mind nearly frozen by fear. She tried to make sense of what Tomás had said—and hadn't said.

His only interest seemed to be the prisoner. And yet he hadn't turned her over to the guardsmen—though perhaps the reason for that was simple. He might not have recognized them as men who did business with the maze.

She wracked her brain for what she knew of the Iberás, and came up blank. If those in his family frequented the red zone, they didn't visit the shapeshifter brothels.

"What's so important about the convict?" Rebekka asked.

Tomás turned toward the front without answering, leaving her imagination to run riot with images of what would happen when they reached their destination.

Ten

ARAÑA'S silence bothered Tir. Not just the physical silence that had settled around her before they left the Were's forest lair, but her emotional silence.

A wall stood between them, blocking her feelings from him. Its presence created a void, a hollow spot that had him reaching up to rub his chest. They'd passed through the red zone to the area set aside for the human gifted without speaking a word.

Tir's lip curled in disdain at the word. *Gifted.* He'd met his share of them over the centuries and found them capable of cruelty beyond measure. Humans were never meant to posses such talent. They were dust, the walking dead, frail and unworthy. They were *less* than the most simple of beasts. They were—

He turned, aware she'd stopped walking. His cock hardened as his eyes traveled over her crouched form and he remembered the feel of her above him, the heated clamp of her channel and the silky texture of her skin.

She was nothing to him beyond useful help, he told himself. But the lie showed itself in the clenching of his jaw, in the flash of anger and need that had him wanting to return to her side and end the silence created by his threat.

His eyes hesitated on the hand bearing the brand, noting the fingerless glove she must have found among the weeds. Realization slid into him like a knife.

He looked around, studied the area and found dark stains on the ground. This was where her family had been killed. This was the place where guardsmen had thought to rape her.

Tir closed his eyes and reached for her mentally, only to be met by a wall of rigid control. She was stronger than most humans, though it had been centuries since he last cared enough about what one of them felt to do anything but try to block them out.

He pushed harder and could almost taste the tears held back, contained in a bottomless well of sorrow. For the first time in what he remembered of his life, he wondered if he had family that grieved when he disappeared. He wondered if he had ever loved another deeply enough that their passing from his life tore a rent in his soul.

He prodded at his lost memory, but there was no echo of pain, no resonance of sorrow. Nothing rose from the darkness.

Tir touched the sigil-inscribed collar, silently reminding himself the *only* thing that mattered was gaining the information that would allow him to translate the tattoos on his arms and achieve his freedom. She was a dangerous distraction, one he couldn't afford.

He watched as she stood and moved away from him, obviously searching for something. She found it moments later, and before she slipped it into her pocket, he saw it was a wallet.

"We've got money for food and lodging now," she said, her subdued voice coming to him on a breeze, along with the scent of her sadness.

Tir steeled himself to wait until she returned to his side. His hands balled into fists in an effort to keep from reaching for her.

He succeeded at the first, but not the second. Her dark pain-shadowed eyes had him cupping her face and trying to smooth the bruised look away with the pads of his thumbs.

Tir leaned in and covered her lips with his, found an unexpected gentleness in himself. She resisted his offer of comfort at first. But with the tender probing of his tongue in a request for admission, he broke through the barrier she'd erected.

Araña softened, opened for him. He tasted her sorrow as well as her strength.

Her hands went to his chest, her palms pressing to his nipples, sending jagged bolts of pleasure to his cock. Lust coiled in his belly as he found the contrast of bare flesh and gloved leather wickedly erotic.

Tir moaned, deepening the kiss. His hands left her face to pull her more tightly against him.

He felt her grief retreat, driven away by the hard press of his body to hers. Desire rose in its place, fanning the flames of his own and making him want to press her to the ground and take her until nothing remained for her but pleasure.

He plundered her mouth until she clung to him. Only then did he lift his lips from hers.

"We need to go to the occult shop," she said.

Tir could feel her desire to escape more than just this place where her family was killed. His arms tightened involuntarily. Denial flared. She wouldn't be free of him until he allowed it.

Araña made herself concentrate on the tasks that lay ahead. "We need to go to the occult shop," she repeated, aware of the steady progress of the sun across the sky.

It could take hours of searching the shop before they'd know whether the information Tir needed was there. And before they sought shelter for the night, she wanted to know if the *Constellation* was still in its slip.

And if Rebekka and Levi are okay, the voice of conscience added, filling her with dread and guilt even as she knew there was nothing she could have done for them. It had been too late to change the future from the moment she'd touched Rebekka's soul thread.

Tir's arms dropped away, but her palms lingered on his chest despite her words. It took more effort than it should have to break the contact, to turn away from the illusion of safety and peace she found in his arms.

She forced herself to start walking, to retrace the path she'd marched at gunpoint. She numbed her mind and blocked her memories, refusing to revisit what she'd seen until she reached the place where the guardsmen's vehicle had been parked.

It was sheer luck they'd driven past the occult shop on the way to the maze. Habit had made her memorize the route. On the ocean there were no signposts, no pedestrians to ask directions of. There were only landmarks close to shore and the stars above.

When they reached the shop, Araña stopped at the edge of the inscribed circle painted in red on the sidewalk surrounding it. The symbols were common enough, wards against noncorporeal beings as well as entities intent on mischief or possessed of evil.

"Can you cross it?" she asked, sweat trickling down her spine at the resistance she felt, the tightness in her chest. It would take effort for her to step over the line.

She hadn't expected to have trouble entering the shop. But it felt as though something in the wards recognized the demon mark.

Tir answered by stepping through the circle and turning toward her, offering his hand. She took it and let him tug her forward.

Her breath left her in a suffocating rush, as if a spell tried to suck her soul from her body and trap it. A whimper escaped at the confirmation she was Hell-bound, and she was left trembling with the single step she'd taken.

"Can you proceed?" Tir asked.

"Yes." It was too late to turn back now.

The spider burned on her shoulder, its fiery heat a reminder that the mark was fused to her being and there would be no separating it from her flesh. Her gaze slid over Tir's bare torso. He was probably safe enough in the occult shop, but he'd need a shirt before they traveled beyond the area set aside for the gifted.

The tattoos on his arms would draw too much attention. They'd make him stand out and would turn him into a target for police and guardsmen alike. Beyond that, it would be better if, in addition to the trapper's knife tied in its sheath to his thigh, he also carried beneath his own shirt the machete that was now strapped to her back and hidden by her shirt.

He pulled the door open. She felt the wards on the threshold, stronger than those circling the building. They pressed on her, as if instead of sucking her soul from her body, these would squeeze, forcing her spirit to flee into some magical trap.

The mark burned hotter. Araña had a brief thought of the demon Abijah, wondering if this was how he'd been captured. Then she forced herself through the warded doorway and into the shop.

A man glanced up from behind a counter cluttered with books. He was slight, pale, goateed. His expression held curiosity about her hesitation at the doorway, but no hint that he'd felt the wards reacting to her.

A clerk, she guessed, not a practitioner, though she couldn't be positive.

Tir entered, and the man's attention went unerringly to the tattoos. His eyes flashed with surprised recognition, sending nervousness skittering through Araña.

She looked away from him long enough to see if the shop was empty. The sight of two men, their hands resting casually on guns worn at their sides, caused her to brace for trouble.

The guns weren't their only weapons. Bandoliers crisscrossed their chests. Only instead of bullets, they held knives and deadly throwing stars.

The men made no movement other than to note her awareness and actions with their eyes. Bodyguards, she thought. Not guardsmen or police.

There was a third presence, the person the bodyguards stood in front of. His identity didn't matter as long as he didn't prove to be a threat.

Araña allowed herself to relax enough to return her attention to the man behind the counter. He was tucking a piece of paper under a book, the nervous swipe of his tongue over his lip and his hasty movements drawing her interest where simply walking away from whatever he was doing would have better served him.

He closed the other books strewn across the counter, leaving her with the impression he was researching something. The lack of a pen or pencil nearby suggested that rather than looking for text to copy for a client, he was comparing whatever was on the paper he'd tucked away to what was in the books.

She'd only been in an occult shop once before, when she'd accompanied Matthew in order to stand guard while he negotiated a job with the owner. But she doubted this place operated much differently. The candles and supplies could be bought, while the books were available to study and, for a price, to have sections of them copied.

Araña shivered at the thought of using spell magic. Much of what was contained in the shop was probably worthless or harmless to someone without the gift for using it, but some of it was deadly, to practitioners and nonpractitioners alike.

The man came around the counter, pale, white fingers worrying his goatee. "Can I help you?"

Araña left Tir to answer, her attention caught by a glassed bookcase near the counter. She edged closer. Inside it were books filled with demon names and rituals for summoning and commanding them.

She shivered and surreptitiously rubbed the spider, trying to ease the burn of it. It was part of her and yet not part of her, a sentient gateway giving a demon access to this world and to a human tool that could be used to bring about suffering and death.

The thought made Araña turn away from the case and the

reflection of her face caught in it. Her stomach knotted and she fisted her hands.

She didn't want to think about what it meant to bear the mark, to have her soul tainted by it. But it was impossible not to consider that the answers to questions that had haunted and shaped her life might be here, in this shop.

The bodyguards eased their stance though they remained alert. Her gaze was drawn to the wall of books behind them.

Shock rippled through her at the sheer number of them—all of them the private journals witches and warlocks kept, shadow books that held their secrets and a record of the power they'd gained in their lifetime.

Movement broke the trance of seeing so many of them in one place. Araña's attention slid from the wall to the man who moments before had been blocked by his bodyguards.

A single, emerald green eye blazed, its twin gone, replaced by scarred flesh in a melted-wax face, as if he'd played with magic and been marked by the fires of Hell.

There was speculation in his gaze as it moved from her to Tir. And what might pass for a small smile before he murmured to his guards, "I've satisfied my curiosity here. It's time to return to the club."

One of the bodyguards peeled away. But rather than walk past Araña and go to the front door, he went to the back of the shop, to a door not immediately obvious until he opened it.

Araña watched as the bodyguard stepped outside. He looked around before giving an all-clear signal and exiting completely.

The man he was guarding and the second bodyguard followed, closing the door tightly so it once again blended into the wall. "Who was that?" she asked, knowing the man had to be both wealthy and powerful in Oakland to be accompanied by openly armed men.

"Rimmon," the clerk said, shuddering, his voice holding fear. "He's one of the vice lords."

"In the red zone?" Araña guessed.

The clerk nodded and licked his lip, reminding her of his earlier nervousness regarding the books he'd been looking through when they entered the shop. Now that they were alone, just the three of them, she saw no reason for subtlety or delay.

Her eyes met Tir's, and for a heartbeat it felt as though they were one person. Perfect understanding flowed between them, like what Matthew and Erik had together.

She took a step toward the counter, gambling that the clerk didn't have inherent magic of his own and wasn't protected by it, guessing whoever owned the store valued only the books enough to ward them.

The clerk squawked, either from her movement toward the counter or from Tir's hands wrapping around his scrawny arms to prevent his interference.

"No," he protested, struggling, his panic increasing as Araña tugged the piece of paper from its hiding place.

Her pulse quickened when she saw what the clerk was researching. Small sections of incomprehensible texts and symbols were scattered on the page, as if someone had randomly reproduced pieces of the whole from memory.

She recognized some of it, could remember tracing over it with her fingertip as she and Tir lay together. Her heart slid into a racing beat as her thoughts went immediately to the vice lord who might even now be setting an ambush into place outside the shop.

"Who's this for?" she asked, turning the page so Tir could see it.

His face hardened in sheer ruthlessness. Intentionally or unintentionally, his grip tightened on the clerk.

The man cried out, fear pouring off him. "I can't—"

He broke off at the feel of steel against his throat, Araña's action was smooth and unconscious, like drawing breath. "This isn't a cause you want to die for. Who asked you to research what's written on the paper?"

His eyes darted to the left, where her gloved hand rested on his shoulder, instead of to the right, where the crime lord and his bodyguards had disappeared through the unobtrusive doorway.

"Who?" she repeated, numbing her mind and her conscience to what might come next even as she fervently hoped the clerk wouldn't force them to hurt him.

"Father Ursu," he said, sagging in relief when she pulled the knife away from his throat and sheathed it.

The name held no meaning for Araña. She glanced at Tir and found his eyes narrowed.

Realization came to her then as she thought about how he'd healed her after she fought with the dragon lizard. There was no cure— either magical or medical—that would have been able to save her.

Many would view what he'd done as a miracle.

She'd assumed he was being taken to the maze. But what if he'd been bound for the Church instead? He'd be priceless to them.

Her gaze moved to the books she'd ignored in her hurry to retrieve the paper. They were old, created well before the world was forever changed.

All but one of them had writing on the cover like she'd seen in Erik's history books. She remembered the pictures of artifacts and parchment texts with script common to the place where The Last War was said to have started, a distant part of the world once known as the Holy Lands.

The book title she could understand made her stomach knot as she automatically translated it: *Demonios del Vieje Mundo*, into "Demons of the Old World." Unerringly her hand went to where the spider lay on her collarbone, hidden by her shirt.

Her thoughts shifted, telescoped. What if Tir had only been able to heal her because she carried the demon mark? What if the Church's interest in him had nothing to do with healing?

She shivered, comparing the spider's reaction to Tir with its reaction to the demon Abijah, how it accepted Tir and seemed to seek out his touch while it cowered from Abijah.

SPIDER-TOUCHED   143

Her attention shifted to the band around Tir's neck. What would happen if he were freed from it? Would he kill indiscriminately? Or would he kill only those who deserved it?

"The priest wants the texts and symbols translated?" Tir asked the clerk, drawing Araña from the turmoil of her own thoughts.

"Yes."

"When did he make his request?"

"Yesterday, when the shop opened."

"You've found what he wanted?"

"No."

"How many of the books are left to search?"

The clerk's gaze skittered to the counter. "Only those. They're the last."

Tir released the man. "Then we'll look through those. You'll stay with us."

A short time later they left the shop without having found anything useful. As they walked, Araña wondered why the Church was also seeking a translation of the tattoos on Tir's arms.

Did they hold the key to killing him or banishing him from this world as well as to freeing him?

Her hands went to the sheathed blades. Her fingers rubbed over the smooth hilts, trying to draw comfort from them but not finding it.

Was he a demon? Is that why the spider allowed him to touch her? Is that why she'd been forced to join the thread of her life to his in the dark heart of the fire?

Tir stopped and gripped her upper arms when they were out of sight of the shop, imprisoning her and making her shudder, not from fear, as the clerk had done, but from needy longing. "You're quiet," he said.

"Yes."

Questions crowded her mind, but the courage to ask them deserted her. She had secrets, too. Things she didn't want to share. But could she really help free him if he meant to wreak havoc on the world? Could she add that weight to all the suffering she'd already been responsible for as a result of her demon gift?

Tir fought to keep his fingers from tightening painfully on Araña's arms. Her tendency to withdraw was back despite the heated scent of desire and the soft molding of her body to his.

The longer he was with her, the more attuned to her emotions he became. They brushed against him, became almost a whisper of her thoughts in his consciousness.

Her silence wasn't comfortable. It rubbed him, made him feel raw and on edge.

The thin wall shimmering between them was intolerable. He wanted her open, as trusting when she walked at his side as she was when she lay underneath him, thighs splayed, her body welcoming his, holding him deep in her core.

"What are you thinking?" he asked, hating that he had no will to stop himself from doing it. Fighting against caring for this human who seemed to be tangling him in a silken web of need.

Silence greeted his question, swallowing it as though it had never been spoken. Dark eyes met his, a black abyss he could lose himself in.

Tir's nostrils flared at the unspoken challenge. His thoughts flashed back to the morning, when she'd taken food from his hand, acknowledging with her act of submission that she belonged to him— body and soul.

They didn't have time for this. Intellectually he knew it. But just as he couldn't stop himself from questioning her, he couldn't keep from stepping her backward, into the shadows, his hands moving from her arms to her wrists and pinning her against what remained of a collapsed exterior wall.

Where before he'd broken through the barrier she erected with tenderness, this time he took her mouth aggressively, plundered it with dominant intent and the hard thrust of his tongue.

Her resistance burned away, melted under the onslaught.

He claimed her cries. Refused to grant her breath that didn't come from him. And in doing it, bound himself more tightly to her.

"Tell me what you were thinking," he ordered, his cock throbbing, urging him to force her to her knees, to demand she worship him with her mouth.

"I was wondering if you're a demon," she said, and with a thought he found he could tell where the spider riding her body was. It rested on her palm, pressed to his as he continued to hold her hands pinned to the rough brick wall.

Was he demon? Was that why he could sense the mark? Or had he somehow forged a bond between them when he willingly shared his blood and healed her?

"There have been those in the past who called me by that name," he said. "But I told you the truth when I said I don't know. My memories are locked away by the collar."

He lowered his head and claimed her mouth again, this time gently, wanting her to offer her submission willingly. Wanting her to accept him regardless of what he might be labeled.

She responded with the touch of her tongue to his, a sensuous dance in dark heat that left him light-headed and craving the feel of skin against skin, the sound of her voice pleading with him not only to take her, but to grant her sweet release.

"Does it matter what I am?" he whispered against her lips long moments later.

She shivered, as though some part of her mind continued to fight her body. "What matters is what you'll do when you're free of the collar."

"No less than what you intend for the guardsmen who killed your family and would have raped you. I'll hunt down my enemies and slay them."

He leaned into her, pressing the hard ridge of his erection to the juncture of her thighs. "Tell me, would you have sliced into the clerk's flesh if he'd refused to cooperate?"

Araña would have turned from him if he hadn't been blocking her from movement. He felt her shame as surely as if it were his own, and might have recoiled from it if his rage hadn't quickly replaced it, reminding him of what he'd suffered while at the mercy of humans. He despised them—all of them except her. It would take a lot for him to hate her.

Tir didn't like the power she held over him.

"Tell me," he said, pressing her for an answer. "Would you have forced the clerk to answer the questions put to him?"

"Yes," she whispered. "I don't draw a weapon unless I'm prepared to use it."

Tir released her and stepped away, fearing if he didn't, he would take her against the wall and further delay them. "You wanted to make sure your boat is still berthed where it was left," he said, signaling the end to their discussion.

She nodded, emotions in turmoil, but he preferred their battering against his psyche to the silence and containment. They walked the length of the area set aside for humans with gifts. At its edge there was a store serving as a general market.

Heat surged through Tir when she placed her hand on his arm, stopping him in the shadows. "Wait here and I'll go in and get you a shirt. You'll need it before we go any farther. Tattoos are outlawed in most of the places where the Church has influence and the non-gifted rule. They're reserved for marking criminals."

He and Araña had clung to the shadows where possible, but he'd been aware of eyes following their progress, strangers noting them from behind concealing drapes and shutters. "I'll wait," he said, and watched as she crossed the street and disappeared into the store.

There were others coming and going from the market. Many of them glanced his way, sensing his presence though he did nothing to draw attention to himself.

Was it because the humans were gifted? Or was it so dangerous in this city that they had all become wary prey?

Worry for Araña crept in the longer they were apart. More than once he caught himself rubbing his chest.

He didn't like having her out of his sight. Despite the spider mark and the knives she carried, she was so very mortal.

He took a step forward, only barely stopping himself from going after her. The tightness in his chest grew more pronounced. When had he come to fear her death so much?

Eleven

THE heavy gates bore the same heraldic crest as the flag fluttering from the car's antenna. Private soldiers, wearing black uniforms bearing red lion rampant insignias, stepped from a gatehouse and approached the driver's window, while others aimed automatic weapons down at the car from on top of the wall.

A glance in, and probably a subtle signal later, and the soldiers stepped away, allowing the car Rebekka was in to enter the estate. A second gate and more armed guards followed before she saw the place Tomás called home.

Manicured lawns and bright flowers were a testament to the wealth the Iberás held, as was the house. It would have been considered a mansion in the days before The Last War.

Through the open driver's window, she heard the distinctive roar of a lion. It was answered by another lion, and then a third.

"My grandfather's menagerie," Tomás said.

Bile rose in her throat along with outrage as she thought of

Anton Barlowe and the Weres he held captive in the maze, the creatures he knew Gulzar had tortured until they were trapped between forms. Her hands balled into fists. "Werelions?"

In answer Tomás tugged on a chain around his neck and pulled it free to reveal the charm at the end of it. "Animals. Pure lions."

The driver parked next to another dark car with deeply tinted windows, and whether by his action, or Tomás's, the locks on the back doors disengaged.

When she would have slid from the car, Eston leaned away from Tomás, his arms opening for her. Rebekka hugged the toddler to her, chiding herself, as she stepped onto the grounds of the estate, for taking comfort in holding him as though he were a shield.

Elegance. Wealth. Beauty. They were in every direction she cared to look—as were the walls protecting them.

"There's no point in trying to escape," Tomás said. "At night lions roam the entire area between the inner and outer walls."

He didn't expand on the statement further or point out the impossibility of her gaining freedom. He didn't need to.

Even if she should somehow manage to get past the guards, walls, and lions, the estate was set far enough away from the reclaimed heart of Oakland to make getting there through predator-filled forests impossible. She could use her gift to calm warm-blooded animals and Weres, if she had time to establish rapport, but they weren't the most deadly creatures prowling the night.

The front door opened and a uniformed butler stepped outside. His face revealed nothing, though Rebekka saw his spine stiffen in disapproval, as if he thought Tomás was in the company of a low-class woman who'd managed to seduce an Iberá then present him with a bastard child.

Rebekka's stomach revolted, and she quickly blocked thoughts of her mother and her own birth. She stood straighter, forcing herself to enter the house as if she were a guest instead of a prisoner.

A priest stood in the foyer, his attention on an elderly man in a motorized wheelchair. Both of them glanced up, but it was the priest who sent dread curling through Rebekka by asking, "How is it she's got the trapper's child?"

"She was there when the truck was ambushed," Tomás said.

"Where's the prisoner?"

"She claims not to know, Father Ursu."

"Was she willing to venture a guess?"

"No."

"Not surprising. She's one of the gifted, and a witch's pawn at that." The priest's eyes narrowed and Rebekka felt the full force of his attention. "She carries something evil with her, a token perhaps."

"Search her," the old man said, directing his command to the butler who now stood within striking distance of Rebekka.

Father Ursu held up his hand, halting the butler's movements. "Allow me to handle this matter at the church. I can dispose of the item there and question her about the ambush."

Icy fear washed over Rebekka as she imagined an Inquisition-like room and doubted she'd leave it alive. She wouldn't betray Levi or Araña, but if she could otherwise use the truth to gain her own freedom . . .

"I don't know who he is or where he would go," she said, unable to keep the terror from her voice.

"But you freed him all the same," the priest said.

"From the chair he was tied to and the cage inside the truck. But he was in chains when I left. None of the keys on the trapper's ring fit the locks on the shackles. There was nothing I could do for him. The guardsmen were drawing near. It was too dangerous to stay."

Father Ursu looked at the old man, the man Rebekka guessed was the Iberá patriarch. "Is it possible Enzo is mistaken? Could someone in the guard have taken the prisoner and perhaps sold him to Anton?"

The old man shook his head. "No. Enzo's spies would have told him. He's been collecting information on those who disgrace the integrity of the guard for years. His efforts have doubled in preparation for cleaning house when he is finally in a position to do so. There were shackles at the site. If she speaks the truth, then there's no need to involve her further in this matter."

Father Ursu placed his hand on the old man's shoulder. "She speaks the truth but she plays with it as well by making it sound as though she was the only one present when he was removed from the trapper's truck. Tomás saw at least one other, a man, and told us he thinks there might have been a third person there, too. If she doesn't have the information we want, perhaps her friends do. The sooner they're questioned, the better."

"Who were you with?" the Iberá patriarch asked Rebekka.

Fear threatened to close off Rebekka's throat. "I won't tell you his name. He left at the same time I did. He doesn't know any more about the prisoner than I do."

The old man's eyes settled on the child she held to her chest then shifted to Tomás. "Where did you find her?"

"Near the Mission. I recognized Eston, then her, when they passed on a bus. Guardsmen were chasing her by the time I caught up to them. They said her companion had killed one of theirs. But they didn't see her get in the car and I don't think they suspected me of harboring her. I thought it better to bring her here and send word to Enzo in case she's wanted for other crimes."

The patriarch nodded in approval. "You made a wise decision, Tomás. Until Enzo is named head of the guard and able to cleanse it of those who don't deserve to wear its uniform, all of them must be looked upon with suspicion."

Father Ursu said, "The time for restoring law and morality to Oakland is close at hand, Carlos. Enzo gaining control of the guard is just the first step. Your continued presence on the council is more critical than ever before. The prisoner needs to be found, quickly and quietly. We need answers. Let me deal with the matter of finding out who her companions are."

Cold sweat drenched Rebekka's skin at the persuasiveness of the priest's voice. To see the guard cleaned up . . .

She might have willingly offered to help them recapture the prisoner except she knew only too well how little the laws applied to the wealthy and powerful. And she would never trust the Church, which held that Weres were abominations originally created by forbidden science and by gifted who dabbled in black arts and bred with animals.

The Iberá patriarch's attention returned to Rebekka, but his question was for the priest. "You say she's gifted. What can you read of her ability?"

There was an almost imperceptible tightening of skin at the corners of Father Ursu's eyes, a subtle tell Rebekka might not have noticed if she hadn't spent much of her life around Weres. "A healer of some type, but given the witch's evil she carries with her and her presence when the trapper was murdered, her gift has most likely been tainted and turned into a thing of darkness."

"By all accounts the trapper's death was well deserved," the patriarch said. "The guard would have killed him if they'd caught him transporting dragon lizards. Just as the Church would put its former priest to death for any number of sins he's committed before and since creating the maze."

"I won't argue that point with you, Carlos. It's always been the purview of both state and Church to punish sinners when necessary."

"My gift is to heal animals," Rebekka said, remembering the lion roars she'd heard when they entered the estate and desperately hoping the revelation of her talent would keep her from ending up in Father Ursu's care.

Interest sparked in the old man's face. "Ah, that would explain her presence at the ambush, Derrick, which any other time I would have applauded, given what was intended for the animals on that truck. She'll stay here for the night as my guest."

The priest openly frowned. "Time—"

"Is of the essence," the patriarch interrupted, his voice now holding the imperious tone of a man whose personal power couldn't be ignored, even by the Church. "No one is more aware of it than I am, though I do share your concern about whatever witch's evil she might carry on her."

To Rebekka he said, "If you'll kindly remove it from your pocket, then I'll have you shown to your room and brought a change of clothing suitable for joining us at the evening meal."

Caught in the fear of being taken to the church, Rebekka hadn't given much thought to the token in her pocket. Her mind had been paralyzed, locked in finding a way to survive without betraying Levi. But now she was loath to give up the inscribed pentacle.

Too late she remembered standing in the occult shop with Annalise and glancing down at the book in the witch's hand, automatically memorizing the short spell requiring candle, blood, and token. *Should you need to use it in order to summon help, change the last word to* aziel.

The butler moved closer. He'd unobtrusively picked up a tray, and now he held it in front of her. Rebekka easily imagined him doing the same to another guest, taking a weapon perhaps, or something else banned from the patriarch's presence.

There was no choice—not if sacrificing the token kept her out of the Church's care. She placed it on the velvet-lined tray.

Father Ursu stepped forward, as if he intended to take possession of the pentacle, but the butler was already turning away, his movement allowing the patriarch to see the token before it was taken from the room.

It was another defeat, and as with the others, the priest's voice held no acknowledgment of it. It remained smooth, unperturbed. "Do you think it's wise to keep it here, Carlos?"

The patriarch laughed. "Surely I can be trusted to keep something so insignificant safe. It bears the Wainwright sigil, one that automatically marks it as evil in the Church's view. If it were truly harmful, the healer wouldn't be able to carry it. Now, as much as I hate to admit it, I need to rest before the evening meal is announced."

"I'll take my leave then." Father Ursu glanced at Eston. "What of the child? Surely you don't want to be burdened by it. Can I be of assistance there? He differs from those typically accepted into our ranks, but considering your support of the Church, he'd be accepted and raised for the priesthood."

Carlos Iberá snorted. "And have everyone wondering which of my children or grandchildren produced a bastard?"

"My word alone would be enough to have him taken in."

Rebekka's arms tightened reflexively, making Eston wriggle and fuss in protest. "He's got a mother," she said.

"A pathetic creature destined for a life of poverty and abuse," Father Ursu responded, confirming her guess that he had been at the trapper's compound.

For the first time she wondered what his interest in the prisoner was, and why—given the Church's power and that of the Iberás— they hadn't brought the chained man to Oakland under private guard.

"Leave the boy here for now," the patriarch said after a long pause.

"Very well. The rest of my evening is spoken for, but send word if you need me."

"Of course."

Tomás opened the door so the priest could depart. A moment later the butler returned and escorted Rebekka to a room with no locks, either on the inside or the outside.

AS Araña emerged from the shop, relief slid through Tir, cutting away his worry and leaving need in its place. He took the offered shirt when she reached him, but instead of putting it on, he crowded her, maneuvering her into what privacy could be found beneath the leafy canvas and shade of the tree.

"Give me the machete," he said, tormenting them both with the command.

He nearly doubled over at the sound of her soft whimper and the slight tremble of her fingers as she obeyed him by opening the front of her shirt so she could remove the harness holding the blade's sheath in position along her back.

His hands balled into fists to keep from reaching out and pushing her bra out of the way so he could look at her breasts. If he saw them, he wouldn't be able to stop himself from touching, suckling.

His cock throbbed at the sight of the leather straps against her skin. She was so utterly feminine. And yet she was a warrior, too. A survivor.

When she'd freed herself from the harness and handed it to him, he secured the weapon and felt the warmth on his back from where it had been held against her skin.

He put the shirt on, leaving it unbuttoned.

Their eyes met and held. Heat flared between them, fierce and consuming.

Her hands went to his chest, fingertips stroking his nipples and sending spike after spike of painful desire straight to his cock.

Liquid fantasies formed and re-formed in his thoughts. Quicksilver fast. Mercury-like.

Her dark eyelashes lowered, but Tir didn't mistake it for a show of submissiveness. He shouldn't allow her any power over him, he told himself, but found it too easy to imagine fighting this battle with her over and over again, enjoying it each time they were so engaged.

"Button it," he said, bracing himself for torment and only barely suppressing a moan when her fingers trailed down his chest and then over the front of his pants as she grasped the bottom of his shirt.

She obeyed. Slowly.

The curtain of her hair hid her expression as she closed his shirt. But her emotions told him the truth.

He struggled to keep his breathing even as her scent intensified with each button.

Her face lifted as she worked her way up his chest.

Satisfaction filled him at the sight of her flushed cheeks and wet, parted lips.

His cock jerked, leaked. A pant escaped despite his intention to remain stoic. Another followed when she reached his neck and her knuckles brushed against the inscribed collar.

Tir grabbed her hips, pulling her to him. It was sweet torture to have her against him but separated by clothing.

If he were free, his memory and his power restored, he'd take her to a safe place and keep her there. He'd insist she remain naked so he could look upon her at will, touch and take her throughout the day and night.

Her hands returned to his chest and settled over material-covered nipples. "The bus will be here in a few minutes," she said. "We should take it to the edge of downtown. Otherwise we'll lose too much of what's left of the day."

Tir was loath to let her go. His hands left her hips, sliding upward until they cupped her face. He brushed his thumb over her moist bottom lip and nearly came when her tongue darted out to caress him before she captured the end of his thumb in her mouth and sucked before releasing it.

"Turn around and I'll braid your hair," she said, her voice husky, her nipples hardened points against the front of her shirt. "You'll draw less attention with it tucked into your shirt."

He took her lips in a lingering kiss before obeying her, then shuddered at the feel of her fingers combing through his hair, weaving strands of it into a new fantasy. A fantasy where he crouched naked in front of her, his testicles hanging free between his thighs, his cock touching, rubbing against her smooth mound and soft belly while her pouty nipples brushed against his chest as she freed his hair.

A moan escaped, and he could feel the way it shuddered through her, going from her fingertips to her cunt. And somehow he knew the spider was there, waiting for his mouth, his cock, his touch.

She pulled the collar of his shirt out and slid the braid through the opening to snake down his back. When she stepped to the side, Tir fought the urge to capture her hand in his in order to maintain the physical contact. He continued to fight it as they walked to the bus stop.

Silence reigned between them as they stood with others who were also waiting for the bus, but it wasn't the emotional silence he'd come to abhor. It was the silence of caution.

He felt the surreptitious gazes of those around them. If he consciously chose it, he could feel their emotions as well.

They didn't interest him. Not beyond assuring himself they posed no threat.

He relaxed to enjoy the caress of a breeze. Araña's scent mingled with that of flowers and trees, the earth itself, all of it becoming the sweet smell of physical freedom.

Tir hooded his eyes and lifted his face toward the heavens. The endless blue called to him, as if he could soar in its heights and become a part of it, forever above the earth and those who inhabited it.

Sunlight struck him, and he basked in the feel of it against his skin. He wouldn't be shackled again. He'd see all of mankind destroyed before he allowed himself to be at the mercy of humans again.

The sound of a heavy diesel engine cut across his thoughts. Around him, those who waited for the bus shuffled their belongings and prepared to board.

He turned his attention to the street and watched the bus round a corner before slowing to a stop nearby. Fear spiked through Araña, along with quickly suppressed grief, her emotions echoing through him as if they were his own.

Tir reached for her, took her hand where moments before he'd denied himself the contact. Her fingers tightened on his, the sole, silent acknowledgment she gave that boarding the bus was difficult. And then she pulled away in order to pay their fare.

He followed her, allowing her to choose their seats. When he sat next to her, he cupped her chin, forcing her to meet his gaze. "I won't allow you to be harmed," he said, keeping his voice low but making sure she heard the depth of his pledge, the promise that settled into every fiber of his being.

Emotions bombarded him. So much pain and guilt it was nearly overwhelming.

"Stop," he said. "You can't undo the past."

"I know."

She escaped his grip and the snare of his eyes, and looked down, drawing his attention to the well-worn wallet in her hands. Her fingers traced the seam, the edges, trembled slightly as she opened it and removed the folded bills it contained.

"You should have money in case we get separated," she said, counting out half of it, touching the denomination marks as she spoke the numbers out loud in case he was unfamiliar with the currency.

He wanted to deny they'd ever be separated, but he knew it would be a lie. She pressed the bills into his hand and he took them. Then she slid the wallet back into her pocket and turned away from him to look out the window.

A fist tightened around his heart. He edged closer, conscious of being watched, chafing at not being able to divert her thoughts and ease her with the joining of their bodies. His fingers tangled in her hair. But rather than force her to face him again, he combed through the silky locks, stroking the back of her neck.

His mouth whispered kisses against her cheek each time she flinched when a camouflage-painted vehicle passed. "Tell me about Matthew and Erik."

She stiffened at the sound of their names, but Tir didn't allow her to retreat. "Tell me," he repeated, touching his lips to her earlobe, gently sucking it.

Her breath hitched, desire and pain mingling.

His free hand settled on her stomach, and he wished they were alone so he could slide his fingers beneath the waistband of her pants and cup her bare mound. He didn't want her to feel anything but happiness and pleasure.

Before he was forced to ask her for a third time, she said, "They took me in when most wouldn't have. They taught me what I needed to know in order to one day survive on my own. They made me believe in myself, in my worth despite . . . the things that set me apart. I loved them. I would have died in their place if I could have, even if it meant eternal damnation."

Tir's fingers tightened in her hair unintentionally. Jealousy scorched through him, along with violent denial at the idea of her giving up her life.

He forced himself to loosen his grip on her hair, to slow the agitated race of his heart. The heat of his reaction dissolved with the lash of her sadness across his soul.

Tir's lips went to the corner of hers. "They wouldn't have wanted you to surrender your life for theirs."

"I know," she said, her voice barely audible. "Matthew told me to live for all of us. It was the last thing he said to me before he was killed."

Tir pressed a kiss to the corner of her lips before easing away from her and watching as the city of Oakland was slowly revealed.

Hardscrabble poverty gave way to lesser poverty, and then to wealth. Estates gave way to the downtown area, where buildings rose in defiance of the past and citizens walked the streets.

Araña finally turned from the windows. "We should get off at the next stop."

There were cursory glances in their direction as they left the bus. Speculative appraisal, but Tir could sense no threat.

"Which way?" he asked, smelling the ocean mixed with diesel fumes and roasting meat.

She indicated an alleyway. "There will be fewer people if we take whatever shortcuts we can and get to the road that runs along the waterfront."

He nodded and followed where she led, content to turn his attention to keeping them both safe. When they reached the bay, Araña stopped well before where piers extended out into the water and docks hosted container ships being loaded and unloaded.

"I can see the *Constellation* from here," she said, pointing to it. "She's in the second slip from the end. This side."

"Stay here. I'll see what I can learn."

Her fingers lightly shackled his wrist, and the restraint sent heat surging to his cock. "Be careful."

Amusement filled him, flowing into his chest along with a warmth he didn't want to look at too closely. He caressed her cheek with the back of his hand. "Humans have far more to fear from me than I have to fear from them."

Worry remained in her dark eyes, tugging at him, threatening to delay him. He made himself turn and walk away from her.

Tir approached the dock. He was careful to keep his head ducked and his face turned away from the camera mounted on the lamppost near its entrance, though he had no idea whether it was possible for his image to be captured on film or not.

The long-sleeved shirt chafed his skin after centuries of wearing minimal clothing. Its collar felt as tight and constricting as the sigil-inscribed one it hid.

He was confident he could recover Araña's boat. But as he moved farther and farther from her, he hated knowing he'd left her un-guarded.

The city wasn't her home. Already it had proven unsafe for her.

He thought of the bloodstains on the ground she'd searched ear-lier, the strength it had taken for her to return to the place where her family had been killed. For centuries he'd despised humans, looked at them and seen only the worst of their natures, but she was different.

She hardened his body and softened his heart. She made him *feel*, and the emotions were uncomfortable, contradictory. Unwelcome. And yet when he was with her, he hated having any barrier between them.

It was only when he stepped foot on the wooden dock that she left his mind completely. He could feel dozens of open stares, and more that were hidden. A thick-necked man emerged from a small concrete building, pig eyes darting suspiciously.

"What's your business here?" he said, the salt-sweat smell of him arriving along with his question.

"I'm interested in buying a boat," Tir lied. "Are there any for sale?"

"Might be," the man said, eyes traveling over Tir's clothing in an effort to assess his wealth.

Tir did something he hadn't done in centuries. He consciously opened himself to the man's emotions.

They poured over him like oily refuse. Greed and suspicion dominated, mixed with a craving to feel flesh yield and bones break under meaty fists.

The temptation to end the human's existence flashed through Tir like a lightning strike. Ragged and bright and primal.

Restraint came with great difficulty. It came only with thoughts of Araña waiting for him, worrying for him.

"I'll investigate on my own," Tir said, eyes boring into the man's, letting him glimpse his own death in them.

The man stepped back, sensing something. Or perhaps he was being monitored by the camera as well.

A hatchet-faced man with an aura of authority emerged from the same concrete building as the dockhand. He took a step toward them.

The man in front of Tir said, "This way," and turned, leading Tir directly to the boat he'd come to look at.

"It's for sale?" Tir asked.

"Auction is tomorrow morning. Nine o'clock sharp. Cash. Unless you've worked out the terms of a barter beforehand with the guard."

"I want to see belowdecks."

The dockhand glanced back toward the concrete building. The hatchet-faced man was still standing there, watching.

"It's unlocked."

Tir boarded the boat. It was old but well maintained. And though there was no evidence of Araña or the men who'd been her family, Tir could see their presence in the care they'd taken.

Where there was wood, it was smooth and waxed, beautifully preserved. Sail covers and bags were faded and weather-worn, but meticulously mended, stowed, and tied.

Belowdecks a safe stood open, revealing shelves empty of valuables. Closet doors were the same, attesting to the fact that anything personal or valuable had been stripped from the boat.

Rage filled Tir. He felt the violation as if it were his own.

The boat was more than transportation to Araña. It was her home, a place that represented freedom and security—and while Matthew and Erik lived, happiness and family.

Tir returned to the deck and then to the dock, grateful the pig-eyed attendant was gone and not there to tempt him into venting his anger. He headed back toward land, taking in everything he could of his surroundings.

He noted the lights mounted on poles, which of the other boats were occupied, the landmasses and shorelines, as well as the distance to the docks where moored container ships and boats belonging to the powerful were patrolled by heavily armed men.

It was difficult to determine all of the security measures in place, or the danger involved in stealing the boat. But he was confident he could overcome them. Humans didn't venture out in the night unless they had reason to—and then only if they were heavily armed and well paid.

The real problem lay in where to take the boat, where it could be safely hidden until their business in Oakland was finished.

Tir glanced at the sky. The sun was well into its descent.

Tension radiated from Araña when he rejoined her in the alley. "She's been confiscated?"

"Yes. They auction your boat tomorrow morning."

Her eyes went to the *Constellation* and her hands fisted. She glanced at the heavily patrolled piers where the wealthy kept boats.

He could feel her gather her control and wall up her emotions. "If I'm lucky, whoever buys the *Constellation* will keep her berthed where she is. I don't know these waters well enough to know where it's safe to leave her until I'm ready to go home. Getting her back will have to wait."

A protest sounded in Tir's soul at the thought of Araña leaving him, or thinking she could. When she would have turned away, he halted her by curling his fingers around her forearm. "We have until nightfall to find a place to hide the boat. If we do, I'll recover it for you tonight."

"It's too dangerous," Araña said, unable to bear the thought of Tir being recaptured. She'd rather lose the boat than see him in chains again. "Even if we learn of a place to hide her, there's no time to watch and note the routines of those guarding the port and the docks."

From Matthew and Erik she'd learned the importance of planning. Of having patience and watching, spotting the glitches in security that would allow a thief to both venture into another's territory *and* escape it with whatever prize was sought.

Tir's fingers tightened on her arm. "Do you think I can't deliver on my promise to you?" he said in a silky voice, masculine affront seething, sliding into her through his touch.

Araña hid a sudden smile. In that moment he reminded her of Matthew, and there was no pain in it.

She did what Erik would have done, subconsciously modeling her behavior on his. She moved into Tir, and he released his punishing grip in favor of pulling her against him.

Twelve

ARAÑA wound her arms around his waist and hugged him to her. She ground her pelvis against his.

His hands moved up her back to tangle in her hair. His lips descended to settle on hers in a fierce, dominating kiss, a show of power she acknowledged and acquiesced to.

She yielded, melted into him. Whimpered as moisture flooded her channel and escaped from her slit.

He deepened the kiss, moving to pin her against the wall in a primal demonstration of strength that made her feel exquisitely feminine.

She wanted to shed her clothes and welcome him into her body. To kneel in front of him and take his cock into her mouth in a show of ultimate submission.

"I need you, Tir," she whispered when he allowed her breath, her plea covering more than just the desire she felt for him.

She'd craved touch all her life, but now that she'd known his, she knew no other would satisfy her. "I don't want you to be injured or enslaved because of me."

Tir's hands left her hair to cup her face, then slid downward to cover her breasts. He rubbed his palms over pebbled nipples, making her moan, before smoothing them down her sides to settle at her waist.

Her womb fluttered and her cunt lips grew more swollen. She rubbed her hardened clit against his erection.

His fingers tightened. "Stop or I'll take you here. There's not much time if we hope to find a safe place for your boat."

A shudder went through her, but she obeyed, forcing her mind back to what was important. "Levi and Rebekka are the only people I know in Oakland. We can go back to the red zone and see if they're at the brothel."

Her passion cooled with thoughts of Rebekka and the remembered vision. Worry slid into her gut and coiled there, waiting to change into guilt.

Tir's eyes darkened. "The Were left me for the guardsmen."

Araña didn't deny the truth in his statement, but she countered it with a question. "Would you have done differently in his place? Especially for someone you thought was human? And a criminal?"

Tir's nostril's flared. "I would see mankind wiped from the face of the earth if it were left to me." He leaned in abruptly. Close enough so their breath mingled. "Except for you. You I would allow to live."

"There are plenty of humans worth saving," she whispered, thinking of the men and women Erik and Matthew called friends, those who'd accepted her among them, the outlaws and outcasts who held to their honor in a harsh world.

Her hand went to Tir's chest. She felt the hard, fierce beat of his heart. "Not all of us are like those who held you captive."

"Then pray it's not up to me to decide whether they live or die, Araña." He stepped away from her but circled her wrist with his fingers.

She thought they'd go directly to the bus stop. Instead Tir pulled her into a tiny eating place not far from the waterfront.

Her stomach reacted by growling, her mouth by watering, her hands by automatically going to the knife hilts.

Rough-looking seamen clustered around a mismatch of salvaged tables. Their faces were tanned, leathered, unshaven, and more than one of them wore the tattoos of a criminal.

They undressed her with their eyes and Tir stiffened at her side. "It's okay," Araña murmured, comfortable despite the glances. She'd been in plenty of diners and bars like this one, where men who lived and worked on the water gathered. "We need to eat before we go to the brothel. This is a good place to do it."

There was little chance of guardsmen wandering in for drink or food. Only trouble would bring them, and these men didn't want trouble, not of that kind, not in a city like Oakland. And if someone were curious enough or bold enough to approach Tir, thinking he was a pimp . . . then perhaps they'd be able to gather information on how frequently the docks were patrolled and what manner of predators roamed them at night.

Araña allowed Tir to guide her to a stool along an L-shaped counter separating customers from a cook and a server. At his silent urging, she took the open seat against the wall while he took the one next to her.

Grease spattered as baskets laden with cut potatoes were dropped into deep pools of cooking oil. Flames jumped as fish were tossed on grills.

"You ready?" the server working the counter asked, stopping in front of Tir.

Stained pictures hung on the wall next to where the cook was busy slapping food onto plates and passing them to an older woman to deliver to those waiting at tables. Prices next to the pictures, as well as crude writing, noted what the diner served.

Beer. Fish. Fries.

The catch of the day was salmon.

"Fish," Tir said.

The server's gaze flicked to Araña then to the male customers crowding around tables. "Your woman eating or she here to work?"

Tir's nostrils flared at the question. Araña put her gloved hand on the bunched muscles of his thigh in a soothing gesture.

"She eats. Fish for her, too."

The server shrugged and told Tir the cost of the meal. His expression said he thought Tir was a fool for paying with cash from his pocket when he had a woman who could cover it by working in the alley on her back or knees.

Tir turned toward Araña, and within a heartbeat, eyes smoldering with hostility changed, the flames of hatred giving way to heat as they looked at each other and remembered their last meal together.

Liquid desire pooled in her labia with thoughts of breakfast and his feeding her by hand. Color rose in her cheeks.

Silence stretched between them. The need to touch was countered by the feel of strangers watching and the necessity of remaining alert to their surroundings.

"Later," Tir murmured, and she gave a slight nod before escaping the intensity of his gaze.

Their food arrived in an unceremonious slide of plates along the counter and a clatter of forks. They ate, and as they did so, interest in them faded, except for five men who sat huddled over their beers, whispering and nudging one another, passing something she couldn't see around the table until finally one of them lurched to his feet and approached.

A few steps away from Tir, the man doffed his tightly woven knit cap and held it in both hands. Grit clung to the grooves in his skin, and his fingernails were outlined in dark grime. His eyes dropped to where Araña's gloved hand remained on Tir's thigh, only partially obscured by the counter.

Sea-chapped lips pulled away from tobacco-stained teeth. "My friends and me, we was wondering if you're selling time with the woman. 'Cause—"

Tir stood. The man backpedaled, fingers lifting away from his clutched cap in a gesture of peace. "Sorry, no offense meant."

Araña touched Tir's arm, her stomach muscles tightening at the returned interest the encounter had generated, the attention she felt on her gloved hand and the speculation it would arouse. "We can go now," she said.

He turned away from the retreating man. "You've had enough to eat?"

"Yes. For now." Their plates were both empty, none of the food wasted.

They left the diner. The five men followed them out almost immediately.

Tir freed the top buttons of his shirt as they walked, so he could retrieve the machete strapped to his back if necessary. "Let's return to the bus stop using the same route we took to the docks."

Araña's hands curled around the handles of her knives. "They'll split up and try to trap us in one of the alleys."

Tir laughed. "I look forward to it."

She glanced at his face and read anticipation to match his words. *So be it*, she thought, closing her mind to any hint of conscience. The men following them were bringing death on themselves.

Araña turned, entering the first of the alleyways that would lead them to the bus stop. In her mind she traced the remainder of the route and considered the best spot for an ambush if *she* were the one planning it.

The men from the diner weren't as patient. Or as stealthy.

She heard the pounding of footsteps moments after she and Tir crossed a narrow street and entered a second alley.

"Stop. This is as good a place as any," Tir said, sliding the machete from its sheath, its blade gleaming wickedly.

Araña drew her knives as their attackers entered the alleyway from both ends. Three to the left. Two to the right.

"You won't need your weapons," Tir said, stepping in front of her, crowding her so she was forced backward between him and the wall. "I won't allow you to put yourself in danger needlessly."

His arrogance aggravated her as much as his protectiveness pleased her. "Move," she said, pressing her knuckles into his back instead of the tip of her knife he probably deserved. "I can hold my own."

"I know, but in this instance, there's no need for you to."

The men advanced, knives in their hands, sure of themselves and growing more so the closer they got. On some silent signal, arms went back to the left and right, then shot forward hurling blades.

Tir blurred into motion, so fast, so smoothly efficient, that before Araña could step forward and follow his attack with one of her own, he'd knocked the thrown knives from the air and moved into the offensive.

It was a fluid dance of man and weapon, his movements a poetry glorifying the righteous slaying of his enemies. Blood coated the sides of the buildings within seconds. It pooled, surrounding severed limbs and soaking into clothing. It painted the cracked and broken pavement and whatever trash it touched. And in the midst of the carnage, Tir stood unscathed, unbloodied.

For an instant Araña thought she saw the air vibrating around him, recognizing his supernatural nature even if he himself didn't remember what he was. He looked up and their eyes met. Heat and frigid cold washed through her, desire and primal fear combined. He was a ruthless warrior whose beauty held perfection as well as savagery.

"Let's go," he said.

She almost obeyed without question, Erik and Matthew's training deserting her until she had the strength to look away from Tir.

Then instinct guided her, habit. She crouched down and quickly went through the closest man's pockets. There was paper money, enough of it that he could have paid for a shared prostitute if that's where the men's true interest lay. It was slick with blood and folded around stubs from a gaming club.

Araña left it, though she knew Erik and Matthew would have chided her for doing so. She moved to the next man, the one who'd approached them in the diner.

There was a paper folded into fourths in his shirt pocket. She opened it and trembled at the sight of her own face staring back at her.

A reward was being offered to anyone who came forward with information leading to her capture, or who braved the warning that she could kill with a touch and brought her to the maze themselves. *Alive.* She was worthless dead.

Tir took the paper from her and read it before crumpling it and tossing it aside. He cleaned the machete with the dead man's knit cap then sheathed it and stood, his fingers a steel band around her arm as he forced her to her feet.

"Let's go," he repeated, his voice dark with fury. "Let's find the Were and the healer."

DINNER was a formal affair, silent and somber for the most part, unlike anything Rebekka had ever experienced. There were no jokes—civilized or ribald. There were certainly no raunchy retellings of client requests or descriptions of anatomical shortcomings or abundances—the things she'd been exposed to in the human brothel she grew up in and the Were brothels she worked in.

There were no children present, though she noted their absence because of Eston's. Janita, the lady's maid who'd brought fashionable clothing along with a matching necklace to the room Rebekka was in, had remained to escort her to the dining room. She'd insisted on taking Eston to be fed in the kitchen, saying The Iberá believed children should join the adults only when they proved themselves ready for the privilege.

Surreptitiously Rebekka glanced at those gathered at the table.

The women wore expensive jewelry and elegant evening dresses, but they still seemed to be shadows of their husbands or fathers or brothers. The men talked among themselves, primarily of business and news from other cities.

Everyone deferred to the patriarch.

Servers came and went, unobtrusively, silently seeing what needed refilling and what needed to be whisked away.

The food was beyond imagining in its abundance and presentation. Rebekka had never known hunger, not as so many others had, but she was still nearly overwhelmed by the feast that was apparently nothing more than an ordinary meal to the Iberás.

Despite her tense stomach, she ate. Committing each flavor, each delicious bite to memory and hoping she would be granted freedom or find a way to escape so she could look back and one day savor at least this part of the experience.

No one left the table. Not when their dessert dishes and coffee cups where taken away, not even when the patriarch's place was clear of dinner trappings.

It was only when he said, "If you'll excuse me, I think our guest would enjoy seeing the lions," that the members of his family were dismissed. They rose, bidding the patriarch good evening before going to the suites and sections of the estate they called home.

Rebekka noticed then, that The Iberá was seated in a regular chair. When the last of his family members had departed, the butler who'd taken the witch's token away on a tray entered the room with the motorized wheelchair.

Rebekka looked away, allowing the old man his pride and dignity. Prisoner she might be, but she was also a healer, and strangely indebted to the Iberás for keeping her from being captured by guardsmen and turned over to the maze, and for not surrendering her to Father Ursu.

The hum of a motor signaled the wheelchair was in operation. Rebekka stood and looked at the patriarch again.

"Come," he said, and she followed, seeing him for the first time as a healer would. Seeing how his aura of command and power and wealth had hidden his frailty before.

Beneath the expensive material of his trousers and shirt, the muscles in his legs and left arm were atrophied. As she watched, the hand resting on his lap twitched in an involuntary spasm, making her realize with a start that he hadn't used it during dinner. It twitched again and she saw him sit straighter, as if he could will his body to cooperate, even as the fingers operating the chair controls trembled slightly.

Pity slid through Rebekka. A name came to mind. *Lou Gehrig's disease*—after a famous baseball player who'd lived and died centuries before The Last War—a cure for which had never been found.

Despite Tomás's earlier claim, she thought the patriarch would lead her onto the grounds and show her lions held in cages or moat-surrounded enclosures. Instead they took an elevator then traveled down a hallway to pass through a doorway leading to the same walkway along the top of the interior walls that was patrolled by private militia.

Rebekka's breath caught when she saw a pride of lions lounging in the area between the inner and outer walls of the estate. There were six females and a male, all magnificent. Seeing them made her heart ache as she was reminded of what had been done to Levi, and what he'd given up when she healed him.

As if picking up on the tenor of her thoughts, The Iberá said, "Our goals aren't so different, yours and mine. We'd both like to see an end to the maze and the red zone that spawned it."

Rebekka resisted the urge to refute his assumption. The red zone had always been more home to her than the area set aside for the gifted. It was a harsh, often cruel place, a decadent, vice-ridden playground for the wealthy and powerful, but it was also a sanctuary of sorts for the Weres who couldn't live among their own kind or among humans.

The patriarch took her silence for assent. "Did you know that the early believers of the Church were once thrown to the lions? There's always been a cost for battling the darkness inside man."

He turned his head to look at her. "There's still a war going on for the souls of those in Oakland. The maze is a symbol of that evil, and Anton, with his demon, proof of how bold and powerful God's enemies have become."

Rebekka couldn't keep her silence. "And what of the gifted? The Church might accept us in public—for political purposes—but they haven't truly turned away from their doctrines. The early Christians looked to Exodus and spoke of not allowing a witch to live, but that edict has been expanded to mean that anyone using unnatural powers or secret arts should be put to death. Do you think I don't know Father Ursu wouldn't hesitate to kill me, whether I answer his questions or not?"

"The Church is made of men," The Iberá said. "They'd have us believe they're infallible, but they're not. They crave power without balance, but allowing them to have it would be a mistake. A strong, uncorrupted guard and police force diligently enforcing the law will provide that balance. As will a governing council made up of those who can both accommodate the Church and stand against it when necessary. There's room in this city for those gifted who don't consort with evil."

The patriarch leaned toward her, his eyes intense, like a hawk's. "If Satan acts through some of them, then God has touched others. A healer should never hunger or fear for their life. They should live in comfort as a doctor or veterinarian would, and be held in high regard."

Below them the male lion began to roar. He was answered by a lion on the other side of the compound.

"Come, there's more for you to see," the patriarch said, touching a lever and propelling the wheelchair forward along the walkway surrounding the main estate and grounds.

They passed an area set aside for private guards to live and train in, as well as three additional lion prides in different sections of the outer estate. When they reached a building to the left of the main house, the patriarch touched a button, summoning the elevator, and they descended. "This is the veterinary facility. Tomás and his father surprised me with a lion for my birthday."

No expense had been spared, either on equipment or furnishings. A heavy steel door slid open and The Iberá ushered Rebekka through into a room where a huge male lion paced.

Hunger radiated from him, and pain. He stilled, golden eyes immediately focusing on Rebekka, drawing her to him.

Without thinking she went, pressing calm into him as she approached, telling him without words she wanted to help him. The lion signaled his acceptance by sitting, then leaning against the front of the cage.

He opened his mouth partially and Rebekka thought the source of his pain lay there. She reached through the opening in the bars and as soon as she touched his muzzle, knew her guess was right.

Infection raged at the root of a canine tooth. It was already starting to perforate bone and spread to soft tissue. She concentrated on the area, calling on the lion's immune system to attack and absorb, then drawing on like tissue to fill the pockets created by pus and bacteria. When it was done, he gave a purring rumble of appreciation before turning to feast on a deer carcass she hadn't noticed in her hurry to get to him.

"I envy you your gift," the patriarch said, reminding her she wasn't alone. "Not just to be able to heal them, but to be able to touch them."

He wheeled the motorized chair around, pausing at the steel door for Rebekka to join him, then pausing again as he directed her into living quarters as elegant as those in the main house. "This is kept ready for the veterinarian, though he rarely has need of it. It could be yours, and the child's. Eston would have a better life with you than he'd have otherwise. The maid assigned to you would be yours as well. You could travel to other estates, escorted by my private guard, and be paid well to use your gift."

Rebekka's hands fisted the expensive fabric of her borrowed dress. "In exchange for betraying my friends?"

The Iberá batted the question aside with his good hand. "I'm interested only in recapturing the prisoner you claim to know nothing about or have any allegiance to."

Would your answer change if you knew Levi was Were and Araña branded? she wondered, but didn't voice the question. "Why? Why is he so important?"

"That doesn't concern you."

"And if I don't help you, you'll turn me over to Father Ursu for questioning?"

"You've had a long day and the child probably needs your attention," the patriarch said, touching the control so the chair moved forward, toward where the elevator stood open. "Think about my offer as you tend to him."

Thirteen

ARAÑA bowed her head so the hood of the dark cloak they'd purchased after the attack shielded her face from view. The heavy material made her feel trapped, and in a fight it would hinder her ability to draw her knives quickly and strike fast.

The only place she knew to look for Levi and Rebekka was the brothel. But as she and Tir approached it, dread built with each step. The healer wouldn't be there. Araña was as sure of it as she had been that Erik would die in Oakland when she first saw the city rising out of ruin.

"It might be better for you to go in alone," she said, slowing at the end of an already deeply shadowed alleyway. "Some of the brothel's clients probably frequent the gaming clubs. One of them might have seen me run the maze."

Tir's hand tightened on hers in response and he kept going. His harsh *no* held the same steel as his grip.

Two hyena-faced Weres served as doormen and bouncers. They opened the doors into a leather-and-fur waiting room hosted by a madam with boar tusks and small black eyes in a round human face.

She swept Araña and Tir with a quick, assessing gaze and grunted before saying to Tir, "You pay full price regardless. A quarter if the woman watches. Half if she works my whore. Full price if my whore works her."

Women lined up without being told. Their clothing left little to the imagination and their appearances ranged from fully human to mostly animal.

"I'm here to see Levi or the healer," Tir said.

The madam's eyes hardened. "There's no healer here. We don't have any use for the gifted except as paying customers. If it's Levi you want, then he should have met you outside."

Araña slid her hand beneath the folds of the cloak. The gesture had two men stepping into the room through doors on either side of the parlor. Their mouths opened in animal threat to reveal razor-sharp teeth.

They retreated when she drew out several bills from the wallet and, keeping her head down, offered them to the madam. "For your trouble. Where can we find Levi?"

The woman grunted and took the bills. "Unless you want to keep paying so you can look at the girls, go outside. I'll have him located and sent to you."

They left, and Levi joined them a few minutes later. If he was surprised to see they'd survived, it didn't show. "Let's walk," he said, turning without waiting for an answer and heading in the direction of the boundary between the red zone and the area set aside for the gifted.

When he was out of the hearing range of the Were doormen, he said, "Rebekka was captured."

Acid rose in Araña's throat, hot with her guilt. "By who?" she asked, already knowing.

"Guardsmen, but Gulzar, Anton and Farold's torturer, was in the area as well."

"When?" Tir asked.

"This morning, as we were taking the child to the Mission."
Levi's face contorted in furious agony. His lips parted in a silent,
impotent human snarl. "I should have hunted the man in the cab
with the trapper. He must have overheard us talking about what to
do with the child and gone to the maze with the information. The
guardsmen and Gulzar were lying in wait for us."

"She was taken to the maze?" Araña asked, her skin becoming
chilled with thoughts of Abijah, her guilt flaying her at the thought
of the healer being raped by guardsmen or convicts or the demon.

"I don't know where she was taken, or even if she lives. None of
the men who frequent the gaming clubs and come to the brothels
have mentioned her. Pictures of those running are often posted early
to stimulate betting interest. We separated. My intention was to draw
the guardsmen and Gulzar away and kill any of them I could so Rebekka could escape with the child."

"Did you recognize the guardsman?" Araña asked, thinking of
Jurgen and Cabot and her intention to kill them before she left
Oakland.

"Two of them, but not the third. I succeeded in killing one
guardsman before I escaped the area. Rebekka works tonight. If
she'd managed to escape, she would have come to the brothel, even
if she had the child with her. The prostitutes depend on her, and
while she's here, she's under the protection of the vice lords who
own them."

He glanced up at the sky and quickened his pace. Araña did the
same and said, "We need safe shelter for the night." She didn't think
it would be on the *Constellation*.

"It can't be at the brothel, not unless you're willing to pay for a
room and a whore."

Despite Levi's waiting in the woods when she escaped the maze,
Araña couldn't bring herself to tell him about the reward being
offered for her. She'd lived too long among outcasts and outlaws—
men and women whom circumstances might turn into bounty

hunters—to willingly reveal there was a price on her head. "A recommendation then."

He considered the request for several long moments before saying, "Rebekka has a house in the gifted area. She rarely goes there and never speaks about it. If she were here, she'd offer it to you." The last held some of the same guilt Araña felt.

"You've checked to make sure she's not hiding there?" Tir asked.

"Yes. There was no sign of her." Levi's fingers flexed in a lionlike gesture of claws being sheathed and unsheathed. "If you intend to eat, you'll need to buy food at the stall up ahead. You won't have time to get it elsewhere."

"We'll stop," Tir said.

At the small shop, Araña hung back with Levi and kept her face hidden as Tir bartered for bread and cheese. Her mouth watered at the sight of the fresh fruit, but buying it would deplete their resources.

He rejoined them and they continued walking. When they were well away from the food seller, Tir said, "Araña's boat has been confiscated. It'll be auctioned in the morning and most likely be gone from its berth by the end of the day. I intend to steal it tonight. Is there a place along the red zone where I can hide it?"

Levi's answer was a lion cough of amusement. "Vampires guard the area at night, under contract with the dock owners as well as some of the cargo ship owners. If you managed to slip past them and steal a boat, the harbor is patrolled by private security, guardsmen, and police. If one of them spots you, they'll hold you in place with machine guns then board at daybreak. And if you're foolish enough to make a run for it and dodge them by going into the outer harbor, they'll blockade you and leave you to your fate."

"And that fate would be?"

Araña couldn't help but smile at the arrogant, masculine confidence in Tir's voice.

"The harbor is filled with ruins. Even in daylight it's nearly impossible to avoid hitting metal sharp enough to rip open a ship. If you manage it, you'd most likely be killed by the vice lord who controls it. He lets very few boats in that aren't his own or haven't paid well for the privilege."

"But he lets some in?" Araña asked, hearing Levi's qualifier and experiencing a small flare of optimism. She couldn't offer the vice lord money, but she had the skills of a thief to barter.

Levi shrugged. "I don't know. But I wouldn't count on making a deal with him, not if rumors are true. They say he's consumed with finding a cure for his daughter. She's said to have the wasting disease."

Pain lanced through Araña, a sharp, unexpected thrust as she thought of Erik. They'd come to Oakland seeking a cure for him. Seeking a miracle. If the vice lord's daughter truly had the disease—

Her heart skipped and stuttered its beat with the memory of Tir saving her from certain death after her fight with the dragon lizard. His hand tightened on her arm, warning her to remain silent as he asked, "What's the vice lord's name?"

"Rimmon."

Araña missed a step as the melted-wax face of the man in the occult shop immediately came to mind. Erik and Matthew had never been believers in coincidence.

"Where can I find him?" Tir asked, his voice holding no hint as to whether or not he remembered the name and the man, though Araña suspected he did.

"He's usually at his club. Temptation. It's a Victorian on the same street as all the others like it."

There was a subtle hesitation in Levi when they reached the sigil-marked boundary of the area set aside for the gifted. His jaw muscles tensed and his posture stiffened, though he didn't flinch as he passed through the wards.

They traveled in silence, staying close to the border for a while, then cutting through a neighborhood where the majority of the houses had collapsed around trees taking root in what had once been living rooms.

Wild grass and flowers sprouted on fallen roofs. Dark green vines with poisonous, bright red berries slowly crushed rusted cars and old fences under their weight.

Rebekka's house stood alone, isolated. They approached cautiously, though there was no evidence of it having been visited by guardsmen or those in the employ of the maze owner.

Levi pulled a key from his pocket and unlocked the door before giving the key to Araña. "There's another one in the kitchen drawer."

He pushed inside and they followed. The house had a dusty, closed smell, verifying what Levi had told them about the healer seldom visiting.

Araña expected Levi to leave immediately. Instead he prowled the tiny house like a large, restless predator. She went to the kitchen and took Erik's wallet from her pocket, blocking the grief that came from handling it, fortifying herself with Matthew's words as he'd told her to run.

She removed Erik's boat keys and placed them on the counter before pocketing the wallet. She opened the drawer and found Rebekka's second house key, along with paper, pencil, and extra candles.

Impulsively she pulled out the paper and pencil. Tir set the food down on the counter and took the keys. Anxiety tightened her chest.

"I should be offended you have so little confidence in me," he said. "But I find your worry for me oddly arousing."

"I want to go with you, Tir."

"No." His mouth found her neck and sent a pulse of pure need to her cunt. "You'll stay here until I return."

When she didn't acknowledge the command, his lips were replaced by his teeth. They closed on her skin in sharp demand and remained there until she said, "I'll stay as long as it's safe."

Tir rubbed his tongue over the place where he'd bitten. A caress and not an apology.

"You'll speak with the vice lord before you go for the boat?" she asked.

"Yes." Neither of them mentioned how he'd done the impossible and saved her from dying after her fight with the dragon lizard.

Heat rose in Araña's cheeks when she realized Levi stood across the counter from them, his arms folded across his chest. Embarrassment at having been so lost in Tir that the Were was able to get within striking distance without her noticing made Araña pick up the pencil and begin drawing. It wasn't a conscious decision, but with sure strokes, Jurgen's face appeared on the paper.

Levi's arms dropped to his sides. "Jurgen," he said, and the same hatred Araña felt was in his voice. "There's always a need for a healer when he visits the brothel. He went after Rebekka."

On a separate piece of paper she deftly drew Cabot, the man whose cock had shriveled at the sight of the spider on her bare mound. "And him?"

"Dead."

Araña allowed herself a moment of satisfaction before pulling another sheet of paper from the drawer. The image of the man she'd seen in her vision was as real to her as the others.

Beside her, Tir tensed so subtly that if their bodies hadn't been touching, she wouldn't have known it. On the other side of the counter Levi shook his head, the brown-blond tones and length of his hair making him momentarily resemble the lion Rebekka said he could no longer become. "He wasn't there."

"He's not the third guardsman or the man you call Gulzar?" Too late, Araña realized she should have hidden her surprise and puzzlement.

Tawny-colored eyes narrowed. "Why did you think he would be?" Levi asked.

Guilt lashed at Araña. Suspicion appeared in Levi's eyes, telling her he smelled the emotion on her. She saw no point in lying. "I had a vision this morning, before we left your lair in the forest." She touched her finger to the stranger's image. "He was in it."

"And Rebekka?"

Araña's guilt intensified. "I saw the three of you on the bus. The man emerged from the guardsman headquarters and bought a pastry from a vendor. He was eating it when the bus passed with Rebekka and the child in the window."

"That's all?"

"I didn't see anything of what happened after that."

The truth, and yet so much less than it. But even Matthew and Erik, who she'd loved and trusted, didn't know all of what carrying the demon mark meant.

Levi leaned forward, the gold of his eyes molten with turbulent emotion. "Use your gift to find her."

Araña's heart skipped a beat. "I can't."

The Were snarled. "Can't or won't?"

"Can't."

"You can try. If it hadn't been for her, you would have escaped the maze only to become food. Humans don't survive a night outside, even if they get out of the red zone and into the forest." His gaze darted to the spider now on the back of her hand. "Against fur and fang and supernaturals, you'd die just as easily as any other."

Araña knew he could hear the thunder of her heart and smell her fear. "I have no control of my gift."

Levi snarled again. "Then get it. Go to the Wainwright witch. It was Annalise who told Rebekka you'd be running in the maze."

The pencil snapped in Araña's hand as the image of the old witch who'd sent Erik and Matthew to their deaths flashed into her mind and brought a killing rage with it. "What does she look like?"

Levi's eyes narrowed. "I only caught a glimpse of her. She's got black hair with a skunk streak of silver down the middle of it."

Araña dropped the pencil halves on the counter. Not the old witch or the pregnant one, then. "Are there others?"

"There's never only one witch. I don't know if there are others by the same last name. What does it matter?" There was a sharp edge to Levi's voice now. "The Wainwright witch has already demonstrated an interest in you. Ask her to help you get control of your gift."

Sweat coated Araña's skin at the thought of willingly entering the heart of the flame. She'd only make it worse by attempting what Levi wanted her to do. And to trust a stranger, a witch . . . "I—"

"Will think on it," Tir said, his hands settling possessively on her shoulders. "There's nothing any of us can do to help the healer tonight."

Levi's muscles bunched. His eyes bored into Araña's, in challenge and anger, with a hint of condemnation—as if he could smell her cowardice. The muscles in his jaws worked as if he intended to argue, but he left without saying another word.

Araña pulled away from Tir and went to the door. She closed it against the approaching night and wished she could shut out her conscience as easily.

She turned and found Tir directly behind her. The heat of lust remained, but it was overlaid with the chill of unshared secrets and unspoken suspicion. "You recognized the man I drew in the third picture."

Tir leaned in, bracing his hands against the smooth wood, trapping Araña. Proximity and the mix of their emotions made for a dangerous, volatile combination. "And your guilt over the healer's fate pummeled me. Tell me about the vision and why you blame yourself for her misfortune. What could you have done to prevent it?"

"Nothing."

It was truth and lie entangled. He sensed it. "Tell me why your conscience flays you."

Araña turned her face away from him, evading, stirring to life something deeply primitive inside him, something that didn't want to allow her to hide any part of herself from him.

Tir touched his lips to her ear. "Don't fight me," he warned, part of him willing her to do just that so he could assert his dominance. "You won't win. Tell me the truth about your visions. Tell me why they lead to your guilt."

Araña stiffened in his arms. "And will you tell me how you recognized the man I drew? Or should I guess?"

It was his turn to become tense, and that tension grew when she said, "You weren't bound for the maze, were you? You were bound for the Church and someone connected to the guard was involved. That's why the priest has the clerk at the occult shop researching the marks on your arm. They want to use you to heal, to create miracles."

The precision of her guesses was testament to her intelligence. He'd been used in that manner for centuries—and the threat of being used that way again would remain until he was rid of the collar.

Already he'd come to believe Araña wouldn't willingly betray him. Not after remaining behind to free him from his shackles as guardsmen drew closer. Not after lying with him and welcoming him into her body. Not after sharing what little wealth she owned after finding the wallet.

But if he gave her Tomás's name and spoke about the lion, she could well do something foolish in her concern and guilt over the healer's fate. How hard would it be to locate a wealthy family that kept exotic, dangerous beasts?

Even searching for the information would divert her attention away from the task of finding the texts that would free him. He couldn't allow it. He couldn't risk her. For all he knew, guardsmen, Church, maze owner, and Tomás's family were all working together to recapture him.

She could keep her secrets, for now. Just as he intended to keep his.

Tir's mouth settled on hers. Her lips were petal-soft against his, though she refused him entry and resisted him with the stiffening of her body. Ferocious desire surged through him, bringing with it all the fantasies he'd harbored during the day, all the possessiveness he felt when it came to her.

He shifted his hands so one was freed while the other kept her wrists pinned to the door. Her heart thundered against his chest. But the shiver of erotic fear he felt in her negated any protest she might voice.

Her heated, sultry scent swamped him, burning away all rational thought. And with a harsh moan he invaded her mouth, cupping her jaw and applying pressure, forcing the barrier of her teeth to lift so his tongue could push its way through firmed lips.

If he thought she'd yield, he was mistaken. She fought him, but the battle was waged on a sensual field.

Hours had passed since they'd lain together next to the fire, since he'd fed her in a primitive display of male dominance and female submissiveness. His hand left her jaw, his fingers ruthless as they unbuttoned her shirt and shoved her bra upward to free her breasts.

She cried out, her back arching; her nipples hard, tight points; her body betraying her. He took a dark areola between his fingers and swallowed her moans as she responded to his touch.

His penis throbbed against the front of his pants. His cock screamed, not only for freedom, but for the feel of her mouth on it.

I need you, she'd whispered in the alleyway near the dock where the boat was moored, and he'd wanted her then and there.

Tir released her nipple. He brushed his knuckles over her flat belly on the way to her waistband.

As he undid the thin leather belt she wore, he imagined using it on her. He'd get the truth from her then.

The image of punishing her nearly sent Tir to his knees. Had he always had such fantasies, or had his time in human captivity darkened his hungers to match those of his captors?

Her hips bucked when he opened the front of her pants and slid his hand into her panties. "Yes," she whispered, widening her stance, moaning as he cupped her smooth mound.

Tir pressed his fingers into her slick channel and fought the siren call to touch his lips to her lower ones, to thrust his tongue into her sheath. "Please," she said, pushing into his touch, rubbing her swollen folds and hardened clit against his palm, driving his fingers deeper.

His mind was a confusion of conflicting desires, but one dominated, the need to free his cock from its painful confinement. She cried out in protest when his hand left her wet, heated flesh. He swallowed the sound, loved the way it slid down his throat, filling his chest before sending molten lust to his penis and testicles.

He jerked her pants downward and then opened his own, nearly coming when his cock head touched her bare flesh. His fingers went automatically to his shaft, and for an instant he was tempted to grant himself relief, to coat her skin with his seed.

His penis hadn't stirred at the brothel. It hadn't filled in the centuries when he'd been presented with women, both willing and unwilling alike, but with Araña . . .

He wanted her. When he was with her, he could barely think of anything else but taking her.

Tir's lips left hers in order to trail kisses along her jaw and up to her ear. He fucked his tongue into the sensitive canal, his fingers tightening on his cock, sliding from base to tip in time with the wet probing.

"Let me touch you," she whispered, the muscles at her wrists flexing as she tried to escape his grip. "Let me take you in my mouth."

In a heartbeat, everything left his mind but one need, one purpose—to fuck through her sultry lips and press his cock head to the back of her throat, to feel her tightening on him, sucking him, swallowing him.

He released her pinned wrists. "Do it," he commanded, resting his forearm against the back of the door, nearly whimpering himself when her hand chased his away from the hard length of his erection.

He quivered as the feminine hand he'd seen wield a knife closed around him in a firm grip. He jerked when the pad of her thumb gathered his escaping arousal and rubbed it into the smooth head of his cock.

She went to her knees gracefully and nuzzled her cheek against his length. The spider was there as well, blending seamlessly into her skin.

A moan escaped when she turned her head and brushed her lips to his trembling, eager flesh. "Araña," he said. Her name curse and pledge. Demand and plea. And she smiled against him and let him feel the hint of her tongue—the torment of pleasure denied.

"Take me in your mouth."

Her soft laugh made lust boil lava-hot in his veins. On a snarl, his hand fisted in her hair. "Do it."

She touched her tongue to his length again, stroked, called what blood remained in his body to his cock. His gut tightened in a wave of panic, that he'd come like some untried youth. He growled her name again, his buttocks clenching, fever sweeping through him as he fought to keep from begging, to keep from throwing himself on her mercy.

Araña had never felt so powerful as she did in that moment, kneeling in front of Tir, positioned like a supplicant for him to command.

She reveled in his harsh voice. In his ragged panting as he struggled for breath. She could barely remember what had led to this.

It didn't matter. All that mattered was touch—what she gave to him and what he returned. She'd been starved for it, had rarely allowed herself even to dream of it.

Now all that mattered was feeling Tir's skin against hers. A lifetime with him would never be enough.

She cupped his testicles in one hand and weighed them in her palm. Remembered the stallion she'd once seen mount a mare—and fantasized about Tir taking her that way. Sinking his teeth into her flesh as his flanks pistoned and his cock thrust hard and deep.

Her other hand tightened on his throbbing shaft. She licked along his length, savored him.

He smelled like the forbidden. Tasted like sin wrapped in undeniable temptation. And the sound of her name coupled with the harsh rasp of his breathing as he ordered her to take him into her mouth, to suck him, was more beautiful than any choir of angels. It spoke to her soul, filled it, as if she'd somehow bound them together the night she'd touched her thread to his in the heart of the flame.

Araña relented. Not because he commanded it, but because she desired it. Because she wanted to hear his cry as he came and to taste the hot wash of his seed as it pulsed down her throat in molten jets.

She took him in her mouth, looked up at him and memorized the harsh lines of his face as he thrust between her lips.

Their eyes met and held, dark and light blending in a carnal taking, bleeding into each other with primitive intensity.

Shallow thrusts became deeper ones. Pants became moans then grunts as she lashed him with her tongue, threatened him with the feel of her teeth against his cock, dedicated herself to swallowing him whole.

He came like a bolt of lightning. Savage. Uncontrollable. Wild. A force no human would conquer. A force only a few survived.

And she took what he gave, her hands leaving his cock and testicles in favor of holding him to her. Her nails digging into his buttocks in a sharp reminder that she might be on her knees before him, but she wasn't conquered.

He hardened again almost as soon as he'd spent himself in her mouth. On a growl he pulled from between her lips and lifted her, held her against the door and thrust his cock into her channel with such ferocity she cried out.

"Mine," he said, covering her mouth with his, pushing his tongue through the seam of her lips and growing more feral when he encountered the taste of himself there.

Araña clung to him as he pounded in and out of her sheath.

There was no thought of fight or resistance. There was only the merciless climb. The scream of release. The sweet lassitude that came afterward. And the tenderness she'd come to need as much as she did his dominance.

He nuzzled her, kissing her gently, the door the only thing enabling them to remain upright at the conclusion of their sensual battle.

"I need to leave if I'm going to arrange a safe berth for your boat and then retrieve it."

"I want to go with you."

"No." The denial was delivered with a kiss. "I don't want to worry. Stay here. Stay safe. The night holds nothing I'm afraid of."

But I'm afraid of losing you. Of what you've come to mean to me.

She volunteered neither.

"The smaller key is for the boat engine. The other is for the cabin."

He kissed her again before stepping away from her. They straightened their clothing, not taking their eyes off each other.

When he opened the door, she said, "Stay safe." The words she'd always exchanged with Matthew and Erik whenever they parted company.

"Stay here until I return." The steel edge of command was back in Tir's voice.

Then he was gone. The door locked behind him.

And the waiting began.

Fourteen

TIR slowed as he neared the Victorian. It was the only house on the street where people weren't gathering at windows, watching the daylight fade from the false safety of clubs with names like Sinners, Greed, and Envy.

The collective emotions of the elegantly clad humans in those clubs reached out, clawing at Tir's mental shields, the patrons like a single vicious creature hungry for pain and suffering instead of food.

The knowledge that they hid their true natures within beautiful bodies and cunning minds reinforced centuries of his hatred and disdain for them. They were *less* than the most simple of beasts. They were unworthy of his attention—except what might be required to rid the earth of them.

He turned his thoughts to the club in front of him. Temptation.

The sign identifying it was elegant, an engraved invitation to sin that contained both warning and promise. Curtains instead of people fluttered at the still-open windows, the sound beckoning like an

insidious whisper, one whose breath held sighs of pleasure and the
sweet scent of opium.

Like the other clubs, bouncers stood on either side of the door.
But unlike the others, these were dressed in expensive suits, as was
fitting for ushers to a party, or a funeral.

Tir climbed the steps and stopped in front of them. "I'm here to
see Rimmon."

"You've got Lord Rimmon's marker?" the bouncer to the left
said. "Or someone else's?"

"No."

Interest flared in cold eyes. "Then the only way you'll get in is if
you're willing to risk a cage fight and pay your way by entertaining
Lord Rimmon's guests."

Tir shrugged. "As long as the fight doesn't delay me unnecessar-
ily. I have other business to attend to tonight."

The second bouncer's smile was as cold as his companion's eyes.
He opened the door to reveal a woman standing there. "Take him
to Lord Rimmon. No detours."

The woman nodded and turned, exposing a dress cut away to
reveal her back, its skirt slit so each step afforded a shadowy glimpse
of her woman's folds. *Temptation*, Tir thought, but his cock didn't
stir at the sight of her cunt.

Other women waited along a curved staircase, their dresses
equally revealing, their bodies adorned with jewelry. One of them
stepped forward to take the hostess's place as he was led away from
the foyer.

Period pieces graced the rooms they passed. Men and women
sprawled on couches and chairs, some of them engaging in sexual
acts while others watched or conversed with fluted glasses in their
hands.

The woman turned toward Tir, her white gloves extending to
her elbows, her dress plunging to reveal deep cleavage and the coy
hint of pale pink nipples.

She reached for him, as though she intended to loop her arm

through his and press her breasts against him, but faltered at his expression. "I'm happy to attend you," she murmured. "But if another escort would better please you, it can be arranged, assuming of course that Lord Rimmon allows you to remain as his guest."

Tir didn't respond, other than to force his mind to remain on the task at hand rather than straying to thoughts of Araña and what they'd done together before he left. Her body was the only one his craved, her human life the only one he cared about.

The sweet smell of opium slunk into the hallway, mixing with that of hashish. Wallpapered rooms gave way to hazy, dim ones where gaunt men and women hovered over specialized pipes, smoking substances that had claimed human souls for centuries.

Conversation gave way to mumbling and then, as Tir moved deeper into the club, to shouts as dice were thrown and a roulette wheel spun. Smoke-filled rooms became dark paneled ones. Tapestries yielded to exotic silk and then to red velvet and the smell of cigars.

Men gathered around gaming tables, calling out numbers and calling for cards, praying to Lady Luck and cursing her, ice clinking in their glasses, the noise they made blending into that of the next room, a hybrid mix of gentleman's club from the long ago past and sports bar from the days before The Last War.

Flesh pounded against flesh, the sound of violence instead of lovemaking. Large-screen television sets were positioned so those at the bar and in front of it could watch as two boxers fought in another part of the country.

An empty cage dominated another section of the room, a circular arena meant for fighting. Tir took it in at a glance before he found Rimmon.

The vice lord sat on a raised dais in a shadowy corner, the rest of the room fanning out in front of him as though he were a king sitting on a throne. His face was made nightmarish by the flicker of candles set in sconces on the wall on either side of him.

Rimmon spoke to the woman sitting on a cushion at his feet,

her arms wrapped around his elegantly trousered legs, her head cushioned on his lap where his hand stroked over honey gold hair as if she were a pet. She was dressed similarly to the hostess Tir followed.

When Tir reached the edge of the dais, she rose to her feet and walked away with the female who'd accompanied him. The vice lord's attention remained on them, his single emerald-colored eye alight with appreciation. "They're magnificent creations, aren't they?"

"Women?" Tir asked, not trusting the brandy-smooth inflection in Rimmon's voice.

Rimmon laughed and shifted his attention to Tir. "Humans. I find them simply divine. But then, I always have. They're my downfall, the temptation I can't seem to turn away from. After seeing the female you were with earlier . . ." The burning green eye found the sigil-inscribed collar. "But perhaps I'm mistaken. Perhaps your time spent among humans hasn't been as pleasurable as I imagined."

Tir stiffened, sensing a trap wrapped in temptation. The vice lord's words hinted at hidden knowledge, the possibility of finding out what he'd been before his enemies trapped him in flesh and wrapped his memories in darkness—if he was willing to admit to such a weakness to the being in front of him.

Rimmon was no mortal, despite his appearance.

When Tir didn't respond, Rimmon waved casually at the cushions scattered on the dais. "Have a seat. Since I extended no invitation for you to visit my club, I assume you're here as a petitioner? Or better yet, as a penitent?"

"I'll stand."

A smile twisted Rimmon's face into a grotesque mask. "Ah, pride. What would it take to break you of it, I wonder? And make no mistake, I'd take great pleasure in doing so, almost eternal pleasure. But of course, it would come with suffering to match. That's always the way, isn't it?"

Rimmon leaned forward onto the armrests of his chair, his hands settling on the lion claws carved into the old wood. "I'm not someone who believes in coincidence. There is a game being played here, of that I am certain. But are you part of it? Or a pawn?" And like light striking a different facet in the same stone, the gleam of amused speculation in Rimmon's emerald eye hardened into ruthlessness. "What name do you go by?"

"Tir."

"Tir. It's a name I've heard whispered, but what it might stand for eludes me at the moment. And somehow I doubt you intend to enlighten me. So rather than waste the night exploring how you came to be at the occult shop at the same time I was there, I ask, what is it you want from me?"

"I want to bring a boat into the waters you control and leave it there, knowing it will be guarded until I reclaim it."

Rimmon blinked and leaned back in his chair, not bothering to hide his surprise. "You do prod me into curiosity. And if I choose to grant this favor? What will I gain from it?"

Rather than place his trust in the Were's rumor about the vice lord's daughter, Tir said, "What would you ask of me?"

Rimmon laughed. "Do you expect me to ask that I be restored to my former glory? Is that the sweet temptation you bring with you to my club? If so, then you've failed. There is something I want more, something that will cost you not just the boat if you manage to bring it safely into the harbor, but the woman I saw you with earlier if you're unable to deliver on your promise."

"And the promise you'd have me make?" Tir asked, not bothering to keep the menace from his voice in response to the vice lord's threat against Araña.

"Heal my mortal daughter. Fail and I will keep your woman in my bed until by some miracle she gives me a child. An eye for an eye. It has a familiar ring to it, doesn't it?"

Fury surged through Tir at the thought of Araña underneath the vice lord, her legs splayed, her channel filled with another man's cock. It took all his control not to lunge forward—and had Rimmon been human, he wouldn't have managed it.

Tir clamped down on his anger, though possessiveness pulsed through him with every heartbeat. There was little risk; in his centuries of captivity, he'd unwillingly cured others of the disease.

"I will heal your daughter."

Rimmon signaled, and a server appeared with a hand-drawn map spread flat on a tray. The vice lord traced a route winding through wreckage, his finger stopping on a spot deep in the harbor. "If you're successful in getting the boat to this point, my men will greet you. They'll stay with you until morning. Then we'll see if you can do what you say you can."

ARAÑA paced endlessly, moving from one barred window to another and staring out. The house was larger than the *Constellation* and yet it confined her in a way the boat never did.

More than once she caught herself rubbing a hand over her heart, as if somehow it would cease beating if something happened to Tir.

It wouldn't, she assured herself, refusing to contemplate it.

She avoided looking at the candles flickering in holders mounted on the wall, but she was less successful in deflecting Levi's impassioned words, in steeling herself against thoughts about Rebekka and, with them, her own guilty conscience.

Araña's stomach tightened with images of the healer huddling in the same cell she'd been in as she waited to run the maze. A cold sweat added to the chill of the house as she pictured the scorpion-marked demon, the cruelty in his eyes as he'd launched himself past her to savage one of the convicts. Without any effort at all she could remember the tortured screams of the men in the maze, the seemingly endless sounds of torment following her into freedom.

Goose bumps rose on Araña's flesh as minutes lengthened like long shadows and guilt slid through her, ripping away the thin scab covering a hundred memories of the lives she'd touched when the demon gift trapped her in unwanted vision.

She turned away from the window, her gaze settling unconsciously on the fireplace. A dusty bundle of wood waited only to be lit in order to ward off the cold and fear that came with nighttime and the ceding of the world to the supernaturals.

She'd never looked willingly into the flame, had never sought its heart and the place where whispered voices were a rushing stream underlying a thousand strands of color. Did that make her a coward?

Yes, her conscience whispered.

No, Erik and Matthew had counseled without fully understanding what it was she faced. To them, fighting the gift was the better way to deal with it.

Araña closed her eyes. Candlelight danced on the back of her eyelids, sinuous, like the movements of a snake.

Even without the flickering, she was aware of each place where fire drank the oxygen and fed on wax. In the close confines of the room, it had its own voice. It sang to her, telling her she had only to call and it would come to her.

A shudder went through her, the remembered screams from the maze blending seamlessly with those she'd heard the last time she called the fire to her.

She crossed her arms. Hugged herself but failed to find comfort in it.

She longed for the feel of Tir's touch. Ached for the caress of his hands and lips.

The spider nestled in the scarred flesh of the brand, and she thought about the demon Abijah *becoming* the scorpion he wore. How, trapped in the vision place, her insubstantial form felt spiderlike.

More than once she'd had the fleeting sensation that without the hindrance of flesh she could live forever in the heart of the flame, endlessly weaving lives together to create the pattern the future would take. Only in that place was there a unity with the mark—and only then until the pain started, forcing her to do the very thing that burdened her with guilt.

What would it mean to willingly enter the vision place? To accept the demon gift that had caused her so much suffering? Would she gain control of it if she did?

The image of Rebekka holding the child in her arms as she walked away from the ambush wreckage rose from Araña's conscience. Many would have left the child, or abandoned him as soon as they reached the city. Just as most would have denied her shelter the night she ran from the settlement, a mob at her heels and bearing a brand on her hand.

She regretted never asking Erik to help her find a way to gain control of the demon gift, for never telling Erik the full truth of the visions. He'd guessed there was more to them.

How many times had he let her browse through books of magic before surrendering them to the rich patrons who'd paid to have them stolen?

How many times had she fought back the urge to unburden herself, to seek absolution for the pain and suffering she'd caused?

Too many to count. And always she'd avoided talking to him by telling herself she didn't want to burden him with the knowledge—when the truth was so much more frightening for her. She hadn't wanted to face the inevitable question. Had she touched the strand that was his life? Or Matthew's? She'd been terrified of losing the family of her heart, the only home that had ever offered her safety and love.

Coward, she called herself, opening her eyes and going to the fireplace, crouching on the floor in front of it. Behind her she heard the soft whisper of flame dancing on wax, begging for her to turn and look at it, to use the gift that came with the demon taint to her soul.

Araña's hands balled into fists, and though she didn't feel it move, the spider reappeared on her cheek. Did it choose the position to remind her of Tir pressing his lips to it, brushing his fingers over it, unafraid? Was its intent to summon her courage and urge her to face the flame freely?

She lifted her hand to her cheek and traced the outline of the spider with a fingertip. Even without a mirror, without any change in the texture of her skin, she could trace it exactly.

Her hand dropped from her cheek, going instinctively to one of the knives. By touch alone she knew it was Matthew's.

Araña's stomach churned at the thought of going to see Annalise Wainwright, of asking a witch for help with her gift. By Levi's description, Annalise wasn't one of those at the bus stop, but with little money and all of it necessary to survive, Araña knew she'd have to bargain the use of her gift for any training the witch might be able to give her.

Her other hand settled on the second knife, Erik's, and the now-familiar pain of loss clogged her throat. If she ever encountered the witch from her long-ago vision, the old woman who'd sent them to the place where Erik and Matthew were killed, she didn't think she'd be able to still her hand.

What could the witch do to her? Her soul was already damned to the fires of Hell.

A shudder went through her as the image of the demon Abijah rose in her mind, only to slide away with memories of Rebekka ushering her into the tiny room at the brothel, offering the use of her bed and her clothing.

That night the demon gift had shown her Tir. Ultimately it had led her to the ecstasy of knowing another's touch.

She glanced once more toward the window and the quickly approaching night. And then, before her courage deserted her, she mentally called the flames licking at candle wax. Directed them to consume the wood in front of her.

The fire caught with a *whoosh*, filling the silence of the room with the crackling of burning lumber. Araña's hands tightened on the hilts of the knives, drawing strength and comfort from their having belonged to Matthew and Erik.

With a thought, she found the spider positioned over her rapidly beating heart. *I am not a coward*, she told herself, holding Rebekka's image in her mind as she looked into the fire and sought its dark heart.

It welcomed her instantly and held her for long moments in the black of a void filled with utter silence. Phantom flames buffeted her, tracing limbs that didn't exist, as if trying to force her to face the full truth of her nature by licking over the same spidery shape she'd traced with her fingertip.

In the unseen distance, where demon place and physical world met, she thought she could feel the wild pounding of her mortal heart trying to summon her spirit back to her body. But the silence and the darkness held and she willed herself not to fight it.

If she had any hope of undoing the harm she'd already caused Rebekka, then she had to keep her mind clear. She had to act quickly, before the pain rose and she grabbed wildly at the threads in order to make it stop.

Silence finally yielded to the rushing blend of a thousand whispered voices. Black nothingness became an endless choice of color.

Doubt filled her. Panic threatened to follow.

Araña struggled to remember the exact color of the thread that was Rebekka's life.

Too late she realized she should have faced the painful memories arising from her previous visions. She should have examined each of them and tried to understand better the array of colors, why *these* souls were the ones she could easily touch.

Now that she'd willingly entered this spidery place of power, she sensed there was an order to it, as if the kaleidoscopic swirl of color was already loosely woven into a pattern. One she was a part of.

A thread caught her attention. Various shades of brown with a swirl of gray. Elation gripped her and she mentally reached for it, thinking it was Rebekka's. But as soon as she'd made it her choice, the brown and gray fell away to reveal tawny gold underneath, as if the healer's touch had masked the truth of the underlying soul.

Mixed in with the gold were thick strands of dark brown and black, a lion's mane. And Araña knew instinctively it was Levi's life she would forever alter.

A wave of panic rose and with it the first hint of pain. She fought to *accept* demon place and dark gift rather than fight against them as she always had.

The pain subsided. She expected to slide deeper into the vision, to become a ghost to Levi's soul and experience the world as it was for him. Instead she remained in the heart of the flame, surrounded by choice, by the whispered voices of a thousand souls.

A black-and-gray thread emerged from a tangle of color, drawing her to it because it ran parallel to Levi's. She hesitated and the strand disappeared. In its wake, pain rose beyond the threshold where it was easily ignored.

The black-and-gray thread reappeared, once again close to Levi's, as if their lives traveled a similar path. She reached mentally for the thread, blocking her mind to the suffering and death her touch had brought in the past.

As soon as the choice was made, the frenetic sense of movement, the wild swirl of color ceased, and a pattern emerged. A thousand connections already in existence, places where lives touched and crossed—altering destiny.

Soul threads changed color subtly or not at all. Merged and split, giving birth to new lives. Ended.

The sight of it awed Araña, mesmerized her. The power pulsing through a carpet of woven color enthralled her. And even as she watched, there were subtle changes to it, choices made or turned away from.

For an instant she felt peace, pleasure in the gift she'd always considered a curse, a demon taint marking her soul as belonging to Hell. Then the pattern disappeared, the colors melting, fading into a blackness that took her into the future she'd wrought when she touched Levi's life to another.

A dark-haired stranger stood face-to-face with Levi. In confrontation? In meeting? The ruin of corroded trucking containers and twisted steel gave no context.

There was movement behind Levi and the stranger, or perhaps sound. They turned, and Araña silently screamed.

Jurgen and another guardsman were there, tasers in their hands. The barbs hit Levi and the stranger before they had any chance of defense or escape.

Both fell to the ground and began convulsing. Araña had only a glimpse of the stranger's body starting to change shape before he faded from her awareness as though his future no longer touched Levi's.

A heartbeat later, she understood why. Levi's back arched violently, as if the lion trapped in human flesh was making one final attempt to escape, shredding through muscle and internal organs, so desperate for freedom it would destroy itself in an attempt to gain it. And then Levi went completely still, his eyes unseeing, glazing over as Araña's cry pulled her from the vision.

Fifteen

THE door locks clicked into place as Tir reached the sidewalk in front of Temptation. Windows slid shut and a low hum warned that additional protections were in place.

Along the street he heard other doors being closed and barred against the night. In the shadows he heard the stirring of predators and felt their anticipation as if it were his own.

Let them attack, he thought, removing his shirt and baring not only the tattoos on his arms, but the machete in its sheath along his back. He rolled his shoulders, glad to be free of the confining material. In the short span of a day he'd learned to hate the feel of it against his skin.

His impulse was to discard the shirt. But the image of Araña emerging from the store coupled with the knowledge she'd used money she could ill afford in order to purchase it stayed his hand.

Phantom fingers tightened around his heart with thoughts of her. Only the presence of the feral animals and hidden Weres kept him from reliving the moments of intimacy they'd shared or slipping into fantasies of things they'd yet to do.

The beasts lurking in the alleyways between the clubs were cautious. They clung to the darkness, assessing him from a safe distance.

Perhaps it was his lack of fear. Or perhaps they sensed he was something other than human. They held back, though Tir knew they'd eventually grow bolder.

He tied the shirt around his waist then freed the machete from its sheath. Behind the glass of bay windows, human voices merged, swelling into a tidal wave as their hungry attention fixed on him.

The last of the sun's rays faded, leaving the night illuminated by floodlights positioned at the corners of the Victorians so the street between them became a gladiatorial arena.

The bloodthirsty didn't have long to wait. A single word rose above the ocean sound of murmured voices.

"Out! Out! Out!"

Tir felt the hidden Weres and feral animals grow more excited as their focus shifted away from him. The voices chanting "Out" came from a club in the middle of the block, a place painted in shades of yellow. Sinners.

Like the clubs surrounding and across from it, the Victorian's windows were unmarred by bars. Well-dressed patrons gathered, their jewelry sparkling, their hands curled around colorful drinks in expensive crystal glasses, their glossy red lips opening and closing in unison.

The shouts reached a crescendo then stopped abruptly, leaving a dark, hungry silence.

The club's front door locks disengaged, the sound a gunshot in the street.

Inside the club a man began screaming.

The door opened. Screams turned into pleading and the sounds of a struggle that disappeared under a roar of applause as a man was ejected from the house.

He stumbled down the stairs and fell onto the sidewalk. The door closed and its locks engaged again before he could scramble to his feet.

Feral dogs slipped from the alleyway, made bold by the easy prey they'd come to expect. The human saw Tir standing just inside the floodlights' reach, the machete held loosely at his side. And like a sinner looking for a savior, the man lurched forward.

He made it two steps before a sleek, brindle-colored mongrel launched itself into the air. Beast and human went to the ground, the man's scream ending in a wet gurgle followed by ripping fabric, then low growls as more dogs joined the first and they fought among themselves for entrails and muscle.

Tir turned away and stepped into the darkness. He walked at first, because he didn't want to suffer a delay by drawing the waiting Weres and still-hungry dogs away from their feeding ground. But when he no longer felt them trailing him cautiously at a safe distance, he began running. And just as he'd experienced in those moments after Araña freed him from the shackles around his wrists and ankles, he rejoiced in the movement, in the smooth play of muscle over bone.

Instead of the sweet scent of forest and the dance of sunlight in shadow, he inhaled the ocean-wet scent carried on the breeze. He basked in the coy caress of muted light as the moon slid in and out from behind clouds. And he thrilled at the faint sound of frightened heartbeats as he passed houses where humans were trapped in prisons of their own making.

Some instinct, some part of them, noted his presence. Something deeply ingrained in them understood that the barriers they built wouldn't protect them against him should they deserve his retribution and he be free of the collar around his neck.

He felt it in the spike of their fear, their emotion and his reading of it unconscious on both his part and theirs, as though some unfathomable, inescapable connection existed between them despite how much he despised them—all of them but one.

His cock stirred, as it did anytime his thoughts turned to Araña. He allowed his mind to linger on her, to replay those moments when she knelt before him like a supplicant, her lips inches away from his hardened cock and her eyes dark pools of desire. Seductress. Sorceress.

His.

Tir quickened his pace. Worry crept in like fog off the ocean. Araña was alone, and he didn't trust the Were not to betray her if it would mean the return of the healer.

He neared the alleyway where he and Araña had been attacked earlier in the day and slowed at the sound of shuffling, dragging.

A bone cracked. He could hear gnawing. But there was an absence of emotion. There was none of the hot animal energy that had radiated in the dark alleys between the Victorians in the red zone. He edged closer, curious to see what roamed the night along with Weres and feral dogs.

Hunched humanlike figures crouched over what remained of the men he'd killed after leaving the diner with Araña. Three or four of them to a corpse, their claws serving as knives.

They were naked, gray-skinned, and riddled with pustules. Hairless and nearly skeletal.

Jikininki.

The word escaped from the depths of inaccessible memory.

Ghouls.

They'd stripped their meals of clothing. But they took no pleasure in eating what they'd stumbled upon in the alleyway. They felt nothing—or nothing he could read from them.

As one, they became aware of Tir, and he lifted the machete in silent warning.

Something passed between the ghouls.

The first of them rose from the crouched position, a male whose penis was shriveled, his testicles wrinkled and dark like prunes. He shambled forward, tongue licking a too-small mouth.

The others followed. Males and females both.

Surprise flashed through Tir at their willingness to leave their meal and come after him. Did they think he'd turn tail and run? Did they believe they'd eventually overtake him? Or that once he was down, they could swarm over him and subdue him with their greater numbers?

He backed away from the alleyway entrance in order to give himself room to slay them. They didn't falter, even after the first of them reached him and he decapitated it with a single swing of the machete.

Bodies piled up in front of him, forcing him to retreat further where their attack hadn't. The machete blade glowed blue in the moonlight, its color spreading, deepening with each ghoul he struck down, until finally it was like holding a shard of dark ice.

Even as the last of those from the alleyway was dealt with, Tir could hear the shuffling sounds of more ghouls coming toward him, drawn to the battle. With a start, he realized he would spend all night battling them if he chose to make a stand.

He lowered the machete and sidestepped the massed corpses to jog through the alleyway, past the half-eaten remains of the humans who'd thought to kill him and take Araña back to the maze.

At the end of the alleyway he paused only long enough to ensure he didn't emerge in a crowd of ghouls. When he found it clear, he continued forward, alert for the icy breath of air that would warn of a vampire's presence.

He felt it against his skin as he neared the pier where Araña's boat was tethered. He stopped, once again lifting the machete in silent warning, its blade continuing to glow blue in the moonlight.

The vampires emerged from darkness worn like a cloak. Three of them. All male. All elegant and beautiful where the ghouls had been misshapen and revolting.

They halted in front of Tir, just beyond the reach of the blade. One took a step forward, not in threat, but to serve as a spokesman.

He lifted his hands, palms out, saying, "We wish no argument with you. Your business here is your own and we won't interfere."

"I intend to take a boat."

"As I said, we won't interfere. In any way."

They pulled the night around them and ebbed away like a cold spot in the ocean. Tir lingered for a moment in contemplation, his eyes going to the camera positioned on top of the lamppost. Would it capture his likeness if he stepped foot on the dock?

He'd never seen a picture of himself, though over the years his captors had come into his cell on occasion and photographed him, sometimes repeating the action several times during a single day and making him wonder if, despite being held to a human form, something of his true nature prevented his image from being trapped on film.

There was risk if he was mistaken. He'd seen the consequences earlier when a simple meal led to an attack in an alleyway.

Tir's attention shifted to the water. He was very much aware of the nuances the vampire's promise held—neither to hinder *nor* to help.

If he chose to avoid the dock in favor of swimming to the boat, he'd survive. That was a given. But he didn't know what predators lurked in the water, and instinct urged him to avoid its cloying embrace.

Decision made, he strode forward. If there were watchers, he didn't feel their eyes on him.

Wood creaked underneath his feet. His steps echoed staccato-sharp in the darkness.

There were lights along the pier where emptied cargo ships waited to be loaded. Beyond it was the muted sound of a boat engine as guardsmen or police patrolled the channel.

Tir reached Araña's boat and sheathed the machete in favor of freeing the mooring lines. The sound of the patrol boat grew louder, though the cargo ship continued to block it from view. A floodlight's beam danced along the water, spearing through the night like a harpoon hurtling toward prey.

The cabin was locked. Tir didn't take the time to open it.

He moved quickly to the engine and used the smaller of the keys Araña had taken from the wallet. He slid it into place, and hesitated only a heartbeat before turning it, deciding to make a run for the outer harbor rather than chance that the patrol boat was merely making a routine pass.

The engine came to life with a powerful throb. Knowledge pulsed through Tir, information beyond what any acolyte had shared with him, as if anything a human could know belonged to him as well.

Tir maneuvered the boat away from the dock and headed toward the mouth of the harbor. The floodlight speared him just as he prepared to accelerate.

"Halt!" a voice blazed over a loudspeaker.

Tir ignored the command. He gunned the engine so the boat surged forward aggressively.

Bullets struck the water behind him.

The patrol boat's growl increased, matching that of Araña's boat.

Tir increased his speed further.

A machine gun rattled. Then something louder fired.

A projectile soared overhead, landing a hundred yards in front of the boat and exploding.

Tir altered his course, abandoning the straight line in favor of weaving back and forth. The boat shook as it hit turbulent water and Tir fought to maintain control of it.

More projectiles were fired.

The voice continued to order him to stop.

Tir pressed forward, racing along the inner harbor channel, passing what had once been the middle harbor.

At the point of land separating middle from outer harbor, he saw another boat speeding toward him, as if it sought to cut him off before he could reach the security of open waters.

He veered right, as he'd intended, and sped along the debris-filled mouth of the outer harbor.

Bullets slammed into the water inches behind him, warning him he couldn't decrease his speed until the last instant, when he changed course abruptly and slipped through a narrow passage-way formed by the rusted, wrecked hulls of boats destroyed in The Last War.

Behind him the patrol boats stopped, no longer in sight. The growl of their engines seemed to deepen in frustration at the escape of prey and the inability to attack further.

Tir turned his attention to navigating the treacherous waters. The landmarks on Rimmon's map rose up, marking his passage as he moved farther into the harbor.

Cormorants perched on buoys and abandoned vessels, their tur-quoise eyes noting his presence, their inky blackness broken by flashes of white on their necks.

Some of them launched skyward at his passing. Tir pressed on, expecting a boat piloted by Rimmon's men to emerge from the dark-ness. But when he reached the place he was to wait, one of the cormo-rants landed on the bow. And then another. And another. Until there were five of them.

Feathers dissolved into tanned flesh, beaks into aristocratic noses. Birds became men wearing feathered headdresses.

Skin-walkers.

"Drop anchor here," one of them said. "We'll remain with you until first light. Then Rimmon will come for you."

RAOUL held the mug of beer to his mouth and finished the last of it, liking the flush of euphoria the drink gave him, the feeling of empowerment. He needed to slow down, he told himself, then im-mediately shrugged off the thought and lifted his hand, signaling the bartender to send a waitress.

He could handle the alcohol. And he had all night to take care of business, as long as he didn't cause trouble.

The doors were locked. He and his prey were trapped together.

There was plenty of time to approach the lion he now knew was named Levi.

Raoul smiled in the darkness of the booth. Seeing Levi enter the brothel moments before sunset was pure luck, considering how he'd almost given up his search. It was as if the hand of fate and justice had touched him.

After the failure this morning near the Mission, he'd worked all day to come up with a better idea for finding out where the demon-possessed human and the branded female were, and capturing them without involving guardsmen. Levi was key to that plan.

Humans. He could understand how the lion had escaped the trap Anton and Farold had arranged, but a woman burdened with a child—pathetic.

A waitress stopped next to the table. She was topless, revealing two rows of teats down her torso, ten in all, though they were tiny and her chest flat. She was available, for a price—there to serve more than drinks and food.

Raoul could smell semen on her and see it streaking the insides of her thighs beneath the short skirt. But there was no answering trace of feminine arousal.

"You wanted something?" she purred, mouth opening to show tiny fangs, her eyes glowing catlike in the dim light of the brothel bar.

Barefoot she would be much smaller than him, making him think she was lynx or bobcat, or perhaps the descendent of cats who'd once tied their existence to humans. On heels she was the right height for patrons to bend her over a table and take her from behind.

Raoul wasn't interested, not in taking some grotesque cat-shifter caught between forms. Before the night was over he'd pay for a fuck, but he intended to visit one of the whores who looked human.

"Another beer," he said, handing the waitress his mug.

She took it and walked away, heading toward the bar. A rank-smelling human stopped her midway. One hand snaked under her skirt to fondle her buttocks. The other pawed a row of teats, fat fingers settling to pluck at the nipple above the waistband of her skirt.

A sluglike tongue licked over his lips. "I'm in the mood for pussy."

"Payment up front," she said. "The bartender collects."

"I want to see what I'm getting first."

He didn't wait for her to respond. The hand on her teat dropped to the hem of her skirt. With a quick jerk upward, she was bared to the man and his table companions.

"Show me your hole," the human said, his sluglike tongue making another pass over his lips and leaving them glistening with spit. "If it ain't small, I'm not interested."

A sharp bark of laughter escaped Raoul. But in a bar full of shapeshifter outcasts and human perverts, no one gave him more than a fleeting glance.

The human probably has a tiny cock, Raoul thought, his lips curling in disgust.

There'd been times when he'd been desperate enough to take his wolf form and fuck one of the female mongrel dogs Hyde used for tracking, but he wasn't so desperate that he'd stick his cock into this whore, even if it was hardened at the sight of her cunt.

The bartender gave a subtle nod, and one of the bouncers sitting at the end of the bar rose from his stool and moved to the table. "Touching the girls costs money. Consider yourself warned."

The human let the waitress go. "How much if I want this one?"

"Negotiate with him," the bouncer said, tilting his head toward the bartender.

The human took a moment to hold a discussion with his companions, then stood and went to the bar. The waitress followed, lingering there long enough for Raoul's mug to be refilled.

The bouncer had reclaimed his stool by the time she got back to Raoul's booth. He paid her for the beer. She remained next to the table, a finger toying with one of her teats, drawing attention to the down fuzz surrounding it.

"You sure I can't do anything else for you? Maybe give you something to eat?" She leaned down and purred. "Or eat you."

He didn't doubt she'd prefer to service him instead of the fat-fingered human—even if there was no hint of sexual interest in her scent. "I'm full," Raoul said, thinking about the man he'd killed as the sun began to set. Whose shoes he now wore and whose money lay folded in a thick wad in his pocket. Whose entrails had been a satisfying meal for a wolf, the stomach heavy with steak and potatoes.

With a shrug, the waitress returned to the bar. There was a brief conversation with the bartender before she went to the table where the slug-tongued human stood waiting.

His clothing was stained and dirty, his fly open, allowing more of the stench from his unwashed flesh to fill the room. Stubby, thick fingers curled around a cock that reminded Raoul of sausage-sectioned pig intestines.

He expected the waitress to bend over. Instead she crawled onto the table and splayed her thighs, the movements making the skirt ride up to reveal her slit.

Despite himself, Raoul's hand slid beneath the table. He gripped himself through the pants that had once belonged to Hyde, stroked up and down as one of the human's companions positioned himself in front of the waitress's mouth and his penis disappeared between her lips.

The man who'd negotiated with the bartender came at her from behind, his pants riding low, revealing the dark shadow of his crack against pale white skin. He thrust into the woman and began pumping violently—as if he'd been too cheap to pay for more than a few minutes of time.

His face lifted, growing ruddy with his exertions. His mouth opened and spittle escaped with each panted breath.

The man's companion came first, his grunts like those of an ape. The waitress turned her head and spit a gob of jism onto the table, ridding herself of it as the man behind her bellowed in release.

He pulled out, his wet cock gleaming like a trophy in the dim light. Raoul turned away, his eyes going to the doorway leading into the area where women waited for clients to select them and negotiate their services with the madam.

His hand slid from his cloth-covered erection to the wad of paper money in his pocket. *It would be better to wait*, he told himself, and smiled when moments later Levi walked into the bar.

Raoul gave Levi a moment to settle on one of the bar stools before approaching and taking the seat next to him. Levi turned. Lion yellow eyes bored into Raoul's, telling him to leave.

He fought the urge to bare his teeth, belatedly remembering his show of subservience in the woods. His licking of the healer's foot before slinking away in order to hunt for the escaped prisoner and the woman.

With a small whine he dropped his head. In the scent-filled bar he hoped the truth of his nature would be lost on the Were.

"I've been looking for you since yesterday afternoon," he said, careful with his words in a room full of shifters who would retain their excellent hearing despite their defects.

He touched his finger to his neck, tracing it along the imaginary line where the witch-charmed silver had trapped him in wolf form. "I wanted to thank you, and the healer. I'd be dead if you hadn't helped me."

Levi's eyes narrowed with suspicion. "What else do you want?"

Raoul shook his head. "Nothing. Except to thank the healer. Is she here?"

Levi's face hardened. The air filled with the scent of rage and worry and guilt. "No."

Raoul's surprise was unfeigned. "What happened to her?"

"She was taken."

Raoul suppressed a growl. He wouldn't be surprised to learn he'd been double-crossed by Anton. It would explain why he'd had to remain in the backseat with Farold as the guardsmen went in pursuit of Levi and the healer. "By who?"

"Guardsmen. Or the maze owner."

Raoul licked his lips, channeling all his nervous energy into making himself believable, into baiting the trap he thought Levi might willingly enter.

Just like seeing the Were enter the brothel, it was pure luck Raoul had caught the faint trace of a werelion's scent on Farold's driver, Gulzar, and with a few questions, a touch of feigned admiration, the tattooed criminal had bragged about trapping two brothers not far from Oakland and turning them into monsters to run the maze.

That one of the created weremen ultimately escaped while the other remained . . . Raoul could easily guess the reason Levi had ambushed the trapper's truck. And that reason, coupled with the guardsmen's failure, had formed the seed of an idea that would ultimately lead to him returning to his father's compound and mate a wealthy man.

Learning the healer was missing only added greater strength to Raoul's plan, though now he modified it, using her as well as what he thought he knew of Levi's motives to bait the trap.

"If she's in the possession of the maze owner, I might be able to help free her," Raoul said.

"How?"

Raoul glanced around the room, only partially pretending a wariness of being overheard. But when Levi didn't suggest they go somewhere to talk privately as he'd hoped, he forged ahead.

"A year ago my brother traveled here by the same route I was taking when you came across me," Raoul lied, laying the groundwork. "I think he ended up in the maze. From what I've been able to learn, he might still be alive. I've heard the maze owner is hunting an escaped prisoner whose arms are tattooed with the names of those he's killed."

Levi abruptly stood. "Follow me."

Raoul hid his smile as he followed the lion out of the bar and into a small office space. As soon as the door closed, Levi asked, "Anton wants the prisoner who was bound to the chair?"

"Yes." Raoul shivered for effect before embellishing with lies. "I was there when he was brought to the trapper's compound. The settlement where he was finally captured was afraid to execute him. They thought he was most likely demon-possessed.

"I heard one of them say they'd used the warded collar around his neck to hold the demon inside the prisoner, but they were afraid it would be freed once he was killed. That's why they offered him to the trapper and paid for him to be transported to Oakland. They'd heard the maze owner has an enslaved demon who hunts. They thought like would kill like."

Raoul licked his lips, his eyes meeting Levi's then skittering away for effect. "I heard what you said in the truck. You thought the prisoner was dangerous and should be left with keys to free himself and go his own way. He smelled human enough to me. But it could be because of the collar. When your companion, the one bearing a church's brand, insisted on freeing him, I thought the churchmen and the settlement police who gave him to the trapper must be right about him being demon-possessed. Then when I heard the maze owner was searching for him and also for the woman—"

"Anton is searching for the woman?"

Raoul retrieved the paper he'd first seen when he went to the maze. He passed it to Levi, reliving his surprise at recognizing her and seeing she was worth money to the maze owner.

As the lion unfolded and studied the reward offer, Raoul sought to close the trap he'd carefully constructed. "If I didn't think my brother was alive, I'd leave Oakland and never look back. But if there's a possibility I could free him by exchanging the woman or the escaped prisoner . . . They're human. And except for the healer, I've never met one whose life is more important than a Were's."

Levi glanced up from the paper. Molten gold eyes seethed with turmoil. "Anton and Farold can't be trusted."

Which was not the same as warning Raoul to stay away from the human with the brand. Raoul only barely contained his jubilation. "I have to take a chance on being able to keep them from double-crossing me. I'd never forgive myself if there was a possibility of freeing my brother and I didn't take it. I'll try to include the healer in the trade even if I'm only successful in recapturing the prisoner and not his branded companion. I owe the healer that much."

Levi crumpled the paper in his hand, balling it in his fist. "I need to get back to work. You won't catch the prisoner by yourself, and if you involve the maze owner, you'll end up in a cage. There's a bar in this section of the red zone. It's got a skinned human nailed to the front of it. Ask around and you'll find it. Meet me there an hour before sunset tomorrow."

Raoul hid his smile and managed to keep it from his voice. "I'll be there."

Sixteen

ARAÑA stood at the window and witnessed the dawn slowly pushing aside the darkness and weakening the predator's claim to the
outside world. The night had seemed interminable, a heavy shroud
imprisoning and suffocating her, trapping her in fear and worry and
guilt.

Tir should have been back by now. But she couldn't wait or go in
search of him or even leave a message, for fear of leaving a trail.

The bread and cheese they'd set aside for breakfast remained untouched, her stomach too tense, her nerves strung too tight to eat.
The vision image of Levi's death assaulted her. Failure and guilt tried
to crush her.

Araña turned away from them. She knew what she had to do,
and she would do it.

Finding the house belonging to the Wainwright witches was
easy. The first person she approached for directions provided
them.

The house was in the center of the area set aside for the gifted.

Dark stones surrounded dozens of tiny windows. Dew caught on elaborate glyphs carved into door and window frames.

A short, wrought iron fence marked a boundary and warned with more sigils that the area was protected by magic. Underneath it ran a ley line.

The ground hummed with it and power licked through the soles of Araña's shoes like a blue-white flame sending nervous energy through her. It danced along her senses with a hint of fire, but not enough of it for her to imagine she'd ever dare to summon it.

She touched damp palms to the knife hilts before opening the wrought iron gate and walking to the front door. A thick brass gargoyle with a ring held in its mouth served as a door knocker.

With a thought, she felt the spider hovering over the pulse beating rapidly at the base of her throat. Araña grasped the gargoyle-held ring and used it.

The door opened immediately, as if the woman standing behind it waited only to see if Araña's courage would fail at the last instant. "I'm Annalise," she said, though the gray streak in otherwise black hair had already identified her as the Wainwright witch who'd met with Rebekka.

"I'm—"

"Araña." The witch's eyes flicked to the spider. "Come inside. I'll show you to the parlor."

There was no true choice. Araña stepped across the threshold, expecting to feel the same pulling at her soul she'd experienced when she crossed the wards protecting the occult shop. Instead she felt a parting, like stepping through a curtain of finely spun silk.

Annalise closed the door, her eyes going to the spider again before saying, "This way."

Araña followed her down a hallway etched with sigils and whose walls were lined with prewar artwork, paintings of naked men and women dancing. Worshipping a goddess who was of the earth. Coupling in rites of fertility that predated any church.

The witch stopped in an open doorway, motioning for Araña to go inside. Araña took a single step and saw the old witch from the bus stop, the one who'd sent Erik and Matthew to their deaths.

Rage engulfed her, flash-fire fast and equally hot.

The knives slid from their sheaths without her making a conscious choice to draw them, but once they were in her hands only a single desire dominated.

Vengeance.

Araña moved forward, uncaring, unthinking about what protections the witch might have in place.

Blind fury drove her—

Into pain so intense it dropped her to the ground.

She screamed silently, writhed in an agony that had no physical expression because she could no longer move any part of her body.

Scream after scream pierced her brain, overlaying onto imagines from the past—the men who'd died from the spider's touch, though they'd been allowed to thrash and flail before succumbing to its poison.

Her vision blurred, narrowing until there was a sole point of focus. The witch hovered above her, curdled-milk eyes staring at her as they'd done at the bus stop, *seeing* her despite the blinding cataracts.

The matriarch murmured something, the language unknown to Araña, and the pain ceased, though the paralysis remained. "Foolish, foolish child to attack me. You remain in this world only because of debts I owe to those who would see you trained in the use of your gift."

Bony fingers delved into a pocket and withdrew, holding a clear, ordinary-looking crystal. The witch dropped it onto Araña's chest, and the spider scurried away from it just as it had done in the presence of the demon Abijah.

"The deaths you thought to avenge served a greater purpose. And the men you think you honor with your mindless violence were rewarded for their sacrifice. If your courage matches your fury, you can determine the truth of their fate for yourself before you seek me out again. Go see the shamaness Aisling. Offer the fetish to her. Tell her that her father wills her to use it in order to escort you into the ghostlands. Tell her she will gain a favor from him for doing it."

A curse followed, or perhaps it was meant as a reminder of a lesson learned. The witch spoke and the pain returned, blocking out all reality and becoming Araña's existence until it fell away abruptly, leaving her gasping, shaking—at last able to move again.

She rolled to her side, her body curling involuntarily into a fetal position and remaining that way until pride forced her knees away from her chest and gave her the strength to rise to her feet. She took a perverse pleasure in finding the knives still in her hands, and didn't sheathe them until she looked around the room and found it empty, the Wainwright matriarch gone.

Movement behind her had Araña turning. Annalise stood at the doorway, expression disapproving. "I'll see you out now."

Araña took a step. Something at her feet glittered, and she looked down to find the crystal on the floor where it had fallen.

Longing held Araña motionless, the desire to see Matthew and Erik overriding her hatred of the witch and her fear of her gift. Pride urged her to turn away from the crystal and all it represented. But the memory of the vision that had brought her to the witch's door at daybreak held her in place.

Before she could change her mind, Araña bent down and scooped up the crystal fetish then followed Annalise to the door. The witch opened it, her face no longer revealing her thoughts, her voice emotionless as she warned, "Inside the circle, those you care for in the ghostlands can touch you without fear. Beyond it neither you nor they are safe."

TIR savored every moment as the night gave up its claim to land and sea and sky in a slow tide of diffuse, cloud-blocked sunlight. Freedom. It sang in his ears with each lap of water against the boat, with each seagull cry. It caressed his bared torso with a chilled, misty breeze that made him want to open his arms and embrace it.

For centuries he'd been trapped in dark catacombs or window-less cells, chained and enslaved, his only glimpse of the dawn what he held in his memories. Never again, he vowed. Never again would he wear shackles around his wrists and ankles and be help-less against humans.

He looked around at the wreck-strewn harbor and felt deeply satisfied at having fulfilled his promise to Araña and recovered her boat. Anticipation formed, swelling his cock as he pictured her ex-pression when he got back to her and told her of his success.

Only the presence of the watching cormorants kept him from taking himself in hand and imagining the tight fist of his fingers was Araña's mouth offering thanks, her cunt offering welcome. The doorway into the cabin offered further temptation, the erotic image of lying on the bed that had been hers and bringing himself to com-pletion, leaving his scent in a primitive marking of territory.

He took a step forward, nearly giving in to the urge before he regained his self-control. Dangerous. She was so very dangerous to him. Time and time again she consumed his thoughts and made him burn—not for absolute freedom, but for her.

Tir turned away from the doorway. He closed his mind to the demands of the flesh, redirecting his energy instead to pulling up the anchor.

Two of the cormorants left their stations on what remained of a sunken container ship. But rather than joining him on the boat, they dove into the water after fish.

Birds and not skin-walkers, Tir thought, glancing at the remain-ing cormorants, though he didn't try to determine which of them were men mimicking their totem guardian.

The low purr of a powerful motor turned Tir's attention toward the shore. He started the engine, unwilling to leave the boat where it wasn't easily accessible.

A sleek craft appeared moments later, emerging from a narrow space created by jagged pieces of metal rising out of the water like sunken mountain peaks. Rimmon was piloting the speedboat, his bodyguards near him, one holding a machine gun, the other a launcher of some kind.

"So you made it," Rimmon said, circling the *Constellation* like a shark circling prey. "Now we'll see if you can deliver on your promise or whether I'll enjoy the companionship of your woman."

Tir resisted the vice lord's taunt and the temptation to violence, and Rimmon laughed, as if feeding on Tir's fury, before saying, "Follow me. Don't deviate from my path or you'll sink the boat you've sold a portion of your soul to save."

Tir followed, skirting hazards and guessing there were more he couldn't see, their path revealing how unnecessary it was for Rimmon to hold the harbor with armed boat patrols. Only someone well acquainted with it or guided through it would have a chance of reaching shore.

Rimmon was climbing onto the pier as Tir brought the *Constellation* alongside it. Two men dressed in the same manner as the bodyguards stepped forward and helped Tir secure the lines. When it was done, Tir went to Rimmon's side. The vice lord said, "My promise covers protecting the boat from theft or damage only. Not determining who has a right to board her, or keeping whoever occupies her safe."

Tir shrugged, his thoughts moving beyond healing Rimmon's daughter and going to Araña and the continued search for the tattoo translations. "Let's get on with it."

"Yes. Let's see if pride goes before a fall in your case."

The vice lord led him to a car, the bodyguards going ahead to open and close the back doors before taking up positions in the front seat. The interior smelled of leather and hashish and sex, much like the club Temptation did.

They left the port area, and at the edge of the red zone were joined by two other vehicles, open jeeps carrying armed men. It surprised Tir at first, but upon reflection, made sense.

Despite Rimmon's nonhuman status, his ruined face was testament to the damage fire could do to him. A man who controlled a harbor was probably subject to attack from those who served the law as well as those who wanted to carve out a crime empire of their own.

Beyond what called itself civilization, they climbed into the hills. The vice lord grew more remote with each mile.

A stone house with floor-to-ceiling glass windows became their destination. It sat at a canyon edge, defying man and nature and whatever god the vice lord might answer to.

The vehicles stopped and the guards exited. Those in the car with Tir and Rimmon opened the back doors, then closed them again, trailing the vice lord and Tir into a house that smelled of incense and spoke of luxury.

"This way," Rimmon said, climbing stairs carpeted with a rug woven by human fingers centuries earlier.

He led Tir down mural-painted hallways filled with winged creatures, humanlike and inhuman, coupling with mortal women. At the end of it, the vice lord paused in front of a door as if gathering his strength. A knock announced his presence before he entered the room with absolute confidence.

"I've brought someone to heal you, Saril."

Tir followed. A woman sat in a cushioned chair in front of the window, bundled in a heavy quilt though the room was almost unbearably hot. She was young, no older than Araña, her face ethereal, beautiful despite the bones shown in stark relief, as if some sculptor had captured her in porcelain and absolute stillness.

The vice lord crossed the room to her, his fear palpable. "Saril!"

She stirred at the command in his voice. And he repeated it, his fingers white on the armrests of her chair.

Her eyelids fluttered as she fought the sleep that would ultimately slide into a coma and then death. When she won the battle to wake, Tir saw the green fire of her father's eyes.

"I've brought someone to heal you," Rimmon said.

"Another one?"

"This one won't fail as the others have."

"And if he does?"

"That's not your concern."

"I'm not like you. I won't let you hurt people in my name."

"You have no say in the matter."

Anger tightened her features. "Just as my mother had no say when she caught your attention?"

The vice lord abruptly caught his daughter's chin in his hand. "This argument grows tiresome. She came to me willingly. And left willingly—carrying a child she then proceeded to hide from me until it was almost too late. An attempt to heal you will be made, whether you want it or not, whether you feel it taints your soul or not. If progeny came to me easily, then perhaps I'd allow you to die some foolish, noble death, but at the moment, you are my sole living descendent."

He released her and turned away. Tir thought he meant to leave the room. Instead Rimmon crossed to the nightstand and took up a sheathed sword.

The hilt was blackened, and when Rimmon drew the blade, it was charred as well, as if it had burned in the same inferno of fire that had tried to consume the vice lord. "If she dies in your presence, I will strike you down."

It was only when Rimmon returned to his daughter's side that Tir could see the script etched into the blade, and the sight of it sent icy fear through him, some deep recognition that the weapon's bite could grant him the true peace of death he'd sometimes thought would be preferable to captivity.

The vice lord said, "Heal her."

But it was his daughter who answered instead of Tir. "Not with you in the room."

Rimmon's lips curved upward in a twisted parody of mirth. "As you wish, Saril. But it changes nothing."

He left without speaking to Tir again. And for a moment Tir and Saril studied each other wordlessly.

Her gaze traveled over the tattoos on his arms, eyebrows making a faint move to draw together as she puzzled over what crimes they might represent. Finally she broke the silence by saying, "I'm sorry you're involved in this. He has a long reach. Even if you manage to escape from the house and get away from Oakland, he'll find you. But if you want to attempt it, I won't call out to him."

Her words rebuffed Tir, making him take a step backward—as if centuries of judgment were under attack. Until Araña, he'd never met a human willing to put herself at risk to offer him a chance at freedom.

"I'll heal you," he said, drawing the knife at his thigh, wanting to be done with it.

Her gasp was faint, as was her flinch. But the emerald green eyes never left his as he stepped forward.

"Give me your hand."

She struggled to free it from the heavy cocoon of quilts, using a strength born of sheer determination to lift it. And even then, she could hold it only inches away from her lap.

Tir took it and felt the fine tremors going through her, the icy chill, as if the grave already claimed her. Deep in the past, among the shattered remains of his earliest memories, were those where warrior priests used him to heal this disease, though it had been called a curse in those days.

There'd been prayers said as his blood was mixed with crushed berries and placed in special vessels set aside for the purpose. There'd been exaltations to a deity who'd ignored Tir's plight even as his blood was used to heal those who served and paid homage to the god.

But the gods of the humans who'd held him captive meant nothing to Tir. And though he could remember the incantations, they weren't words of power to him.

He knew only one way. And his jaw clenched as he remembered the excruciating agony he'd experienced when he restored Araña to health. He knew, as surely as he knew it would require all his strength not to kill Saril, that his suffering would be made worse because he willingly healed.

Tir closed his mind to it as he slashed across Saril's palm and then his own. He thought instead of his freedom, focused on the ancient parchment containing centuries of translations, as he wove their fingers together, pressing wound to wound.

Madness threatened to engulf him. Discordant notes tore through his mind like daggers ripping and shredding, spreading disharmony.

The urge to lash out was nearly unstoppable, but he fought it, willed himself to save the violence for when he was free of the collar and could wreak vengeance on those who deserved it.

He battled against the desire to scream. The muscles of his neck tightened, choking off the sound of his suffering and, with it, his breath.

Sweat poured off him, slowly leaching away his mindless, pain-driven fury.

And finally he was free of it.

Tir dropped Saril's hand. Her eyes held awe, gratitude, reverence.

"The music," she whispered, tears escaping to trail over her cheeks. "I've never heard anything so beautiful."

Tir turned away from her, disconcerted by her expression.

He moved toward the doorway, intent on making his escape. She stopped him mid-stride by saying, "Are you looking for them? The papers covered with glyphs and texts?"

He was beside her with no memory of having returned, the knife held against her jugular vein as Araña had held the knife to the clerk's throat in the occult shop. "What do you know about them?"

Saril's gaze remained steady though he felt her fear. "A picture came, when you were healing me. I thought the pages were musical scores at first. But then I realized it didn't make sense for me to see an image unless you were concentrating hard on one."

Color tinted her face. Her voice softened. "I'm sorry if I stole your thoughts. I didn't mean to. I'm a Finder. Sometimes it's hard for me to *stop* being what I am."

Thick lashes lowered to mute the emerald green of her eyes. "If you're searching for them, I'll help you. My debts are my own, not my . . . not Rimmon's."

Tir stilled completely. Did he dare trust her?

He pulled the knife away from her throat, feeling an unwelcome sting of shame—and recoiling from it as he'd done when he'd felt the same in Araña after she'd held the clerk at knifepoint.

Tir sheathed the blade to delay answering. Was it foolish not to take advantage of this unexpected opportunity? Or the wise avoidance of a neatly laid trap?

Her illness wasn't feigned. Nor did he think the exchange with the vice lord had been an act put on for his benefit.

He glanced away from her and saw his reflection in a mirror. The collar around his neck caught the rays of the sunlight coming in through the window, mocking him, turning the instrument of his enslavement into something a human would wear as jewelry.

When he looked back at Saril, he made his decision. "The papers themselves aren't important. They probably no longer exist. What I'm searching for is what was once written on them. The translations for the symbols inked onto my arms."

Saril's gaze dropped to the tattoos. She pushed off the heavy comforter and leaned forward, studying them for long moments before she used the arms of the chair to get to her feet. "I need my scrying bowl."

Tir backed up to allow her room to move. Saril crossed to the dresser and lifted flowers out of what he would have labeled a squat vase, had he been interested enough to notice it. She shook the flowers gently to reduce the amount of water clinging to their stems before setting them aside. "My mother always said the best way to hide something valuable is to make it seem ordinary and put it in plain sight."

Saril picked the bowl up and returned to the chair with it. Up close, Tir could see the lettering, something old, in a language that seemed familiar to him, as if he'd once known its meaning.

She bent over it, and he could feel the totality of her concentration. If she chanted, he didn't hear it. If she closed her eyes, he didn't see it. The workings of her gift weren't obvious to him.

One moment ebbed into the next, like the slow trickle of a stream. He saw no change in the water. But when she lifted her face, her smile was one of triumph.

"I'm not sure if the papers are the originals, but pages holding the same information are bound in a book bearing the seal of the Knights Templar. It's here in Oakland, at L'Antiquaire."

THE new day brought a renewed sense of dread to Rebekka. She might be called a guest and allowed to wander the estate freely, both inside and outside, but she knew she was being watched for any attempt to escape, as surely as she knew her only hope of it was recovering the witch's token and using it.

She didn't forget she was a prisoner or that after allowing her a night to think about his proposition, to experience the comfort and security the wealthy took for granted, The Iberá would expect her to say yes to his offer of protection and employment. He'd expect her to name Levi, and tell him everything she knew about Araña and how they came to ambush the trapper and free the shackled prisoner.

Her answer hadn't changed, despite the temptation presented to her. This wasn't her world. It was as foreign to her as San Francisco and life as a vampire's servant would be. Her place was in the red zone, where her gift made a difference in the lives of the Weres who had no choice but to prostitute themselves in order to survive.

Rebekka's chest tightened with the knock on her door followed by the appearance of Janita. She rubbed her knuckles against the stiff fabric of the day dress she'd been provided.

"You look beautiful in that outfit," Janita said, smiling and picking up Eston when he held out his arms to her. "The Iberá wishes to see you in his study. If you're ready, I'll show you the way before taking the little one to the kitchen for his meal."

"I'm ready," Rebekka said, unable to hide the nervousness in her voice.

Janita tsked. "You have nothing to fear. Carlos Iberá is a fair man. A good man. He takes care of his own. My family has been in service to him since he was a baby like Eston. When my cousin was accused of a crime he didn't commit, The Iberá interceded and saw that justice was done."

Rebekka nodded in acceptance of Janita's assertions and resisted the urge to worry the fabric of the dress as she left the room. At the doorway to the study she placed a kiss on Eston's cheek before he was taken off for his breakfast. Her heart squeezed at the sight of him disappearing around the corner, then nearly ceased beating altogether when she entered the patriarch's office and a guardsman rose from a chair across from The Iberá's desk.

He was heavily decorated, austere and autocratic. And in her fear she missed the family resemblance until the patriarch said, "This is my grandson, General Enzo Iberá. Tomás's uncle."

The general bowed slightly and said, "A pleasure, I hope."

Rebekka didn't miss the nuance. She focused on The Iberá, careful to avoid looking directly at the credenza where she'd caught a glimpse of the butler's velvet-lined tray with the token exactly where she'd placed it. "I can't accept your offer," she said, taking the offensive. "And even if I did, it doesn't change anything. I don't know where the prisoner is."

The patriarch seemed unfazed. "I'm sorry to hear that's your initial decision. I haven't lived so long by not being persistent. As to the other, I believe you when you say you don't know what happened to the prisoner. Your friends might have a different answer, however."

"My friend left when I did and didn't go back." She gave a quick, nervous glance at Enzo before adding, "The prisoner was still shackled when we fled as the guardsmen were approaching."

"Someone remained behind," General Iberá said. "It's only a matter of time before we locate both that person and the one you claim is your friend. We know the child calls you Bekka. We've had men canvassing the gifted area since daybreak. None of the gifted has yet to admit they know of a healer who takes care of animals, but before long one of them will. The prisoner didn't get out of his chains by himself. Tell us who freed him and, because of it, might know where he went."

Rebekka's throat tightened in fear. "I can't."

"Your answer grieves me," the patriarch said, and his response seemed genuine. "I'd hoped—" He waved it aside. "No matter. There's time yet for you to change your mind both on my offer to remain here and on helping us find the escaped prisoner."

"Grandfather—"

"No. Her gift isn't one to be thrown away casually, Enzo. If you'd seen her with the lion your brother and Tomás gave me for my birthday . . . Go ahead and take the steps we agreed on."

The general nodded in acquiescence and pulled ink pad and fingerprinting card from a pocket. Rebekka backed up a step, only to find the butler had entered the room unnoticed and stood ready to restrain her, if necessary.

"Allow me," Enzo said, reaching for her hand, his voice courteous despite the steel in it.

Rebekka took a deep breath and allowed him to fingerprint her. It could take him days, perhaps weeks, to find the identification papers she'd been required to file when she homesteaded in the area set aside for the gifted. And even if he located them, Levi wouldn't go to her house and Araña didn't know about it.

When it was done, the general left, and Rebekka accompanied the patriarch to breakfast. *There's hope*, she told herself, thinking of the token left out in the open rather than tucked away in a safe or hidden somewhere.

Her hope was short-lived. The butler announced Father Ursu's arrival just after the meal concluded but before she'd left the table.

"Forgive me for arriving unannounced," the priest said after he was shown to the less formal room where they'd eaten the morning meal. "The situation has grown more urgent, Carlos. Anton has learned of our interest in the prisoner. He's made it known that he's willing to pay a bounty for information, capture, or the prisoner's corpse."

From his vestments Father Ursu pulled out a piece of paper and placed it on the table. "That's not all. He's also circulating this."

The priest's eyes flashed with victory at Rebekka's reaction to the picture of Araña. "Your guest recognizes her," he said. "The woman managed to escape the maze even with the demon pursuing her. She wears a brand on her hand said to belong to the Church. Anton believes she's with the prisoner. We don't have the luxury of time any longer. Let me take the healer when I leave."

Rebekka's heart rabbited in her chest and her stomach roiled with the food she'd just eaten.

"Not yet," the patriarch said, but his words held the possibility that, in the end, he would be willing to turn her over to the Church.

"Carlos—"

The Iberá held his hand up. "We can discuss this again later. Come, I want to show you something I discovered in an old journal I'm currently reading. There's record of two urns like the one once housing the demon Anton commands. They might be of interest to you should the Church ever be in a position to get its stolen property back." To Rebekka he said, "If you'll excuse us."

She nodded, but remained seated, unsure she could stand without trembling, but also wanting to follow their progress audibly and confirm they traveled down the same hallway she'd taken earlier to The Iberá's study.

At the patriarch's mention of the urn and the demon, a terrible certainty had settled on her. She'd never studied witchcraft, but it seemed likely a demon freed yet still subject to human command could be trapped and held again.

Rebekka remembered Annalise's words at the occult shop clearly. *A woman will run tonight as well. It is beyond our control as to whether or not she will escape. But should she survive, she will be as important to you and the . . . man . . . who waits outside for you, as she is to us.*

At the time she'd dared to hope the Wainwright witches wanted the destruction of the maze or might be persuaded to involve themselves in it. She hadn't contemplated their motives for enlisting aid should Araña escape the maze, because she had no basis for forming an opinion. She'd spent little enough time in the area set aside for the gifted and none of it around witches like the Wainwrights.

Then later, after it was done and Araña was safe, when she'd returned to her room and learned about Anton's plan to acquire a dragon lizard and set it against Levi's brother, she'd preferred to remain ignorant about the brand Araña wore or the spider-shaped mark Araña claimed made it dangerous to touch her.

But now, as Annalise's words reverberated, with a refocused emphasis on Araña's importance to the Wainwrights, Rebekka couldn't shake the idea that they knew about Anton's possession of the urn and its connection to the demon. She couldn't rid herself of the certainty that the witches believed Araña could gain it for them, perhaps knew by the brand on her hand she was capable of accomplishing it.

Rebekka shivered at the idea of commanding a demon. And yet hope churned in her stomach along with fear. If the demon could somehow be trapped in the urn, then all the plans and dreams she and Levi held about freeing his brother and the others could be realized.

It was common knowledge Anton employed no guards because the demon couldn't be defeated or subverted. It was the demon who patrolled the buildings and grounds. If the demon were no longer there . . .

Rebekka got to her feet and returned to her room, wanting to think and expecting to find Eston.

Instead she found a teary-eyed Janita.

"What's happened? Where's Eston?"

"I'm sorry, there was nothing I could do. I tried to bring him to you so you could say good-bye, but I was told no, it wasn't allowed. Enzo took him with him when he left. The Iberá ordered Eston sent away."

"Where?"

Janita brushed tears away. "I don't know. None of us do."

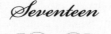

Seventeen

TIR knew the moment he reached the healer's house that it stood empty of anything living. No emotion emanated from it, especially not Araña's.

The excitement that had brought him here so she could accompany him to the bookseller's shop became a cold, gut-wrenching fear before flaring into white-hot fury.

If anything had happened to her . . .

He entered the house, steeling himself for what he might find, then sagging as relief swept through him when there was no blood, no body. No evidence of a struggle. Nothing to hint she'd left unwillingly or an enemy had been there in his absence.

The drawings she'd done for Levi were on the counter, next to the uneaten bread and cheese he'd placed there. A pile of ash in the fireplace was all that remained of the wood burned there the night before.

Her cloak was also gone, as if she'd left the house on an errand of her own choosing. There was no note. But its lack didn't mean anything other than she was being cautious.

He couldn't stay, not when he was so close to gaining his freedom. Yet he prowled the tiny house repeatedly before going to the front door.

Her scent was everywhere. Evocative. Tempting. Taunting him with the memory of her on her knees before him.

A different type of heated fury flared inside him as he left. Something dark and primitive, bringing with it a demand she be punished for defying him when he'd ordered her to remain in the house until he returned.

THE shamaness's house was freshly painted white adobe with a gray tile roof. It was small, the yard well tended. Flower boxes overflowed with color beneath the windows and on the porch. Tomato plants stood tall along one side, towering over vines holding squash and cucumbers. Songbirds flew to the ground from nearby trees, then back again, while chickens scratched and pecked, looking for food.

Like the witches' house, a fence marked the boundaries of the property. It bore protective sigils similar to the ones carved into the door frame. And like the witches' house, there was no symbol announcing what manner of gifted human lived in the house.

Araña had found it only by asking strangers for directions, her heart racing each time she approached someone, fear gathering in her chest that they'd be in possession of her picture and would seek the reward being offered for her.

The fingertips left bare on her gloved hand glanced over the hilt of a knife before going to the fetish in her front pocket. She felt no magic in the crystal, nothing to suggest it was a powerful amulet. And yet it must be.

Tir should be back with news about the boat. She longed for the safety he'd come to represent, for the feel of his arms around her and the strength she gained from his touch. But the desire to see Matthew and Erik again, to be absolved of the guilt she carried over their deaths, kept her from delaying by going back to Rebekka's house.

Araña's hand curled around the crystal through the material of her pants. Memories of the men who'd meant everything made her heart ache and her throat tighten on tears of hope and sorrow.

She opened the gate and stepped onto the property. A breeze swirled around her, bringing with it the unexpected scent of hot sand and desert spice.

Gauzy curtains billowed as it passed through an open window. From somewhere inside the house a woman laughed then abruptly went silent—the reason obvious as Araña reached the porch and looked through the bars of the protective outer door.

A man and woman stood embracing, their passion a scorching heat wave that had Araña's body crying out for Tir's. The woman's low moan made Araña feel like a voyeur. She started to back away, only to stop when the woman laughed and extricated herself from the man's arms, saying, "There's someone at the door, Zurael, as I'm sure you already know."

They turned toward her, and Araña was momentarily stunned by their beauty. Both had long hair, the woman's blond, the man's black. He was shirtless, his body deeply tanned.

Araña's fingers rubbed over the sheathed blades of her knives, the habit so deeply ingrained she was barely aware of it until the man's hand curled around the woman's arm when she would have stepped to the door.

"No, Aisling," he said, halting her with a murmured warning.

It was then that Araña saw the serpent coiled around the shamaness's forearm, its head flattened on the back of her hand, so lifelike it took her a moment to understand it was a tattoo.

A deep sense of foreboding settled in her chest. Her attention shifted back to the man. Zurael.

Inhuman eyes of melted gold met hers. But it was the glimpse of the small, matching serpent on the side of his neck that sent fear slithering through Araña.

Demon, she thought, and realized the spider had reacted to Zurael in the same way it had to Abijah and the scorpion he wore, by sliding down to rest at the base of her spine as if cowering in the presence of a greater power.

There was a subtle change in the—in Zurael's expression, as though he recognized something in her as well. His face hardened. "What do you want?" he asked, his voice holding a harsh warning. "Who sent you?"

Resolve stiffened Araña's spine. It was too late to retreat now. It had been too late from the moment she'd seen Oakland. And knowing what fate waited there, hadn't told Matthew and Erik and pleaded with them to abandon the search for a healer there.

"The Wainwright matriarch sent me."

Araña slid the fetish from her pocket. She held it up so the shamaness could see it through the bars of the outer door, and noted how Aisling's eyes widened in surprise.

"The witch said to tell you that your father wants you to use this crystal in order to escort me into the ghostlands. She said if you do it, you'll gain a favor from him."

Zurael growled, "Aisling," but the shamaness ignored the refusal he'd infused her name with and said, "Come in. The door is unlocked."

Araña entered the house and found the same desert spice and hot sand scent the breeze had held. She gave the shamaness her name, along with the fetish.

Aisling couldn't seem to take her eyes off the crystal, as if it held some secret in its icy heart that only she could see. With a low growl, Zurael put his arms around her waist, pulling her backward against him until there was an unbroken line where their bodies touched.

"Send it back," he said, his voice low and menacing. "I warned your father against making you his pawn again. I won't allow you to risk yourself."

"I'll be safe. Using his name to enter the ghostlands will ensure it. And I'd be foolish to throw away the offer of a favor."

Zurael hissed, a serpentlike sound that sent fear skittering along Araña's spine. She balled her hands into fists to keep them from curling around the handles of her knives.

The shamaness tore her attention away from the crystal. "What is it you seek in the ghostlands?"

"The fate of my family. I want to see for myself that the Wainwright matriarch told the truth when she said they'd been rewarded in the afterlife for the taking of their lives." There was no masking the emotion from her voice.

Sadness came to Aisling's face, making her look delicate and vulnerable. Her hand closed around the crystal. "When did they die?"

Araña's throat tightened as images from the fight with the guardsmen scrolled past. "Three days ago. The day we arrived in Oakland."

"Do you have something belonging to them?"

This time she allowed her hands to curl around the dark hilts. "Their knives."

Aisling nodded. "That will work."

"I'll accompany you into the spiritlands," Zurael said.

Amusement replaced the hint of sadness still lingering on the shamaness's face. "And leave our physical bodies unguarded?"

A muscle spasmed in Zurael's cheek. The gold of his eyes took on a deadly cast. "I could forbid it."

His threat was met with a laugh. "You won't."

"If anything happens to you—"

Aisling silenced him by turning in his arms and pressing a kiss to his lips before pulling from his embrace. She reached out, probably intending no more than to offer a touch of reassurance or encouragement, but Araña jerked away.

"It's not safe to touch me. Not here anyway. The witch, Annalise, said it could be done in the ghostlands as long as I stay in the circle."

The shamaness's eyebrows drew together in contemplation rather than fear. She worried her bottom lip with her teeth then finally gave a small nod. "I think I know what needs to be done in order to escort you there. This is something you want to do now?"

Araña's mouth went dry and her heart kicked into a hard, rapid, throbbing pace. "Yes."

Aisling shared a glance with Zurael. His frown was scorching, but he locked the barred door anyway, then closed the solid front door and secured it as well.

"This way," the shamaness said, leading Araña to a room that had obviously been created for the sole purpose of journeying into the ghostlands.

It seemed little more than a huge closet with a dirt floor. Fetishes perched at the edges of shallow openings carved into the adobe wall at the corners. They were so lifelike Araña thought they would come alive if filled with the spirits of the creatures they represented.

Bear. Raven. Serpent.

Spider.

Only Aisling's voice instructing her to sit pulled Araña from the black-onyx thrall of the last fetish.

She sat, cross-legged in the restricted space, and became aware of the glyph-marked wood turning a soft, dirt floor into a well-protected altar.

The shamaness sat next to her, assuming the same compact, cross-legged position before leaning forward and tracing a symbol into earth that smelled of delta waterways.

Araña expected Aisling to draw a circle, but apparently the single sigil in combination with the perched fetishes and the glyph-inscribed wood enclosing the dirt was enough.

When the shamaness was satisfied with what she'd drawn, she turned slightly, her expression solemn, her Angelite-colored eyes meeting Araña's and holding them. "It'll take a blood sacrifice, yours I think, to free you from your body enough to enter the spirit-lands. The only other time I've accompanied someone like this, it took their death. I can't guarantee it won't require yours as well. Do you wish to proceed?"

Araña felt calm. She wouldn't die here. She wouldn't die like this. When the demon who'd marked her with the spider claimed her for Hell, it would be in terror and pain, in fire. "Yes."

The shamaness nodded. "Cut yourself with the knives one at a time and hand them to me, giving me the names of your family members as you do so."

Araña didn't hesitate. She pulled Erik's blade from its sheath and sliced across her forearm, welcoming the pain.

A memory welled up with the blood. It flowed across her consciousness as metallic-scented red slid across deeply tanned flesh, making Araña think of those early years when Erik was teaching her to read. How he'd listen to her stumble and struggle through the words each evening until finally they came smoothly and effort-lessly.

"This blade is Erik's," she said, passing the knife to Aisling before drawing Matthew's blade and cutting a line parallel to the first. Memories surfaced with the strike, learning of a different kind. From the very first, Matthew had concentrated on teaching her how to wield a weapon, how to defend as well as attack.

He'd cut her a hundred times. And she could still remember the pride and satisfaction on his face the day she'd finally drawn blood—sending him into the cabin for a lecture from Erik and stitches, because even though she'd succeeded, she was still unskilled in con-trolling the extent of the damage she inflicted.

"This one belongs to Matthew," Araña said as the blood from the second cut mingled with that of the first.

Aisling took it, dropping the fetish into Araña's hand. "Use this as a focus," she said. "Close your eyes and picture them."

Blood streamed over Araña's wrist and pooled in her open

palm, surrounding the fetish and making her think of a buoy set in a red sea.

She closed her eyes and let the memories come, images as unfettered and uncontrolled as the wind.

There was a pulling sensation, much like the one she'd experienced at the doorway of the occult shop—as if something attempted to suck her soul from the body housing it, but she didn't fight it.

Sweat poured off her skin as the hot burn of the spider mark spread to encompass and define every inch of her, making her feel like a living flame.

Cold air swirled around her, buffeting her, attacking then retreating. Finally making her aware of its touch on her naked flesh.

Araña opened her eyes to gray nothingness, like being lost in thick fog. A glance downward revealed the truth of what the shifting mist had hinted at.

Her clothing was gone, including the fingerless glove. In the land of spirits, the brand on her hand glowed black-red, like a brick of charcoal.

Movement to her left made her stiffen, but it was only nothingness giving way to the shamaness and bringing with it a quick swell of relief.

"I probably should have warned you," Aisling said, noting the blush stealing across Araña's cheeks. "Only those who call this world home can manifest clothing here."

Araña gave a small nod, unsure of what to expect next. "I don't see a circle," she said, and a man's voice responded, cutting through the grayness like a foghorn. "I believe that's my cue to appear."

He stepped into sight, eyes dancing with unholy glee as he made a point of studying their nakedness. His face was marked with a criminal's tattoos, and for an instant, Araña wondered if Matthew or Erik had introduced her to him in one of the outlaw settlements or boat towns, but her artistic ability allowed her to memorize features, and his didn't seem familiar to her.

"I like your choice of company, beautiful," he said, focusing his attention on Aisling. "Light meat and dark meat. My mouth waters. What a tempting, succulent feast you'd both make. If I was willing to pay the price, of course."

The man gave a mock sigh, his lips turning downward in an exaggerated frown. "I'm afraid I've got more than enough on my plate at the moment. So I'll have to content myself with my fantasies." His smile became sly. "I hope you don't mind sharing your starring role with your friend."

He turned and the band around his neck Araña had thought was crude jewelry became a twisted metal cable trailing down his back and disappearing into the fog. It slithered behind him as he walked, playing out to form a large circle.

When the cable finally met and crossed, color and texture and shape filled it, altering reality by changing nothingness into a sandy beach surrounded by a black ocean. A man shimmered into existence, a robed figure who sent an inexplicable surge of fear and pity through Araña.

She stepped back even as Aisling rushed forward, whispering *"Aziel"* as she wrapped her arms around him. And then his presence no longer mattered to Araña.

Erik and Matthew rose from the sea and stepped onto the beach as though they'd been swimming. Water glistened and sparkled, dripping from their hair and streaming down bare chests and onto the ragged, worn-out cutoffs she'd so often teased them about.

They smiled and opened their arms, and in her joy she was unself-conscious about her nakedness as she hurled herself forward, able to do what she'd never been able to do before, embrace them without fear of killing them.

A sob escaped, wrenched from the depths of her soul and opening the floodgate to her tears. Her body shuddered with the onslaught of emotion.

"Hush. Matthew and I are fine," Erik murmured, stroking her hair and pressing kisses to her temple. "Better than fine."

"You're wasting time with your crying, girl," Matthew said, his voice gruff with his own unshed tears and his hand tightening almost painfully on her arm as he fought to keep his emotions in check.

Araña inhaled on a long, shaky breath. They smelled the way they always did, like boats and surf and sunshine.

She pulled away far enough to look up into their beloved faces. "I'm sorry," she said, the words holding all her guilt and pain. "I—"

"Stop," Erik said. "You're not to blame. Going to Oakland was a gamble. I would have died soon anyway. You know that. There have only been a few cases where someone's been cured of the wasting disease, and those have been called miracles."

The sand swirled up, as if issuing a warning. Matthew rubbed his stubbled cheek against her smooth one. "Live in the moment. There are no guarantees beyond it. Isn't that what we taught you?"

"Yes." Her arms tightened on them. "This place—"

"We're not allowed to tell you anything beyond that we're okay," Erik said.

"You're together?"

"Yes," Matthew said. "And what we've found here is better than either of us expected after death. It's better than we deserved. That's no lie."

The guilt and sadness and pain drained away with Matthew's use of their private code. If he'd said they were telling the truth then she would have known it was the opposite.

More sand joined that which was already dancing and spinning above the ground. "We don't have much longer," Erik said.

Out of the corner of her eye, Araña saw Aziel gliding toward them. "I love you," she whispered, saying the words they'd so rarely spoken out loud to one another, unable to stop herself from clinging to them as if she would remain with them or drag them back to the world of the living with her.

It was Matthew who answered gruffly, "You know the feeling is mutual." And Erik who laughed softly at Matthew's response then spoke the words she needed to hear, "We love you. Always."

The cloaked figure had nearly reached them, bringing fear and darkness with him. His shadow was the black sea Erik and Matthew had risen and stepped out of, now coming to reclaim them.

Matthew kissed her. Then Erik did.

"Don't let your courage fail you," Erik said, his voice little more than a whisper spoken in the night as Aziel reached them. "Matthew and I did some terrible things when we lived. You were our redemption." And then they were gone and Aisling was there beside her, both of them standing in the eye of a ferocious desert storm.

The sand swirled around them, gaining in speed. Golden granules gave way to gray nothingness. The roar of the wind became the screams of the dead, hurtling Araña's soul away, returning it to its flesh housing, to the small room with a dirt floor that smelled of delta waterways, to the place where the demon Zurael stood guard in the doorway.

Araña left moments later, after reclaiming the knives and giving the crystal fetish to Aisling. Her thoughts swung like a pendulum, between all that had happened since leaving the healer's house, and the anxious need to return to it and find Tir waiting there, safe, the boat secured.

The emotions she'd experienced in the ghostlands still had the power to make her throat clog and her eyes burn with tears. She wasn't sure she could put into words what it meant to her—to see Matthew and Erik again, to be able to embrace them and to know they didn't burn in the Hell those who controlled her early childhood would have prophesized for them—but she wanted to try.

She wanted to wrap her arms around Tir, to breathe in his scent and feel the hardness of his body against hers. She wanted to share her joy with him.

Even the prospect of returning to the witches' house in order to gain control over her gift couldn't suppress the giddy feelings of relief and happiness, the unburdening of the heavy weight of her guilt over Matthew and Erik's deaths. Only the empty house had the power to do that.

Araña knew Tir wasn't back as soon as she reached it. There was no movement at the window, no door opening, no demand to know where she'd been or why she'd risked capture by leaving.

Fear clutched at her, squeezing her stomach in a tight fist. She forced the fingers of icy horror to open as she went inside to verify the truth of his absence.

She refused to believe something had happened to Tir. She told herself his delay meant only that he was paying whatever price the vice lord demanded for safe harbor for the boat.

Araña left, her destination the witch's house. A chill swept through her at the thought of facing the Wainwright matriarch again. There'd be a price to pay. And she feared it would be her very soul.

Eighteen

L'ANTIQUAIRE was a long, narrow building, the sole survivor in a block where bombs or munitions had destroyed its neighbors and human scavengers had plundered what remained. Small barred windows on either side of the front door were coated in grime that had probably built up in the centuries since The Last War.

A heavy steel door was the only opening set in the back of the building, the untrampled appearance of the vegetation creeping toward it making Tir think it was seldom used.

The remoteness of the shop's location surprised him. He'd thought it would be in the center of town, closer to where guardsmen and police were headquartered and the wealthy walked the streets without fear of losing whatever riches they carried on their person.

Instead, L'Antiquaire was at the far edge of where humans without gifts had settled. It was one final residential neighborhood away from the border marking the remotest section of the gifted area, and relatively near to where the forest began.

Tir returned to the building's front, wary, wondering again if this was a trap set for him by Rimmon and his daughter. Frustration and uneasiness seethed inside him. For all his dealings with humans, this world was unfamiliar to him, and without his memory he had only his instinct and his reason to guide him. And they urged caution.

Even in the days before the war and plague, the famines and droughts, and the emergence of the supernaturals, rare books were things to be killed for. And afterward, when humans burned them to stay warm or destroyed them because of what they contained, they'd become even more valuable.

It made no sense that a place like this—a shop where something as old and valuable as a tome bearing the stamp of the Knights Templar—would be located here. If Araña were with him—

Tir snarled, cutting off the thought. Already he was too deeply entangled in the silken webs of desire she'd spun around him. He was here and he would recover the book without her aid.

Still, he used caution in approaching the shop and stopped just beyond the doorway. The smell of books greeted him, musty and old, reminding him for a moment of the catacombs that had been his prison for centuries.

There were symbols carved into the door frame, generalized protections all the buildings in Oakland seemed to have and others that made him think of those he'd seen at the occult shop. Neither kind caused him concern. It was the glyphs interspersed among them that reached into his darkened memory, as if they'd prod him to—

He clenched his fists in frustration. The knowledge remained submerged, and the only way he would recover it was to step through the door, past the sigils, and gain possession of the book.

Tir reached with his mind for the emotions inside the shop and found awareness. Someone inside the building knew he was at the door, but they neither feared him entering nor anticipated it. If there was curiosity about his purpose or why he lingered beyond the heavily barred screen door, then it was buried in other thoughts.

Safe enough, Tir thought, glancing one last time at the glyphs stirring his memory before entering the building.

The musty, dry-parchment and old-book smell was magnified inside the crowded shop. The air was thick with it, yellowed by the diffuse light coming from lanterns holding spell flame instead of true fire.

There was little room for anything other than shelves. They reached from floor to ceiling, creating tiny aisleways that would slow down a man of his size and keep anyone larger from exploring the stacks altogether.

A heavy, battered wooden desk was the only furniture visible. It was pushed into a corner to the left of the doorway but seemed to serve only as a place for books waiting to be shelved. If there was a method governing how the books were organized, it wasn't immediately obvious to Tir.

He expected the shopkeeper to emerge from the stacks, but when one didn't, Tir chose the middle aisle and moved deeper into the bookstore. His shirt grew dusty as he brushed against the tomes on either side of him.

Unlike those in the occult shop, the books here were mundane and not magical. History and literature. Science and politics. Texts that might have been in any library or home in the days before The Last War.

He reached the end of the row of shelves to find the aisleway he'd been traveling along blocked by the beginning of another row. A narrow gap allowed him to step to the side and proceed forward, giving the shop the feel of a maze-like warren.

Tir frowned, as puzzled by the shop's layout as he had been by its location. It seemed to invite theft—or worse.

He kept going and finally emerged from the tight confines of book-laden shelves, only to find even more books, though these were scattered on tables in an area set aside for restoration. An old man glanced up, his gray-green eyes faded with advanced age.

"What can I help you with?" he asked, the hand holding needle and thread pausing over the book he tended.

Tir moved to the table where the old man worked. Up close he seemed even more frail and defenseless. "I've come for a book that's in your possession."

"Do you need me to find it for you?"

It took effort for Tir to tamp down the wild surge of emotion. For centuries he'd dreamed of this moment. "If you could."

The bookseller placed the needle and thread on the table and came around to stand next to Tir. "Describe it as best you can."

"Easy enough. It bears the stamp of the Knights Templar on its cover."

The bookseller startled, then shook his head. "I don't know how you learned I was in possession of that particular tome, but I'm afraid it's already been sold."

Tir's hands curled into fists. How could the book be gone when Saril had seen it only a short time ago and assured him before he left that she saw only the present with her gift?

"Who is the buyer?"

"Virgilio Cortez."

"He's here in Oakland?"

His question was met with a puzzled expression. "Virgilio rarely leaves Los Angeles."

Sudden insight made Tir ask, "Has he taken possession of the book?"

"Not yet."

Satisfaction purred through Tir, though he continued to be puzzled by the shopkeeper's lack of concern for his own safety. "Then I will see the book."

The old man shook his head. "That's not possible. Virgilio is quite strict in his requirements. Items purchased for his private collection are taken out of circulation immediately. The only way I can allow you access is if he or his designated servant grants me permission to do it."

Tir's hand dropped to the knife strapped to his thigh, Araña's words sliding through his mind. *I don't draw a weapon unless I'm prepared to use it.*

"You will show me the book."

He let the old man hear the promise of death in his voice. But some unexpected, foreign impulse made him add, "And I will protect you from the consequences of it."

There was the briefest flickering of fear in the bookseller, as though his advanced age made the prospect of death's embrace frightening only at the gateway of its claiming. Stooped shoulders straightened, a signal he intended to meet his fate bravely. "I can't allow you to see it without Virgilio's blessing."

Tir pulled the knife from its sheath. Centuries of captivity darkened his mind, renewing the hatred in his soul and reminding him of his pledge to seek vengeance. He would do what was necessary in order to gain his freedom. Pain could make even the most devout of humans break.

The catacombs had once rung with their screams and tortured admissions of manufactured guilt. And he had offered this man a choice when he himself had never been offered one.

"Last chance," he said, voice guttural, harsh.

The old man started to speak. Whatever he might have said was lost in the opening of the steel door, in his sudden, deep fear as a pregnant woman entered the back room, her greeting of "Thierry" cut off, strangled.

Here is a weapon I can use against him, Tir thought. But before the intention could take root, a black-haired, brown-skinned girl-child slipped inside, stopping Tir's heart with her likeness to Araña.

A blink and the child's features became her own. But it was too late. The image of Araña growing heavy with his child, bearing a daughter that looked as she did, had shocked him to his core and scattered the hate festering in his soul.

Tir sheathed the knife, knowing Araña would turn away from him and accept death rather than welcome him in her arms if he harmed this woman and child whose only crime was being loved by the bookseller.

He would gain the book by another means, he decided, and thought instantly of Araña's picking the locks, freeing him of his shackles.

He was reminded of his own pronouncement at the stream. *I believe I'll find what I seek in Oakland. Otherwise you wouldn't have found your way into my dreams.*

The bookseller said, "Talk to Draven. Perhaps there's some service you can perform for him in exchange for his intercession with Virgilio. Only Virgilio and his High Servant have the combination to the safe the book is in."

Tir gave a curt nod, his eyes quickly scanning the room and finding a line of safes set into a wall. He didn't know who Draven was. It didn't matter.

Araña had lived among thieves. She was one. If she couldn't open the safe, then she could help him locate someone who could.

Tir left the shop through the steel door set in the back wall. He hurried toward the healer's house, telling himself his rush was dictated by what he'd found at L'Antiquaire. But the stirring in his cock and the worry in his heart called him a liar.

ENTERING the witches' house again was harder, so much harder than stepping into it the first time. The paintings and antiques had no power to distract Araña, and though she forced her hands to hang loosely at her sides—away from the knives—she doubted she was successful in appearing relaxed.

She expected Annalise to lead her to the parlor again. Instead the witch took her deeper into the house, only stopping when they arrived at a sigil-painted door with a bloodred pentacle in its center.

Magic hung thick and heavy in the air, as if centuries of conjuring had soaked into the wood before spilling out into the space in front of the door.

When Annalise opened it, revealing a narrow, dark stairway leading downward into utter darkness, Araña took an involuntary step backward. Despite her time with Matthew and Erik, the fear beaten and prayed into her during her formative years returned as if she'd never been free of it.

Hell and damnation waited at the bottom of the stairs. It waited for anyone who took up with witches and played in their dark magic.

Araña could almost see Hell's flames shadow-dancing on the walls, black and hungry for her soul. The prospect of taking the first step downward made her skin crawl and grow clammy, threatening her resolve to gain control of the demon gift.

"Levanna waits below," Annalise said, voice empty of inflection.

Araña's stomach knotted, forcing the acid-hot taste of fear into her mouth, and without her meaning them to her hands curled around the knife hilts.

The witch said, "Only agreements entered into long ago spared your life earlier today. They won't protect you a second time. A single human life span passes without notice to beings whose existence spans eternity. Failed tools and plans are easily set aside and replaced by new ones."

Araña's fingers tightened on the smooth leather of the hilts before she made them uncurl and ordered her hands away from the false security of the knives. She closed her mind to fear and blocked out the voices from the past, the sermons shouted from the pulpit and delivered with the lash of a cane.

Her reasons for seeking out the witch hadn't changed. Levi would die because of her unless she gained some control over her gift. Her next victim could easily be Tir.

She took the first step downward. Then a second. And a third. Fully expecting Annalise to close the door and trap her in darkness.

But if the witch was tempted, she didn't act on it before Araña reached the bottom of the stairs and found a hallway instead of a room.

A single candle beckoned at the end of it, bloodred, the flame whispering, *Come to me.*

It was like a vision summons, only Araña's body answered instead of her soul, moving steadily forward, unwilling to turn back or deny the fire's command.

Her heart thundered, not the phantom beat she imagined in the dark center of the flame, but the real squeeze and release of muscle.

The Wainwright matriarch waited in a room of flickering candles set at each star-point of the pentacle drawn on the floor. She was draped in black, moon-faced and milky-eyed, like a spider waiting in a web. "So you returned. Perhaps you're not a foolish child after all."

"Will you help me gain control of my gift?" Araña asked, her throat so dry it took effort to push the words into the air between them.

"You have to enter the place where the Spiders weave if you want to learn."

Araña's eyes glanced at the candles, positioned one at each apex of the pentagram. If she'd allowed herself to think about it at all, she would have guessed she'd have to go to the very place she'd spent a lifetime trying to avoid.

She had no way of knowing if the matriarch would lie or tell the truth, but she couldn't stop herself from asking, "Will I be able to undo something that hasn't come to pass?"

"Perhaps. Perhaps not. That is not for me to say. Where you go is not a place I can enter now. Another waits to teach you the things you need to know."

A chill swept through Araña as she imagined herself coming face-to-face with the demon responsible for the spider mark. "Who?"

Goose bumps rose on her arms with the witch's laugh. "Nothing you can offer is worth what it would cost me to speak that particular name out loud. If you want answers and knowledge, then enter the place where the Spiders weave." A gnarled hand emerged from the black folds of her garment. In it was a vial full of liquid. "I am here to assist you in finding the true gateway and to ensure the shell of flesh so painstakingly created to house your spirit will not host another's."

Araña felt as though a wall of ice encased her heart. A silent scream of *no* came from the depths of her soul.

Levanna lifted the vial higher and the candlelight bounced off it, turning dark liquid into a thousand strands of color. "The choice is yours. My obligation extends no further than offering you a way to enter the place of Spiders and keeping your physical body safe until your return."

Araña's gaze flicked to a candle flame and back to the vial. "I can enter on my own, through the fire."

"That's your gift, to be able to enter a realm no human can. And your curse. To have the gift limited because you're bound to mortal flesh and can't enter it fully."

The witch indicated the pentacle drawn on the floor, serving as an altar much in the way the shamaness's fetish-surrounded dirt floor had. Wax pooled at the bases of the candles and spread like blood-stains, reminding Araña of the blood she'd willingly shed in order to enter the ghostlands.

She thought of Matthew's use of their code to tell her he and Erik were truly okay, and Erik's parting words. *Don't let your courage fail you.*

"What's in the vial?"

"A rare poison. It separates the soul from the body."

The ice encasing Araña's heart so each beat was labored spread, freezing her lungs. "*Bòcòs* use it for creating zombies."

"Yes. But it won't be used for that purpose this day. Choose. The spell allowing you to safely enter and return through the gateway will last only as long as the candles burn."

Araña looked at them again, seeking their hearts. Unlike the candle in the hallway that had beckoned her forward, whispering *Come to me*, the ones set at each apex of the circle-inscribed star were silent, leaving the choice up to her.

She wanted to turn away and hurry from the house. She couldn't.

The reasons for coming to the Wainwright witch hadn't changed. Her ignorance when it came to her gift had entangled Matthew and Erik in this web. It had led to Rebekka's capture and would lead to Levi's death. She held out her hand for the vial.

"You will pass quickly into the world beyond," the witch said. "I won't catch you if you choose to remain standing."

Araña took the vial but couldn't bring herself to sit at the matriarch's feet. She moved away, stopping in the center of the pentacle.

Against her fingers, she could feel tiny lines etched into the glass. Bile rose in her throat as she opened the vial. She doubted she could physically swallow its contents—until the cognac scent reached her.

The poison might have been designed for her. It made her think of home—the cabin and not the boat—of times spent in front of the fireplace, curled on a chair across from Erik, both of them reading while Matthew worked on whatever project held his interest.

Poisonous or not, she lifted the vial to her lips, drinking its contents before lying down. But as numbness came, starting with her limbs and moving into her core, it wasn't Matthew and Erik she thought of, it was Tir.

Until she'd been forced to join the strand of her life to his, she'd never known the ecstasy and pleasure of touch. She'd thought she craved it then, but that desire was nothing compared to what she felt now.

Her heart rate sped up then abruptly slowed as the poison reached her chest. Blackness formed at the edges of her consciousness, her body trying to spare her from the panic of not being able to breathe. The darkness moved in. It reminded her of the sea surging ahead of Aziel in the ghostlands to reclaim Erik's and Matthew's spirits.

She thought fleetingly of the spider, and knew true fear when, for the first time in her life, she couldn't feel it at all. And then, just as she became aware that her heart had slowed to the point where it didn't seem to beat at all, the witch loomed above her holding an unlit candle, her words nearly drowned out by the babbling stream of sibilant whispers. "Call the fire."

With a thought Araña did. Flame leapt from each of the five candles at the apex of the pentagram to form a sixth point above her, a fiery gateway she slid into as easily as if she were returning home.

Unbidden the dream came, the first dream, the spider's birth dream—only it was different than before. There was no separation of soul and mark, no it and her. She and the spider were the same, a thing without form in the dark heart of hellfire.

Around her it hissed and crackled. It roared with fury and power, with the desire to destroy as well as create, and she burned with it.

Into the fire flew a raven. The black of its body absorbed the heat and its eyes became glowing pits of red.

Its presence created a storm of howling and shrieking. Flames leapt higher, as if trying to draw its attention. But it ducked and wheeled, ignoring them as it dodged grasping hands of fire and came unerringly to her.

Its beak opened, and she filled with hungry anticipation, knowing somehow that when it spoke her soul name, it would separate her from the fire and wrench her from the place where all life began.

There was no memory of a journey, no sense of a physical form, but Araña saw the world as if through the eyes of the raven. It perched on a limb outside an open window.

A deep, unnamed dread filled her as she recognized the settlement where she'd spent the first twelve years of her life. Always before, the spider's birth dream ended just after the raven's call gave it form, merging with the memory of pain as it burned its way outward to appear on her flesh. Now it continued.

Two men stood at the bedside of a woman who'd already been

dressed for burial by the midwife who hovered near a beautifully carved cradle. One was a church elder, the other a man who'd always shunned her.

Gingham curtains fluttered peacefully, in sharp contrast to the words being spoken in the room by the younger man. "Let Satan take the child the same as he claimed the mother giving birth to it. It was conceived in sin. All I have to do is look at it to know it isn't mine."

"You'll damn yourself by calling on Satan," the elder said. "The child is innocent of the mother's sins."

"If it lives, I won't claim or raise it."

"If it lives, I'll see that it's raised by those who won't spoil it by sparing the rod as happened with the mother."

The raven hopped along the branch, its movement drawing the attention of the people in the room.

"A bad omen," the midwife murmured. "Death waiting on an unclean soul."

The man whose pale, silver-blond hair was almost the same shade as his dead wife's, visibly shuddered. The church elder said, "Superstition is blasphemy against the Lord." But he touched one hand to the man's shoulder and extended the other to the midwife. "Join me in praying for forgiveness for any evil that's entered our thoughts because of this birth and death, and for the child, that it will be welcomed into God's loving arms should it not survive."

They prayed, and filed from the room at the conclusion of it, none of them glancing backward at either the corpse awaiting burial or the infant left unattended a few feet away from its dead mother.

The raven jumped to the windowsill. It cocked its head, listening for the sound of approaching humans. Hearing none, it soared across the room to perch on the cradle.

Araña saw it then, why the man was so sure the child wasn't his. Instead of pale skin and silver-blond hair, the infant was dark, its hair and eyes black.

Its mouth opened and closed in a cry too weak to hear. Its tiny hands were balled into fists as if it fought to live even as the raspy sound of its faint breath marked the struggle.

The raven opened its beak and emitted a harsh cry, the sound of it carrying a word buried deep inside, a name. Araña.

She felt herself taking form, emerging from the raven's mouth as a spider, sliding downward toward the baby on a fine silken thread.

The infant stilled the moment she touched its skin. Its death the harbinger of her birth.

She felt the flutter of its soul departing as in spider form she crawled into the baby's open mouth and took up residence in a shell of flesh that wasn't her own.

There was the hard kick of a heartbeat returning. The gasp of lungs filling. And then a cry announcing her arrival as the human soul hadn't had the strength to do.

No! Araña screamed silently, denial filling her, driving her out of the scene. Breaking her contact with it as though she'd been riding the thread of her own life in the same way she'd done hundreds of others.

For a shimmering instant she was without true form, as she always had been in the spider's place, but then the physical shell she still wanted to believe was her own gathered around her, shocking her.

Instinctively she sought the mark with her thoughts, and her horror deepened when she felt her cells start to break up—as if they'd re-form into a spider in the same way the demon Abijah became the scorpion.

"No!" she shouted, and her voice joined the whispering stream around her, drawing her attention away from the whirlpool turmoil of her own emotions and to the tapestry in front of her. It extended for as far as she could see, its detail sharper, its texture richer than the carpeted pattern she'd glimpsed the first time she willingly sought this place.

"Your time here is finite," a voice behind her said. "The candles in the other world burn down rapidly."

Araña whirled to find a woman standing there in the robes of a desert dweller, the fabric concealing all but a dark slash of face and eyes as black as Araña's own. "Who are you?"

Nineteen

THE woman tugged at the material covering her head, pulling it away to reveal features nearly identical to Araña's, save for the wrinkles at the corners of her eyes and the spidery threads of gray through her black hair.

"I am the one who first gave you life, only to witness your being slain by the god's warriors, your soul cast back into the fire until a Raven could find the name forged for you, and you could be reborn—not as you once were, but to serve our kind in a different manner."

"No," Araña said, denying the woman's words. She'd accepted the mark, accepted that it tainted her soul by turning her into a tool for the demon, but this—

"No." She couldn't be a demon.

"It doesn't matter whether you believe or not. Your life serves us. You live bound to human flesh by the will of The Prince."

Ice slid through Araña's veins at the mention of the name, but also a thin, desperate sliver of hope. How often had she felt the lash of a cane against her back and heard the fervent prayers accompanying it in an effort to drive out the taint placed on her soul by the Prince of Lies, the Great Deceiver? She had no reason to trust the being standing in front of her, no reason to think the demon's words or appearance were truth.

Araña forced her mind closed to everything but the purpose that had made her seek out the Wainwright witch and freely swallow poison so she could enter this place. "Will you teach me how to use my gift?" *My curse.*

The demon pulled the folds of material back in place, leaving only the thin strip of flesh and dark eyes revealed. "I will give you the knowledge you need to possess. Come. Not much time remains."

She turned and walked alongside the tapestry. Araña followed, realizing as she did so that she could sense the passage of time vividly now. They were moving from the past into the present, the babble of indecipherable voices growing louder with each step.

The demon stopped in front of a section of the weave. And somehow, Araña knew if she could find her own soul thread and touch it, she would see herself lying in the center of the witch's pentacle with the Wainwright matriarch standing guard. She looked ahead, into the future, and the patterns shifted subtly, then shifted again, as if despite what might be done in this place, life could not be so easily controlled.

"Until you are freed from the shackle of human flesh and able to exist in a noncorporeal form," the demon said, "you won't enter this place again or see the complete weave of lives. Your gift will remain limited."

Training and the hardships she'd endured growing up kept Araña from reacting to the comment, from revealing she'd seen this tapestry before, as a carpet sweeping out in front of her.

The demon's hand lifted to hover just in front of it. "Do you hear the whisper of their true names?"

"I hear a rushing stream."

"Choose a thread and focus on it, but don't allow yourself to touch it mentally."

Araña felt a trickle of sweat down her back. A lifetime of resistance paralyzed her. Acid burned her throat at the thought of destroying a life.

She swallowed and focused on an orange-green thread with hints of brown. It was a struggle not to merge into it. But slowly the babble of voices faded away, leaving only one, an unknown man's name. It repeated itself over and over again, as if death would come if it ever ceased being spoken.

Araña pulled away from it mentally and turned toward the demon. "How can I find a particular soul if I can't see the pattern?"

"Your reach is short unless you travel deeper and deeper into the heart of the flame. Physical proximity is compounded by the ties those souls have to others."

The answer sickened Araña, but it also explained why she'd so often seen the damage she wrought. Those who were close to her would always be at risk if she couldn't control the gift. "And if I want to change a pattern?"

"Not all of them can be changed. Some are held in place by powers other than ours, just as some threads can't be seen or, if seen, can't be touched. To predict how a single change will affect an entire pattern takes centuries of study by those dedicated to it. In your human life span, without the ability to enter this place as you are now, you will never be able to accomplish it. The candles marking your time here have almost burned out. Tell me which weave you wish to alter and I will use it in teaching you."

Araña's stomach muscles tightened hard enough to cramp. Ruthless fingers squeezed her heart. She was terrified that telling the demon would lead to something worse for Levi or Rebekka. But there was no real choice. And so she revealed what she'd done when she entered the vision place in an effort to help Rebekka.

"To change his fate you must start at the outcome you wish to undo and work backward, searching through all the strands and picking the one which will divert the course of the Were's life if it's touched to his. It's a complex task and your time is short—as it will always be. Your human body will draw you back to it with pain."

The demon stepped forward, into the future, and pointed, saying, "Here is the Were's thread."

Araña recognized it and understood by its abrupt end that she was looking at the instant of Levi's death. Another thread ended at the same time, the black-and-gray of the dark-haired stranger tasered along with Levi.

Near them, entangled but not ending, were two threads. The guardsmen.

Jurgen and the stranger.

She focused on them one at a time. The red-mottled-with-black strand belonged to the stranger. Salim.

The purple-twisted-with-blue belonged to the man she'd vowed to kill. Jurgen.

Araña followed Levi's strand backward, into the past, and found her own at the moment where he and Rebekka had been waiting for her in the woods.

Her thread called to her like a living flame, and it was almost impossible to resist merging with it. She wanted to follow it to the place it originated. To see for herself that the scene following the spider's birth dream of fire was real, and not a demon trick, a lie meant to turn her into a more willing tool.

Instead she went forward. She saw the blue-black of Tir's at the place she'd seen him in her vision, then again at the ambush site.

His life thread disappeared and reappeared only when it was alongside hers, often so close it bled into the hues of her flame-colored thread. *Some are held in place by powers other than ours, just as some threads can't be seen or, if seen, can't be touched.* She thought Tir's supernatural nature was the reason his was so elusive.

Araña moved forward, to the moment where she and Tir and

Levi were at the healer's house. Tir's thread remained hidden beyond that, what happened after he left to recover the *Constellation* a mystery.

But in the future she saw how Jurgen's soul strand paralleled the black-haired stranger who'd died with Levi, crossing it once before both the stranger's and Levi's threads ended.

She found the flame of her thread on the tapestry. It didn't intersect with Levi's again. Or wouldn't unless she altered the pattern. And altering the pattern was what she intended, that and killing Jurgen.

Araña held a part of herself back as she mentally touched the gold-brown of Levi's soul. He was at the brothel door, waiting or leaving or simply standing guard, it didn't matter.

She reached out her hand to physically touch the flame color of her own strand. The demon said, "With that choice you will return to your flesh prison without knowing what changes you wrought."

"Will I encounter Levi at this place in the future?"

"Yes."

"Then that'll be enough," Araña said, trusting in the outcome she'd accomplish with her knives far more than in the demon standing next to her or the gift that had always been a curse.

She altered the future by touching her life to Levi's. There was only the briefest impression. Early dusk. Levi opening the brothel door into the alleyway. A soiled newspaper tumbling over her foot. And then she felt a shock of joy as name and spirit and body fused together, rousing her as the five candles on the floor around her guttered and went out.

SHE was back. Tir felt the turmoil of Araña's emotions as soon as he reached the rubble-free ground marking the beginnings of the healer's yard.

Relief swept into him that she'd returned safely, followed by heat, lust, a tide of feelings that began and ended with her, and had since the moment she first breached his mental shields to invade his dreams.

The promise of freedom made every sensation all the headier. His cock throbbed, thick and full from the knowledge he was only steps away from her.

He'd take her as soon as he got inside. Then take her again before they left for the bookseller's shop.

It was a few hours less than a day since he'd been with her last, but it was too long. He was anxious to be inside her, to have her beneath him, thighs splayed, midnight black eyes heated in sensuous welcome.

He jogged the last few feet and took the stairs in a leap, only to halt at the front door and remember how he'd prowled the house earlier when he found her missing. How her absence had given birth to something dark and primitive, something that demanded she be punished for defying him when he'd ordered her to remain in the house until he returned.

She was mortal. Human. Vulnerable.

A blink and she could be gone from his life forever. With his blood and his vigilance, she could remain by his side for eternity.

Possessiveness and desire were a liquid-fire heat pouring into his bloodstream and pooling in his testicles, making his penis pulse so violently a drop of arousal escaped its tip.

His mind flashed back to the child and the pregnant woman at L'Antiquaire, only it was Araña's face overlaid onto the stranger's and onto the little girl's. He wanted a child with her in the future. When he was free, his need for vengeance satisfied.

Tir unlocked the door and entered the house. She'd cleaned since returning. The scent of wood soap and fresh air made him think of the *Constellation*.

She'd showered. Moments earlier. He smelled shampoo and felt the fine hint of mist against his skin.

He didn't call out. She knew he was back. He sensed it in her, but instead of challenge or sexual invitation, it was confusion, distress, the longing for comfort that assailed him.

Tir stripped the shirt off as he crossed the tiny living room and went into the bedroom. He nearly doubled over at the sight of her standing naked in front of a mirror secured to the wall.

"What's wrong?" he asked, meeting her gaze, no longer able to bear the confinement of trousers when his cock ached unmercifully.

He kicked off his shoes. The machete fell to the floor as he crossed to her. As did his pants.

"I went to the witch's house," she said, their eyes locking in the mirror.

The desire to punish her for worrying him returned. But the need to touch her, to hold her in his arms and feel the press of her skin to his, overrode it.

Tir's hands went to her waist, then up, to cover her breasts. The hitch of her breath inflamed him further. The way she melted into him very nearly had him burying his face against her neck and finding her opening with his cock.

"You should have waited for me to accompany you."

"I couldn't."

His fingers tightened on her nipples in rebuttal. She argued with the press and rub of her buttocks against his hardened shaft, by covering his hands with hers.

"What happened?" he asked, no longer able to resist kissing her neck, her shoulder, brushing his lips over the spider that appeared like a deadly pet, also seeking his attention.

She shuddered. Her distress spiked. Her eyes became haunted.

"Tell me," he said, letting her feel the hint of teeth, a silent promise he wouldn't let her evade his question as he had the last time they were together.

"Do you think it's possible I'm a demon?"

Surprise allowed the laugh to escape. That was his only excuse. She stiffened in his arms, but her hope wiped away any affront his reaction might have warranted. In the mirror her gaze flicked to the hated collar around his neck then met his again. "You knew Levi was Were and Rebekka one of the human gifted after encountering them at the ambush site," she said.

His lips went to her ear. He traced the delicate outline of it before sliding his tongue in and out of the sensitive canal.

She arched, pushing hardened nipples against his palms and smooth buttocks against his groin. The longing for comfort he'd felt in her earlier melted into the need to feel him inside her, the desire to be so closely entwined it would be difficult to tell where one of them ended and the other began.

Tir moaned, wanting the same thing, nearly yielding to the demands of his body and hers. "You're human. Fully human."

He had never thought the words would give him such satisfaction. But at the moment he found her mortality arousing, her fragile, feminine form unbearably pleasing.

"Then how do you explain the mark?"

He shrugged. "A geis perhaps. Or a curse. Now tell me why you think you're a demon."

Araña shivered; her cunt clenched and nipples ached. The birth dream seemed just that—a dream, an illusion so far removed from reality it no longer mattered.

Lies built on truths, especially hidden ones, were more powerful than those formed without basis. Looking back on it, she wondered if perhaps a part of her had always known the man and woman raising her weren't truly her parents, despite what she called them.

No matter what she did and how hard she tried to be what they wanted, there'd been underlying coldness and suspicion, a reserving of love. It had been easy to attribute it to the demon mark, but now . . .

If it lives, I won't claim or raise it.

If it lives, I'll see that it's raised by those who won't spoil it by sparing the rod, as happened with the mother.

That much of what she'd seen in the vision place she believed. Her back bore the evidence of it. And Tir's suggestion of a geis made her think of her birth father's curse. *Let Satan take the child the same as he claimed the mother giving birth to it.*

How could this not be her body? She knew every inch of it, its strengths and weaknesses, what it was capable of doing, of enduring, its craving for touch—for Tir—*her* craving.

"It doesn't matter," she said. She'd accomplished what she set out to do when she went to the witch's house.

Tir's fingers claimed her nipples again in a punishing grip. Her cunt wept from it, wept with the need to have him inside her, and had since the moment he stepped through the front door.

"I already intend to punish you for leaving when I told you to remain here until I returned," he said, sending erotic fear whipping through her. "Do you want to make it worse?"

Lust coiled in her belly, a dark need she wouldn't have thought possible, given the scars marking her back. "The witch opened a gateway to the place the visions take me. When I entered it I saw . . . my own birth. I *was* the spider, a demon taking possession of a human body, a newborn child's body. I felt her die as soon as I touched her. I—"

"Have no reason to trust a witch," Tir said, his hand sweeping downward, over her belly to cup her mound.

His fingers delved into her slit. His palm rubbed over her stiffened clit. "Does it feel as though this body belongs to another?"

"No," she said on a moan, grinding against him, the muscles of her sheath clenching hungrily on him. "No."

In the mirror his face became taut, his eyes nearly as dark as hers. His mouth found the topmost scar on her back and his tongue traced its length, sending a lash of ecstasy to the soles of her feet. "Would a demon allow itself to be punished so severely?"

"I killed them in the end, the night I was branded."

He sucked. Bit. Left his own mark on her. "If they still lived, they would meet the same fate at my hands."

She whimpered in protest as his fingers left her channel. Closed her eyes as they plunged in again.

The sharp sting of his teeth preceded his command. "Watch."

She watched. Her breath growing short with each fuck of his fingers into her sheath. Each rough caress of his palm against the tiny head of her clit.

Her hips jerked. Her skin grew slick with sweat.

"Please," she whispered.

And he asked, "Would a demon beg?"

"No." And as if to prove she was no demon, he made her beg repeatedly, taking her to the edge of release and backing away, tightening his grip on her to keep her a prisoner in front of the mirror until need was her only reality.

But even when he finally allowed her to orgasm, the need wasn't satisfied. She turned in his arms and pressed her mouth to his, rubbing her passion-slick folds against his cock as she undid his braid so his hair cascaded down his back. "The sheets on the bed are clean. I want you inside me. Take me there."

Tir cupped her cheek and the spider came to him. His cock bathed in her liquid desire. His buttocks clenched as he fought the temptation to lift her in his arms and carry her to the bed.

Her command was nearly impossible to disobey. He wanted to feel her underneath him, wanted nothing more than to slide into the heated paradise of her channel.

A glance at the waiting bed nearly undid him. Punishment can wait, his cock urged.

Tir touched his lips to hers. "I told you to remain here. There's a price on your head. And despite the spider, you're mortal. Human." *And I can't lose you.*

"I had to go."

It was her lack of remorse that tipped the scales. His hands went to her sides, then pushed under the curtain of her hair.

She shivered when his fingers traced over the first of her scars.

Fear spiked through her, but he knew it wasn't memories of being whipped as a child that prompted it.

Her fear was erotic, the emotion generating it primal, dark, exquisitely feminine—and he felt the instant she controlled it, backed away from it. "Did you recover the *Constellation*?"

Tir laughed, both at her question and her mistaken notion he'd allow her to escape the hunger that mirrored his own.

"Of course. The vice lord guards your boat, though he was careful to limit his obligation. It begins and ends with protecting the *Constellation* from theft or damage. He's not responsible for determining who has a right to board or for keeping its occupants safe."

"That's good enough."

"Yes." His hands caressed her back, his fingers hesitating over each scar ridge to count them.

"Fourteen," he murmured when he reached her shoulders, his eyes settling on the pants she'd left draped over a chair, on the thin leather belt she wore. "No one will ever have the right to touch you this way again. Except me."

"Tir—"

"Tell me you don't want it. Tell me you don't want to replace the memories of those whippings with the punishment I intend."

She shivered. Her scent intensified, as did the desire surging back and forth between them, unchecked by any mental barrier.

A step, a quick tug, and he held the belt. "Put your hands on the mirror."

Dark, dark eyes met his. Flashed with the brief consideration of defying him, then were hidden by her lashes before she turned and obeyed.

He stepped forward to push her hair over her shoulders and nearly came at the image of her in the mirror. She was the picture of submission with her head bowed. But she was also primal woman, the original seductress with her hair caressing the curves of her body, drawing his eyes downward to her glistening, swollen folds.

If he touched her again, he wouldn't have the strength to resist taking her. Already the delay was costing him, punishing him with testicles pulled tightly against his body, with the threat of greater agony if he didn't find his own release soon.

He stepped away from her. Lifted his arm and brought the belt down across her back, checking his strength so pain bled into pleasure for her.

"One," he said, then struck again, continuing to count out her punishment with each rise and fall of his arm.

Her soft cries were a white-hot lash across his soul, the sight of her wet inner thighs and eager, trembling body a torment that turned it into a feat of endurance to reach the number he'd settled on.

With each strike, the past lost its power over Araña. Each of the lashes Tir administered was like a lick of flame, burning away her memories. Eradicating the pain and humiliation. The fear and overwhelming guilt of having her soul tainted.

Beatings given in chilly silence or ranted condemnation, done with a cold heart and unforgiving hand, were a nightmare replaced by fantasy.

Need spiked through her each time Tir brought the leather of the belt across her back, his harsh breathing echoing her own, telling her he was just as affected by the punishment as she was.

It was freeing. Equally enslaving. And as her nipples tightened to the point of pain and her channel spasmed, she could smile while thinking about something that had once terrified her. She could look forward to something that had once made her hang her head in shame.

From Tir, she would welcome punishment. Come to crave it.

"Fourteen," Tir said, finally able to drop the leather belt.

His skin was slick with sweat, his chest rising and falling as quickly as hers. With a groan he pulled her against him, buried his face in the silky blackness of her hair and pressed kisses to her neck, her shoulders, the scars and heated flesh of her back.

Her shiver mimicked his. Her hunger was part of his.

"Please, Tir," she whispered. "Don't make me wait any longer. Come inside me."

He carried her to the bed and followed her down onto it, rolled so she straddled him, the silky length of her hair against his thighs and stomach an erotic whip making his penis pulse and leak. Her fingers entwined with his, holding him to the mattress in sensual enslavement, and he allowed it.

She leaned forward and his mouth answered the silent summons of hers. Their tongues tangled in an ecstasy of reunion as she positioned her opening against his cock head. It was like being engulfed in flame, caught in a primordial force that could level mountains or create them. A thrust and they were joined, mindless to anything but the urgency to move, to lose themselves in each other, to become a single entity bound together in pleasure.

REBEKKA had paced the walkway on top of the inner wall for so long the lions no longer looked up as she passed their enclosures. She'd agonized and argued with herself—not just about Eston's fate, but hers as well. She'd tortured herself with images of what would happen if the patriarch decided to turn her over to Father Ursu. Gifted or not, in the end The Iberá would do it if she didn't accept his aid and his cause.

What was it about the prisoner that made him so important? Anton Barlowe's interest she attributed to his desire to strike out at the Church and the Iberás, because between them, they'd clean up the guard and work toward revoking the sanctioned lawlessness of the red zone.

But what was Father Ursu's interest in the prisoner? It was more than simply helping a wealthy patron attain something he wanted, it had to be for the priest to be so insistent on questioning her.

Rebekka closed her eyes and lifted her face toward the sun, hoping it would warm the ice at her core. Images played through her mind, starting with the messenger arriving at the brothel with the witch's token.

It all seemed like a delicately woven trap, yet looking back on it, she couldn't have made any other choice but to help Araña. If she hadn't, then Anton would be in possession of the dragon lizards and Levi's brother would be dead.

She opened her eyes at the sound of an approaching car. Her heart rate sped up at the sight of the sedan bearing the emblem of the guard.

The gate leading to the section of the estate reserved for the private soldiers swung open as the car reached it. A uniformed officer emerged from the building, as if he'd been expecting the car's arrival.

He opened the back door and Enzo stepped out. "Are the men gathered for the briefing?"

"Yes."

"We'll get started as soon as I speak with The Iberá. It might be advisable to take the healer, and arrange for Father Ursu's involvement as well."

Rebekka's breath froze in her chest. The general handed the officer a folder.

"There are aerial photographs of the gifted area inside. Go ahead and show them to the men. I've marked the healer's house. We're in luck. She lives close to the red zone border and in an area that's not been extensively reclaimed."

Rebekka remained motionless, not even daring to breathe. Her heart thundered as she tried to convince herself there was nothing in her home that would lead to Levi or the brothel.

Enzo disappeared through the trees shielding the main house from view. The officer retreated into the soldiers' building.

Only then did Rebekka dare leave her position on the wall, hoping to hide. Hoping that if a search was initiated for her, she'd somehow manage to get into the patriarch's study and have enough time to use the token to summon help.

Twenty

ARAÑA lazily traced one of Tir's tattoos. In his arms she felt safe, complete, at peace. Time stopped when they came together physically, forming a wall of contentment that separated her from fear and reality.

"You were gone a long time," she murmured, pressing a kiss to his collarbone.

"Are you hoping for additional punishment by reminding me of your own absence?"

Her cunt spasmed, and the telltale escape of arousal answered his question. Feminine pleasure surged through her when he rolled on top of her with a moan, as if he couldn't resist the call of her body to his.

Tir pinned her hands to the mattress. The feel of her underneath him never failed to stir his possessiveness. The sweet smell of her desire was a distraction he seemed destined to battle endlessly.

He should have been completely sated, but the more he had her, the greater his craving became. "I came back for you after healing Rimmon's daughter, Saril. You weren't here, though since then you've cleaned the healer's house."

"Matthew's habit. He cleaned when he worried. Where did you go?"

"Saril is a Finder."

Araña's heart leapt against his chest as she understood the significance of his statement. Her joy washed through him, only to be followed by a wave of confusion as her gaze went to the sigil-inscribed band continuing to enslave him. "The translations didn't hold the answer?"

A muscle spasmed in his cheek as he thought of the unexpected arrival of the woman and child, and the image of Araña that had flashed into his mind in the shop. She weakened him. Because of her, he'd stayed his hand. He'd walked away instead of using a weapon presenting itself to him.

"I wasn't able to see the book containing them. They're in a safe and the shopkeeper claims only the buyer and his servant have the combination to it."

Araña's smile was sunshine arriving in a burst of joy. "What kind of safe?"

Her excited happiness was infectious. "You can open it?"

"Safes are what I do best. And alarm systems. They're the only things I could do faster than Matthew and Erik."

Tir realized that for the second time in as many minutes, she'd spoken of her family and the mention of their names didn't rake her with guilt and pain. He'd felt only a fleeting sadness, barely a shadow of emotion. Her visit to Annalise Wainwright had done some good then. "The witch helped you with your gift?"

"Yes."

"At what price?"

"None to me."

He didn't like the answer. "Whose then?"

Araña shivered. "A demon's, I think."

He liked that answer even less. "Promise you won't visit the witch again unless I'm with you."

"I don't intend to go back."

The truth but also a refusal. He rose onto his elbows, acutely aware of the feel of her flesh against his own, the ready willingness of his penis to lodge itself in her wet channel and extract a promise from her in a most pleasurable way.

"Araña," he started, only to feel the sharp spike of adrenaline piercing his mental shields and coming from beyond the house.

Tir acted instinctively, rolling to his feet and pulling Araña to hers. "Get dressed. We need to leave."

She obeyed without question, her movements smooth, efficient, well practiced.

They left by the back door, crossing the street in order to take cover among the houses too badly damaged to be reclaimed by other gifted. A moment later they heard the rumble of diesel engines approaching, converging on the house from all directions.

"We can't risk getting caught out in the open," Araña said, climbing through a thin curtain of vine covering what had once been an upper-story window.

Tir followed her into the cramped space. His fury stirred to life. If the Were had betrayed them—

Two sleek cars came into view, traveling toward the healer's house from opposite directions. Tir's attention was drawn to the flags fluttering from their antennas. Each bore a red lion rampant in an elaborate shield set against a gold backdrop.

The cars stopped at either end of the healer's house. Uniformed men got out of them and stood at the ready, the red lion sewn onto the front of their black shirts visible from a distance.

A final man joined them, this one wearing a guardsman's uniform, the decorations against his chest indicating he was a man of high rank. "Everyone is in position," he said. "Those of you using live ammunition fire only as a last resort. We hit with tranquilizers first—especially on the primary target and any Were that might be in there with him. Tasers are for backup. Use with caution. They might make the situation worse. Understood?"

There was a murmur of assent. Tir glanced at Araña to see if the words had carried to her as well. She gave a slight nod.

Moments later another car turned onto the street, black with heavily tinted windows. It stopped directly in front of the house. A chauffeur got out and opened the passenger door. Tir stiffened at the sight of the cassocked figure who emerged.

"Your men are ready, Enzo?" the priest asked in the same power-filled voice he remembered from the trapper's compound.

"They're ready."

The high-ranking guardsman drew his gun and signaled his men forward. They moved on the house with professional precision.

The locks on Rebekka's doors were no match for the tool one of the uniformed men used on them. And despite the seriousness of the situation, Tir smiled when he felt Araña's unwilling admiration of the man's skill and her covetous desire to possess the tool allowing for such easy access.

It was over within minutes. The men seemed to exit the healer's small house almost as soon as the last of them had passed through the doorway.

They took up positions near the cars they'd arrived in. The high-ranking guardsman was last to emerge, carrying the drawings Araña had done.

He stopped next to the priest. His face was grim.

"Cabot Lavene was killed the other day near the Mission," the guardsman said, showing the priest the first of the images before sliding it to the bottom. "This is Jurgen Reichs. He's one of those I've been watching. It won't be hard to prove his involvement with the maze."

That picture went to the bottom. The priest visibly stiffened at the final image, the one Tir knew belonged to Tomás. "Have your grandfather turn the girl over to the Church for questioning. Impress on him how dangerous it is to delay."

"I'll speak with him. In the meantime, I've left four of my men inside and ordered others into positions where they can watch the approaches to the house."

"Good. You'll be in touch with me later?"

"Yes, by phone if not in person. I'll press my grandfather to make the transfer before nightfall, but I suspect he'll put off a decision until the morning, arguing Tomás is safe enough as long as he remains at the estate."

The priest nodded then climbed into his chauffeured car. The others got into the cars that brought them, and a moment later the street was empty, the house left as a false beacon of security.

"They'll probably have men stationed near the red zone," Araña whispered. "And they'll position themselves along the most direct route, expecting us to come that way. If we keep to the ruins, we can cross the border—"

"There'll be no need to worry about them at all once the bookseller's safe is open and the translations are in my possession."

"And what about Levi? What if he comes here and walks into a trap meant for you?"

Tir's nostril's flared as he felt the weight of her judgment against him. He leaned forward abruptly and tangled his fingers in her hair. "What of the Were? In the forest he left me shackled for the guardsmen to find. He argued against freeing me."

"And you would have risked your life if your positions had been reversed? Your freedom when it seemed like a foolish waste? He could have turned us away last night or betrayed us. Instead he told you about Rimmon and what you might face when you went to recover the *Constellation*."

"Unless he provokes the men waiting in the house, he'll be tranquilized and captured. What then, Araña? Do you think he won't betray me in exchange for his own freedom and the healer's?"

The sting of her disappointment in him lashed across his soul. She said, "These are your enemies. Not theirs. When I drew the picture of Tomás, you guessed who might have Rebekka. You—"

Guilt slapped him, making him snarl. "Even now I don't know *who* or *where*, though with time she *can* be found."

Araña's eyes darkened into endless black. Resolve and determination slid up her spine, throbbing so deeply he felt it pulsing through him. "She might not have time. The Church is no friend of the gifted. I'm going—"

"No." Fury at the idea of her risking herself made his voice harsh. "I'll find the healer. I'll rescue her from *my* enemies as soon as I'm free of the collar. The Were, too, if he's unfortunate enough to stumble into this trap."

Araña's relief melted over Tir, along with her pleasure in his promise. It should have angered him that her emotions so often became his. It should terrify him that her will could become his own. But instead he found himself fighting the urge to push her onto her back, the need to eradicate all remnants of their argument making him want to cover her with his body and feel her underneath him.

His mouth settled on Araña's and she willingly parted her lips for him. Her tongue greeted his, sliding against it in a sensuous celebration of intimacy restored.

He could spend an eternity with her and never have his lust sated to the point where he would desire another female. Even in their cramped, debris-strewn hiding place, he wanted to free his cock and join with her.

Tir forced himself away from her. "There's not much of the day left. We need to go to the bookseller's."

It pleased him that physically parting seemed as difficult for her as for him. Her dark eyes hid nothing from him. They smoldered with desire. Caressed him.

"You're right, we need to go," she said, sending a lick of flame along his cock when she glanced downward and wet her lips with her tongue.

"Araña," he growled.

Her smile held feminine satisfaction. Her eyes, when they lifted and met his, held an awareness of the power she had over him, how thoroughly she'd enslaved him and made him a prisoner to his need for her.

"That look invites further punishment," he said, urging her from the hiding place before lust delayed them further.

They clung to ruins where they could. Several times they were forced to duck into shadows by the sound of a diesel engine, followed by the passing of a sleek car carrying the gold flag with the red lion rampant.

Eventually they passed out of the area set aside for the gifted and into neighborhoods where groups of houses had been reclaimed. Dogs barked, announcing their passing. Children looked up from evening chores of gathering food from gardens and chasing chickens into well-protected coops.

Older children drove cattle and sheep down the street, returning from a day in the forest, or maybe from a day spent guarding the animals as they grazed among rubble.

The residential section gave way to what had once been a business district. A goat rounded the corner in front of them, its eyes wild with fear, the bell tied to its neck clanging as it sped past.

Tir drew the machete as quickly as the knives appeared in Araña's hands. They approached, bracing themselves for whatever predator might charge after the goat.

Instead there was the panicked bleating of more goats, the shout of a boy, and then the horrible, abrupt sound of silence.

They surged forward, around the corner.

Tir had no name for the things he found there. But Araña did.

"Chupacabra. Goat suckers."

The creatures were reptile and mammal combined, leathery skinned with sharp spines running down their backs, their fangs driven deep into the throats of two goats and a boy barely in his teens, their cheeks puffing in and out as they drank blood.

"He's still alive," Araña said, rushing forward and willing to take on all three of the creatures.

Tir passed her, though he doubted it would make a difference. The boy no longer struggled.

The closest chupacabra lifted its mouth away from a goat's throat and screeched in warning, flashing its bloody fangs. It screeched again when Tir kept rushing toward it, then sprang away like a kangaroo, emitting a sulfur stink an instant before the machete sliced through the air where the creature had been.

He kept going, trusting Araña to watch his back. The second chupacabra jerked, nearly severing the goat's head from its body in its hurry to get away from Tir.

The third, smaller and probably less dominant than the other two, followed the example of its companions, abandoning the boy it had been forced to take as a meal.

Arterial blood sprayed out in an arc of red. Tir reached the body and could almost feel the soul hovering free, thinning, slipping away.

Too late, he started to say. But before he could utter the words, Araña's sorrow at being unable to save the boy washed through him, the intensity of her emotions striking so deeply he acted without thought.

Tir sank to his knees and opened his mind, accepting the pain. He touched his hand to the boy's torn throat and *willed* it healed, *willed* the soul to return to the still warm flesh.

The machete fell from numb fingers. He was only vaguely aware of it, only vaguely aware he hadn't used his blood to heal.

Pain nearly crushed him to the ground. He fought against crying out and revealing his weakness. Then Araña was there beside him, her touch feather-soft on his back, but it was like life-giving fire, adding strength, adding her will to his, and the combination was undefeatable.

The boy cried out. He opened terror-filled eyes and rolled away from Tir's hand, then scrambled to his feet, taking in the dead goats before fleeing.

Tir turned his head and found his lips only inches away from

Araña's. Hunger rose like a victory cry, flaring between them, tightening their bodies.

He wanted to take her. *He would take her.*

But they were too close to the bookseller's shop now to delay. And he needed time to think about what had happened with the boy, what it meant that her desires had so completely become his own. Never before had he healed by will alone.

"Another block and we'll be there," he said, standing, dragging her to her feet, unable to resist crushing her mouth with his, tangling his fingers in her dark hair and holding her to him as his tongue thrust against hers, dominated hers until she melted against him.

He freed her then and started walking, the confusion of his thoughts yielding to anticipation with each step closer to the bookseller and the text that would finally free him from the cursed collar.

Araña walked next to Tir, filled with awe and wonder, happiness over what he'd done. He'd saved a child, spontaneously, when there was nothing to be gained from it other than the satisfaction of having done something good.

He'd saved a human at a cost to himself. Despite his efforts to hide the pain it caused him, she'd seen it, sensed it.

Araña glanced at his face, her eyes caressing the elegant lines, hungrily storing each nuance in her memory. Her fingers itched to take up colored pencils and capture his likeness, though she doubted she would ever be able to re-create his beauty on paper.

In moments he would be free of the collar. She might doubt her ability to draw him fully, but she didn't doubt her ability to open the safe containing the translations. From the first time Matthew showed her a safe and challenged her to crack it, she'd never failed at opening anything that used sets of numbers to control the locking device, or in the case of alarm systems, to engage or disengage them.

Her gaze dropped to her hand and the spider. She'd always thought her ability with combinations was simply a knack made better with practice and usage, much as Erik and Matthew could pick any lock almost as soon as they'd inserted a tool into it. Now she wondered if her ability was a result of the demon mark. Unlike the mechanics of picking a lock, combinations were *known*, they were part of the already woven threads of the past.

Araña's palm glanced over the hilt of Erik's blade. A knot formed in her throat, not for his loss—she'd come to terms with losing him and Matthew—but what it would mean when Tir regained his memories and his powers.

Would he still want her? Desire her? Would he discover he had a mate elsewhere? Children? A family that would shun him if he chose to keep a human at his side?

Araña closed her mind to her worries in favor of studying her surroundings as they passed through ruined buildings that had once housed shops. L'Antiquaire came into view near the edge of the forest.

The remoteness of the bookseller's location sent the first trickle of uneasiness through her. And when they reached it, Araña's gaze went automatically to the sigils carved in the doorway.

It was like being doused with icy water. Her breath caught. Her skin chilled into gooseflesh. "You don't recognize the symbols?" she asked above the erratic pounding of her heart.

"Some of them." He touched the common ones, the ones meant to ward against evil and certain types of supernatural beings.

Araña's hand shook slightly as she lifted it to the wood, forcing herself to trace the glyphs Tir hadn't and speak the names they represented. "Tucci. Tassone. Torres. They're vampire family names."

She traced others on the opposite side of the door. "Laurent. Rios. Michel. They've offered their protection, too."

Tir's husky laugh was almost enough to melt the ice encasing her at seeing the glyphs. His fingers curled around her arm, turning her to face him.

The knuckles of his other hand grazed over her cheek in a caress. "And you've got my protection, Araña. I had no trouble with the vampires I encountered at the dock. They allowed me to pass and recover your boat, though if the Were is to be believed, they were paid to guard the area."

Her heart gave a jolt and her hands went to his chest. "You didn't tell me you encountered vampires."

Tir shrugged. "It wasn't worth mentioning."

"Perhaps not. Vampires take business matters seriously, just as they do their promises. If they let you pass at the pier, it was because they *could* under the terms of the agreement they'd negotiated with the dock and ship owners. It doesn't change the danger represented by the symbols around *this* door."

Her eyes strayed to the protection sigils. "See the marks after each name? They're a pledge that justice will be administered even if it takes centuries to accomplish. They're a warning that the punishment they administer might encompass the enslaving and killing of not only the person guilty of a crime against them, but every living descendent and every blood relative."

"If it will calm your worries, I'll promise not to harm the bookseller." He kissed her in a rough display of masculine dominance and arrogance. "You will open the safe, Araña. And you will trust me to protect you from the consequences of it."

In the end she knew she would do as he requested. She'd promised to do this for him, just as he'd promised to recover the *Constellation* for her. But fear drenched her all the same.

He reacted to it by stiffening beneath her palms at the implied lack of confidence in his ability to keep her safe. His face became a harsh mask.

She touched her lips to his in supplication. "Trust me to try negotiation first," she whispered, rubbing her fingertips over hardened masculine nipples.

Tir's nostrils flared and his eyes narrowed, but in the end he gave a slight nod before leaning forward to issue a sensual warning against her ear. "When this is done, I'll take you so thoroughly there'll be no room left for doubt or fear."

Araña shivered as the threat sent heat sliding into her belly, thawing some of the chill as they stepped into the shop. "Did the bookseller tell you who owns the book?"

"Virgilio Cortez."

Optimism built on the heat from Tir's sensual threat. She didn't recognize the name. Maybe Cortez was human. "Is he a vampire?"

Tir countered by asking, "Does the name Draven mean anything to you?"

Her steps faltered, not just at the mention of Draven's name, but at the smell of books and the sight of so many of them crammed onto overstuffed shelves. "He's head of the Tassone family. They rule in San Francisco."

"Then Cortez is most likely vampire. Before I left here, the bookseller suggested there might be some service I could perform for Draven in exchange for his intercession with Virgilio."

Tir stepped into a narrow aisleway between shelves. Araña followed, her optimism growing and allowing her to smile for the first time since seeing the vampire family names carved into the doorjamb. "It's possible the bookseller knows of something Draven wants."

As they maneuvered through a rabbit warren of shelves, fleeting images of Erik and his books passed through her mind. He would have loved this place. And Matthew would have grumbled more loudly the longer they were in it.

The stacks opened into a work space. Araña immediately sought the safe with her eyes, barely taking in the figure of the old man hunched over a table. She found a row of them set in brick and mortar, and even without taking the first step toward the wall housing them, she knew each safe would have a vampire sigil on it.

Her attention swung back to the bookseller. He looked up, and shocked recognition replaced all else. "Thierry?" she asked.

Faded lichen-colored eyes studied her face for a long moment before dropping to the gloved hand. "You're Matthew and Erik's girl, Spider, if I remember correctly."

"Araña."

He gave a small nod to acknowledge the translation. "Are they in Oakland, too?"

Her throat closed for an instant. "They were killed here."

"I'm sorry to hear that." His glance traveled from Tir to the bank of safes, then back to her. "Considering the company you're in, I can guess your reason for being here.

"I don't doubt you can do what you intend. Erik could have, and the last time I saw him, he bragged you were better at it than him. But I know Matthew would have made sure you know how foolish it is to cross a vampire. The Cortez family isn't a powerful one, but the others will stand with them."

Tir stiffened at her side and Araña took his hand in hers. She stood taller with pride that Eric had bragged about her accomplishments to this man both he and Matthew had once used when it came to dealing with vampires. "I'm prepared to negotiate for access to the book. Will you mediate?"

The bookseller studied Araña and Tir's clasped hands for a long moment. She suspected he was remembering Matthew's warning not to touch her because of the demon mark.

As if her thoughts summoned it, the spider moved to the back of her hand, its sudden appearance startling Thierry. He glanced up. "I'll assist you. Have you ever dealt with a vampire before?"

She saw no point in lying. "No."

"Then let me make a suggestion. Because Virgilio is the lesser vampire and the book of relative unimportance to him, it would be acceptable to summon Draven's human High Servant, Thane. He is available during the daylight hours and can enter into certain contracts on behalf of Draven. He's certainly qualified to negotiate with both you and the Cortez representative on this matter."

"How do I contact him?"

"I'll send a message, now if you wish."

Tir stirred restlessly. "This will be settled tonight."

The shopkeeper gave a slight shrug before moving away from

the table. Araña thought he'd disappear into the stacks and send his message via magic or human runner. Instead he opened a drawer and pulled out a cellular phone.

It surprised her—but only for an instant. The technology had existed well before The Last War. Even children were said to have routinely carried them in the past.

In her lifetime she'd never seen one of the phones except in history books or magazines that catered to the ultra-rich. But it made sense that vampires—many of whom had been alive for centuries before the world was changed forever—would have saved and guarded some of the towers for their own use, and that a man who dealt in old, valuable books, and was protected by a great number of vampire families, would be able to contact them using technology rarely available to humans.

As Thierry spoke into the small device, Araña released Tir's hand and moved to stand in front of the safes. She'd been right in her guess. Most bore the mark of a vampire family.

From behind her Thierry said, "You're in luck. Thane is on this side of the bay. He'll be here shortly."

She turned. "Do you have a suggestion about what Draven might consider a fair trade for his intercession?"

The bookseller shook his head. "I'm sorry, no."

Twenty-one

THANE entered a short time later, accompanied by bodyguards. He was everything Araña would have expected of a High Servant. Deadly beauty and lethal charisma combined.

Tir came to her side, equally beautiful and equally deadly, though Araña hoped the situation wouldn't escalate into violence. Thane's eyebrow lifted at Tir's action, his storm gray eyes glittering with amused speculation—until something cold and alien passed through and they were left the color of smooth steel.

The hair on the back of Araña's neck stood. She shivered, remembering Matthew's speculation that a vampire could take possession of a High Servant's body in daylight.

"Any deal will be with the human," Thane said, his voice indicating there was no room for negotiation, his gaze settling completely on Araña. "I've already spoken to Cortez's man and he's agreed in principal to allow you access to the book, as long as it doesn't leave the premises and is returned to the safe in its existing condition. What do you have to barter with?"

"I'm a thief."

"Draven rarely requires the services of a thief. But your skills might be put to a different use. What are they?"

"I'm good with safes. And alarm systems."

Thane's smile was more savage flash of teeth than anything else. "Then perhaps we can deal. The question is, how good are you? Good enough to succeed when the penalty for failure will be death?"

A low growl came from Tir. His arm snaked around her waist, pulling her back to his chest in a possessive, protective gesture that made Thane's amusement reappear.

Thierry said, "She's good enough."

An elegant eyebrow lifted again, this time in obvious surprise. "High praise indeed, coming from you."

"What's does Draven want done?" Araña asked, sweat trickling down her back.

Thane snapped his fingers, and a smallish man she hadn't noticed stepped from behind one of the bodyguards. He held a museum catalog. It was old, the date on its cover indicating it was for a show taking place in San Francisco during the days when The Last War raged, before the world knew it truly marked the end of civilization as it had been.

At a nod from Thane, the man opened the catalog to a faded, glossy page with a ceramic urn that had once been part of a traveling collection. Despite its obvious worth, the sight of it filled Araña with deep uneasiness.

It was wide at the bottom, narrow-necked, and sealed with both stopper and wax. Writing covered it, like the tattoos trailing down Tir's arms, though none of the sigils on the urn resembled the ones he wore.

"Draven wants this destroyed. It will shatter easily, as long as it is done with willing intent and by human hands."

The sweat coating Araña's skin grew chilled. "What's in the urn?"

"As you will discover if you accept the task and succeed in getting to where it is currently being kept, the stopper has been removed. If it's with the urn at all, it is of no consequence and doesn't fall within the scope of the bargain. Only the urn does. Draven wants to assure himself it can't be used again for the purposes it was created."

Araña glanced at the description beneath the picture. It held no additional information, but served to remind her that the urn had been part of a museum display in San Francisco *before* the supernaturals emerged from hiding.

Vampires were said to have a noncorporeal form. They were said to be very nearly immortal. Perhaps one of them had once been trapped in the urn.

She licked suddenly dry lips. "Where is it?"

Thane's smile was a shark's, his gray eyes equally merciless. "In the possession of Anton Barlowe, the maze owner, who lives in a house wired with an advanced alarm system and is, as you might know, guarded by a demon. That's why I ask if you're good enough, and say if you aren't, you will die. The demon will kill you. Or his master, Anton, will.

"Or Draven will see it done if you enter into a contract with him and then fail to deliver what you promised. Success provides the only possibility of remaining alive. As I said a moment ago, Draven rarely has use for a thief. I am aware of details regarding *how* entering Anton's house might be accomplished. If you are willing to attempt it and guarantee the urn is destroyed in the prescribed manner, then Draven will intercede on your behalf with Virgilio Cortez."

Araña suppressed a shudder as the image of the demon rose in her mind, sending the spider scurrying to the sole of her foot. The prospect of facing Abijah again made her legs threaten to give out. An icy fist squeezed her chest as she remembered fingers ending in curling, wicked claws, leathery black wings against an evening sky, and the coppery smell of human blood on his skin.

Tir's arms tightened around her waist. From what seemed like a long distance away, she heard her own voice say, "We'd have to have access to the book belonging to Cortez *before* going after the urn."

At some subtle signal, the small man closed the museum catalog and retreated from sight. Thane's arctic-cold eyes bored into hers. "I have no problem allowing for a couple hours' grace with respect to the book, and wording the agreement accordingly, as long as you agree to complete the task within three days' time, the beginning of which is marked at tonight's sunset."

The merciless smile reappeared. "Be very clear. Your task isn't finished until the urn is *willingly* destroyed by *human* hands. They can be your hands, or another's, it doesn't matter. But if I were in your position, I wouldn't risk failure by delaying to see it done. If you need a few moments to discuss your decision with your companion, by all means, take them."

Araña didn't need a moment. She saw no real choice. If Thane left without an agreement and she broke into the safe, the vampire families would unite to mete out their punishment, and she didn't doubt their reach extended into the ghostlands where Erik and Matthew were. They wouldn't stop hunting her until they'd administered their justice—a justice that would probably see Tir in chains again.

If she agreed, and because of the translations, Tir's power and memory were restored, then—

"I will protect you," Tir said, stroking her cheek, directing the next at Thane. "Your enemies are mine."

Thierry chose that moment to mediate on her behalf as he'd agreed to. "Thane has indicated he's in possession of certain details, which I assume relate to the maze, and more particularly Anton Barlowe's security. Since it's in Draven's best interest you succeed, Araña, it would be appropriate for Thane to share what he knows so you can more properly assess the proposed job before giving him your answer."

Thane's laugh held genuine amusement. "So she was clever enough to get you working on her side—it bodes well for her chances of surviving if she agrees to a contract with Draven."

He snapped his fingers again. The small man reappeared and placed paper, pen, and a wooden box on the table in front of Thane.

Thane took up the pen and drew what Araña had already seen for herself once—a security gate opening into a fenced driveway and leading to the building where Jurgen and Cabot had sold her to Farold for the maze.

"This building serves as office and prison," Thane said. "It also contains living quarters for those who assist Anton as well as those who are required by law to be on the premises at certain times."

With quick strokes he sectioned off a portion of the building to the right of the counter where she'd been forced to stand as money was counted out and her picture taken. "This is Farold's apartment. The front office area extends into it."

He drew a larger square, then two curved lines creating a path between the two buildings, though Araña remembered seeing only a wall when she was taken through the front door at gunpoint.

"A fully enclosed walkway leads from the office in Farold's living quarters to Anton's house. There's a door on either end, both alarmed, both unlocked using a keypad."

Thane retracted the ink tip with a click and traced the route from the main office space, through the portion of it in Farold's apartment, through the tunnel and into Anton's house as he said, "This is the best chance anyone has of getting into the house and upstairs to the study, where the urn is kept.

"There are no windows facing the red zone outside Anton's house. What windows there are all face the maze. The bottom floors are barred and the entire yard fenced to prevent hunters or runners from straying or attempting to kill him. Not that many would dare.

"The demon patrols the maze as well as all the buildings on the grounds, and as you have cause to know, he can be both corporal and incorporeal."

Araña stiffened at his allusion to her encounter with Abijah. Thane's eyes became a gray swirl of amused condescension. "Surely you don't imagine Draven must supplement his income by collecting bounties on those who've escaped the maze. The fact you managed once and made a big enough impression on Barlowe that he wants you back is enough to qualify you for this job, even without Thierry's recommendation, though I'll admit to being surprised when I entered and saw you here."

Matthew and Erik's training kept Araña from missing the bigger picture. There was no way Thane had gathered all this information in the short time between Thierry's call and his arrival at the shop. "How come Draven hasn't gone after the urn before now?"

"Who says he hasn't?" Thane countered.

"Has he?"

Thane considered his answer for a long moment, then said, "No. The timing has not been right, until now." His eyes became the cool of steel gray. "Do we have an agreement, or do you need a moment to decide?"

A remembered conversation from her time at the maze slid into Araña's mind, her subconscious already planning how she would accomplish this seemingly impossible task.

We'll allow her two knives in the maze and give Abijah permission to play with her all night if the convicts don't kill her first.

Why not add a caveat that Abijah can't intentionally kill her unless she's escaping the maze? If she survives his attention, that'll make her next run a profitable one.

Done. Abijah has his instructions.

"I agree to the terms," she told Thane.

"Then I'll prepare the contract."

Araña closed her eyes and soaked in Tir's warmth as she listened to the sound of a pen scratching over paper. Her stomach churned with thoughts of facing Abijah again.

Taking comfort in Tir was a show of weakness, one that would have gained her a severe frown from Matthew, but she didn't force herself away from the haven of Tir's arms until Thane's sardonic voice said, "If you're ready . . ."

The document was short and simple, exact, and created in duplicate. It covered not only her agreement for services to be rendered for Draven, but Virgilio Cortez's restrictions with respect to the book.

Araña read it before accepting the pen Thane offered and adding her signature beneath his on each page. When it was done, Thane said, "One last thing."

His hand went to the wooden box. With the flick of his wrist it opened to reveal a syringe.

"Roll up your sleeve and hold out your arm," he said, lifting the syringe from its bed of satin.

Araña's heart pounded in her ears like a violent surf. When she hesitated, Thane motioned toward the signed papers. "They're not official until I press the Tassone seal to them. That requires blood."

A glance at Thierry, who'd returned to his work at a nearby table, gained her a solemn nod. She rolled up her sleeve and held out her arm.

Elegant fingers clamped down, forcing a vein into prominence, the material of her shirt keeping Thane safe from the spider.

Araña looked away as the needle slid through her skin and the syringe filled with blood. She expected Thane to store her blood in the satin-lined box. Instead he plunged the needle into his own arm and injected its contents into his vein. The sight of him doing it made her feel light-headed, nauseous. Sweat broke out again, icy and frightening.

"Done," he said, calmly snapping off the needle and dropping the used syringe into a wastebasket at the end of the desk.

Thane lifted the satin bed the syringe had been resting on and retrieved an official stamp. He pressed it to both copies of the contract, leaving the red-ink seal of the Tassone family—a serpent holding an apple in its mouth, the three segments of its S-shaped body impaled by an arrow from a point behind its head to just before the tip of its tail.

The small man stepped forward to put the stamp away before reclaiming box, pen, and one of the signed contracts as Thane went to a safe. He opened it and removed a bound book, then returned to place it in Araña's hands. "You have until sunrise to examine this in accordance with the terms of the agreement, and until sunset in three days to fulfill your obligations."

"I understand," she said, clutching the book to her chest and waiting until Thane left before offering it to Tir.

He stroked her cheek with the back of one hand, the emotion in his eyes something she'd never forget. "This will take some time."

"We've got until sunrise."

Tir leaned forward and pressed his lips to hers. A thousand sentences crowded in, tangled in emotion so acute only two words could emerge. "Thank you," he said, taking the book from her and sitting at the desk, opening it.

It smelled of leather and the smoke of oil lamps, until he reached parchment texts placed behind others centuries younger. There he found the scent of desert and incense, of a past so ancient it was only a whisper, marking the very dawning of human civilization.

Araña's hand settled on his shoulder, her fingers stroking nervously, her worry vibrating into him. He looked up from the old parchment and took her hand, carrying it to his mouth and placing a kiss against her palm.

"All will be well," he said, guessing her promise to the vampire was the source of her anxiety. "The Finder's gift is a true one. These are the pages I remember."

Her eyes went to the faded ink and foreign symbols, none of which matched what was on his arms. He pressed another kiss to her palm. "If I could free them from their binding and place them in their correct order, it would speed the process. But even then, it would still require time and concentration to untangle the incantations. I may well need until sunrise to accomplish it."

Araña glanced at the tiny grime-coated row of windows near the room's ceiling and knew she couldn't stay. She felt confined, agitated. Thoughts of Levi and the brothel kept crowding in, along with images of the guardsmen and the dark-haired stranger from her vision.

Was tonight the night where her path crossed with theirs? Or was it merely the approaching dusk, and the knowledge it would soon be too late for her to leave the building that had her anxious?

She didn't know. She couldn't be certain. When she'd been standing in front of the tapestry with the demon, she'd known only that she was in the future.

"I'll wait for you at the boat," she said, pulling her hand from his, not daring to tell him she intended to go to the brothel.

His frown told her he didn't like the idea. She leaned in and touched her lips to his cheek, unconsciously mimicking the strategy and words Matthew had so often used with Erik. "If I stay, I'll drive you crazy with my pacing."

Tir turned his face, capturing her mouth in a fierce kiss and her hair in a firm grip, holding her there until the need for air forced them apart. "I'll come to you," he said, releasing her, and she escaped the room before he thought to make her promise to go directly to the boat.

REBEKKA matched the rose in front of her to the page holding a description of its origins. Whatever arguments Enzo had made to The Iberá about taking her with him during the assault on her home, they hadn't been persuasive. No one had come looking for her, though there wouldn't have been much need for a search.

As soon as she'd emerged from the walkway elevator, intending to find a hiding place, the butler had been there, a cold, austere shadow holding a wealth of carefully concealed suspicion. His presence was followed by a series of maids, including Janita.

They'd offered to bring her food or drink, to show her to the music room or the art room or the television room. They'd suddenly needed to attend to housekeeping chores in whatever room she settled in, until she'd finally been driven back outside, where at least she could pretend she was alone as she wandered among beds of carefully tended roses.

It was there she'd heard the heavy throb of diesel engines marking Enzo and the Iberá private militia leaving the estate. It was there she'd seen movement at a window and crouched automatically, her fingers stroking the butter-smooth petals of a rose as if it held all her attention.

Curtains parted. Glass windows were opened by the butler, revealing the patriarch sitting behind his desk in the study—and giving Rebekka a glimpse of much needed hope. If he left, even for a few minutes, she could slip in from the gardens and reclaim the token.

Hours had passed since she'd returned to the house and made her way to the library, expressing a great interest in roses to the maid who quickly appeared, and taking one of the tomes about them out into the garden on the pretext of learning more about the bushes planted there.

Her fingers tightened on the book each time she heard a vehicle come in or leave through the gate the private army used. Had they found Levi? Or Araña? Or the prisoner?

If so, she didn't think they were on the estate. Enzo would have prevailed then and had her sent for.

The scent of roses grew more cloying as her tension mounted. Her eyes ached from reading about them, but she wanted to be prepared if she was questioned and had to feign enough interest to avoid suspicion.

She was far enough from the main entrance that the guards no longer paused as they noted her presence in the garden. There were stretches of time when none of them were visible on the wall at all.

If only . . . Rebekka's heart tripped into a desperate race when she saw the patriarch leave his desk. The moment she'd hoped for had arrived.

She checked the wall, and her breath caught at the sight of a guard there. His back was to her, as if he was watching the lions on the other side.

The horrible scream of prey dying confirmed her guess. The sound was followed by lions roaring throughout the compound.

Rebekka bolted for the study and clamored through the open window, only to hear the sound of approaching footsteps. There was no place to hide except underneath the patriarch's desk. She curled into a ball, skirts tight against her legs, the book on roses clutched to her chest.

She thought it must be the butler entering. He paused in the doorway, as if the scent of roses had left a trail leading to her hiding place.

Rebekka didn't dare breathe. If she could have stopped the wild pounding of her heart, she would have.

He moved into the room and closed the windows. Locked them. Lingered for what seemed like an agonizing eternity before leaving and closing the door behind him.

She didn't move for fear he stood just outside, in the hallway, to make sure his suspicions were unfounded.

The clock on the patriarch's desk ticked loudly. Elsewhere on the estate, another tolled, announcing the half hour and serving as a warning the dinner hour approached. Janita would be looking for her now.

Rebekka forced herself from underneath the desk. The token was where she thought it would be, still lying on the velvet of the butler's tray. She grabbed it.

Sweat made her palms slick and her clothing cling to her. She started to leave, only to remember the conversation between Father

Ursu and The Iberá about the demon in Anton Barlowe's possession.

An old, leather-bound journal was sitting on the patriarch's desk. Rebekka opened it to a bookmarked page. Scratchy, handwritten text filled the right side of it.

The trader, Domenico Cieri, arrived in port today. He had in his possession two urns he claims were recovered from an archeological dig centuries ago and held in a private collection until financial disaster led to them being sold. They look authentic, like something from the Holy Lands, and the glyphs—I'll admit, bumps rose on my arms when I traced my fingers over the symbols carved into the first of the urns.

Both are said to house demons, and it is a tantalizing prospect, though I continue to remind myself Domenico is a bit of a charlatan.

The first urn is sealed. Domenico claims (not knowing the full extent of my interest in such matters) that one need only be courageous enough to open it and a winged, tailed horror will appear to do the bidding of its new master. Of course, even the most ignorant of acolytes knows commanding a demon is not so simple (though of course I didn't point this out to Domenico as it's much wiser in these times not to do anything to draw the Church's attention).

Demons have no love of humans and will expend as much energy twisting and evading and turning a command into something to suit their own purposes as obeying it.

The second urn is unsealed. If it did indeed once contain a demon, then there is no guarantee it is still bound to the vessel in any way. Scholars (dare I say, practitioners) of such matters are divided on this, and with good reason. Without the correct incantations or knowledge of the demon's name, the results can be deadly.

Still, the urns are tempting, though of course, I listened to Domenico as one would listen to a tall tale at the bar. Tomorrow I'll make arrangements for their acquisition, through the usual intermediaries so their purchase can't be traced back to me.

Rebekka scanned through the rest of the entry. There was nothing more. Whoever the journal belonged to originally had moved on to list other items in the trader's possession.

To the left of the entry, on the back of the preceding page, were sketches of the urns. Rebekka tried to memorize the images but quickly realized she'd never be able to describe the swirling sigils and unfamiliar symbols.

She was tempted to take the book, but its loss would be immediately noticeable, more so than the token. Reluctantly she closed the journal, only to open it again and cringe as she tore the pages containing the entry and the sketches from it. She tucked them into a pocket of her dress before shutting the book again and going to the door.

She held her breath and strained to hear any sound beyond the thick wood. Nothing, and she couldn't afford to stay longer or escape through the window. If there wasn't a search in progress for her yet, there soon would be.

Her hands trembled as she twisted the doorknob and slowly pulled backward, creating a tiny space. She heard footsteps and the sound of the patriarch's motorized chair coming toward the hallway containing the study. Heart lodged in her throat, she darted from the room and slipped into the library several steps away, huddling next to the door so she could get to her room as soon as it was safe to attempt it.

"It's time to turn the healer over to the Church, Grandfather," Enzo said as they neared the library door.

"Allow me to do things my way. I've got months yet before the disease will kill me. If the prisoner is not what we believe he is, if his blood won't heal me, then there won't be a miracle and hurrying will have accomplished nothing. If you'd seen her with the lion—"

"There were drawings at her house. Two of them were of guardsmen I recognized. They're men I'd marked for trial with a recommendation of the death penalty because of their involvement with the maze. One of them has already met his death. He was murdered near the Mission at around the time Tomás intercepted the healer. The third picture was of Tomás."

Rebekka pressed the fisted hand containing the token to her mouth to keep from making a sound. The drawings had to belong to Araña, and she couldn't have known about the house unless Levi took her there.

"You believe an attempt will be made on Tomás's life?"

"I think it's possible. The prisoner saw Tomás when he went to the trapper's compound to look at the lion. Even blindfolded, as Father Ursu insisted be done on the second visit, the prisoner would have recognized Tomás's voice."

"I'll send Tomás away."

"That would be wise. And the healer?"

There was a long pause. Instead of an answer, the patriarch asked, "What of the child? Is he back with his mother?"

Relief gave Rebekka a moment's respite.

"Yes, the unit I sent was in range of our newest cell tower an hour ago. They'll be back shortly."

The study door opened and they went inside. Enzo said, "Grandfather, if it could be any other way, I wouldn't lobby so hard for this, but so much is at stake. Not just your life and Tomás's, but all you've worked for, all the Iberás have stood for since our ancestors started reclaiming Oakland from anarchy and lawlessness."

"I know, Enzo. I know."

"Then let me take her. I can insist on being present when she's questioned. Perhaps she can even be brought back here afterward. We can't wait. The restoration of the guard and the elimination of the red zone are within reach. But if the prisoner disappears or Anton Barlowe takes possession of him, it might be decades before we're this close again."

There was a long silence. "I'll speak to her one last time. If my effort to enlist her aid fails, I'll allow you to take her to Derrick.

Close the door. Let me gather my thoughts for a moment and share them with you before we proceed."

As soon as she heard the click of the study door, Rebekka fled to the room assigned to her.

Janita looked up, a smile on her face. "Good, you're here. I was getting worried. Hurry! Hurry! Let me help you out of that dress. Your bath is drawn and your evening clothes set out for you."

"I need to be alone," Rebekka said, practically shoving Janita from the room then pulling a heavy wooden chest containing handmade quilts in front of the door. It wouldn't hold against a true assault, but hopefully it would hold long enough.

Janita pushed and encountered resistance. "What's wrong? Please, at least tell me what's happened to upset you."

"I can't."

There was another push. Soft, and then Janita's footsteps hurried away.

Rebekka scoured the room for what she needed. Candles and matches were easy. But a knife—

Foolish, foolish, foolish, not to think ahead and plan.

She lit the candle on the dresser and pressed the witch's token into the wax so the flame danced on either side of it, turning it black. Her eyes desperately sought something sharp, anything, skipping over the handheld mirror to settle on an expensive bottle of perfume provided for her just as the clothes she wore had been, as if by wearing them she could fit into this world.

Rebekka picked the bottle up and smashed it against the corner of the dresser, breaking it without drawing blood. She would have preferred that she had, so she wouldn't be forced to drag the sharp edge against her skin.

She slashed and held her hand over the token, squeezed so a drop of blood fell for each word of the spell. Rather than tamp down the candle flame, her blood fed it, making it leap hungrily upward as if it would wrap around her hand and consume her.

Rebekka reached the last word and hesitated, knowing instinctively it was the most powerful, the one word whose use was
irrevocable—but in the end she gave in to the inevitable, preferring
to take her chances with the witches instead of the Church. She
spoke what she feared might be the name of a demon. Aziel.

He chose his moment to arrive. Not appearing until the chest
was shoved away from the door with force, and both the patriarch
and Enzo had entered the room to take note of the token and the
candle.

Then it was as though a rent appeared in reality itself, tearing
an opening between two worlds so a shrouded figure could step
through it.

Aziel carried a staff and the aura of death. His face was darkness
itself.

In the hallway, Janita fainted without a word. The Iberá fumbled
with his single useful hand, struggling to pull the crucifix from beneath his starched and buttoned shirt.

He spoke a litany of Spanish, but Aziel only laughed. "Your
prayers have no power over me. But your death will serve as a warning to your grandson. It will serve as proof of my resolve. The
healer is to be safely delivered to the witch's house and those in your
family who survive you will cease hunting the tattooed one, or
every man, woman, and child bearing the name Iberá will enter the
ghostlands."

The sigils on Aziel's staff came alive. He stretched the end of it
toward The Iberá, only to halt a hair away from Rebekka's chest
when she stepped in front of the patriarch and said, "No. I don't
want his death on my conscience."

The black hood holding no visible form tilted, birdlike. "And
you, Carlos Juan Iberá, if I honor the healer's plea and allow you to
live, will you be required to answer for the death of your entire
family?"

"No," the patriarch said, sounding like the old man he was.
"No."

The sigils on the staff turned from red to icy blue. Rebekka gasped as it plunged forward, passing through her body like cold light to touch The Iberá. "Forget your answer and suffer the consequences," Aziel said. "Your fate is now bound to the healer's. Take her to the witch's house and consider your search and your part in this done."

Twenty-two

REBEKKA had no way of knowing if the Wainwrights expected her or not, though she imagined they knew she'd used the token, and perhaps the spell summoning Aziel was *meant* to have her brought to their home.

Was he a demon? She still didn't know.

He'd struck fear in her heart. But he hadn't felt *evil*.

Then again, what evil she'd experienced and witnessed had been done by beings of flesh and blood, not formless dark.

She rubbed her palms over the stiff fabric of the borrowed dress. The Iberá had insisted she keep it, along with the matching jewelry, and she hadn't stopped to argue, though she was glad to have the bundle of her own soft, frayed clothing in her lap.

It had been offered through the window of the chauffeur-driven car by Janita, who'd recovered from her faint and cared enough to retrieve it and see that Rebekka had it before the car pulled away.

Tears leaked from Rebekka's eyes. She couldn't stop them. She was safe. Free. Everything that had happened seemed like a surreal nightmare though she knew it had been real and her peril no illusion.

The token was like ice where it pressed between dress and flesh. Aziel's parting words to The Iberá were burned into her memory.

His fate was tied to hers.

It wasn't a responsibility she wanted. His wasn't a world she would ever feel comfortable in.

Liar, a small internal voice whispered, reminding her of the lions and the value the patriarch placed on her gift, the genuine caring she'd seen in Janita's face when she picked Eston up and carried him off for his meal or told Rebekka she looked beautiful in the elegant, expensive dresses.

Rebekka rubbed the tears away. At least Eston was back with his mother.

Perhaps that's what had made her step between Aziel and The Iberá. Or maybe it was the patriarch's repeated reluctance to turn her over to the Church, until the very end, when Tomás was threatened.

Rebekka didn't know. Maybe she'd never know. Or maybe it was a healer's nature—the same nature that had seen The Iberá's atrophied and useless limbs and wanted to restore them despite her status as a prisoner.

The chauffeured car pulled to a stop in front of the witch's house. Rebekka got out quickly, not waiting for the driver to open the door—though *he* waited, as if she were the guest The Iberá had named her, and didn't drive away until she'd passed through the wrought iron gate and reached the front door to have it opened for her.

"Come in," Annalise said, leading Rebekka to a small room just off the foyer.

Rebekka sat, then stood, uncomfortable in the presence of so much magic pressing in on her. "I should be at work."

Annalise folded her hands over her knees but didn't rise from the chair she'd claimed. "The Weres are lucky to have you."

Rebekka found herself lowering to the settee. Memories crowded in, of the caged werecougar freed during the ambush and forced to choose between human and animal forms, of Levi, who'd had to do the same, of the countless others she'd *fixed* but couldn't truly cure.

She'd wondered, flirted with the idea of asking the witches for help with her gift after accepting the token, had come to suspect they wanted the demon in Anton's possession. Her mouth grew dry with the question she was ready to dare despite her fear of the answer.

"I can't heal them completely. My gift isn't strong enough, and because it's not, they remain trapped between forms, or are forced to choose between them."

Annalise leaned forward, her eyes holding Rebekka's. "There's a war brewing between supernatural beings, not unlike the one occurring at the dawn of human creation. Depending on its outcome, the world as we know it may change again. As alliances are forged, healers will emerge who can make those Weres trapped in an abomination of form whole, able to shift completely as they were always meant to do. You are one of those healers."

"If I'm willing to pay the price."

"There is always a price to pay. But sometimes it's in the choices made."

"Is the escaped prisoner one of the healers you speak of?"

"That remains to be seen." Annalise got to her feet. "I imagine you're worried about your friend, the Were who accompanied you the other day. He is out of harm's way for the moment, but it would be wise to send for him. A messenger is waiting."

Sudden fear swept into Rebekka. She stood. "I'll go to the brothel myself."

"As you wish," Annalise said, though she made no move to escort Rebekka to the front door.

Rebekka took a step and halted. Unbidden, Aziel's words to the patriarch came to her, like a hint left for her to discover. *Consider your search and your part in this done.* As if this was an elaborate game, the very web she'd once fleetingly thought herself trapped in.

Choices. She'd chosen to ally herself with the Wainwrights the moment she'd pocketed the token in the occult shop and memorized the spell. She'd wondered what it would cost to be able to cure the Weres fully, so they could shift between perfect forms.

Maybe she couldn't know the cost ahead of time. Maybe she could only go with her heart and do what she considered right at each juncture, as she'd done when she stepped between Aziel and the patriarch without agonizing over the decision.

Rebekka tugged a flowered handkerchief from the pocket of her bundled pants and handed it to Annalise. "Levi will come if this is sent with a messenger."

"I'll need the token as well."

ARAÑA raced toward the brothel. Fear crowded her when she saw the hyena-faced Weres standing on either side of the door instead of Levi. Sweat coated her skin, and the demon's warning in the vision place raged through her mind like fire consuming dry tender. *With that choice you will return to your flesh prison without knowing what changes you wrought.*

Was this the wrong day despite the increasing uneasiness and urgency she'd felt at L'Antiquaire and after leaving it? Or was Levi's absence proof she'd changed the pattern leading to his death?

Araña pulled the cloak around her more tightly, making sure the hood and the tilt of her head shielded her face as she went to the front door. One of the Weres opened it—and there was Levi, so close that in another moment he would have been where she'd expected to find him.

He reached out as if to take her hand, then remembered the spider and indicated they go to the right instead. Lewd comments from the prostitutes followed them down a hallway of glass-fronted rooms.

Inside, male and female Weres plied their trade, servicing humans who paid to get something they couldn't otherwise, while

others paid to walk the halls, watching them. At the corner Levi
indicated a turn to the left, and they traveled a corridor marked by
closed doors as well as open ones allowing glimpses into rooms containing only a bed.

"So he didn't survive his attempt to recover the boat," Levi said
in oblique reference to Tir's absence.

"He survived and found a hiding a place for it."

Levi stepped into the last room before the hallway ended. "So
you're here because of Rebekka. You used your gift to find her."

"I attempted it." Araña's mind closed against the images of Levi
dying. "Rebekka's not at the maze. A private army stormed her house
today. A guardsman general was with them." A life lived among outcasts and outlaws kept her from mentioning the priest who'd urged
Rebekka be turned over to the Church for questioning. She couldn't
be sure Levi wouldn't trade Tir for the healer.

"Did you recognize any of them?"

"No. The cars they arrived in sported flags, a red lion rampant
against a shield with a field of gold behind it. The soldiers had
the same image on their uniforms. Do you know who the crest belongs to?"

Levi shook his head. "No. But it should be easy enough to find
out."

"Tir and I will do what we can to free her. And if it's possible,
we'll free the Weres held at the maze. I made a bargain with Draven
Tassone through his High Servant. Fulfilling it will require me to
break into Anton Barlowe's house."

The statement was met with silence rather than amusement.
"You'll die in the effort."

"Or die if I fail to accomplish it."

Levi shoved his hands into his jacket pockets. "How long do you
have?"

"Three days."

"Not even one," Levi said, "unless you want to take on the traveling magistrate's armed guards. By noon tomorrow the magistrate will arrive with those he's judged guilty elsewhere, criminals he'll turn over for the administration of their punishment. At least half of them will end up at the maze. The law requires the magistrate's guards remain with them to ensure they get a fair run, and to certify justice was carried out either by their deaths or their experience in the maze."

Ice slid down Araña's spine as she remembered Thane drawing the office building and saying, *It also contains living quarters for those who assist Anton as well as those who are required by law to be on the premises at certain times.* He must have known when he gave her three days' time to accomplish Draven's task that she really had much less of it.

Araña touched the knives for comfort. It could be done. Tir was immortal, and the next time she saw him, he would be free of the collar, his power restored.

But she hadn't lived with Matthew and Erik so long and not learned the value of gathering information when she could. "How many usually guard the maze grounds and buildings?"

"Anton doesn't bother with guards because the demon protects him."

"I saw only Farold, Anton, and the demon when I was held," Araña said. "Who else is there?"

The gold of Levi's eyes darkened in hate. "Gulzar." It was more growl than word, a savage pledge of revenge Araña recognized and understood only too well.

"I'll help you by doing what I can and sharing what I know," Levi said. His hand emerged from a jacket pocket with a crumpled piece of paper. She guessed what it was, the notice putting a price on her head.

"I know about the reward," she said when he would have given it to her.

Golden eyes lightened with surprise. "Then you took a big risk coming here. The same humans who enjoy watching Weres hunt in the maze come here and play out their fantasies of being superior by fucking them."

Araña shrugged. Levi said, "There's someone else who might help. A man who thinks his brother could be in Anton's possession."

The black-haired stranger she'd seen die with Levi in her vision came to mind. "Who?"

"Raoul. The werewolf bound for the maze and freed in the ambush."

"Do you trust him?"

Levi opened his mouth but closed it without saying anything. His face hardened as he gave serious consideration to the question. Finally he answered, "I don't know."

Araña didn't know either. Logic said the Were might be an ally. But the way his soul thread crossed and paralleled that of Jurgen's suggested he might not be.

The door being jerked open kept them from saying anything more. Three drunken men stood in the entranceway.

"Room's ours," one of them slurred, pushing through his companions and tugging a doe-eyed prostitute into the room behind him.

The second man followed, unzipping his trousers and pulling out his cock.

The third also stepped into the room. He squinted at Araña, recognition struggling to swim to the surface of his alcohol-saturated brain.

"There'll be more like these," Levi murmured, stepping in front of her and blocking her from sight. "It'd be better if this discussion continued tomorrow."

Araña ducked out of the room, careful to keep Levi between her and the brothel client. He was right. The hallway that had been empty minutes earlier was now crowded.

The dark cloak made her stand out. Taking it off was even riskier.

"This way," Levi said, pressing his thumb to a spot on the wall.

There was a click followed by a panel sliding open. Araña's heart began racing in anticipation as the staircase she'd climbed to Rebekka's room was revealed, and beyond it, the unobtrusive door into the alleyway between brothels.

"Don't come back here," Levi said, crossing to a keypad. "Given the assault on the house, I can guess where the two of you will be staying. I'll be there shortly after sunrise."

He entered a code. Another lock clicked open.

"We'll see you then," Araña said, releasing the cloak and letting it hang as it would. Her hands settled on the hilts of her knives as she stepped outside, into a surreal moment where past and future came together, where a breeze picked up, bringing with it the scent of curry and the rustle of paper as a soiled newspaper tumbled over her foot, signaling the moment when the hunted became the hunter.

RAOUL felt a thrill of victory as the breeze reached him, carrying the scent of prey into the shadowy alley where he waited to see if Levi would emerge to keep their agreed upon meeting. He'd searched relentlessly all day, following the lion whenever he left the brothel, in the hopes Levi would lead him to the escaped prisoner.

Every turn had been a dead end. Every moment spent in Oakland an assault on his senses.

He was tired of paying for whores who stunk of other men and pretended pleasure, or stared out of vacant eyes as he thrust in and out of them.

He was tired of the noise and the stench of humans.

Even the ease with which he could hunt here in wolf form, feasting on those foolish enough to stray into his path, didn't reduce the growing call to return to the compound surrounded by miles of forest and the human female who would soon smell of him and not his father.

He'd barely noted the cloaked figure going into the brothel. But his interest was aroused when he saw her slip through a side door. And then when her scent reached him . . .

Raoul opened his mouth slightly, letting air coat his tongue with the taste of woman and sex. She'd been with the demon-possessed human recently. She'd held her body open and let him spend his seed inside her.

It had marked her. And unlike the brand on her hand, there was no hiding it—at least not from a Were.

She was secondary prey, not as important to him as the escaped prisoner. He'd line his pockets with the reward Anton offered for her if he could, but he'd sacrifice her if necessary.

Raoul's lips pulled back in a feral smile. With a fresh trail, he could easily track her, and he would. The only question was whether to leave the hunt until after he'd met with Levi, or to take it up now.

Alone he could subdue the female. She might be deadly skin to skin, but he had the armor of his fur if necessary, though he'd have to be careful. Even in the red zone he'd be fair game in anything but a humanoid form.

His attention swung back to the brothel. Perhaps it would be better to wait, at least until he learned whether Levi had taken the bait and decided to help him turn the prisoner and the woman over to the maze owner.

As if on cue, the lion emerged from the brothel. Raoul averted his eyes, wary the other Were would feel the intensity of his gaze and find him lurking in the shadows.

It was far harder to suppress his anticipation. Would Levi head toward the bar and their meeting? Or would he decide to go to the maze and attempt to trade whatever information he had to Farold or Anton in exchange for the werelion they held there?

The woman must have come to the brothel and spoken to Levi, delaying him. Otherwise Raoul would have expected Levi to leave earlier in order to get to the meeting place in time to make sure it was safe.

At the end of the street, a waif-thin young boy changed from a run to a walk as if fearful the shapeshifters who controlled and worked in the whorehouses wouldn't be able to stop themselves from pouncing.

Raoul laughed silently. Stringy muscles and narrow bones, he'd killed a boy just like this one at dawn and left the carcass for scavengers after finding there wasn't enough meat to waste his time trying to eat it.

The boy approached the brothel, squaring his puny shoulders as if preparing for their ridicule and taunts. "I'm lookin' for a Were named Levi," he said, his voice still a child's.

"I'm him," the lion said, leaping down the steps in a graceful bound.

"Got a message for you. From the healer, Rebekka."

Raoul snarled in frustration at seeing his trap ruined. If he'd been close enough to rip the boy's throat out, he would have, just to keep him from saying more.

"Where is she?" Levi asked.

"With the Wainwright witches." The boy extended his arm, offering a tattered handkerchief. "The healer wants you to come to her there. She sent the cloth, so you'd know the message was real."

The boy opened his hand, revealing a darkened token. "This is from the witches."

"What do they want?" Levi asked, not taking the coin.

"Nothin'. They said if you didn't want to take it, showin' you was good enough. I'm to return it to them before I go home."

"And if I take it?"

"Then you can pass through the wards at the border of the red zone without pausin'. And you can come see the healer without worryin' about spells and such."

"So they're offering safe passage?"

The boy shrugged. "I reckon. I don't know. I'm just deliverin' the message."

"Did you see the healer?"

"Sure, least I think it was her. She told me her name and said I was to tell you the trapper's son was back with his mother."

A low growl sounded in Raoul's throat before he could stop it. He should have killed the toddler when he had a chance. If the messenger boy spoke true, then in all likelihood the compound was already abandoned, Eston's mother gone and spreading her legs for some human male who offered protection.

Everything Raoul had been working for seemed lost in a single cruel sweep of fate as Levi took the handkerchief and token, then headed toward the red zone border without even a glance in the direction of the bar where they were to meet.

Raoul fought against changing form, his muscles strung tight in his fury. He wanted to chase the lion down and slay him, to slaughter the messenger boy as well. But reason prevailed.

He left the alley and found the scent of the prisoner's woman. Sex-laden, marked. Easy to follow. And in doing so, he found he wasn't the only one who'd recognized her.

His path crossed with two guardsmen as they emerged out of a brothel bar moments after the cloaked figure passed. He recognized them both—the one named Jurgen, and the other, Salim, who'd been driving the jeep when they tried to intercept the healer and the Were.

Another time Raoul might have decided it suited his purposes to kill the humans competing for the same prey, especially since these particular humans were responsible for letting the healer escape with Eston. But already he was adapting, realizing there were other females he could take for a mate. Virgin females who could be bought or stolen or captured.

Claiming his father's woman would have been the ultimate in victory, the ultimate vengeance. Taking her would have satisfied him the way pissing on his father's corpse had, but if she was already soiled by another human—

"You'll take a third of the reward?" Jurgen asked, breaking into

Raoul's thoughts and verifying his suspicion they were all after the same prey.

Tasers. Netguns. Pistols. It took only a second for Raoul to inventory the weapons they wore on their belts openly because of the insignia patches sewn onto their shirts.

"Equal shares," he said, agreeing to the partnership though he didn't trust the guardsmen any more than they trusted him.

"Good." Jurgen touched his netgun as their prey turned a corner ahead of them. "You take the street to the right of her. I'll go left so she can't use the alleyways to get away from us. Salim here will catch up to her and drive her forward. If she keeps going she'll hit the open space near the maze. I can net her there, then taser her until she's real compliant and real helpful about answering our questions."

Salim's hand settled on his gun. "What if she comes at me? I'm not going hand-to-hand with her. Not after what she did to Nelson."

"Nelson touched her pussy. As long as you don't do that, nothing's going to happen to you."

"Farold said—"

"Shut the fuck up already. Shoot her and kiss off collecting any money. Even if she lives, a gun going off is going to bring the vice lords running to claim their take. Don't get close if it's going to make you shit your pants. Just let her know you're coming after her and keep her moving so I can use the netgun."

"Okay, okay," Salim mumbled.

"Split up," Jurgen said as they reached the street parallel to the one their prey had turned on.

FEAR spread through Tir like an inky black stain. His jaw ached from unconsciously clenching it as he worked his way through pages of long-dead languages, translating one symbol into another and then another and another, until he came upon a word he could speak and whose meaning he knew.

Prayers. Invocations. Incantations.

All of them using his blood to heal. Most of them turning it into something separate and living, something that could be offered like wine in a cup without his presence being necessary.

His emotions swirled like a building storm. For centuries he'd kept his sanity by imagining himself in possession of the translations. And now—

The tattoos on his right arm were translated and none of them unlocked the collar or made it disappear.

Terror grabbed and twisted his guts—that he'd have the same results when he finished transcribing the glyphs on his left arm.

He stood abruptly, his chair scraping over the floor, a harsh, abrasive sound that jerked the bookseller from his own tasks.

The promise of violence gathered around Tir, and he caught himself looking upward. Stopped himself from raising his arms as if he could call out to the heavens and bring bolt after bolt of lightning down until nothing remained of mankind but smoldering ash.

Araña had bargained with the vampire's servant. She'd made an agreement that might well cost her life, all because he'd been convinced these texts would free him and allow him to protect her.

Tir suppressed a scream of rage and frustration and fear. The muscles on his neck stood out, pressing against the collar as if by sheer force of will alone he could rid himself of it.

His hands balled into fists as he wrestled his emotions under control. Whether the remaining texts held the key or not, he needed to finish the translations and go to Araña.

He should never have let her out of sight to begin with. Caught up in the promise the book represented, he'd forgotten his thoughts when he returned to the healer's house and knew Araña was back. A blink and she could be gone from his life forever.

*   *   *

HEAVY boots crunched rough gravel behind Araña, making no effort at stealth. Eyes bored into her back, almost inviting her to start running.

The footsteps sped up as she did, gaining slightly but still in no hurry to catch her. Not surprising.

There were people around. Vendors closing up their shops and stalls. Messenger boys on their bikes or on foot, hurrying to turn their coin into shelter for the night and food.

Her enemy wanted her alive.

She was counting on it.

A risk. But an acceptable one.

She walked in shadow, her hands caressing the hilts of the blades. The sweet promise of vengeance was a siren song she couldn't ignore, the desire to kill Jurgen a black lust coating her heart and spreading through her veins. Maybe she was demon after all.

She glanced back. Instead of finding Jurgen or the black-haired stranger she thought was the werewolf Raoul, it was the guardsman whose soul thread was red mottled with black. Salim, who she'd seen in the vision of Levi's death.

Herding her.

Premonition or instinct, it didn't matter.

When the roles of predator and prey were interchangeable, traps could work both ways.

Erik and Matthew had taught her the value of a backup plan.

Araña started running.

A shout went up behind her.

She didn't look back again, even when her ears told her a second man had joined the first. But she smiled, and ran faster, angling to the north and east, to the place where she'd emerged from the maze on the night she escaped it.

She gambled that her pursuers didn't want to draw attention to their hunt by firing their guns. And the gamble paid off.

The opening that had been guarded by the spider was bricked

off, but in the grove of trees in front of it, the slick knots resembling cancerous growths remained, spaced out along the path, one to a bough—just as they had been the night Gallo watched another prisoner stumble into the trap thinking he'd reached freedom when he escaped the maze.

Araña hesitated only long enough to glance back at her pursuers. Jurgen was steps ahead of his companion.

A fitting end, she thought, not needing to feel the slide of her knife between his ribs to have her thirst for revenge satisfied.

She darted forward, into the grove.

Above her, leaves trembled slightly, but she was left alone, as she had been the night *she* escaped the maze and took this path to freedom.

A scream marked the moment her pursuer followed her into the deadly trap. Araña stepped from the path, turning to crouch behind elephant-eared plants.

Softball-sized spiders slid downward on silky strands of thread, leaving the tree limbs smooth, free of their unnatural blemishes. There could have been twenty of them, or forty, hurrying to aid the one that had jumped to immobilize their prey when he passed underneath.

Not Jurgen. Perhaps he'd sensed a trap and yielded the lead to his companion. Or maybe his companion's misfortune came from surging ahead before reaching the trees.

Either way, the guardsman named Salim lay screaming for help, unable to thrash or move his limbs because of the subduing poison the spider on his neck was injecting into his bloodstream.

Jurgen pulled his taser gun and fired it into the body of the spider. If it felt the jolt, either of the barb or the charge that followed, it didn't show any sign of it.

The first of the other spiders reached the paralyzed man and began using the trailing length of silk it had descended on to bind his ankles together.

"Hurry, oh god, get it off me, Jurgen."

Araña left her vantage point, merging into shadow with the intention of circling around and killing Jurgen while he was occupied with the spiders.

Instead of firing on even the first of them, Jurgen kept his pistol aimed for an attack. "There are too many of them. I don't have enough bullets to take them all out."

"Shoot them! Shoot them! Please, you can have my share of the reward."

Jurgen jettisoned the taser cartridge and holstered the weapon in favor of drawing a knife. "Looks like that's mine already. Besides, this will keep them busy."

The rest of the spiders massed like a living carpet and slowly began covering Salim. Jurgen's attention shifted, eyes searching for Araña in the rapidly darkening forest.

He ignored Salim's terror-filled words and cries until Salim began shrieking, "Kill me. Oh god, Jurgen, kill me. Don't leave me like this."

"Sorry, Salim, I don't know if they like dead prey."

Jurgen probed the shadows, directing his next words at Araña. "Just you and me now, bitch. Time to come out and play."

Araña answered the call, darting out and slashing at his back—finding body armor but drawing first blood on his upper arm.

The pistol fired as he reflexively squeezed the trigger. It fired again, an angry shot as he cursed.

She was already gone. Waiting for another opportunity.

Jurgen was no stranger to hunting in the forest. He used the evening darkness and soft loam to his advantage. Avoided the bones littering the path and hid the sounds of his movement in Salim's sobs and mewling cries.

Retreat wasn't an option even if Araña had been willing to consider it.

The open space and rubble-strewn ground between the grove and the reclaimed area of the red zone made that route an unwise choice.

Jurgen would use the gun now. If not to kill, then to incapacitate.

She could go deeper into the woods, taking a long detour and circling back to where Tir had told her the *Constellation* was moored. But doing it risked getting caught out in the night.

It left Jurgen alive to hunt her again.

This would end here. Tonight.

Araña picked up a human skull with strands of silk still clinging to it. She tossed it into a cluster of dried vine, distracting him long enough for her to move in, this time going for his legs, slicing across the back of his knee. Disabling him.

Jurgen screamed and fired, grazing her. It was a shallow wound, but it put the scent of her blood in the air and forced her to retreat.

Gasps of pain blended with his curses. He'd have to pause long enough to stop the bleeding, to fashion a crutch.

To decide.

Stay or leave.

It was already late enough for the feral dogs to be hunting.

If he was lucky he might make it to safety.

She moved in, not willing to allow him the choice.

He was silent now.

Hiding.

The creatures who called the forest home were silent, too. Waiting.

Only the sobbed prayers of the fallen guardsman drifted through the dusk. Eerie and surreal.

Araña crept forward, slow and cautious.

Adrenaline coursed through her, and heightened senses caught the flash of movement. She was already slashing before her mind identified her attacker. Werewolf. The one freed in the ambush.

Raoul.

Blood sprayed hot across her chest. Hers she thought at first, until the wolf's body fell away, her knife going with it.

She'd severed the Were's jugular, the move accomplishing it one she'd practiced so many times with Matthew that it needed no thought.

Sudden weakness drove her downward, onto her knees next to the furred corpse. Blood poured over her hand.

She stared, uncomprehending at first.

Hers, she realized. Heart rate spiking, pumping more of it through the place where the Were's fangs must have punctured her artery.

She had minutes before she'd bleed out.

She dropped her second knife.

Increasing weakness and loss of focus made it a struggle to free her belt and get it around her arm. Ropes and knots were second nature because of the *Constellation*. All she needed to do was—

Pain slammed into her, a thunderous blow to her head knocking her off her knees and to the ground.

The belt fell away from her arm.

Blood pulsed, escaped in a rush again.

Jurgen crouched over her, rage and victory in his eyes as he held his gun to her forehead, the bare skin of his wrist only inches away. "Tell me where your companion is and I'll let you tie the artery off. Otherwise, bitch, you bleed out."

Too late.

She was cold. So very cold.

She could barely feel her arms and legs.

With a thought she found the spider.

It hovered over her heart and seemed to grow larger, as if it stretched to meet the blackness forming at the edges of her consciousness, as if it were anxious to escape the tether of a mortal body.

No! she screamed silently, impressions flooding her mind.

Tir finding her in front of the mirror after her visit to the witches and showing her with pleasure just how thoroughly bound together her soul and flesh were.

The spider repeatedly seeking his touch.

The sense of unity she felt with it when she entered the vision place.

At the edge of death, all denial slid away. There was no separation of soul and mark. They were mirror images of each other.

Her acceptance of it brought the fusion of name and body, mind and spirit. And using the mark was as easy as drawing her knife.

It came to her hand, to her fingertips—a manifestation of who she was, what she was. And with the last of her strength she touched the bare skin of Jurgen's wrist.

He jerked away from her, the bullet from his gun hitting the dirt next to her head. And then he was screaming, writhing. But there was no room for satisfaction. Only regret.

Tir, she wept, her last thoughts of him as darkness engulfed her, bringing with it heat and the roar of the fire calling her home.

Twenty-three

ARAÑA. Her name whipped across Tir's soul. Suddenly. Intensely. Making him rise from the chair so violently it crashed to the floor.

The force of his need to go to her refocused his fury, his terror at having translated the last of the glyphs and found no hint of how to free himself from the collar.

She was hurt. Dying.

Whatever bound them together, so often turning her emotions into his, was stretching, thinning, dissolving.

Regret swamped him. Hers morphing into his.

It was acute. Excruciating. Destroying.

The sense of loss drove him to his knees, the bookseller and shop fading away as if they no longer existed on the same physical plane he inhabited.

No! Tir screamed silently. Willing Araña healed as he'd willed the boy attacked by the chupacabra healed. Willing her whole, safely returned to him.

His scream of pain became one note among a thousand of them—jarring, discordant sounds creating an agony unlike any he'd known.

It lasted a lifetime and an instant.

Ended abruptly. Completely. As if the choice whether she lived or died was no longer in his power to change.

He rose to his feet. Shaky, swaying, empty of all emotion and thought, all awareness, until the bookseller's movement brought him back to the present.

"Return the book to the safe. I have no further use of it," Tir said as he hurried toward the door, toward the boat where Araña had said she'd wait for him.

"WAS revenge as sweet as you thought it would be, daughter? Was it worth the price you paid to gain it?"

The demon's voice pulled Araña from blackness and into the same long corridor with its ever-changing tapestry where they'd met before. But unlike before, the threads were a vision seen through the shimmer of flames. They were like a reflection on water, there but not there, just as she was there but not there.

She was truly formless, her body an illusion created by her mind as it clung desperately to the memory of who she'd been.

Soon all vestiges of it would be burned away. She knew it as surely as she knew the demon behind her shouldn't have been able to stop her descent into the fire.

It wasn't the Hell she'd been threatened with and beat because of, or the place of eternal damnation and torment she'd been taught to fear, but the molten womb of the birthplace she'd dreamed about. And it held no terror for her, only the promise of rebirth.

Her soul had no place among the living, the proof of it was in front of her—in the fiery thread that extinguished in a flare of blue, as if in the instant of her death, when she'd called Tir's name, he'd been aware of her passing and called her name as well.

Araña's gaze lingered for only an instant before searching for the blue-black thread that was his. There was joy in not seeing it—in knowing the texts had contained the incantation to free him from the collar. But there was pain, too, intense regret at not having had a chance to say good-bye, to feel his body joined to hers one last time as they shared a final kiss, shared breath and spirit before being parted.

"Look further into the future if you want to see his life enter the weave again," the demon said, and Araña obeyed, feeling the phantom tightening of her throat when she saw the thread enter the pattern. Disappearing and reappearing only when it was alongside another, this one jagged ice where hers had been flame.

"Is he free of the collar?" she asked, afraid she already knew the answer by how closely the twining of the two threads mimicked the way hers had done with Tir's.

"No. Perhaps his future companion will discover a way to free him. Perhaps not."

Araña felt the sharp stab of jealousy, but still she asked, "How long until he has another chance at freedom?"

"Do you care so much? He's the enemy of our kind. In all likelihood he would have killed you if he'd gained his freedom from the collar."

Memories swelled up, swamping Araña in moments of tenderness and passion, companionship and possession, filling her with bittersweet emotion that she'd never experience any of it again with him. "He wouldn't have."

"You sound so sure, daughter. But once you would have sworn vengeance against him in the same way you did to honor the two human men you loved."

"Never."

Tir's name was so thoroughly woven into her soul she knew she was incapable of killing him.

Her confidence was met with laughter. "Once you would have looked at the collar around his neck and viewed it as a victory by the

House of the Scorpion. You would have celebrated Abijah en Rumjal's accomplishment along with the rest of us."

Shock sliced through Araña, as well as the faded remnants of terror. "The demon the maze owner commands?"

"He may well be demon by now," came the cryptic reply. "He's been bound to human will for thousands of years. He remembers all the deeds he's been forced to perform along with what came before. If the collar is removed, our enemy will also remember our shared history."

There was a roar, a sudden burst of air and power, like fuel added to fire, and it carried Araña to the past.

She recognized the imagery from the art history books Eric had cherished and she'd so often studied. Only instead of dreams captured in oil, scenes rising from the imagination of devoutly religious artists, instead of it being captured myth, she understood it was reality.

Men—mortal and those cast in supernatural light—fought side by side with angels, their faces resolute as they battled demons who looked like Abijah. Demons who bore images of spiders and serpents, cardinals and ravens, as well as scorpions on their skin—and others who looked fully human save for the marks that were a manifestation of their spirit's nature.

"He thought of himself as a holy warrior," the demon said. "It's written that healing was the greatest of his talents, but he turned away from it, preferring to kill instead. And when he couldn't kill, he saw us enslaved and held by humans. He lives because of alliances we've made with powers beyond The Prince's domain. And because it's fitting he endure the torment and horror he once so readily sentenced us to."

Araña closed her eyes, unwilling to search out and witness Tir's deeds even though the memory of it would soon be burned away. Whatever power the Spider demon used to hold her from the flames, it was weakening. She could feel the pull to leave.

"How long until he has another chance at freedom?"

"Three hundred years. Four hundred. The weave changes and

the woman has yet to be born. She won't be if we can prevent it. She wouldn't serve our cause or pledge herself to The Prince as you would have."

"I'd never bow to Satan."

The demon laughed again. "That would be a terrible sight indeed. One of our kind—and a daughter of my House—bowing to the angel who is now the god's adversary."

The response startled Araña. She turned from the battlefield, and it faded away as if it had never been. In front of her stood the demon, dressed as it had been before, in concealing robes with only black eyes and a small strip of skin revealed.

A raven perched on the demon's shoulder. And beyond both of them, a magnificent city rose, shimmering like a mirage, in an endless expanse of sand.

"This is the kingdom you were born to," the demon said. "This is our paradise and refuge. Our prison set deep in the ghostlands.

"We are the children of Earth, the Djinn, given life from its fiery womb so we can protect it. But now we wait and plot, and dream in exile of one day being able to return and reclaim what is our birthright."

"Djinn?" Araña asked, searching her mind, her memory, finding nothing though the word resonated within her.

"We existed long before the alien god arrived and thought to enslave us and give us over to his mud creations as familiars. When we resisted, the god forced The Prince into the image Abijah showed you and named him demon.

"The Prince was the first to be called by that name, but it's come to serve us well. In the millennia since then, the humans have followed the example of their god.

"They've conjured up thousands of nightmare creatures and named them demon. And along with their wars and their false prophets, knowledge of us has disappeared from human memory and history. They no longer remember how we once walked among them, able to take no form as freely as we could take any form."

The shimmering, beautiful city began to disappear, its buildings consumed by translucent flames. And like the candles burning in the witches' circle, Araña knew time was running out. The roar and pull of the primordial fire was growing stronger, harder to resist—or want to resist.

"I grieved the first time I witnessed your death," the de—the Spider Djinn said. "This time, as I stood in front of the tapestry and watched the outcome of your human choice, my anguish was tempered by the knowledge a Raven would soon follow you into the fire, and you would be reborn among us.

"I didn't know then that you'd touched your lips to those of our enemy and, in doing so, shared breath and bound a part of yourself to him. In the moment your spirit was freed, he used his greatest gift to heal and preserve the human shell you've been tethered to.

"Because it was a vessel created for you, the Raven can guide your spirit back to it and you will live again among those who've feared and hurt you.

"Or the ties binding you to our enemy will burn away in the fire and you can once again walk among your kind, in our kingdom.

"By The Prince's will, it is your choice."

Live for all of us.

Matthew's words found her, holding within them the love that had sustained her and the only home her heart had known—until Tir.

Memories of Tir made the decision easy. Thoughts of how she'd found him in the trapper's truck, shackled and tethered to a chair, and how earlier in the day he'd healed a human child when there was nothing to be gained from it.

If she'd once lived for vengeance, she realized now its price could be too high to pay. And if she and Tir had once been enemies, she'd learned that the past might be better put aside and a different future forged.

"I want to go back to him," she said.

The pitch black eyes of the Spider Djinn who claimed to be her mother showed no emotion. "As you will," she said. "But know this. If you betray us by speaking of us or revealing our existence, The Prince will send assassins belonging to the Scorpion House and they won't fail him. He will order your name struck from the books of our kind and those of the Raven's House will be forbidden from ever returning you to us."

"I understand."

"Then the choice is made. Perhaps you will still come to serve us as you were meant to. Use your gifts wisely. Use *all* of them."

"Will you continue to teach me?"

"Perhaps, daughter. Call my name when you next enter the Spider's realm. I am Malahel."

Araña understood, as she hadn't before, that from the moment she'd climbed onto the *Constellation* and seen the unnamed port city in her vision, she'd been meant to come to Oakland and encounter Abijah and Tir.

"Why don't you free Abijah?"

"The human he's bound to is one we can't touch, not from our prison, and not while he refuses to leave the one he created for himself with the maze."

"And Abijah, why doesn't he kill Anton?"

Malahel shuddered. "Doing so would make him *ifrit*. One whose name can no longer be spoken out loud and whose spirit can't be guided back and reborn into a new life."

"Will he be freed if I kill Anton?"

"Perhaps. Perhaps not."

If the Spider Djinn cared at all about Abijah's fate, it wasn't reflected in either answer or voice.

Araña could feel how little time she had left before the choice she'd made would no longer matter against the consuming nature of fire. "Will you tell me how to free Tir?"

The raven stirred, ruffling its feathers.

Malahel turned her face toward it, and something passed between them before the Spider Djinn's attention returned to Araña.

"Abijah knows the incantation. You have his name. If the maze owner is dead, and the moment right, you can gain the information you desire."

"I can't speak in the language Anton uses."

"His use of it is a conceit."

The last of the kingdom city behind Spider and Raven went up in flames with a *whoosh* that engulfed everything—burning away moment and scene like a match put to paper—turning reality into a rush of heat and the hungry song of the fire, then nothingness until Araña opened her eyes to descending nightfall seen through a canopy of trees.

The stench of death surrounded her. Blood and feces and urine.

Goose bumps pimpled her skin, making her realize how cold she was.

Her shirt was soaked in blood, both hers and her enemies'.

But the Dji—Malahel hadn't lied. She was whole. Healed. Strong.

Araña found her knives among scattered bones and leaves. She got to her feet, sheathing them, taking a last look at Jurgen and the Were.

The soft sound of sobbing and whispered prayers reached her. She retraced her earlier steps, going to the place where the remaining guardsman, Salim, who she knew only from the vision she'd changed with her visit to the witches' house, cried in a cocoon of silk. There were twenty or thirty spiders around him, protecting their prey as others scurried along the branches on either side of the path, anchoring the threads that would allow them to lift their meal and suspend it where other predators couldn't get it.

The spiders let her approach, parting to create a path through their midst, those displaced climbing onto the cocoon.

Perhaps he deserved this fate. Perhaps he didn't. But Araña couldn't walk away and leave him to die slowly.

She drew the knife, and the spiders converged on him, completely covering him. They lifted the front part of their bodies, telling her by their action they would protect their prize even from her.

Use your gifts wisely. Use all *of them.*

If there'd been fire here, she could have used it as a weapon. But in doing it, she would have betrayed a gift of trust, a birthright forged for her in the womb of Earth's fire, where her nature was chosen.

Instinctively she willed the mark to her hand, then concentrated on the spiders, asking them with pictures if they'd let her cut away the silky threads of the cocoon.

They answered with movement, parting again but only enough to reveal a small patch of silk above the guardsman's heart.

His fate was out of her hands. But she could grant him mercy.

Araña drove the knife in, accepting the spiders' offering.

Then she turned away, racing the nightfall and hurrying toward the *Constellation*—and Tir.

THE scent of blood made Tir's heart stop beating for an instant as he entered the boat's cabin.

The air was heavy with it.

Were.

Human.

Araña's.

She was safe. Alive.

The sound of the shower was testament to it. The way terror had morphed into relief as he ran, making him stumble and nearly fall, had told him, but until he saw her, held her . . .

A faucet was turned and the water stopped. A moment later, the door separating them opened.

She was naked. Beautiful. Her skin glistening, as if she'd known he was waiting and been in such a hurry to get to him that she had only allowed herself a cursory sweep of the towel over wet flesh.

Dark, dark eyes consumed him and made him burn as though he'd stepped into the heart of a primal fire.

He shed his clothes without being aware of doing it. Closed the distance between them, helpless against his need to hold her, to touch his skin to hers.

"Love me," she whispered. Command and plea. Inescapable desire stripping away any thought he might have other than to obey.

Tir lifted her into his arms, his mouth against hers, their tongues rubbing and twining in carnal bliss, in a ravenous joining of breath and soul.

His cock strained upward toward her, licking across his belly as each step toward the bed brushed the wet tip of it across his abdomen.

It was more than lust. More than the sating of physical desire.

If he'd lost her . . .

Her fingers touched the collar enslaving him, transmitting regret. Worry for him. Fear only barely masking a deeper terror.

"Don't," he said against her lips, wanting to lose himself in her, to become a willing prisoner to the passion that eradicated all reality other than the touch of flesh to flesh, soul to soul.

Tir placed her on the mattress and followed her down, no longer content to taste only her lips. He trailed wet, hungry kisses to her breast and reveled in the way her back arched, thrusting hardened nipples against his mouth, her body begging for him to suckle with the same fervor her words did.

He laved. Bit. Sucked. And grew more aroused as she writhed, pressing her heated cunt to his belly, adding her honeyed arousal to his own.

She cried out when he left her breast and kissed downward. But when he lifted his head after tormenting her with the shallow thrusting of his tongue into her navel, he erred in underestimating her, in forgetting how ruthless a warrior she was in her own right.

"I want to put my mouth on you at the same time," she said, wriggling out from under him, making his hips buck. The erotic images suddenly bombarding him hardened his cock further, leaving his testicles burning with the need for release.

Savage, feral determination swept through him when she would have pushed him to his back and taken the dominant position, crawling down his body and tormenting him before pleasuring him.

He grabbed her and pulled her underneath him, not allowing her to linger over his chest or nipples, not allowing her to tease. His forearms pinned her thighs to the mattress, holding her open so he could breathe her in, savor the sight of her glistening folds.

Even as he watched, the color of her aroused flesh darkened, beckoned. And it was all he could do to resist its call. He'd be lost as soon as he buried his face against her cunt, helpless against anything she wanted of him.

"Now, Araña," he said, commanding rather than begging, forcing steel into his spine as her lips and tongue found his cock.

Pleasure rippled through Araña, his so easily becoming hers as she willingly obeyed him by pressing her mouth to his rigid penis and measuring its length with kisses and sinuous rubs of her tongue against hardened flesh.

Tir was everything to her. Unlike the truth of the spider mark, it hadn't taken death for her to accept how important he was to her. Part of her had known from the very first, in the heart of the flame when she'd touched the strand of her life to his.

There'd never been any other choice for her but to fall in love with him, to need only his touch, crave it with a desperation that made it easy to turn away from the promise of power and a home among the Djinn.

His cock pulsed, wept for her just as her cunt throbbed and cried for him. She wanted him, ached for all of him, his body as well as his heart, his present as well as his future.

Fear clawed at her, but she forced it away, refusing to consider what lay ahead just as she'd refused to seek his image among those battling and slaughtering her kind in a past mankind no longer remembered.

His hips bucked when she took him into her mouth. She sucked, only to stop and once again tease along his length with her lips and tongue and teeth, fighting against taking him completely until he touched her in the same way.

Each lash was erotic agony. Each caress a test of Tir's strength and resolve.

Death had come for her in a heartbeat, and for a while, as he ran, he'd thought it had taken her. Now he wanted to savor his victory over it. He wanted to hold her beneath him and soak in the heat of her, to fill himself with her cries of pleasure, with the taste and scent and essence of her.

But he was powerless against the punishing ecstasy of lips and tongue and teeth on his cock. He couldn't resist her pleading with him to love her by putting his mouth on her.

Tir relented and lowered his lips to her heated flesh. He took her erect clit and thrilled at the way her hips jerked, bucked as she fucked the tiny organ into his mouth in the same rhythm as his cock slid into hers.

Satisfaction buffered the raw edge of his passion—until she swallowed, taking him deeper, sucking him harder.

With a growl he left her clit. He lapped his tongue through the silky moisture of her slit, plunged it hard and deep between her swollen cunt lips.

The bond that sent her emotions swirling into him, that had nearly destroyed his sanity in the moment she almost died, allowed him to feel her pleasure, the ecstasy she found in his touch—only *his* touch.

He wouldn't part with her. Couldn't. Even the thought of it burned away what remained of his control.

Tir fucked her with his tongue. Shoved it into her tight channel as he held her open, his cock doing the same to her mouth. And even when she came, it wasn't enough of a claiming.

He pulled from her mouth before he spewed his seed. He forced her onto her elbows and knees, though she went willingly, provocatively spreading her thighs, offering herself to him, feeding a bestial urge to mate.

He covered her. Thrust into her.

Rutted like the stud his captors had so often tried to make of him.

Her moans and panted pleas sent him into a frenzy. Had him convulsing in exquisite victory as jets of semen rushed through his cock in a lava-hot rush to her womb.

He wouldn't lose her again. Now and forever, she was his.

Tir collapsed, his arms locking her to him, holding her back to his chest as his penis remained inside her, trapping his seed in her sultry depths. She shivered against him, but he knew it was in pleasure, in reaction to the intensity of their lovemaking.

He pressed a kiss to her shoulder, her neck. A question forced its way through the aftermath of desire. "What happened?"

She shivered again. And this time he knew she was remembering. Fear tried to chase away the heated remnants of lust. He tugged a blanket over them.

"What happened?" Tir repeated, his arms tightening around Araña in a silent warning he wouldn't let her avoid his question.

Araña closed her eyes, savoring the heat of Tir's body, the protective, possessive feel of his arms around her, the intimacy of having his cock still lodged inside her.

What should she tell him? What could she tell him?

Nothing about the Djinn. She didn't doubt The Prince would send Scorpion assassins as terrifying and deadly as Abijah if she spoke about her kind.

"I led the guardsman who sold me to the maze into a copse of trees near where I escaped from it. He was with two others. Another guardsman and the Were from the trapper's truck."

"Raoul," Tir growled. "They're dead?"

"Yes." She delayed the moment when they would need to talk about going into Anton's house by rubbing her palm over the tattoos on his arm. "What do the glyphs mean?"

"They're prayers to use with my blood."

She heard the savage anger in Tir's voice. "For healing?"

"Yes."

She ached to tell him Abijah held the key to freeing him from the collar. But just as she couldn't tell him what she'd learned of her own heritage, she feared what he would do with the knowledge.

Abijah might be bound, but he was no less powerful or deadly for it, while Tir was vulnerable. Fear stuttered through her chest as she thought about what tomorrow would bring—and the choice awaiting her if they managed to get into the maze and then into Anton's house.

Malahel's warnings whispered through her mind, along with the words Tir had spoken before they'd come to Oakland. *Keep your secrets as long as they don't involve me. But remember this, if I find they make you my enemy, not even the sweet temptation of your body will save you from my vengeance.*

Araña took a steadying breath and forged ahead with the plan she hoped would lead to Tir's freedom without putting him in the path of the Djinn who'd enslaved him. "When I was held at the maze, Anton summoned the demon and ordered him to bring me to the front of the cage. The demon didn't move to obey and Anton commanded him again, in a language I didn't understand.

"It made me realize the demon wasn't a willing participant in the maze. Later the demon refused to answer a question until Anton repeated it three times. When he did answer it, Anton's assistant Farold suggested a caveat be added to whatever command the demon has to obey when it comes to those running the maze. He suggested the demon be told not to intentionally kill me unless I was *escaping* the maze. If I'm breaking *in*, and the demon sees an opportunity to be free if I can kill Anton—"

"Don't think you're going in alone."

"It's our best chance."

His teeth found her shoulder and administered a rebuke. "If I thought you'd agree to leaving Oakland and forgetting your promise to the vampires, I'd force myself out of the tight heaven of your channel and head for the bay and open waters right now."

There was an edge of truth in Tir's comment, as if he'd contemplated forcing her to leave. "I can't," she said, the image of Erik and Matthew rising from the black sea of the ghostlands pressing in on her.

Araña entwined her fingers with Tir's and regrouped, her heart racing as she remembered the hungry pull of the flames, the desire to reunite with them and the shimmering promise of the Djinn Kingdom.

"I was dying," she said. "You saved me. You healed me."

Tir's fingers tightened on hers. "And promised myself that from now on I wouldn't let my vigilance waver, even for a moment. You're so very mortal. So vulnerable. A blink and you could be gone from my life forever."

Her heart thundered in her chest at what his words implied. She turned in his arms, putting aside the need to convince him to let her face Abijah alone, at least for the moment.

Araña smiled when Tir grunted in protest at having his cock forced from her body. Even now, after all they'd done together, she found him too beautiful to look at and yet so enthralling she couldn't look away. He was masculine perfection, the epitome of unfathomable power.

If he remembered his past, would he look on her with hatred and revulsion? Would he regret touching her, lying with her?

A fist squeezed her heart, sending pain spiking through her chest at the thought of losing him. She refused to believe he would kill her if he learned she was Djinn, but she couldn't stop herself from stroking a fingertip over the collar.

"I nearly died today in my hunger for revenge. If I asked it of you, would you turn away from seeking vengeance against the one who put this on you?"

"Don't ask it of me," he warned.

"I can't promise I won't."

And because she wanted him to have the words, she added, "I love you."

Tir rolled so she was underneath him, his cock once again buried deep in her heated channel. Her emotions flowed into him, fierce and aching, compelling. Devastating in their intensity. He touched his lips to hers, whispered against her mouth as his hips moved, beginning a slow climb to shared ecstasy. "Love doesn't begin to encompass all I feel for you."

Twenty-four

RELIEF spread through Rebekka as Levi came into sight. Seeing him made her escape from the Iberá compound more real than the chauffeured drive or the moments she'd spent in the room off the foyer with Annalise Wainwright. Seeing him allowed her to believe life would return to normal—an illusion that lasted until the witch standing next to her on the porch said, "The matriarch thought you and the Were would be more comfortable staying elsewhere tonight. She's arranged for an escort to the shamaness's house. It's safe to speak in front of him, but don't ask his name."

The comment took Rebekka's eyes off Levi, and she startled at the man now standing where moments ago there'd been nothing but shadows and a raven perched in a tree just beyond the gate marking the boundary of the Wainwright property.

Shapeshifter, she thought, but even from a distance, she knew he was nothing ordinary. He was clothed, where a true shapeshifter wouldn't have been. More telling, eyes the color of a dense forest blazed with inhuman fire, while a stylized raven marked his cheek.

"If all goes well," Annalise said, "I will speak with you again in the future. You may keep the token in the Were's possession as a symbol of alliance; it no longer holds a spell capable of bringing help."

Rebekka nodded and Annalise went inside, leaving Rebekka free to hurry into Levi's hug and barrage of questions. Before she answered the first of them, she glanced at the stranger who leaned against the oak tree where he'd once been perched.

Levi stiffened. A low growl emerged, only to be met by a laugh.

The man pushed away from the deep shadow and approached. "That's hardly the appropriate greeting for the poor escort and messenger boy charged with ensuring you spend the night in a place free of trouble."

"Who are you?" Levi asked, making Rebekka cringe.

"You'll have to trust the little healer when she tells you I mean you no harm, though as a courtesy to Aisling and her prince of a mate, it would be best if we appeared on her doorstep before full dark arrives."

Rebekka gave Levi another quick hug then disengaged, saying, "We can talk as we walk."

Lion gold eyes issued another warning to their escort before Levi took up a position next to her. And as they walked, she told him what had happened since they parted upon seeing the guardsmen and Gulzar near the Mission.

When she reached the part where Aziel had appeared, Levi produced the blackened token and handed it to her. He stopped in his tracks when, moments later, she got to the end of her story, telling him, "Annalise prophecies a war between supernatural beings. She claims healers will emerge who are able to do what I can't for those trapped between forms."

"What you can't do *yet*," their raven-marked guide said, causing them both to look at him, though he neither looked back nor stopped walking.

Levi let the stranger advance a block before he took a step.

Rebekka doubted even ten blocks would be enough distance to keep their escort from hearing their conversation.

"Is he right?" Levi asked.

"Yes."

"What do the witches want from you?"

She curled her fingers around his arm. "They didn't ask anything."

"Yet. They involved you in their schemes from the first, by sending for you. You could have lost your life, either at the hands of the guardsmen or the Church."

"Because I *chose* not to leave Eston in the truck for guardsmen to find," Rebekka said, and she wasn't sorry for that choice. Just as she wasn't sorry they'd ambushed the trapper or waited in the woods to offer shelter to Araña. "If not for the witches, Anton would have dragon lizards and Cyrin would be dead."

Levi snarled at what Anton had planned for his brother. She squeezed his arm, hardly daring to mention the dream they shared of freeing the animals and Weres held at the maze, but she didn't know Aisling or her mate, and Annalise hadn't said it was safe to speak freely once they arrived at the shamaness's house.

"I think the witches intend for Araña to gain control over the demon. If—"

"She and Tir intend to break into Anton's house. Araña made a bargain with Draven Tassone. I don't know the details of it."

Confusion buffeted Rebekka. The vampire's involvement was unexpected. "Tir is the prisoner?"

"Yes."

"When will they attempt it?"

Levi stopped her once again, this time putting his mouth close to her ear. "She has three days to complete whatever task she agreed to."

Rebekka's palms grew suddenly damp. "Then they have until tomorrow at noon unless they want to face the magistrate's men as well as the demon."

"I warned her about the magistrate's arrival when I saw her earlier. She and Tir witnessed the assault on your house and she came to the brothel to warn me. Her boat is hidden in the outer harbor. I'm meeting them there shortly after sunrise tomorrow."

Rebekka's breath caught. Her thoughts went to the patriarch, trapped in his wheelchair, his limbs slowly becoming useless. She could think of only one thing Araña and Tir had that could be used for bargaining with the vice lord who controlled the outer harbor. "Rimmon's daughter?"

"I told them she suffered from the wasting disease. If Tir healed her as you think he might be capable of doing, there's no rumor of it yet."

Levi turned away from her and began walking, hands shoved into his pockets and shoulders hunched in an uncharacteristic way. "I contemplated betraying them. I asked her to use her gift to find you. When she claimed not to have control over it, I told her about Annalise sending for you. I told her to seek out the witches and learn how to use her gift. When nearly a day passed . . ."

Levi shrugged. "I was on my way to the outer harbor to see if Tir had succeeded in stealing the boat and making a deal with Rimmon. Then I was to meet with the werewolf we freed. He approached me at the brothel—

"Now I know he lied. He said he was there when Tir was turned over to the trapper. He claimed Tir was a demon-possessed human being sent to the maze."

Rebekka slid her arm through Levi's. "You wouldn't have betrayed them."

"I've thought about little else but the possibility of you being held at the maze and Gulzar—" A shudder went through him. "If Araña had arrived a few minutes later, I would have missed both her and the messenger bringing news you were safe. I might have—"

"No. You wouldn't have betrayed them."

He shrugged again and remained silent. Ahead of them, the stranger leaned indolently against a fence in front of a white adobe house with a profusion of flowers underneath the windows and on the porch.

Rebekka touched her pocket and felt the folded pages she'd ripped from the journal on the patriarch's desk. Choices. Paths taken and not taken.

Sitting across from Annalise, she'd accepted that maybe she couldn't know the cost ahead of time. Maybe she could only go with her heart and do what she considered right at each juncture. "There might never be a better chance to free those held in the maze."

Levi didn't respond until they'd halved the distance to the shamaness's house. "I had the same thought as I passed from the red zone into this area. Vampires aren't known for wasting their resources. Draven Tassone least of all. He would have provided her with information to increase the odds of success. I'll listen to her plan, and if it's a sound one, I'll go with them. You can wait—"

"No. Both the Weres and the animals will need me or they'll end up dying in the traps outside the maze or slaughtered in it when the magistrate's guards and the police arrive and find them loose."

The stranger opened the gate and proceeded to the shamaness's front door. As they neared the house, Rebekka could hear music coming through the open window, an exotic mix of instruments making her think of shimmering desert and primal heat.

Their escort knocked and the door was opened by a man. Rebekka's steps faltered. He had the same otherworldly beauty as their escort, the same hint of ready death.

"Was that the door I—" The shamaness's question was cut off by her laugh, and it remained thick in her voice when she said, "Didn't you warn your father against making you his pawn again, Zurael?"

The teasing question earned her a growled "Aisling" and had their escort's teeth flashing white in the rapidly approaching darkness. He extended a hand toward Rebekka and Levi. "I've brought guests in need of safekeeping."

The shamaness nudged her mate aside and stood in the doorway. He curled a protective arm around her waist, but she smiled and

Rebekka felt welcome. "Come in," Aisling said. "We're just about to sit down for dinner."

ARAÑA brushed her fingertips over a taut masculine nipple and smiled at the sound of Tir's heartbeat speeding up beneath her ear. *Just a little bit longer*, she told herself, savoring the closeness as his words of love continued to sing through her like a musical refrain.

She closed her eyes in contentment and sighed as his fingers combed through her hair, gliding sensuously over her vertebrae, his palms caressing her buttocks at the end of each downstroke. She wanted this forever, but even as she thought it, the knowledge that he'd once killed and enslaved the Djinn pushed her peace aside.

Against her back, Tir's hand stopped moving. "What are you thinking about?"

She longed to tell him, to ask for reassurance. But how could he give it when he had no memory of his past? When he'd already refused to give up his claim of vengeance?

Araña snuggled closer and wedged her leg more firmly between his. None of it would matter if she didn't succeed in the task she'd agreed to. "I spoke to Levi after I left L'Antiquaire."

"At the brothel?" There was no mistaking the purr of menace in Tir's voice.

"Yes."

His fingertips found one of the scars on her back and traced it, sending a pulse of erotic fear through her. "I should punish you. You knew I expected you to go directly to the *Constellation*."

"I told him what we'd seen and heard at Rebekka's house," she said, neither making excuses nor refuting Tir's charge, but unable to hide her reaction to his threat of punishment, not with her clit and bare mound pressed to his thigh. "I also told him I'd made a deal with Draven Tassone. Levi will be here shortly after sunrise."

"He intends to go with us?"

"I don't know. At the least he'll share what information he has. He once hunted in the maze."

She lifted away from Tir so she could see his face. "Normally there are only three people in the maze compound, beside the— beside Abijah." When there was no flicker of recognition, she continued, "By noon tomorrow, the traveling magistrate will arrive in Oakland. Some of his prisoners will be taken to the maze."

"Meaning additional guards," Tir said, also remembering Thane's comment about apartments being available for those required to be on the premises at certain times. "And meaning we need to act before noon tomorrow."

"Yes. Thane was right in his assessment of the best way to get into Anton's house. There are cameras throughout the maze, and cages of wild animals forming a gauntlet at the back of it. The day I was taken there, the guardsmen stopped at the gate and were buzzed in from the front office by Farold after they identified themselves. There are probably others who receive the same treatment, but there's also Farold himself and a helper named Gulzar." Araña smoothed her palm over Tir's chest. "I'm going to use my gift to see if I can find a way to get into the office."

Tir frowned, but didn't protest.

She forced herself to roll away from him and sit up.

He sat as well, pulling her onto his lap, his chest to her back and his arms secured around her. A kiss followed, in the hollow of her neck where the spider stretched across her skin.

Araña glanced at the lantern Tir had lit earlier when they'd left the bed long enough to drop anchor a short distance away from the pier.

Remembered pain and fear pressed in on her as she thought about the night she'd climbed aboard the *Constellation* and seen Erik's death. She swallowed down the emotion and found a smile when Tir said, "I won't allow this if it's going to hurt you."

"I'll be fine," she said, focusing on the flame. Willingly accepting its call.

Almost immediately soul strands settled, forming a carpet spreading before her, as if she could walk its path into eternity. Around her colors and threads shifted subtly. She sensed then what she *knew* had to be true, though she'd never noticed it before. She wasn't alone here.

She had no form, only the spider-shaped illusion she now understood was the manifestation of her soul. The others weren't visible either, and yet the echo of the changes they made to the pattern vibrated through her.

Panic threatened to seize her. For an instant she didn't know where to begin, how to find the threads she was looking for. Then, like a beacon, her own life blazed near her feet, only to disappear. Where it slid beneath the pattern, it was entwined in the blue black of Tir's.

She turned away from the present and the future and looked to the past, followed the bright flare of her own thread until she found the place where it intersected with Levi's at the brothel. There was no subtle movement around her, and in texture the carpet appeared more solid, more vivid, as if now that it couldn't be changed, the full truth and all its nuances could be revealed.

Levi's was the only thread she was certain would lead to Gulzar, and maybe Farold—though she held little hope his soul could be touched here given what Malahel had said about Anton.

Araña traveled further into the past, being careful not to violate Levi's privacy until it became necessary—when it ran concurrent with a pus-colored strand she had only to concentrate on to hear the name she'd been hoping to find. Gulzar.

He had Levi strapped naked to a table slick with blood, instruments of torture and rape scattered haphazardly around him.

Charmed silver wrapped around various segments of Levi's limbs, creating a monster that was neither lion nor man.

Nausea and hate swelled inside Araña. She reached for Gulzar's thread, meaning to grasp it so she wouldn't lose it, but she hesitated at the last moment. She had no desire to see the entirety of his sins, to walk the path of his evil.

She concentrated instead on retracing her imagined steps along the patterned carpet, from past into present. And her desire to kill him grew when she found him in a house in the red zone, a young girl strapped to his table, terror coming off her in waves.

He circled her, as if she were a slab of clay and he was an artist contemplating what he would make of it.

In the immediate past Araña could see the girl's capture.

The location of the house.

The car in the garage with its remote control to open the gated entrance to the maze complex.

The collection of keys that would unlock the office door and the cells housing the animals and Weres, as well as any human prisoners.

Impotent rage held Araña in its grip for an instant as she realized that in her hunger for revenge and her desire to gain it with her knives, she'd wasted an opportunity to learn when she stood in front of the tapestry and asked how Levi's fate could be changed.

"To predict how a single change will affect an entire pattern takes centuries of study by those dedicated to it," Malahel had said upon their initial meeting.

Araña didn't have that kind of time. Neither did the girl.

Pride was a weak barrier against what it would cost both the girl and herself if she failed now. With a thought, Araña cast a name into the vision place. *Malahel.*

A robed figure shimmered into existence though her form was translucent. "I'm impressed, daughter. I hadn't thought it possible you would retain so much of what you once were."

"How do I stop him? How do I kill him from here?"

The Spider Djinn's attention shifted to the pus-colored thread. Araña could feel a phantom presence enter the same mental place her soul traveled. But it was the translucent image of the woman who'd once been her mother that said, "Look for those connected to the girl's life."

Araña looked, and saw immediately that the girl had brothers and a father who were searching for her. Bear shapeshifters who'd left the safety of the forest and joined the other predators in the red zone, though they hunted only a single prey, the human whose scent they'd found where a trap had been set in the woods.

"Touch one of their threads to Gulzar's?" Araña asked, a pit of horror forming at the thought she might relegate one of them to the same fate as the girl's by doing it.

"It's his scent they need," Malahel said. "The girl's won't be easily found outside his house."

Araña found the strand in the closest proximity to Gulzar's and mentally grasped it.

The patterned carpet dissolved into a thousand separate threads.

Panic welled up, but she forced it away, concentrating instead on finding the sickly thread of Gulzar's strand.

It was the sound of his name that led her to him, and as soon as she mentally took his strand, the carpet representing the future returned.

A glance showed the convergence of threads, the extinguishment of Gulzar's life in less than an hour's time, less than it would take her or Tir to get to him.

Araña moved toward the moment, wanting to witness the truth of it.

Pain stopped her before she reached it, shocking in its intensity and unexpectedness.

Malahel's voice spoke in her mind, blocking the pain. *Your body tethers you and calls you back. It can't survive long without your spirit housed within it. Beyond that, this realm belongs to the Spider Djinn. You've mingled your soul with our enemy's and that also limits your time here.*

Araña had always thought the pain was caused by the mark

forcing a choice on her. Now, with a thought, she could feel the strand holding her to her body. With it came an awareness that was real, not phantom.

Blood dripped from her nose and onto her breasts. Tir cursed and willed her back to him.

The vision place itself pushed and contracted, as if it would cast her from the womb where the future was formed.

She knew instinctively she'd traveled here too many times in the span of a few days for it to be easily reached again, at least for a while. And when the pain returned, she couldn't fight it.

"Never again," Tir said as soon as their eyes met.

"I'm okay," she said, finding her nosebleed had already stopped. "And the price was worth it. Anton and Farold's helper isn't at the maze tonight. He's at a house in the red zone. He'll be dead in an hour. The car is there along with keys and gate controller. I can describe the route and you—"

"Will remain here with you until sunrise. Rimmon's promise of protection covers only the boat. I don't intend to allow you out of my sight again until I'm free of the collar."

She opened her mouth to protest then closed it again, knowing it would be futile. Tomorrow, after they'd gotten to Gulzar's house, she'd find a way to convince Tir to let her confront Abijah alone.

"I won't lose you," he said, standing with her in his arms and taking the few steps necessary to reach the bathroom.

He pulled the paneled door of the shower stall open and turned on the water, adjusting the temperature before setting her to her feet.

Her cunt lips grew slick and swollen with the thought of his lathered hands on her flesh, of hers on his. "There's not much room for two people."

Tir urged her underneath the warm spray and joined her, crowding her against the wall, his hardened cock trapped between their bodies. "For what I intend, we don't need much of it."

Twenty-five

"LOOKS like they're getting ready to leave," Levi said as he and Rebekka cleared the last of the tangled ruins that had once been trucking containers and multimillion-dollar cranes.

Rebekka nodded but didn't say anything. The day of the ambush she'd been consumed with thoughts of the child crying in the cab of the trapper's truck and the Weres held in the back of it.

She'd been battling fear at the sound of the approaching guardsmen—and if she was honest with herself—didn't want to look too closely at a man she knew they'd have to leave behind.

But as Tir turned, sensing their approach and nudging Araña, Rebekka *knew* he wasn't human, despite the form he took—just as she'd known the same about Zurael and their raven-marked escort, though Levi had claimed otherwise on their walk to Rimmon's dock.

Surreptitiously she touched the witch's token in her pocket, attributing her newfound *sight* to it, then shivered as she remembered the icy feel of Aziel's staff passing through her chest and her heart.

"How is it you're free, healer?" Tir asked when she and Levi reached the dock.

There was something in his voice that made it impossible not to answer, though Rebekka told him an abbreviated version of what she'd shared with Levi, leaving out what she knew of the urn and what Annalise had told her—only to get a small shock when Araña said, "I encountered Aziel in the ghostlands. The shamaness greeted him with warmth."

"When?" Tir asked. And there was no mistaking the edge of menace contained in the single word.

"Yesterday," Araña answered. "After I visited the witches the first time."

"You let your soul be cast from your body and into the land of the dead?"

"I saw Matthew and Erik there."

There was a subtle change in Tir's expression, but his voice still held a silky promise of retribution as he said, "We will revisit this conversation later, in private, after we accomplish what we must at the maze."

Rebekka resisted the urge to rub her hands over the smooth, worn cloth of her pants. She felt the weight of the token in her pocket, along with the folded pages from the journal.

Between Araña's mention of Aziel and the knowledge she'd visited both Aisling and the witches, Rebekka didn't think she needed additional proof this was the right time to attempt a rescue of the animals and Weres held by Anton, but she still asked, "Will you tell me what you agreed to do for Draven Tassone?"

"He wants an urn destroyed."

Rebekka started in surprise. She'd been sure the witches intended to use Araña to trap the demon and bring them the urn.

Now, framing it with Annalise's talk of war between supernatural beings and the forming of alliances, she considered that maybe what they really wanted was to free the demon and had made a deal with Draven to hide their connection to it.

"The urn the demon is bound to?" Rebekka asked, needing to understand.

Araña went completely still at the question. Tir cursed.

Without it being a conscious decision, Rebekka pulled the folded papers from her pocket and gave them to Araña. "They're from a book in The Iberá's possession."

A glance at the rough sketches and Araña nodded. "These urns are very like the picture Thane showed me." Her eyes scanned over the accompanying entries. She quoted a portion of the passage, "Demons have no love of humans and will expend as much energy twisting and evading and turning a command into something to suit their own purposes as obeying it."

Araña looked up at Tir. "This is why I need to go into Anton's house alone. Abijah will use Anton's command, not to kill me unless I'm escaping the maze, to his advantage. He was granted permission to 'play with me.' It might keep him from investigating what's going on in other parts of the maze."

"No."

Levi spoke for the first time. "The demon's intentions won't matter at all if you—*we*—can't get into the compound in the first place without being seen."

Nothing could have prepared Rebekka for Tir saying, "If Araña's vision proves true, we'll find the man named Gulzar dead in a house he maintains in the red zone. We intend to use his car and his keys to gain access to the office, and from there, Anton's house."

Levi's hands opened and closed as though he still had a lion's claws. "How did he die?"

Araña gave a small shake of her head. "I don't know the exact manner of his death, only that he died last night."

HIS death was brutal, Tir thought a short time later.

Blood trailed everywhere, as if Gulzar had been nicked and chased until the floors were painted red and he'd finally bled out.

And when he could provide no more entertainment alive, his attackers still found another way to make sport of him. They tore him apart.

Pieces of Gulzar were everywhere. What remained of shredded skin and muscle and organs was on the walls and furniture. Shards of bone, none of them bigger than a coin, crunched underfoot as the four of them moved through the carnage, looking for the key chain Gulzar had once worn on his belt.

Tir's gaze kept returning to Araña. Suspicion descended and clung to him. There was more to her visions than she admitted.

Twice he'd seen her bleed as a result of them. Twice he'd thought it was a cost unwillingly paid. But what if it was an offering instead? This violent death was no coincidence.

His hand snaked out when he neared her, catching her arm. "Don't think you can continue to hide the truth about the mark or its vision gift from me much longer."

Araña's fear lanced through him, confirming his suspicions. "I know," she said, unfathomable emotion becoming a wall between them as she reached up and touched the hated collar. "The incantation is in Anton's possession. You won't gain it unless you allow me to go into his house alone."

Her words from the night before slid from the dark place his hunger for revenge lived. *If I asked it of you, would you turn away from seeking vengeance against the one who put this on you?*

Tir's hand tightened on her arm. "Tell me."

"I can't."

Centuries of memories and hate whipped through him, all that he'd endured while at the mercy of humans. "If you prove to be my enemy, not even the love I feel for you will save you from death," he said, knowing it was a lie even as the words left his mouth, but there was no taking them back as Levi and Rebekka stepped into the room with Gulzar's ring of keys.

Levi said, "There's a good chance Farold will be walking in the maze, checking the cameras and traps. It was a habit of his on days when the magistrate arrived in town. We may be able to catch him there. That would leave only Anton and the demon."

Fear for Araña added to Tir's anger over her refusal to tell him what she knew of the incantation. She'd placed him in an impossible situation. Freedom was too close for him to turn away from it. But beneath his hand her bones were fragile, her lifetime finite without his vigilance. She was mortal, and there were no guarantees he would be able to heal her if things went wrong.

As if sensing the violent turmoil of his thoughts, Araña's finger traced the collar. "Trust me to deal with Abijah and Anton while the three of you handle Farold and free the Weres."

Suspicion flared again at her choice of the word *deal*. But this time it was doused immediately, and the hollow place it left filled with guilt and repudiation as he remembered her fear at L'Antiquaire when she'd entered into the vampire's bargain in order to allow him access to the texts, as he thought about her kneeling in front of him in the woods and working desperately to free him of the shackles before the guardsmen reached them.

He leaned in and brushed his lips against hers in apology. "I trust you."

THE car had been in the garage where she'd seen it from the vision place. The gate controller made it unnecessary to do more than slow as they approached the entryway.

She drove—because she knew how thanks to Matthew—and because if Levi was wrong about Farold being in the maze, then the sight of her alone in the front seat and behind the wheel would suggest Gulzar was behind her with a gun pointed to her head.

But Farold wasn't there, or if he was, then he intended to meet the car around back, where trucks carrying hunters or groups of human prisoners were directed.

Araña stopped the car at the side of the building and they all got out.

"How long do you need?" Levi asked.

"If I don't encounter anyone, three minutes to get in and through the first walkway door."

Araña's eyes met Tir's. Her heart thumped in her chest and she fought to hide her fear from him.

"Leave the doors unlocked or open," he said. "As soon as Levi and Rebekka are done, I'll come to you."

She nodded and turned away, resisting the urge to wrap her arms around his waist and bury her face against his chest. To soak in his heat and cling to him one last time just in case it was the last chance she had.

With the keys it was easy to get into the front office where she'd been held at gunpoint by Jurgen. The door between offices was unlocked and she slipped inside to confront the first of the keypads Thane had told her about.

Always before she'd thought she had a knack and was simply picking up on changes of texture and slight discolorations to the keys, using hidden patterns her subconscious detected when she and Matthew and Erik made their detailed studies before attempting a job. This time as she touched her fingers to the numbers, she knew her ability came from her gift, from her connection to the vision place.

A verse whispered through her mind. *He that is unjust, let him be unjust still. And he who is filthy, let him be filthy still.*

Her smile was a snarl of remembered suffering as the hell of her early years finally served her. She recognized the words and knew Anton had set this code from Revelations, the twenty-seventh book, the twenty-second chapter, the eleventh verse.

She punched in the numbers and heard the satisfying click of a lock disengaging. A second later she was inside the covered walkway, the open door triggering lights along the rocked corridor.

Araña hesitated. Indecision plagued her as she folded the paper she'd grabbed when she passed the front counter.

There was a certain poetry in using the notices putting a price on her head to keep the lock from engaging again. But part of her wanted to protect Tir from a direct confrontation with Abijah if she failed.

Hesitation ended with decision. She put the paper between door and jamb, accepted that if she died, she owed it to Tir to allow him a chance to see Abijah and perhaps remember some of the past.

Cold sweat drenched her at the second of the keypads. Her mind was blank—as if this code had been set after Anton gained whatever protection kept his soul thread from appearing in the weave.

Panic welled up. She'd never failed with a lock. Never.

The lights flickered in warning, probably programmed to remain on only for the time it would take someone to travel the length of the walkway.

A feather-soft awareness brushed over the mark now on the back of her hand, causing her to glance up and spot the spiderweb wedged in the corner. The sight of it gave her a rush, the same thrill she'd always gotten when a plan jelled into something workable.

Just as she'd done with the spiders in the copse of trees, she asked in pictures—and was answered by movement.

Delicate, long brown legs covered the distance to the keypad. They reached out and lightly touched a series of numbers before retreating.

Araña didn't hesitate or doubt. She punched in the code and heard the telltale click.

She was in.

Another folding of paper to prevent the door latch from engaging. A few steps.

And then Abijah was there. Appearing from nowhere and immobilizing her as though she were a child and not a woman who had trained and killed.

He pinned her arms at her waist as the serpentlike tail coiled around her ankles and his palm pressed against her mouth, preventing even the sound of her terror from escaping.

Adrenaline spiked and she wrestled against the instinct to thrash. The mark cowered at the bottom of her foot.

She struggled to *think*, to use her mind as both Erik and Matthew had so often counseled when it came to dealing with someone so much more powerful than she was. It hadn't occurred to her that she wouldn't be able to talk to Abijah.

In desperation she took control of the fear and willed the mark to her cheek, to Abijah's hand. He laughed. "Do you think I didn't recognize a Spider? Especially one who looks as you do? Did you think it coincidence that I diverted my attention to the convicts and left you unattended in front of the very exit and trap I knew held no danger for you?"

Talons pressed into her side, piercing the fabric of her shirt but not breaking her skin. His palm slid from her face to curl around her neck, against the sharp, hard beat of her pulse.

"There's something different about you," he murmured, scraping the deadly nails lightly over her throat. "Something that stirs an ancient memory."

She couldn't stop the telltale race as her heart sped up more than she would have thought possible. To distract him she said, "I'm here to destroy the urn, Abijah en Rumjal."

He stiffened at the mention of both urn and name, then laughed. "You might be able to do it, wrapped as you are in human flesh. But the one who thinks of himself as my master would need to be dead and I'm charged with protecting him. One threatening move, one command . . ."

Abijah's hand slid to her belly, the movement suggestive. "And you will become my plaything, whether I will it or not."

Araña blocked her revulsion and parsed through his words, seeing them for what they were—warnings, hints, the twisting of Anton's commands.

Abijah's forked tongue found her earlobe and she couldn't stop herself from shuddering and trying to pull away from him. She staggered when he let her go, though one taloned hand kept possession of her wrist.

A curved nail scratched over the fingerless glove hiding the

brand before tracing along the line where fabric and skin met above the veins in her wrist. Without warning he sliced through the flesh, cutting more deeply than he had when Anton asked him whether she was one of the human gifted.

Blood streamed over her leather-coated palm and off her bared fingers. Abijah's tongue submerged itself in the flow. Yellow eyes flashed to red. "You taste like my enemy," he purred, cocking his head. "Perhaps I won't regret your fate when you fail at your task."

"I won't fail."

His tongue lapped over her wrist again. "Tell me, has he enjoyed his captivity as much as I have mine?"

"He's hated every moment of it and wants his freedom as much as you must want yours."

Abijah laughed, but his eyes remained red. He leaned forward abruptly, and the scorpion mark flared to life on his cheek, only inches away from the spider on hers. "Is that your price for destroying the urn? The incantation I used when I placed the collar on him?"

"No. I'll destroy the urn regardless of whether you tell me the incantation. That's a price *I* have to pay for gaining help from a vampire."

Red eyes faded to glittering yellow. "Your mother was always one for playing deep games, but then she wouldn't have risen to rule her House otherwise."

The tip of Abijah's forked tongue brushed over the spider. "Did you know we were lovers once? Your mother and I?"

"I didn't know anything until yesterday, when I would have died. When I *could* have died and been reborn into the kingdom of our people. But I chose to return."

Abijah's eyes flashed red for an instant. "Because of him?"

"Yes."

He cocked his head. "He will kill you when his memory returns."

An icy hand squeezed her heart, its cold fingers the words Tir had spoken in the midst of the carnage at Gulzar's house. "I'm not his enemy."

Abijah's smile was terrifying. "In all scenarios your mother gains something." He stroked a talon over the spider. "You succeed in your task, I return to her. If you don't, your failure will see you reborn into a place at her side."

He leaned forward to whisper in her ear. "Did it occur to you that freeing him completely was never the goal in this game? The incantation is in parts. Speak some of it and he gains strength and power—enough to believe you've done what you can for him, enough to enable him to protect you until you grow weary of living as a human. Hold back the last of it and he doesn't remember anything about . . . demons."

"No. I won't betray him."

Abijah stepped away from her. "Where do you expect to find the one who calls himself my master?"

She didn't know. Killing Anton had always been secondary to destroying the urn. She guessed this was Abijah's way of helping her without violating the commands governing what he could and couldn't do.

"Upstairs. In his study."

"A good choice."

She tugged at the wrist still in Abijah's possession. He dug his talons in, reopening the wound he'd created. "I've been told you are a permissible plaything as long as you don't try to escape. Given you're the more immediate danger to the one able to command me, I will remain with you. Make a threatening move toward him and I'll kill you. Think of it as a fate preferable to the one you'll gain if I take you prisoner instead."

She nodded and he released her.

As they moved deeper into the house, Abijah said, "If you succeed in performing the vampire's task, I will give you the incantation."

Twenty-six

THE snap of Farold's neck and the sound of Levi dropping the body to the ground seemed loud in the silence of the maze. To the animals that hunted and killed there, it served as a trigger for them to charge the front of their cages and clamor to be let out. For Rebekka it was a signal to move, and move quickly.

A glance at Tir, who nodded from a position allowing him to watch Levi's stealthy attack on Farold, and Rebekka left her hiding place. It helped that she'd done this a thousand times in her imagination, dreamed of sprinting to the caged animals serving as a gauntlet of terror for humans running the maze, and calming them until the Weres could be freed.

She went first to the pack of feral dogs, using her gift to silence them before something went wrong and the demon appeared.

The hyenas were next. Then the cheetah and the bears.

She wasn't telepathic, not as some Weres were. But her gift allowed her to touch emotion, use it to gain trust.

Levi and Tir joined her, their presence and her own rush of

excitement nearly undoing what she'd managed with her gift. A couple of the dogs began barking and she hurried to quiet them. When it was done, Levi motioned and said, "Come on."

A final mental push, trying to convey that freedom was near, and she followed Levi to the metal door leading to the cells holding the Weres.

He jammed the key with Gulzar's dried blood on it into the lock and twisted. A motor hummed to life and the door retracted.

Rebekka's heart lodged in her throat as she stepped inside. It was bad. She knew it would be. The only thing that would have made it worse was if there'd been more Weres held captive. Once there had been.

Cyrin's eyes held only madness as Levi went toward him. Deadly claws at the end of furred arms reached through the bars with the intention of savaging anyone who got close enough to strike.

A flattened, maned face pressed to the cage. Yellowed teeth glistened as he roared.

Torn human carcasses represented what was left of meals, not just in the werelion's cage, but in those of tiger, leopard, and wolf shapeshifters.

Rebekka moved to the bars, working hard to establish rapport. Knowing all of their lives depended on her gift.

Tir's machete was drawn, as was his knife. He'd kill any threat. Including the Weres. Rebekka knew it without it being said.

The werewolves calmed the fastest, and then the leopard and tiger shapeshifters.

For any of them to escape, they needed to work together, to leave together, to use their combined abilities to keep the pure animals in line after they'd been freed from their cages.

Sweat coated Rebekka's skin as she joined Levi in front of his brother's cage. Her head pounded as she concentrated on Cyrin, trying to reach him through remembered emotion, love and loyalty and trust, trying to fix the tears in his mind where human and animal instincts had fought one another.

She used her gift as well as her words, her voice joining Levi's until finally the insanity slid from Cyrin's eyes and was replaced by recognition.

Levi unlocked his brother's cage then and the two of them embraced. Tears streamed down Rebekka's cheeks. If the demon arrived moments from now and killed them, at least they'd had this shining moment of success.

ABIJAH cocked his head as they neared the end of the hallway. Adrenaline surged through Araña when she recognized the sounds coming from outside. The animals were free. She suspected the Weres were, too.

Tir would be coming for her.

She had only an instant at the doorway to access the room. The urn sat on a narrow table against the far wall, directly across from her. Next to it a red candle burned in a shallow blood-filled bowl attached to a platform where a carved deity served as a fetish carrying prayers to the being it represented.

If Anton's worshipped god had truly been present, she doubted she would have heard the fire whispering its willingness to become her weapon. To kill as it had killed once before, on the day she'd called it to her as hot iron was pressed to her flesh.

She couldn't see the maze owner, but from the light pouring into the room and the sounds still coming from the maze, she guessed he was standing at the window, watching whatever was taking place there. She couldn't afford to allow him time to think, or order Abijah outside.

Araña entered the room fast, going straight for the urn.

"Stop her, Abijah! Stop her, Abijah! Stop her, Abijah!"

Three times in rapid succession. Without the conceit of archaic words.

It was a command Araña understood couldn't be disobeyed, and yet not a thorough enough one to keep Anton safe from her.

Abijah's talons curled around her arms, halting her before she'd gotten more than half a dozen steps into the room. He lifted her so she dangled above the floor, seemingly defenseless.

Anton laughed. "Clever, clever demon. Now I understand how you managed to avoid killing the intruders outside. What luck for both of us that your plaything returned."

He glanced through the window. "I fear I'm going to have to let them die in the traps and settle for the woman as a prize. I can't send you after them and risk touching her myself."

The spider rested on her brand in a symbolic acknowledgment of the day ten years earlier that had ultimately led to this one. She'd once thought her ability to summon fire was further proof she was destined for Hell. Now she knew otherwise. It was a gift to one reborn, a thread connecting her to the birthplace of the Djinn.

Anton left the window, passing between her and the flame he'd lit to his deity, and the fire came to her call. It filled the room with his scream as it had once filled another room with the screams of the clergyman and the couple she'd believed to be her parents.

It destroyed Anton's ability to command a Djinn first. Burning away his lips and tongue. Swallowing his throat and filling his lungs with its rage. But unlike before when the fire killed because of her summons, Araña felt no guilt, no remorse. He deserved no mercy.

Abijah disappeared with Anton's final heartbeat, and Araña skirted the still burning body, going directly to the urn. It was a thing of temptation and horror, but she'd known as soon as she read the stolen journal pages that she would destroy it without trying to use it to force the incantation from Abijah. She grasped it, the blood from the wound painting its side as she brought it down on the edge of the table, willing it to break.

A boom sounded. A wash of power exploded through the room as the urn shattered.

The force of it knocked her to the ground and sent shards of glass from the windows to the yard below. It extinguished both candle flame and Anton's burning corpse.

Abijah appeared next to her, standing over her as a man and wearing the robes of a desert dweller. When she would have risen, he put his foot on her chest and held her with an easy strength that warned against drawing her knives.

"He's killed hundreds of our kind and enslaved even more. You risk his life if you free him and he resumes his war on us. I spared him the first time because The Prince demanded it of me. He won't be spared again."

"The time for vengeance is past," Araña said, ignoring the tiny voice reminding her of Tir's warning not to ask this of him.

"Is it?" Abijah asked. "We will soon see."

In a blink he became the scorpion. His tail lashing out, stinging her hand—and then he was gone in a swirl of wind that tore paintings from the wall and sent papers and books to the floor.

Pain spread through her with venom not meant to kill. It was like the witch's strike when she mindlessly attacked—only this agony was the price she paid to gain the incantation.

It flowed into her, segment by segment like a scorpion's tail.

It burned into her—ancient words she would never have been able to remember or speak if they'd been delivered from his mouth to her ears.

Outside she heard destruction raging, the howl of an unnatural storm tearing down walls and flattening anything in its path. But she was held motionless on the floor, unable to do more than smile slightly when Tir burst into the room and knelt next to her, his face harsh with worry.

He put the machete and knife down to run his hands over her as if searching for the source of her agony. "I'm okay," she said, the last of the pain fading when the final words of the incantation were in place.

Tir lifted her into his arms and stood. Through the open space of the window the funnel cloud that was Abijah dissipated, leaving utter calm and stark devastation in its wake—and such intense silence Araña's heartbeat sounded like a bell tolling in her ears.

"Levi and Rebekka?" she asked, delaying her final task.

"Safe. I assume that was the demon making a grand exit. He cut a clear path for them to escape into the woods before circling back to attack the building next door."

"Farold?"

"Dead."

Tir glanced around at the chaos of the office, at the smoldering corpse. He set her on her feet, his expression hardening as he met her eyes. "You said the incantation was in Anton's possession. Where is it?"

Did it occur to you that freeing him completely was never the goal in this game?

You risk his life if you free him and he resumes his war on us.

The incantation is in parts. Speak some of it and he gains strength and power—enough to believe you've done what you can for him.

Tir could live among the outcasts and criminals as she did. The tattoos on his arms would draw little attention, just as the brand on her hand rarely warranted a second glance in the settlements and floating boat cities that were *her* world.

She reached up, intending to touch the face she had already committed to memory.

He grabbed her wrist. Stopping her.

"Where is it?"

Trust me, she'd asked of him.

I trust you, he'd said.

"Abijah gave it to me before he left."

She leaned forward until her mouth was only a breath away from his. "Remember I'm not your enemy. Remember I asked you to put aside your dreams of vengeance because the price for gaining it can be too high to pay."

Tir didn't stop her from pressing a kiss to his lips. "Remember I love you," she said, then began speaking the words Abijah had given her.

Power surged into Tir with each syllable. It came with music, indescribable notes transcending reality and calling for his cells to break apart, to become the spectrum of light, part of a greater whole, to be everywhere and nowhere. Infinite. Without measure in form or time.

It was only when the collar fell away and memory descended that music and cold light were forged into individual purpose. Tir.

Black wings flowed out, tearing away the shirt as they solidified. Along his arms the marks put there by humans disappeared as if they'd never been.

Abijah. He remembered the name now.

It was the name of the Djinn he'd hunted for centuries. The name of the enemy who'd caught him in a trap and enslaved him with the collar.

The desire for vengeance rose up, pulsing through Tir with omnipotent fury until the rush of returned memory and power faded enough for him to become aware of Araña standing in front of him, her dark, dark eyes seemingly soulless, the spider on her cheek marking her as his enemy.

She met his gaze, neither cowering in his presence nor drawing her knives from their sheaths, neither pleading with him to turn aside the past nor cursing him for what he'd once been to her kind. An enemy. A killer.

The knowledge of it was there in her eyes as she stood waiting for him to make *his* choice, just as she'd made her choice when she spoke the incantation to free him.

"Araña," he said, reaching for her, only to have her pushed away as others of his kind appeared in a burst of light, three of them, their wings ranging from snowy white to mottled gold—all of them beings he'd hunted alongside, first to slaughter and then to capture the Djinn so the creatures of mud could rule here.

"Brother," the white-winged Addai said, stepping forward and embracing Tir. "I turned my attention away from this world and a thousand years passed before I knew you'd gone missing. By then it was too late to find you."

Addai stepped away and, with a casual backhand, sent Araña sprawling to the ground at Tir's feet. Without conscious thought, Tir formed a sword. It glowed like the sun but was the frigid ice of deep space.

"Slay her and let's be done here," Addai said. "The humans no longer remember the creatures we were once charged with making their familiars."

"No," Tir said, stepping in front of Araña, protecting her from the angels he'd once called brothers, knowing in that moment he would die with her rather than return to what he'd been. "It's time for our war on the Djinn to be over."

"Heretic," Addai said. "We have encountered others holding that same idea, and they have all met with the fate you have only recently escaped."

With a sweep of Addai's arm, sigil-inscribed shackles appeared next to the collar on the floor between them. Swords to match Tir's came to his brothers' hands and they spread out, flanking him.

Pride flashed through Tir when Araña pulled her knives from their sheaths and prepared to spring to her feet. "Don't," he told her, fashioning a second sword from his memory, remembering its hunger for passing judgment and naming it death.

Music swelled inside him. The notes of a warrior who'd accepted a cause.

Addai said, "I will give you the benefit of the doubt and a chance to throw off the last of whatever spell she cast on you when you were at her mercy. Slay her, brother. Don't make us bind you and return you to the mercy of humans."

Tir's gaze went to Araña's, and he felt her horror for him, her willingness to sacrifice herself rather than see him enslaved again. "No," he said, "that spell is love and its loss is too high a price to pay."

"Well said, brother."

The swords around Tir blinked out as if they'd never been drawn. The shackles and collar disappeared as though there'd never been a threat of them.

Tir freed the power forming one of his blades and offered his hand to Araña. When she took it, he pulled her to her feet and against his chest, his arm going around her waist to keep her pressed to him.

His brothers made no move to attack. Instead they gathered again in front of him.

"This is no trick," Addai said, "but a test. There are those of us who want to live openly here, to take mates and reshape this world. To that end, new alliances are forming. Between angel and Djinn as well as with gifted humans and shapeshifters."

He looked at Araña and bowed slightly. "My apologies for striking a daughter belonging to the House of the Spider. Had you died by my brother's hand, your mother would have you know a Raven waited to guide your spirit back to the Djinn."

"I understand," Araña said, and though Tir couldn't discern her thoughts, he felt her peace and knew Addai's words hadn't surprised her.

"She is mortal," Addai said. "There is only one way you can assure her safety and keep her with you."

Tir closed his eyes. A part of him wept in sorrow. To speak the words Addai alluded to was to cut himself off from the glorious whole of the light that both defined his form and absorbed it. But to do less was to risk Araña and to one day lose her.

For all that she was Djinn, she was also human, mortal, fragile in this harsh world mankind had created from the paradise they'd been given. Her flesh was a prison her soul would flee at the slightest dropping of his guard against it.

Tir turned her in his arms. "Do you want this? There is no going back."

Not that there had ever been a chance of willingly parting from her. She had enslaved him from the moment she entered his dreams then knelt at his feet and freed him from the shackles he wore.

"I want this," she said. "I love you."

"I feel the same for you."

He touched his lips to hers and spoke the forbidden incantation. Separating himself. Limiting himself to *this* world.

She deepened the kiss, and like a pattern made whole, he felt her spirit weave with his, felt the spider twin itself and become a part of him, taking up residence on his chest, above the heart that beat only for her.

Slowly he became aware that his brothers were no longer there, but humans were converging on what remained of the maze. "Where do you want to go?"

"Home."

The word formed an image in his mind. Echoed and became his. *Home*. Not the *Constellation*, but a cabin where laughter and love had saved a young girl's life. Where childish drawings slowly morphed into the beautiful recapturing of the world around her, where books lay on tables alongside knives and guns.

He folded his wings around her and by will alone took her to the bedroom that was hers.

Her joyous laugh filled him with song.

The love shining in her eyes and flowing between them threatened to take him to his knees.

"Araña," he said in a voice that had once sent armies of men to their deaths and made humans prostrate themselves before him.

Don't think I'll allow anyone else to worship you but me, she spoke into his mind, shocking him, replacing images of his remembered past with erotic ones, demonstrating to him how thoroughly their souls were bound.

Dark eyes challenged him, absorbed him as her hands went to his wings, the touch sending liquid ecstasy through the both of them. "I want you," she whispered, opening the floodgate to need and the rush to get rid of clothing.

When nothing remained to separate them, they fell naked onto the bed. His body covered hers and Araña moaned at the erotic feel of his wings against her splayed thighs, at the contrast of soft feathers and hardened warrior.

She wrapped her arms around his neck, buried her fingers in his hair.

She welcomed him into her body as thoroughly as she'd welcomed him into her heart and soul.

And as his mouth took hers in a shared breath, the twin spiders touched, joined as one. Djinn and angel. Fire and ice melting away the past to form a new future.

ABOUT THE AUTHOR

Jory Strong has been writing since childhood and has never outgrown being a daydreamer. When she's not hunched over her computer, lost in the muse and conjuring up new heroes and heroines, she can usually be found reading, riding her horses, or hiking with her dogs.

She has won numerous awards for her writing. She lives in California with her husband and a menagerie of pets. Visit her website at www.jorystrong.com.